Fiona Maazel was a 2005 recipient of a Lannan Foundation Fellowship, winner of the Bard Fiction Prize for 2009, and recognized by the National Book Foundation as one of the best fiction writers under thirty-five. She lives in Brooklyn, New York.

www.lastlastchance.com

Last Last Chance

Last Last Chance

Fiona Maazel

Picador

Farrar, Straus and Giroux
New York

Designed by Jonathan D. Lippincott

ISBN-13: 978-0-312-42831-0
ISBN-10: 0-312-42831-6

First published in the United States by Farrar, Straus and Giroux

First Picador Edition: April 2009

10 9 8 7 6 5 4 3 2 1

Mom, Paul, Ilann

Last Last Chance

i

One

People I love know how to get on with their lives. In evidence: A girlfriend from elementary school was getting married. Day after tomorrow, Plaza Hotel. The invitation was piped in copper and rice, maybe because the bride was Indian. It promised a groom on horseback. This I'd like to see. I knew the groom, which made it tough to imagine horseback nothin'. A horse could make him cry. A horse could make *me* cry. How fortuitous. When the crying starts, blame horse.

I was on break outside the crèche. The view was coops and farmland. Tractor here, reaper there, and, per usual, Wanda Deckman headed my way. She is the chief union steward. She likes to meddle. And, in my case, to paw for information apropos a strain of lethal plague vanished from my father's lab a few months ago. I understood. Miasmic events storming the country were on everybody's mind. There was reason to believe the strain had fallen into enemy hands. Enemies of freedom, the press was saying. I tried to look buoyant.

"Lucy," she said, and grabbed at the card. "Hand it over." Never mind that I'd been fondling the invitation for weeks, it looked like news to her.

I did as told. She studied it and blushed. Not word of the Miasma, just some girl's wedding.

I said it was my oldest friend, though we don't talk.

"Uh-huh."

I said I had regrets, more regrets than not.

"Uh-huh."

"But I do like a good biryani," I said. "Some of the curries, too."

She agreed. Could I have the day off? Sure, have fun.

There was nothing left to say. Stanley Gensch, making for the john, came as a relief. He'd been the bellman and pluckhouse supervisor for twenty-three years, though his job was in peril. It always was. He drank. And, in drink, tended to forget the closing bell, which got Wanda cross and him grousing that double duty prefigured a screwup. No matter. Wanda could nail him with guilt. I'd even heard it myself, them squared off while she declaimed his past, social outcast inmate whose priors she chose to overlook when giving him what's called a second chance, even though this was more like his third or fourth and certainly did not *feel* like a chance since this place, this abattoir, was hours away from life in any direction, a kosher chicken plant that had the remove and dyspepsia of rehab. I had been here two months, four days, nine minutes.

First thing I noticed about the plant: hygiene was king. We wore latex gloves and surgical caps to repel disease. We sterilized our clothes. In canisters bolted to every wall: antibacterial mousse. Broadsides would come down from the office, stuff like, The chicken line cannot be exposed to unhealthful agents. That's the phrase we used: *unhealthful agents*. Listeria monocytogenes *was* a threat. I would read this, and my heart would sink. Because I knew what was on deck. I knew about disease—my dad had worked for the CDC—so yeah, I knew, which made for an uneasy time on the line. I'd developed a clucking of the tongue that kept time with the action of my hands. Some of the other girls got annoyed. They said I was disruptive. And when the brass called me up, they had this to add: The serenity proffered by the line can be had so long as you try.

It wasn't so much the job. My colleagues were fine. The vistas were great. But the feeling was claustral. I'd been exiled, and though I could leave anytime, I felt I deserved this. And that's the thing about exile, you tend to feel extra trapped if you know the comeuppance is just.

In the city, I'd been in sales for high-end retail. Next, I'd dabbled in real estate and estate planning, which have less in common than you'd think. Then I had my fun and slept with Mother's acupuncturist, whose practice foundered on the scandal. We were discovered by a client arrived too soon. Mother, who'd been footing my bills under aegis of Bridge Loan, decided to foot no more. And so, the chicken house. The house as holding tank until a bed opened up for me at a rehabilitation facility down South.

Wanda had hair to the small of her back, sieved through a low ponytail. Mostly white and gray, fried at the ends. She wore glasses. Red plastic. I often found her lost to the occupation of wiping the lenses, which had the boon of redress for awkward moments such as this.

She sat next to me on the step. I tried to stand and was successful at it.

"Did you just swoon?" she said. "Because that is not right. Especially at a wedding. Heels and a bad inner ear, I'm going to call it a *bad inner ear*, can make for a spill on the dance floor, not to mention the disco ball and strobe lights."

Wanda, apparently, had not been to a wedding since 1977.

She gloved herself and, once gloved, snapped the rubber cuffs like maybe she was about to engage in some ob-gyn activity. "Going to the pluckhouse," she said. "Sleep it off. Drive safe—"

I rolled up the invitation and brought it to my eye like maybe I could see something new in the prospect before me. *Inner ear.* Wanda's will to believe was disheartening. But she was just doing her best. I'm sure Mother had begged her to take me in. And who knew, maybe the chicken house really could subtend the path I was on. Maybe it would get me out of rehab. Rehab cost a fortune, and Mother had a habit of her own to finance. Plus, I really, really didn't want to go.

I scoped the terrain and found Stanley across the yard, shouting and throwing up his arms. I thought he might be trying to pep my spirits coach style, so I gave him a thumbs-up, like play ball!, which seemed to satisfy him enough to continue walking to the salting plant. I liked Stanley. We both had death in our families, and the idea of sharing our grief seemed to improve on acquaintance.

It was August. The wedding was on the thirtieth, which seemed odd because who gets married on a Friday? Less odd was that I had no date. I'd had weeks to prepare and yet: no date. Possibly it was because I knew the nuptials would be my last outing for a while, which meant having to find just the right escort, which meant being paralyzed by the onus of having to find Just the Right Escort. Possibly it was because I had no male friends. Most likely, though, it was because the pressure of having to front my well-being for at least five hours was so unsustainable, I'd been hoping the world would end before Friday. Showing up would certainly evidence progress of my own—is there anything more well adjusted than going to your oldest friend's wedding?—but also, come on, what a nightmare.

It was time to frisk the chickens. Alternately, there was my bed, which called out to me with godlike authority. I was under the covers in seconds. Unlike the other staff, I slept on the premises, in more of a barn than house, whose open windows and cracks in the joists let in a breeze I enjoyed, except by morning spindrift was always up in my hair, which made me look more acclimated than I would have liked.

I didn't have many personal items, since I'd left the city in a rush, essentially shoved on a bus by Mother, who blew kisses as the driver pulled out of Port Authority. There was Farfle, my stuffed sweet potato, and tweezers because I cannot live without tweezers, and a cardholder that looked like a recipe box, in which I kept a log of the men I've dated. My last entry was before I came here, when I was participating in a study—pheromones, I think—that paid enough to get me the blast, which became the tryst with the acupuncturist.

The good thing about the log is that it bedecks my heart with the lives I could have had if only. One of the entries was for a guy named Ben, Dirty Ben, who told me he had married a Venezuelan to help get her a Green Card, but that this was not in any way prohibitive of relations between us because she was gay. He could make for a good date at a Hindu wedding, being a free spirit and such. Plus he knew the bride from a Sierra Club summer when they had teamed up and gone door to door, guilting for money. As for me, we'd met last winter in Charleston, at a VA homeless shelter for narcotics recovery. It was absurd, my being there, because five seconds before I was at a department store, looking for sneakers—Chuck T's—until the saleslady was like: Oh, I recognize you from the news, your pop done fouled it up, at which point I got mad, and suddenly there's cops, rehab, and what? The worst I had on me was grass and a locket of smack around my neck. Ben was in for something retarded like Robitussin OD, though I found out later he was just there to get some crystal meth from one of the VA guys. His wife was not Venezuelan or gay, but I slept with him anyway. And since antibiotics are not cheap, and since Ben *knew* he was giving me more than his love, I figured he owed me. Plus he lived in New York.

Next morning at breakfast, there was gossip. Me and the other girls were airing it out. Beyond the compulsory assemblage of lives in slaughter, these talks were the closest you got to feeling a part of things. Sharon Boozel, who oversees desalination and rinse, was saying, with pride, that Stanley had gotten into a fight with one of the rabbis. And just the thought of Stanley, who's a bit of an oaf, sparring with a rabbi made me think that perhaps he wouldn't be such a bad date, either. He was obviously not doing well, and it made me feel tender about him. Probably he didn't own anything but Orthodox duds, but they could pass for a tux. Me, I could always buy something in town.

I headed for the grain silo, which is where he tended to start the day. It was impressive, this steel proboscis of huge affront to the landscape. Alongside the pluckhouse, coops, and satellite facilities, it had a bunker quality you had to admire.

He was not there. He was, instead, in the killing room, in the back, honing a cleaver. It's true Stanley was awkward, oafish, but this was looking more Fatty Arbuckle than *Of Mice and Men*. Also, the cleaver was not our blade of choice. We've got ritual slaughter guys with their perfect knives, and a routine in which a cleaver had no place whatsoever.

"Uh, Stanley, you're looking like a crazy."

"Oh, so now you want to talk to me."

"I always want to talk to you," I said, and flashed some teeth. I wasn't so good with people, but I was trying.

Stanley wore jeans and a T-shirt spattered with blood because when a chicken's carotid, jugular, and windpipe are severed, it's a bloody affair. Thing is, I could still read his shirt. It said: *Stick Up for Chickens!*

Stanley, it seemed, was at the end of his rope.

"You know, most of us around here aren't even Jewish," he said. "I'm not. Clearly *you're* not."

I couldn't decide if I should be taking offense, like I was so Waspy it showed on my face, but also I was thinking if Stanley wasn't Jewish—forget Orthodox—he might not own suitable wedding attire.

"Yom Kippur's in two months," he said. "If I have to watch those guys twirl the birds one more time—"

He was referring to *Kaparos*—atonement—in which Jews take chickens by the feet and swirl them overhead, like a lasso, before the ritual killing. I've been told that since the Hebrew word for *man* and *rooster* is the same, the twirling projects your sins onto the bird. So there's some chanting that accompanies the twirl, something like: This is my substitute, the bird dies, and I am atoned. Guilt figured hugely in Stanley's life, so I decided he was experiencing an upsurge precipitated by the holiday just two months on.

I asked if he was okay.

He asked if a chicken has lips.

I asked if he'd be my date for the wedding.

He said sure.

I said, "Be ready after work."

He said, "Yep."

I smiled, but it did not last. Stanley turned away. I've been told my face remits joy faster than anyone's.

The bride's name was Kamini, which was meany in sixth grade, mini in high school, and Kam after that. When we were twelve, we auditioned for a strip show that played on late-night cable. They told us to come back with nipples. At fourteen, we did nitrous from balloons we got from a guy in the park who liked to say *baaaallup, baaaallup*, and rattle a snake tail. I'd been seeing this man ever since I was five. It got so I was certain he didn't know any English besides *baaaallup*. Then one day his argot doubled so that he'd say *baaaallup, special baaaallup*, and then he had customers and then he had us, and with a combination of mime and mindset we got the picture and were fucked up for hours. Each take from the balloon made your brain pirouette. Kam and I finished ours and sprawled on the grass. Nothing is pastoral in a city, but when you're high, every pony is Icarus, which might explain why when Baaaallup got arrested by cops on horseback, we thought he was going to heaven.

Kam liked to call me Boothe Luce. She was there the day I first tried to use a tampon. Got it halfway in, then decided it was stuck and I was going to get toxic shock and die. Mother was out, which left Kam and my nana from Norway, whose English rivaled Baaaallup's for diversity. I remember her fretting and me crying and Kam swaddling her fist in toilet paper, like a boxer before the fight, and grabbing the string until out it came. There was some oregano in the house we tried to smoke by way of celebration, but it burned like hell, and anyway, Nana Agneth was making lutefisk, so it was time to go. Cod soaked in lye is just not my idea of a party.

We killed water bugs on Kam's roof. For the baptismal ordeal known as the facial, I was in the next bed first time she went through it. She had a dog that could walk on its front legs. We went to the same high school and wrote notes to each other in class that I still have. At sixteen, she had her breasts augmented. Cited mental health on the insurance claim. At eighteen, we were leaving a loft party, us and this guy in a cab, when someone reached in through the window and stabbed our third in the knee. We once got so wrecked at an Irish bar that I agreed to let two old men shackle us to the gridiron in their van so we'd be safe in the back—it was more like a U-Haul than a van with seats—while they took us someplace more romantic. Kam demurred. Her drunken state said: I need to evacuate the contents of my stomach. Mine said: Let's get molested. Hers won. On the walk home, she ralphed in a dumpster while I held back her hair. And I remember thinking this felt like love.

While I was in teen rehab, she sent me letters sealed with turtle stickers. When I got out, she said she'd gotten into a college of repute. And that while I was gone, she'd joined the swim team. Turned out she was good, but her lung capacity sucked.

We had not spoken in a year. Come birthday time, I wished her happiness in my head. I wondered if she was still athletic. The groom was a photographer. Kam, from what I'd heard, was a VP at Ralph Lauren, the youngest ever. I was surprised she had invited me to the wedding. No idea how she even found my address.

It was almost time to go. I had gassed up the car and made hotel reservations for two. Everything was in place, only Stanley was AWOL. No one had seen him since this morning. I was nervous enough, which meant if he was off drinking, I might have to join him.

At five and without the bell, the line broke up. I was assisting the *mashgichim*, who are just guys looking for broken bones, holes, bruises, etc., when the conveyor shut down. I found this poignant, which helped nothing. Gloves were doffed and tossed. A few rabbis slipped out the back. It was like watching people scatter after a funeral because the person who'd kept them together was gone.

Wanda was trying to record negligence as she saw it. The brass were ordering us back to our stations.

I found Stanley in my car. He was smoking a joint I had put in the glove compartment for when the wedding got too hectic or too depressing. I got in the driver's side and pulled out of the lot.

In minutes, Stanley was asleep with mouth ajar. I noticed a fake tooth, but only because it was so much whiter than the others. Have I mentioned he was just over fifty? That he had angina and a cauliflower ear from when he was in a car wreck that killed his wife and dog ten years back? Not that Stanley told me any of this, but what is the chicken line if not a conveyor of story?

"Hey, Stanley?" I said.

He opened one eye.

"It's not mandatory, you know. The twirling and all that. You don't have to go."

"Says you."

I worked into my seat, renowned for a lumbar support system that was just a leather bolus humping my spine.

"You okay to drive?" he said.

"Yeah. All I need is to get us to this wedding, in one piece, on time."

Last I saw Kam was in the Adirondacks, at a chalet nestled in fifty-four acres of forest. She had brought Miss Piggy Pez and a magazine that published articles by famous people about what shit their lives had been until they got clean. She stayed the afternoon. We played pool in the rec room. We watched a film noir in the rec room. We played croquet. I said it was like vacation, and she said but was it working? Was I trying?

Her skin was immaculate. I noticed she had calf muscles. When I smoked, she stayed upwind.

The rehab was fancy and a little dumb, and had supplied every bathroom with Listerine. The day after Kam left, a staffer found me drinking from the bottle, hiding in a shower stall and sniffing the replacement grout for fumes of advisable use. They ditched the Listerine. I got sent home.

In the tunnel to Manhattan, I whacked Stanley awake. I hate tunnels for the same reason everyone who hates tunnels does. If the thing collapsed, I wanted him there to scream with me. He looked ready to scream anyway. The tunnel did not help. I said something about the wedding being at four the next day, and how we had plenty of time to get attired and sober. He said he was game for whatever. We reviewed my story: I worked for the USDA; I was a mole recording violations in one of the country's biggest kosher chicken plants. And Stanley, he was my boy Friday.

I got us to the hotel and parked in a garage. The guy at the desk was looking all around and behind us, like where was the Mr. and Mrs. I had promised?

The bed was a queen. It was late and I thought it best to crash and get up early the next day to prepare. I told Stanley to shower. He said: Come with. I said he was obviously going through a tough time. He said today was the anniversary of his wife's death. I said: Oh, fuck.

He left the shower on for me once he was done and came out

with a towel wrapped around his midriff. There were black and silver curls patterned across his chest.

We fit together nicely, and after, he was sweet about it.

Next day, I took him downtown to a used-clothing store that was still fairly chichi. I made him try on suits. We settled on a double-breasted pinstripe. The saleslady kept asking what's that smell, like she was having déjà vu. We got that a lot. The odor of raw chicken is a bit like resentment: try as you will, it never goes away.

I bought a black dress, spaghetti strapped, with eyelet-sized polka dots. Heels and shawl, but only because Stanley insisted. I was worried about looking just right and got to thinking about Mother's pearl bracelet and how to make my story stick. If I had to go to rehab, maybe I could pretend it was a work-related sojourn. Maybe there were cracker cattle to neutralize down South. Maybe there was mad cow to deal with. So my job, it could seem important. And I could seem needed. If I could just belie the impression I knew people who'd be at the wedding had of me, this venture into the world would be worth it.

I was chewing a fingernail and thinking how to acquire the bracelet and make Stanley's collar sit flat when he took me by the wrist and said, "What's the big deal? We'll go over to her place and get it."

I tried explaining about doormen, which turned into a story about one of the doormen I'd grown up with, this guy Joe, who taught me how to ride a bike in the courtyard, and how he helped me get my dad unhitched from the ceiling fan and later how he went nuts and beat the desk guy, José, over the head with a pipe.

Stanley was dragging me along and noting how fancy this part of town was. When we reached Mother's apartment, I hid because a lot of the door guys had been there for years and some of them would recognize me and it wasn't that I was afraid of getting busted but that I was embarrassed that so much time had passed and I rarely came by to say hello even though these guys, a lot of them, they were like family. Also, my mother. Coming back after a leave was always precarious because I never knew just how bad off she'd be, or how low I'd feel about it.

Stanley left me at the corner and marched into the building. Words were exchanged. The desk guy—someone new—was on the in-house phone and next thing, Stanley was being directed to the elevator. I waited and waited, then tired of waiting and went to a bar down the street where me and Dirty Ben used to hang out and deal. Or he dealt and I bought. I was already dressed for the wedding. I was intending to order a soda, kick up some nostalgia, and split. The bar was one of those city relics around which progress has to arrange itself. Boutiques and bistros cramming the purlieus and at the heart, this dump that hasn't been mopped in sixty years. I felt good in there. I stood out against decrepitude, which was novel. If there was a contrast to be had, it rarely favored me. I checked my teeth in a mirror. No lipstick stains or anything.

I took a stool and waited for someone to show up behind the bar. Instead, I got hands covering my eyes and Dirty Ben saying guess who. So now he was the bartender, which probably made dealing that much easier.

"Well, well," he said, onceing me over. "Drinks on the house! How are you?"

I smiled. It was good to be around people who knew you for what you were. I said I wanted a soda, that was all. I asked how's tricks, which was enough to stifle other thoughts like: My, he looks healthy.

"I'm doing all right," he said. "I make some money here. I'm back in school, trying to get my GED. I got loans and stuff, but on the whole, things are really good. And you? Obviously, I heard about your dad, I'm sorry."

I said thanks, and marveled. He was so happy for a drug addict. I was tempted to join in, like: I'm good, too! I work on Wall Street!

"And the rest of it?" I asked, because how long were we going to play this game?

He laughed and said, "Oh, come on. Ancient history. I got divorced, but I'm engaged now. She's in law school. We want children in the next few years. I work at this place, which isn't so great for staying sober, but I manage."

I think I reared. He squeezed my forearm and said, "You look really good, Lucy. I'm glad we all got out of that phase alive. Because I was worried about you at Kam's wedding. We all were."

Horror cannot describe it, but if I flushed my head down the toilet and drank, it'd be an improvement on the condition of my inner life as it now struck me in that miserable little bar. I'd been told deadly plague was on the loose and that my dead father was to blame. I had groped my way to consciousness in front of several people seeking the halcyon magic of acupuncture. I'd even accompliced a chicken massacre for two months, but this—this was, no. Just no.

"Oh, boy," he said. "You're still out there. Oh, honey," and he lifted my face from the bartop.

The automaton in me had words to share: "The wedding is today, August thirtieth."

Ben shook his head. "The third, sweetheart. August third. A Saturday night. There was a sit-down dinner and yours was the only empty seat. We thought maybe it was too depressing for you."

"August thirtieth. At the Plaza. I am dressed appropriately. I have a date. This is an opportunity for me to do well. I'm not going to ruin it."

"Lucy, wait. I can take you someplace."

I must have walked home like a zombie. Waved at the doormen and gone upstairs. One of them might have said something friendly, but I was so zeroed in on Mother, I heard nothing. I had missed my oldest friend's wedding, and it was her fault. On some other planet for the love of drug? She *gave* this illness to me.

There was only one apartment per floor, so the elevator opened into our vestibule. The front door was ajar.

Mother was laughing it up. Her nose was red and laced with powder. Her eyes were bloodshot. It did not take a genius to figure out what she'd been doing.

As for Stanley, he looked relaxed, sitting on a couch opposite her with a bottle of rye between his legs. I saw the pearl bracelet in his chest pocket, which could only mean Mother had not noticed the theft. But no. It was not like that at all.

He motioned for me to lean in close, then whispered: "I called the police already. Your mother was on the floor, crushing pills and snorting them with a straw. And the way things are in my head, I'd rather be back in a real jail than this."

So he was waiting and Mother was laughing and I was standing there, angry. And anger was good. Anger always seems like a fili-gree atop whatever else you're feeling, viz., I am so fucking morti-fied I want to put my head in a blender, so that the whole shebang starts to feel outlandish and silly. In short, I deflate on a dime.

Stanley looked me up and down. My dress really was pretty. "Lucy," he said, and his face bloomed with ardor. "This is for you."

He retrieved the pearls and held them aloft.

Mother stopped laughing. "A stranger with pearls," she said. In some other movie, she'd have meant me. "I have earrings to go with them. Stanley, right? They're in the safe, help yourself." But then she sniffed the air and cocked her head as if registering a smell, like maybe she'd left the oven on. She lurched for the back room.

I put on the bracelet and bunned my hair. The house phone rang from downstairs. Stanley said, "You know, I still think of my wife every day."

I told the doormen to send the police away. Then I went to see about Mother, who was in the laundry room under the ceiling fix-ture Dad called relief. This was where she'd always smoked, before his suicide and after. She was crawling around the floor, looking for anything white and crumbly. I noticed a pipe jutting from her back pocket. She'd smoke talcum powder if it was there. I called Kam's house. I watched my mother harvest the tile and nose the corners like a truffle hound. On the machine, the groom's voice, which having to hear was three times more painful than I had expected.

"Found some!" Mother said. "Come join me?"

She beckoned me to the floor. I got on my knees to help.

Two

The way the apartment worked, you could cohabit for days and still feel alone. Seven thousand square feet can do that. So even though it was me and Stanley, Agneth, Mother, and Hannah, the place was desolate.

Hannah is my half-sister, seventeen years between us. She probably thinks I'm unhip to the major consensus narrative of adolescent girls today, and if that's what she thinks, she's right. Hannah was born in the nineties. The *nineties*. I find this hard to accept no matter how long I've known about it. As a result, we have a routine, and in this routine we do not understand each other. And this is fine. On days I see it her way, it's only because she's tapped into something primal whose occasion cannot be good.

Returning home in the shape I was in, it wasn't like the second shift come to reprieve the first. My homecomings never were. Only this time, opportunities to fail everyone were in more abundance than ever. There'd been a development on the plague front, two developments, in fact. The first: a letter addressed to a senator from Minnesota suggesting that whoever had absconded with the bacterium knew how to release it. The second—well, it was more revelation than development. What everyone knows: it's been 237 days since vials of plague were stolen from my dad's lab, and 180 days since he took his life. What everyone just found out: The bacteria he cultured are sprightly. They do not degrade in the open air and no antibiotic can kill them. They are, in a word, immortal.

The story broke around dinnertime, which meant someone sworn to secrecy had cracked over the pot roast. We'd been congregated in front of the TV, watching the preview channel. Stanley had been saying, "So this isn't a pit stop? This is our actual viewing for the night?" when came the news crawl at the bottom of the screen and Hannah flipping to CNN, where the anchorman was delivering the latest with élan. What a time to depart from tradition. The anchorman is indurate, he is glacial, the provenance of feeling has never included him, so who the hell was this guy?

I made for the remote, which Hannah shoved down her pants. CNN was her bag. I asked her to turn down the volume. She pointed at Agneth and shook her head. Agneth is eighty-four and under the impression that at the advanced age of eighty-four, one's cochleae frustrate the progress of sound to the relevant hearing organ. Her hearing is fine, but no one likes to argue.

As soon as the anchorman finished the lead, Hannah had an opinion. "This is bad," she said, shouted really. "Bad, bad, *bad*."

I understood her completely. There was even some nodding between us.

On-screen was a picture of our dad, the same picture that accompanied every story about plague, which kind of story tended to inveigh against the scientist on whose watch the disease had toodle-oo'd out of a lab in D.C. We were all agreed that the photo had been doctored to assert in his demeanor something unpleasant. My poor dad. As a senior official at the Centers for Disease Control, he'd been an *eraser*. When a disease got too virulent or contagious, he'd be called in to wipe it out. But he was also a forward-looking man. Why wait for death when you can preempt? He did some work on the side.

Regular pneumonic plague, if untreated, already has a near–100 percent fatality rate. It's easier to get than a cold. And because there was some bioterror precedent here—e.g., the Japanese bombed China with infected fleas during WWII—Dad figured it'd be good to assess the danger. And so did the government. Never mind that his work violated the Biological and Toxin Weapons Convention—like anyone paid attention to that anymore—he was headed for the Nobel. And we were proud, in a Heisenberg's mom sort of way. His questions were simple: Could plague be stabilized? Made to survive in the air for as long as it took to saturate a major city? Could he devise a strain that resisted antibiotics, even if treated immediately? If he could do it, could anyone? Yes, yes, yes, and yes.

"Absolutely," Hannah said. "This is just what we need. First on *my* list."

We fell into that group silence there'd been so much of in the last eight months. The anchorman passed the story to a woman standing outside CDC headquarters in Atlanta. Her hair smacked the mike in the wind. She said the FBI was downplaying the danger, but that sources inside the White House were confirming a high degree of apeshit among senior staff.

The reporter looked weepy. She upheld the cover of tomorrow's *New York Post*. The headline? SUPERPLAGUE. She was reading out 800 numbers to call for more information.

The anchorman asked about the threatening letter. Was it credible? Were there any leads about the author? After all, there'd been several such letters since the theft, just enough to keep the concept of holocaust fresh in your mind, but not enough to spike life insurance. Still, this new letter seemed more ominous than the others, in part because our friends at Dad's lab had been saying the strain would probably hit any day. Someplace up North. Canada, if we were lucky.

Hannah was on her feet. I tried to grab her arm, but she parried. I asked where she was going.

"Her *room*," Mother said, which made me think there was some tension there.

"Jesus," Agneth said. More nodding. "The nightmare continues."

I went after Hannah, whose door was closed. Her *room*, I gathered, was more fort than sleeper. I knocked. The password was *streptococcus*. I had to say it twice before she answered. She was in the bathroom, private facilities, which was just as well. She likes her hands to be clean. Teeth brushed and flossed. Agneth, who is both spiritualist and diagnostician, says Hannah has acute juvenile mysophobia. That it runs in our family and, for emphasis, she'll snap the bands of her surgeon's mask, which she buys in bulk.

Hannah's room was unchanged since Dad died. He'd been helping her plot incidents of West Nile on a map using colored push-pins. Avian flu wasn't much in the news yet; back then, West Nile was the thing. The map took up half her wall. In a corner were toys and a stuffed apple-green platypus.

"Watch the puzzle," Hannah said, and just in time, since I was about to step on what looked like an ulcerated vesicle on some guy's neck. It was a cutaneous anthrax infection depicted in stages. A three-thousand-piece puzzle she'd bought online.

"Hannah, this is gross. Not at all normal. When I was twelve I had a poster of boys who waxed their chest hair."

She stepped out of the bathroom with a towel wrapped about her head. She is fair-skinned with freckles that saddle her nose. Braces are imminent. Breasts are not.

"See my map?" she said.

I nodded. It had come a long way. This time last year, five cases of West Nile had been reported in New York State. Now we were looking at close to thirty, and those only in the boroughs.

"Very professional," I said. "You've got a future here."

"Shut up. I was getting weekly calls from Wanda Deckman until now. You always mess up everything."

She was on her bed. Her hair had begun to leave a wet spot on the pillow. I haven't been around much to see her grow, but I swear her feet didn't hang off the mattress like that a couple months ago.

I said I was sorry. She said, "I've heard that before." I leaned against the wall.

Wanda was one of the last to see Dad before he died. He'd gone up to the plant to check on the CDC's first-line-of-defense chicken initiative, which was meant to trial-run a belvedere for plague. The way it works, domestic fowl are host to viruses that scare the crap out of everyone. Avian influenza and exotic Newcastle disease. St. Louis encephalitis, Eastern equine encephalitis, and the notorious West Nile encephalitis, to name a few. But here's the thing about chickens, they don't get sick from West Nile. They produce a strong antibody response and do just fine. So there you have it, a virus-patrol chicken. Choose six that test negative for West Nile antibodies and use them as bait. Bleed them every two weeks. Euthanize the ones that test positive, necropsy the carcasses, and monitor the results. If a lot of birds are getting hit, trouble's on deck.

The program backed the virtues of the nonhuman sentinel and endorsed spin-off plans for hundreds of other vector-borne diseases. But nothing came of it. The People for Ethical Treatment of Animals got in the way. The bleeding is painful, they said. And the birds don't get to run around. Also, what good is knowing a pandemic is upon us? All we can do is run, and we can't run forever. Seemed like a reasonable gripe until the stolen vials of plague. Since the vials, the People for Ethical Treatment of Animals are America's most wanted.

I straightened up, like I'd just had a great idea. "I'll be going back, anyway," I said. "I'll smooth things over."

"Who's the old guy with you? Is he your *boyfriend*? Because he looks old. What are you doing home, anyway?"

It was the first anyone had asked. "Remember Kam? I came for her wedding."

"Oh, yeah. She was calling here a bunch a few weeks ago. Want a Klonopin? I stole them from Mom."

My body tends to act without prelude. Every time I get with a man, I don't see it coming. Or when I leave the house. Put on my clothes. I just do these things without thinking, which is why I'm inured to alarm. Wake up enough nights in some guy's tub, you stop asking questions. And so do they. But Hannah, she's only twelve. And when I yell, she's shocked.

"Are you out of your mind?" I said. "Those pills can kill you. Where are they? Tell me right now."

But she didn't, and I doubted any password would get me back in her room.

Hannah likes to tell the story so that no one is ashamed: On an expedition to Guatemala, our dad spent one night with a biologist who worked on lethal paralytic shellfish poisoning. She got pregnant, but kept it to herself. Not sure what perversed her ethics—debt, probably—but a couple years later she resurfaced to extort money from Dad or blow the story. Guess she didn't figure on the dispassion with which he regarded his family life. Come D-day, he just accepted the baby into our home with the same indolence you might see in a guy picking up his mail. As for Mother, she didn't even meet Hannah for a day and then only because the nanny, Maurice, had given Hannah's toddler leash enough slack to let her get from the pantry to the living room. Maurice, who'd snuck into the States from Barbados, was always trying to patent habits indigenous to her clan. She'd lash groceries to her body with a fabric sling. Sometimes she wore Hannah that way, all over town. The toddler leash was years ahead of its time, part suspender, part sarong.

Dad had been in charge of hiring our nannies. The arrangement was this: he'd offer asylum, they'd offer themselves to science. It's true that human vaccination trials border on genocide. That as a result of the trials, hundreds of illegal immigrants died and none was missed. But Dad had an answer for everything. If pressed, he'd reason that human trials were the only way to devise vaccines, that many diseases simply do not reproduce in animal hosts. Next he'd refer me to Edward Jenner, who discovered vaccination by noting that dairymaids exposed to cowpox didn't seem to get smallpox. To prove it, he had to zap a little boy with the cow stuff, then with pathogenic smallpox juice. The boy lived. And look at the results: the word *vaccine* derives from the Latin word for cow, rooting a pillar of epidemiology in that most harmless and ridiculous of creatures.

Maurice was spared, though she was frequently ill and once confined in a Level 4 biocontainment hospital suite while Hannah wailed outside the roller rink because no one was there to pick her up. She still has the toddler leash stuffed in a drawer. We miss Dad but don't talk about it.

On TV: rats. Rats whose vectoring of bubonic plague nearly wiped out fourteenth-century Europe.

In short: Here we go again.

"What a time we live in," Agneth said. "Horrible."

I threw a pillow at the screen. Stanley, God bless him, said at least we've got the kosher chickens. Chickens at the plant are safe as can be.

My stomach hurt. Mother had boxed herself in the faux fireplace. She liked to say it was the safest spot come the big one. Also:

From every corner hails word of the Apocalypse. And: If disease doesn't get us, the Big One will. I knew I was not going to last long in this environment, so I looked to Agneth for guidance. She'd taken steps to protect herself from plague by wearing those surgical masks, even though the protection was nominal. Also, she was knitting a kimono, which meant she knew how to experience peace of mind. I thought yarn probably wasn't the best fiber for a kimono, but she told me to take it up with *Vogue*.

Aggie is a marvel. There is a Potatohead affect to the way her body has arranged itself over the years that makes her enjoyable to hug. Also to watch, since when she laughs, her stomach bobs with zero regard for what the rest of her is doing. Her stomach bobs when she's sitting down! I have often found her in the bathroom, coloring in her eyebrows with blue pencil. There is no telling her it's blue. You can't tell Agneth anything. She trucks with mortality better than anyone I know. She is teaching herself Japanese so that in the next life, she has a leg up. I ask what if she comes back a clam. She says it doesn't work that way. That the mind always out-lives the body and can only reincarnate in a brain sophisticated enough to host it.

Aggie has ideas, among them that Mother is hosting Knut the Soft, a ninth-century Viking who had to be carried on a shield, but who still sacked Angers, maybe Nantes, and was pretty good-looking, too. As the story goes, either he ate too much or he was born with Klinefelter syndrome, which meant he had man boobs and soft skin, high cheekbones, and the most fuckable ass in Jut-land.

Hard to tell if Aggie's diagnosis was a compliment or not.

As for me, she would not say whose spirit was manifest in this body of mine. And I was okay with that. Because if I was a faggot Viking, I don't think that'd sit well. Even so, I'd ask if she had thoughts about what I should do to rampart the family against, I don't know, the swell of doom tiding high now that plague seemed imminent.

"Just stay here," she'd say. "Your mother could use you."

"Have things been bad?"

"Yes."

"More than usual? You know how Isifrid gets."

At this point, Agneth would sigh because she does not like me calling Mother by name, which I've been doing for years. Isifrid Clark. My dad used to call her Dizzy Izzy, which was cute until it was true.

"Things have been bad, yes, especially for Hannah. You think it's good for her living here? I'm an old woman. What can I do?"

At this point, I would sigh because there was just so much wrong with Hannah's life. For one, Mother had put her in a day camp called Good-Time Living. As I understood it, the campers were indoctrinated with hate, hate, hate. Racism, jingoism, intolerance. Those and Bible study, which should have nothing in common.

At night, the Hazmat stickers on Hannah's door glowed neon. She seemed to have only one friend, a black girl named Indra, who couldn't possibly attend Good-Time Living.

"Now go talk to her," Agneth would say. "And put some drops in your eyes. At the very least you could act the role model."

Right. Pass the mantle to me. Boy do I look good in this mantle.

I checked my phone. There was a message from Dirty Ben and one from Wanda to say that my abducting Stanley had affronted Dad's legacy. How true. The sentinel surveillance program gave everyone a sense of mission. It was proactive. And for a while, it seemed to give Dad relief from the anxiety of everything else he faced. The labs at the U.S. Army Medical Research Institute of Infectious Disease are notoriously chaotic. Their inventory is a mess. I could probably walk out of there with enough Ebola to wipe out Chicago. Stuff goes missing all the time, and no one gives a shit unless the press makes a stink. In our case, the press made a stink. Dad was indicted, slandered, ruined. The charge? He stole the vials himself. Psychologists said he was a highly patriotic American with plans to arrest the country's march toward hedonism. Nothing like widespread death to reassert the importance in culture of family, tradition, and salt-of-the-earth labor. Other people said he was a eugenicist who'd targeted the poor and colored. The CDC fired him. Hate mail accrued on his desk at home. A local restaurant refused to seat him. A couple months of this, and no one was surprised by his death.

We've all been interviewed. The house has been searched.

Mother had to relocate her stash and paraphernalia to a safe-deposit box downtown. Then the contents of the box were subpoenaed. The Feds, in their mercy, overlooked the stuff. They were looking for plague, not a Tiffany sack of crack.

In the last eight months, I have intended to prepare for the worst. To get the family safe. Each time there's a letter, I swear to get on it. So far, I have researched two gas-impermeable bubble tents.

It was *Narga* and *Glanders* and *African Horse Sickness* before Hannah relented and opened her door. I was disappointed. I'd been trying to accord the number of guesses with how many Klonopins she'd give me.

She was still on the bed, computer open. Her laptop has a seventeen-inch screen because she does not like to squint. She appeared to be toggling between a chat room and a catalog. I watched her type in the numbers from Mother's credit card. When I asked what she was buying, she said Crimean-Congo hemorrhagic fever virus. Freeze-dried and everything.

If she ends up being the next Unabomber, I will not be surprised.

"Klonopin?" I said, because really, what else was there.

"I was *kidding*," she said. "God, you're a mess."

"I know," I said. "I'm sorry."

"Fine. Now can you go?"

And just like that, I gave up. I slunk out the door. Six others lined the hallway, and behind each could have been Agneth. "Agneth!" I yelled. "What should I do?"

But Agneth and Isifrid could not be bothered. They were playing gin in the blue room.

Three

Mother used to have a dog. A Neapolitan mastiff. Her given name was Celina but we called her No Face. She was all slobber and flap. Mother thought she'd been trained as a guard dog, which we hardly needed eight floors up in a doorman building, and which didn't even seem true since No Face was more hog than bouncer. But I guess she looked scary enough. The dead stare. Sorrow of the world. And if she sat on you, forget it. No Face could clear the coffee table and move furniture. Her cheek meat, like drapery, would continue to ripple long after she'd come to a stop. Her paws were big as muffins. No Face and I had a storied past. When I started in on heroin, I got intense about there being people in the house. Had to be empty for me to shoot. Empty and dark. So I'd lock myself in the closet and listen real hard, certain that if there'd been no one home five seconds ago, there was someone home now. Only No Face confused things. I could shoot so long as I knew it was her making noise, but you could never be sure it was her. So I'd lock us both in the closet and listen real hard. Only she had a chain around her neck that drowned out whatever else I was listening for. I'd sit on her like a bench and tell her to can it, but every time she moved, I'd have to start listening all over again. This could go on for hours. It never occurred to me to take off her collar.

Later I'd be on the floor, staring at our ceiling fresco. The will to live might have left my heart, but the fresco still had me. I'd start counting angels and having the talk, like: Look, people, can't you come down and get me or something? Maybe I'd start to cry. Or feel like crying. Either way, No Face would plant her wattle on my chest so the whole thing spread out like batter. I loved that dog more than I loved my parents. Sometimes I figured that between me and death was No Face. Everyone else could live without me, but who'd take care of her the way I did?

When she was six, No Face ate the rubber finger brush I used to scrub her teeth. It lodged in her throat, and she died. Now I wear her collar, even to bed. Stanley has been quick to understand. He still wears his wedding ring. And his wife's earrings, which are diamond studs. He says she was wearing the studs when she died.

Mother says the collar makes me look like a retard. It's been five years, get over it. When we have this talk, it's all I can do not to ram my fist down her throat. I have rage. In a former life, I was probably a jihadi teen.

Stanley disagrees. He thinks I was a turtle. I tried to explain Aggie's theory of the reincarnated mind, but got stuck on his choice. A turtle? Soft on the inside, he said, then nibbled my hip.

The content of our rapport was growing. Our first few days in the apartment, he was tiptoeing around Isifrid and telling me about it. After that, he lost interest. And after a week, he was onto me. He wanted to know me, he said. He wanted to talk. Apparently, we were on a mission to repair things with Kam. I said *he* was on a mission, since I couldn't stand the thought of ever seeing her again.

Whenever we have sex, I swear he talks to his wife. No matter. I am not much into it, either. The social worker at the Listerhab, which is what I call it, said my life's motifs were apathy and armament. I guess this means I cannot enjoy intercourse. Probably I should have asked her to clarify. I remember she said this in a conversation just days before I got released. We'd been having one-on-one sessions that lasted an hour. At five to, a buzzer would go off followed by the exquisitely debasing *We have to stop now*, and the social worker arranging on her face a look both aloof *and* sympathetic. Professional rue. These people have rue down to a science. Sometimes I got so enamored of that look I wouldn't say anything meaty until seconds before the buzzer. The social worker would get peeved. Like I was yanking her chain. But I wasn't yanking, I was enamored. And that was a big deal. Interest in anything but drugs and sleep was a big deal.

The longer me and Stanley camped at Mother's, the more I

wondered what he was doing there. Sometimes I'd ask, noting that we had not called Wanda and that we had no money. But he'd just grin and hit a bottle of rye and next I knew he'd be ejaculating into a cup because he wanted to test his sperm. Bought a kit online. His sperm used to be fine, but he wanted to know for sure that age and alcoholism had not ruined them. His wife could not carry a child, so she had frozen her eggs intending to find a carrier once Stanley dried out, the logic being that dads who are sober fare better than dads who are not. Problem was, Stanley could not dry out. Problem was, Sylvie waited and then she died. I did not like the idea of Stanley gauging his sperm around me because it meant that at any second, he could ask. Like I was in any shape to host a baby. But this is how he got me to talk. If I was talking, he wasn't.

We were in bed. I could hear Hannah on the phone with someone at *Scholastic News*. She was asking about plague, playing dumb and waiting for the guy to let something slip. She thinks the government made up the Minnesota letter to corral support now that a recent poll owed the president's meager approval ratings to disinterest in politics and, coevally, a lust for embattled politicians as seen on TV.

Stanley took my hand and pressed it to his forehead.

"Am I warm?"

I sat up. "Why are you asking?"

"I don't know. I feel warm. What's wrong? Oh c'mon. It's not *superplague*."

"Can you not call it that?"

"Fine, but am I warm?"

"No."

I moved my hand down his chest. He was wearing briefs that for all their sag looked more like shorts, and a V-neck undershirt. His stomach bore the swell of drink fairly well, retaining a tautness that surprised you on contact. His limbs, by contrast, were as toothpicks in the sausage. I found the architecture of his body a source of delight; it was so odd, it moved me.

"Stanley, what if it gets out? It won't, but I'm just saying, what if it does? What would you do?"

"I don't know. I've always wanted to take flying lessons."

He pressed his gut to the small of my back. We spooned.

"Funny," I said. "You're a laugh riot. I'm talking plague and you want to hit the skies. Which, now that I think about it, makes some kind of sense."

"Well, I just don't see the point in speculating. Nothing's happened since the letter. I've got other things on my mind. I've been thinking more about Sylvie and what to do."

I stopped him short. "Yeah? I've been thinking about some things, too. You want me to talk? I'll talk. My heart's broken."

"I figured."

"Really?"

"Of course. Takes one to see one. Now go on."

So I did. I said he was a photographer disguised as a real-estate broker. Eric Ludlow. That he had a tattoo of a bull's-eye at the base of his neck. Ate Captain Crunch for dinner. That when we talked, it was like this:

Eric: Well, my collection of photos is out. Let's hear it for self-celebration amid the suffering—

Lucy: I know! And it's terrific. Puts me in the mood for pudding.

Eric: Let me ask you: What aspect of your life's pleasures is *not* somehow captured by the phenomenon of pudding?

Lucy: I thought you'd never ask. None. None whatsoever.

But mostly, it was like this:

I love you.

Me, too.

Stanley sat up. "What's all that supposed to mean?"

"We understood each other."

"And?"

"And nothing. He got married."

"Married? How awful."

"Yep. Possibly the worst day of my life, except for I didn't know it. *Shhh*, listen."

Hannah was shouting into the phone. Saying the *Scholastic* guy was holding out on her.

"That girl needs guidance," Stanley said.

"And you need to mind your own business."

He began to knead my shoulders. "You still hurting about him? This Eric guy?"

I reached over to the bedside table and took eight Vicodin. Then I held up the bottle. "See these? Nothing hurts so long as I got these."

I slept for sixteen hours. When I awoke, it was a little after three in the morning. Isifrid was up, watching TV in the yellow room. If it's not a quilt show, she's usually watching a program that smuggles in the grotesque under pretense of education. Face-eating Tumor. The Boy Whose Skin Fell Off. Tonight it's a show about the Vikings. Isifrid's got a thing for those guys, courtesy Agneth. In the show, they are reenacting the sack of the Lindisfarne monastery. They have cast men with long hair and pockmarks. When I come in, they are at an excavation site, panning across a skeleton whose ribs are flayed like an artichoke.

"Nice, Isifrid. Oh, jeez, why are you crying?"

But really, I should have known. Her face was all dribble. Not a tissue in sight.

"Here, let me." I wiped her chin with the hem of my shirt and sat next to her on the couch. She balled up and put her head in my lap. Her hair was textured like mesh. It was tinted wet sand; last week was dry sand. So long as the color hewed to a shade of beach, she was happy. Or as happy as Isifrid got, which just meant being divested of the usuals: despair, mania, grief.

Her collarbone jutted into my thigh. It's true, right, that touch is always a crossroads? I tried to put my arms around her and make us a family, but it was more like trying to cradle music stands. Totally awkward. And she had gotten very thin.

I asked if she had more. She nodded at a book on the table, *Why England Slept*. I thought she was trying to tell me something, so I flipped it open. Title page intact—who knew JFK wrote about WWII?—but the rest was gutted. In the well was about a nose of coke. I rejoiced. Then stopped. Mother was never generous with her stash. Normally she kept it in a cabinet above the sink, way up high behind the pitchers. This way, she'd have to mount a chair and remove the pitchers to get at it. The work of retrieval was supposed to be a deterrent, though I saw her on that chair a lot.

These days, I'm not so into cocaine or heroin, because they make me feel alive, and who wants that. Sometimes, if that's all I got, I might even pass, which tonight I did, seeing in the main no reason to alloy the metals of my heart, not with cocaine or anxiety resulting from Isifrid on cocaine. The latter, however, I could not control.

I asked what was wrong, besides the obvious.

"Aggie's sick," she said.

"Is not. I just saw her. She's fine."

"Then Hannah's sick."

I shook my head.

"Are you sick?"

I said no.

"Then it's me. Someone in this house is sick, I can feel it."

I nodded. I'd already seen her cough up black sludge that cleaved to the sink. She wheezed. Had chronic sore throat. Fever, sweats, nausea. But that was just because of drug abuse. Not a real illness, just drugs.

"Do you think maybe you oughta slow it down for tonight?" I tried to put this gently.

"I'm sorry?" she said, like she had not understood me. "Are you *back* from rehab? Is that rehab speak I hear?"

Our dynamic was so convoluted, I didn't have a name for it. But this emotion of hers, it was not scorn. After all, she intended to pay for rehab down South. She even wanted me to go. And I hardly had much choice. Wanda was not going to keep me on indefinitely and hell if I could hold down a job or find a place to live on my own. I was, on a daily basis, entirely too sleepy for such ventures.

"How about you switch to something lighter?" I offered.

But I'd gone too far. She snatched the book from my hand. Looked both ways and fled the room in a crouch.

The voice-over on TV was saying that the redoubtable heathens assailed the Baltic Coast and founded the Russian state. That as pirates, rogues, and butchers, the Northmen appalled all Western Christendom. That they ruled the seas and annexed territory, only to lose everything in the Middle Ages. They lacked colonial sense. They didn't have a program. Without a program, the Ost-men in Ireland disappeared, the Scottish isles reverted to Scotland, the Danelaw in England collapsed, the settlers in Iceland and Greenland died of famine, and the Swedish people of the Kievan state in Russia were folded into Slav culture. The voice-over guy, who also does movie trailers, was narrating with gravitas because herein this arc was a cautionary tale.

TV off, pillows thrown. There was even a pillow moat growing around the TV from how many we kept throwing at it. I called Kam. Her husband answered, none too pleased. His voice made a hatchery of my gut, like little birds pecking away.

"It's for you," he said, and passed the phone to Kam. I'd called before. Mostly at night.

"It's four in the morning," Kam said. She must have had her lips right up against the phone because I could hear her breathe. Her breath stood in for the silence I was supposed to break. I covered the mouthpiece with my palm. I was not going to talk. In no uni-verse was I going to talk.

"Oh, come on, Lucy. You've got to stop this. If you're going to call, at least you need to talk."

Her husband was telling her to hang up. Just hang up, already. But Kam, she wouldn't do that. My antics had always given her the chance to put up with them. I let her forbear, and how many peo-ple could say that of their friends?

"Okay, what is it that you need to hear? That I forgive you for missing the wedding? Sure. Forgiven. There were four hundred people there, you weren't that missed. Okay? Can you say some-thing now?"

No. No I could not. The night our friend got stabbed after we left that party? It was Kam's boyfriend at the time. Thing is, the knifer had been after me because I owed 12K to my dealer and who cared if I was a girl, it was time to pay up. I never told Kam, but she knew. A week later, she wrote me a check, saying her mom would never notice. Only her mom did notice and Kam had to spend every weekend after that helping her pitch celebrity wear on the Home Shopping Network. Mrs. Yalamanchilli had PIs on retainer who'd photograph the outfits the stars were wearing. She'd buy a thousand of same and address herself to the vulnerable women of

America. As the logic went, you couldn't be unattractive while wearing the vintage fichu Kate Hudson wore at Cannes.

I'd been silent on the phone for ten minutes. A fight was brewing between Kam and the husband. He had to get up for work in three hours. This thing with me was getting out of hand. "Fine," Kam said, and then, into the phone, "Get some help, Lucy. I mean it. So you've tried before, try again."

I heard the husband say so long as I wasn't in trouble, Kam should hang up. And Kam say, "Eric, be nice."

Then the line went dead.

I put the phone to my temple like a gun.

As if on cue, Stanley came trotting in with dropper in one hand, plastic strip in the other. He was waving it like a foam finger. "Above twenty million," he said. "*Way* above." He was almost dancing.

So Stanley has live sperm. No small feat when you consider the stats. Just a few decades ago, guys had counts like 150 million per milliliter. Now they average 50 million. Then there's the alphabet thing, which has A sperm swimming forward, fast and in a straight line; B sperm, which zigzag and meander; C sperm, which move their tails but get nowhere; and D sperm, which are dumbstruck. Some sperm like to fertilize in groups, which is like trying to thread a needle with the spool. Some of them look like hammerheads and some have no heads at all. I think laptop technology is to blame but Stanley says it's PCBs. And heavy metal.

"So what now?" I said. "And why are you awake?"

He threw himself on the couch and flung his legs over the arm. The couches in the yellow room were upholstered with tapestry of squires in the grass, sipping tea. If you sat on them too long, you'd get sore.

"I have them tested for speed and movement," he said.

"You can do that at home?"

"No, I need a lab."

"Sounds expensive."

"Very. But I was thinking—"

"Me, too."

"About what?"

"I'm still hurting. Pretty bad, in fact."

"Say more."

And I did.

Eric and I met on a train platform in Speonk. We were both waiting for the 6:15, which never arrived. He had eyes like wet gravel. He wore a black ring on his index. He was also barefoot. Later, he said what made him like me was that I didn't ask about his feet. As if it never even crossed my mind. And I suppose it hadn't. He said he'd been out taking photos of a homeless guy named Shoes who collected footwear in a shopping cart. Eric said he'd given his flip-flops away as payment. So this guy with the pristine feet, he also took photos. And he was generous.

Later I told him I knew it was love when he didn't ask about my hospital gown or giant slippers. He said he'd thought it was cute. I said, Hospital breakout. He said, Well, *yeah*.

When we met, he had a fiancée in Berlin. Kam would tell me it was a bad scene. I'd agree and as soon as she'd leave my house, I'd call him. We'd joke about depression. We'd say: How long is this premature-death joke gonna last us? Eh, just a couple hours more.

But after a few months, it was pretty much like this: I am unreachably in love. I have no emotional life outside the one I live for him.

Me and Eric, we shared. Or *I* shared. I told him about Isifrid, who used to sell hats on the streets of a little town in Norway to feed her six younger sisters. How she fought for everything she has, in stark contrast to her daughter, who is lazy and useless. How in the mornings before school, I used to sit outside her door with a bowl of cereal and wait for her to get up.

Nights, I said, were like this: I sit in the bathroom and sob, but am afraid to wake her because a multimillion-dollar hat company needs a CEO who's well rested.

Growing up, I said, was a minor improvement: At school, I study only if the other kids are doing it. Mostly I pay them to write my essays. I work at the Gap and have my first real kiss with a boy named Al. We are in a stall in the dressing room. The store is closed, we're cleaning up. Security tags arrayed on the floor are evidence of theft, which loss will come out of my paycheck since where was I? Wasn't I looking? I bend down to fetch the tags. I am wearing a skirt and Wal-Mart briefs, which color is sky, which appeal is grandma. Al is seventeen, I am fifteen. This makes him unassailable, so that when he divests me of the grandma blues, I do not resist. He uses his fingers to probe for the hiatus in my skin. I think: *Ow*, and: *I have no hiatus!* After, he kisses me bye.

I start smoking cigarettes with brown filters because the white ones are for girls who think they've got a shot at being pretty.

I have friends whose only sustenance for days is cum.

I kiss girls in front of other girls. Two men fall for me, maybe three. I am comically and wrenchingly obsessed with a guy I work with. If he likes pig brawn steeped in wine, I like it, too. He belittles hair gel, wears socks with sandals, but I do not care. I follow him around all summer until I know his schedule well enough to arrange a meeting I can parlay into an extemporaneous date. Outside Leeanne's Bakery it goes like this—Girl in whose mind love is an option: Hey, what a coincidence! You like Leeanne's, too? Don't they just have the *best* pie? Lemme buy you some pie! Guy in whose forging from the goop of nature her life began: Actually, I just come here to read and catch up on my alone time, you know?

I am crushed, I recover. I become a pothead. I don't date anyone. I am frequently sad, though I do not know why. Diary entries are maudlin.

I drop acid. My parents send me to another boarding school in the country. I have an affair with the cook. We fuck on a drainboard. He teaches me how to make crème brûlée, I torch the sugar scrim and then, by accident, I torch him. Somewhere in Connecticut is a man whose eyebrows never grew back.

I learn nothing all year, and I am afraid of the cafeteria food. I am sad, very sad.

A doctor tells me I lack for potassium and electrolytes. Another tells me that's not it at all. I think of what I can do to make hurt go away. Options usually include doing violence to myself, the way people in the Middle Ages thought that plague was caused by BAD AIR and that the only antidote to BAD AIR was MORE BAD AIR, which is why back then you might have seen hundreds of people sniffing shit on a sewer bank. Guess it didn't work for them, either.

I get myself up to six lines an hour. I sit in restaurant patios and tap ash into my own purse by mistake.

I finally make the switch from coke to heroin, though the love does not last. I blow through every vein I can find.

I date a man who wants to marry me. He says: I love your voice, your touch, your tenderness and grace, your snatches of melody, your fingers interlaced with mine. This kindness is withering. We break up. Later, I am told that I killed off the good part of him.

I meet Dirty Ben. His bisexuality is a turn-on. His diseased genitals are not.

I do horse tranquilizer. I fall apart. I am sleepy. I am longing. I am depressed. I get MORE depressed. I meet Eric. I fall in love. And love is good. Only it's not enough. Not even close, which is what finally does me in. We go to a concert in the park. The music kindles a familiar sensation of loneliness and hurt and need that nearly drives me crazy. I can't take it. I am in pain. I look back and see nothing but THIS. I look ahead and see more. I am besieged by self-disgust. I am blanched and without hope. I cry in his lap. I plead with him to help me. Please help me. Take care of me. Please.

"And that was Eric," I say.

Stanley's mouth is half open. "Jesus Lord Almighty. You are one depressing woman."

"Don't I know it."

"So he got married?"

I nod. "But not to the fiancée. He left her."

"Huh?"

"He met someone else."

"I'm confused."

I shrug and say my love for him is dismantling. That making him laugh, which I did often, gave me the most joy I'd ever had. And yes, that he got married. To my oldest friend, Kam.

Four

Stanley is answering a questionnaire about his ejaculate history for the andrology lab at Cornell. He's looking to me for help. Is it clear and watery? Does it coagulate? He reads from the brochure: *ejaculatory duct obstruction; prostatic dysfunction; severe ipsilateral abnormality*. I stop him at the *hidden testis*. "What the hell is that?"

"No idea. But it sounds bad, right?"

Hannah says he should just take matters into his own hands. That an Integrated Visual Optical System for sperm analysis can be bought online. Windows-based. Plus, she adds, it comes with *swine software*.

Isifrid says fertility is no joke. That she had a hell of a time conceiving me. I suggest maybe her drug use was to blame. She says, Probably.

Hannah wants to bring me to Identity Camp. The summer's over, but Good-Time Living does a family thing one weekend every fall. She says it's like a workshop, and that she doesn't have a whole lotta options. The sleeves on Aggie's kimono taper at the wrist. A yarn kimono with cuffs and gussets. No way she's getting in with the Japanese next life, and no way is she bonding with the parents at Good-Time Living. As for Mother, she's just not up for Christian Identity Camp. So I tell Hannah okay, but ask if I can bring Stanley.

"Only if you say he's our uncle."

"Thanks," Stanley says. "I'm working through my virility over here and you're not helping."

"She's twelve," I say, like that's some kind of defense.

"I *know* what ejaculate is," she says. "More than you, anyway."

I hear the elevator open in the vestibule, which means it's mail time. I used to love mail time during years in which I was oversubscribed to print media whose niche content gave me hope. Like: I know, I'll fix cars when I grow up; I want to collect, hone, and brandish arcane weaponry; I want to *blow glass*. Finally, though, all I wanted was to do drugs, and since magazine paper does not smoke well, me and print media broke up.

Today's delivery includes a letter with a clipping about my dad, circled in red wax marker. We are always getting hate mail, now more than ever. I guess people hate us. Even though the Feds and press absolved Dad retroactively—no one thought a man likely to pinch vials would also commit suicide—people hate us.

Hannah grabs the letter. She's been making a scrapbook. I do not find this funny in the least, though she seems to think it's a hoot.

"Oh, look," she says. "This guy writes that we're all going to hell. That he can't wait to see us in hell."

Izzy wants to know if he's writing from jail. The answer is yes, yes he is.

"You know," Hannah says, "those guys in jail will be better off than us if superplague comes. Fuck."

"Can you not call it that?" I say.

"Language!" Mother yells.

But Hannah is not having it. "Hello? Is anyone noticing that everywhere you turn, someone says he'll see us in hell? That there's nothing out there but a million ways to die?"

As if we don't know. As if she ever talks about anything else. She is obsessed. And now she has to itemize the possibilities. If not the plague, then how about this: Three guys show up at Dodger Stadium with inhalers full of smallpox. One guy contracts untreatable staph in an ICU and spreads it to everyone in his ward, followed by everyone in the world. Mad cow, SARS, Lyme. Terminal strep and Ebola. E. coli. Definitive type 104 salmonella. Each has the potential to kill millions, and the CDC is not prepared. Consider smallpox. If you inhale just a single particle, you're dead. Fever, headache, rash. Ulcers clustered in the lining of your throat and mouth. Abscesses congregated on your skin, parsing skin from muscle. On the inside, a meltdown. The virus invades healthy cells to reproduce. The immune system fights back. The result is organ soup. Patients often die fighting for breath. Heart failure or toxic shock. Lucid till the end and, in the case of hemorrhagic pox, alive while the whites of their eyeballs turn livid and the membranes in their bodies dissolve. All within two weeks.

Hannah is flushed. I worry she's more excited than anxious. But probably not. Probably anxiety has so clotted her brain, the blood has to go somewhere. I am feeling a little pink, myself.

"Remember Dad's simulation project?" she says. "It's all coming true." And with that, she flees to her room. I can hear the lock click from here.

"Poor girl," Aggie says. "So tortured."

I suggest that maybe Hannah was a Vietnam vet. That in a former life, she was a miserable war veteran whose family abjured the government not two weeks after the draft, whose friends were hippies, and whose wheelchair was found in San Francisco Bay, but whose body was not found at all. Aggie shakes her head and says, gravely, "That would be better. She'd suffer less."

I ask what does that mean. I ask who was Hannah. But Aggie's done talking. She says it's time to retire and when none of us moves, she seems appalled. It's seven in the evening.

Stanley wonders how we can understand anything through that surgical mask. I say it's an acquired skill, though even without the mask she's hard to follow. Imagine a Norwegian with sticky lips and no teeth, then imagine this person speaking a foreign tongue, and you've got Nana.

I watch her stuff the kimono and needles into a shopping bag.

After she's gone, Isifrid says, "You really ought to be nicer to her, Lucy. She won't be around forever." She sounds choked up, but that's only because she's yet to exhale smoke from the joint Stanley's passing around. "And you," she says, nodding at Stanley, "you're not helping your fertility with all this grass. You should probably just give the rest to me."

"What about *her*?" he says, and points at me. "Doesn't she get any? I think she probably needs it more than you."

"I'm right here, you know. I can hear what you're saying."

But he just carries on. "Missed her oldest friend's wedding, calls their place every night, the broken heart, I'd want to tune out of my life, too."

"Is this your idea of helping?" I say. "Let's light a candle for my darkest hour in recent memory?"

Mother sits up. "You missed Kam's wedding?"

Stanley and I look at her incredulously, though by now, her absence from the world should startle no one.

"It was awful," Stanley says.

I nod. And Mother, she starts to laugh. She laughs for a solid two minutes. Without apology or effort to stymie this upswelling of glee that has me less offended than bored.

"Oh, that's sad," she says, regaining her voice and sighing.

"Yep," I say. "So much for that. Lucy strikes again."

"Oh, come on," Stanley says. "Don't be so harsh. I think you're doing all the right things. You *are* going to rehab, when is that again? Rehab definitely counts toward putting your life together. There will be other chances to show up."

"Whenever there's space," I say, and reach for my Gatorade. I don't know that I've ever been short on electrolytes, but that doc spooked me for life. "Some spot in Florida. Popular I guess."

Mother snorts. "What gave you that idea? It's in Texas. Get your boots on."

I am chewing on a straw, which drops right out of my mouth.

"That's right. Close to the border. Don't look so horrified. It's not Tikrit."

"Who found this place?"

"Aggie."

"You let Agneth choose my rehab?"

"Would you rather I did it?"

"It's not that hard," Stanley says. "Make a few calls, ask some questions."

Mother shrugs. "No matter now."

Stanley pinches my thigh. "You'll look cute in chaps. Take photos."

"I don't feel well," Mother says. She's looking at Stanley. "Where'd you get this stuff?"

"The park."

"Oh, great."

He looks confused. He doesn't know about the delivery boys who'll door-to-door an eighth and still charge you a hundred dollars. He doesn't know kind from basil. I pat him on the knee and say Mother's just upset about other things.

Is it odd to talk rehab while smoking a joint? I imagine it says something about my level of commitment.

"Texas?" I say. "The desert?"

I look from Mother to Stanley, but neither seems inclined to respond. Perhaps Hannah will be more sympathetic. I excuse myself. I go to her room and walk in. I don't bother to knock or password because I have no hope they will work.

I find her on the floor with scrapbook open. She's got a tower of completed books by the wall. I think she's got every article about Dad that's come out since the theft, plus any news item that even mentions his name.

I see one from the *Tribune & Georgian* about how if the plague hits St. Mary's, Georgia will mobilize. Also, in case of emergency, supplies will be doled out at the Heritage Bank. And just in case you forgot: the plague went missing from Dr. Michael Clark's lab in December of last year, etc., etc.

I ask if I can help. She says, "Suit yourself."

There's a Ziploc of clippings that need a home. I overturn the bag and start sifting. I'd like to tell Hannah that saving such things will not help her turn the corner on grief. Or that articles demonizing our father will not help her remember him any better. But then maybe this is her process, and who am I to interfere. My instincts about how to care for other people are worthless.

Do I have a process? I remember the morning I found his body, I'd eaten a blueberry muffin. I'd woken up, intending to secure a job of value so that at least someone in this family could feel good about himself. I'm pretty sure Dad was still in his robe when I waved goodbye. No kiss or anything, just a wave from the door to the kitchen because I'd grab a muffin on the way to every temp agency in the city where I'd cop to skills like medical billing and the Internet. Internet proficient is what I was calling it.

Of course, I had to find the agencies, locate the power button on my laptop, and forge a résumé, so by the time noon rolled around I was still at a café, pulping muffin crumbs with a spoon. But I was hopeful. The months before had been so lowly, I'd really thought we were coming out of it. Dad was up before nine. Mother was the most sober I'd seen her in years. And Hannah, she was doing some PI work, wanting to exonerate Dad, but also maybe to find him out, because in the long run, it was way better if he had the vials than if some nut had them. Or some nut likely to bioterrorize the country. There was much ransacking of his stuff, which he did not take well. A part of me worries this is what tipped him over, that his own family doubted him. But we didn't doubt. It was just fear. Which is what I experienced when I found him suspended from the ceiling fan. I can still picture the verdigris furrowed into his neck—rope burn, I think—and one foot that had lost a slipper, fallen to the tile. Also, the police removing his body in a tarpaulin sack. Just what sort of process gets you over that? I really think the articles are a bad idea.

I ask Hannah if she's certain she wants to be doing this. "Look," I say, and hold up a piece from the *Los Angeles Times*, "this one makes like Dad had bad blood with the higher-ups."

"Totally untrue," she says, and glues it down.

The phone rings. I hear Mother hollering, saying it's my friend from Dad's lab. We talk for thirty seconds, but it's enough. I get back to Hannah, and when there's another call for me, it's Dirty Ben. I pick up in the yellow room. He wants to know how I am. Fine. What's new? Nothing. You feeling any better? I dunno. The conversation lurches thus until he mentions Eric. Now I am all ears. Did he say anything about me?

"You really need to stop calling them."

I am incensed. My nerves are starting to go. "Lemme tell you something, *Ben*." And I tell him good. Only I lose the anger real fast. I say, "You know I was only with Eric once, right?"

"Luce, this really isn't any of my business—"

"—but that one time, I was sober. You know I never had sober sex before? I was always too afraid. Like I was about to be found out somehow."

"Lucy—"

"—but with him, it was different. And forget the sex part. I mean across the board. You have any idea what that's like? After so

much time alone to have someone you can actually talk to? Someone who isn't repelled by your inner life? Someone who maybe actually cherishes it?"

"Yes. But he's married, honey."

"I know. And no one is at fault, except me. Kam didn't know
what I felt, I didn't tell her. Didn't tell anyone. I'm just not one for
talk, I guess."

"But you two have been friends since you were ten or something."

"So? You've lived in your apartment for, what, six years? How
intimate are you with the wall?"

"You are not a wall."

"It's a metaphor."

"You are not a wall."

The sigh that booms out my mouth startles us both. A booming
sigh.

He says, "I told Eric you mixed up the dates, if that helps."

"But I did mix them up. What, he thinks I missed it on purpose?
Oh, God. This humiliation never ends."

I stand up to regroup. The coil between phone and cradle is so
long, I could probably swaddle myself like a mummy or skin stump.
I pace. Over the years, many specialists have told me I need to feel
the feelings. But when the experience of hurt begins to feel like a
dry heave, I think you do better to suppress with all you got.

"Lucy," he says.

I answer. "It's fine. I'm fine. I'll stop calling them."

"You can call me, instead."

If this is meant to hoist my mood, it has the opposite effect.

"You still there?" he says. "Hey, do you want to come with me to
a meeting?" He means a twelve-step thing, which seems pointless
at the moment.

"Not really. I hate hearing all that crap over and over. Besides, I
got rehab coming up, so I'm good."

"That is ridiculous. But look, you know where to find us when
you change your mind."

I love his certainty. As if when I see the light, he'll be waiting.
We say bye. I say it as if I've just been denied a lolly by my mom.
He says it like a married guy who's got a future.

I listen to the dial tone, and then to Agneth and Isifrid, who've been eavesdropping on multiple extensions.

I know what Izzy's thinking so I say, "Not a chance. Ben's done with our kind. He doesn't deal."

"How tedious," she says, and hangs up.

This leaves me and Agneth. "Agneth," I say. "What the hell am I going to do? What are we gonna do? I just got a really scary call from the lab."

"And I don't want to know. I'm going to bed," she says, and hangs up.

But I find this unacceptable. Down the hall from the kitchen, down another hall, and to the right is her room, itself the largest of three earmarked for the domestic live-in help. A hundred years ago, I bet it was adolescent serving girls riven with syphilis. During my family's tenure, it was the nannies, and after that, a trio of empty rooms Agneth commandeered for purposes that seemed to change yearly. She once had a terrarium going, for plants that needed little to no sunlight. Later, she let Hannah devise an exer- cise room for her Peruvian guinea pig, never mind that the pig was lethargic. And timid. For instance, no way was he getting in that high-rise hamster wheel or, for that matter, the nine feet of piping Hannah had put down. So the room was a bust and anyway, the pig, Tesla, died shortly thereafter from an erupted blister made fatal by previously undiagnosed hemophilia. Agneth shut the door on the room after that—the space was tainted—which left her with sleeping chambers that adjoined the last room, which is where I find her now. She is sitting at a table, hunched over a giant square of posterboard.

I ask what she's doing. She says did I knock? I rap my knuckles against the wall and sit down.

"You can stay, but I don't want to hear any plague talk."

I notice she's opened a new box of surgical masks. I notice ten unopened boxes in the closet. We both know these measures are absurd. Like the plague can't penetrate a synthetic dime-store membrane of the sort veiling my nana's respiratory apparatus.

"Fine," I say. "You'll find out soon—"

But she tut-tuts me, which has the effect of defeating whatever urge I had to talk at all.

I lean over the board. It is so large, it occupies the entire table, which seats twelve.

After a moment I cannot resist and say, "Nana, what the hell is this?"

"Have a look," she says, and hands me a magnifying glass. The print is legible from close range but the glass is welcome. I scan a section of what appears to be a diagram. "Okay," I say. "This is the most chaotic family tree I've ever seen. Who are these people? And why are the dates all messed up?"

I see her grin and think: You have got to be kidding. I walk to the end of the table and sure enough, there's Knut the Soft right alongside Izzy's name. So this is our family tree with ornament. I see Knut, I see the peasant waif who was Knut before Knut, and the cave guy who was the peasant. It stops there, which means I am very much wanting to say something about the newt who became Knut, but Agneth seems so serious about these matters, I do not risk it. And anyway, I'm losing my sense of humor the more I peruse the tree.

"Hannah was a flagellant?" I say. "You made her a flagellant? Good grief, that's horrible."

"*I* didn't make her anything. And it's worse than horrible. But it helps me understand her better."

"Oh, come on. Is this how you explain away everything? We are who we are just because we're channeling some other person's ethic?"

She stands up with more vim than should be allowed a woman of her age and drapes a sheet over the board. "Wait," I say. "I didn't find myself. Where am I on the tree?" I start to lift the sheet but she snatches the hem from my hand. I step back. "Are you saying I'm worse than a flagellant? What, was I Mengele?"

She thinks I'm kidding and says, "Don't belittle phenomena you cannot understand. But to answer your questions: yes, reincarnation accounts for many things."

I sit on the floor, cross-legged. "You know, it's convenient the way you use it to absolve people. Like Izzy can't help herself because she's some pansy Viking. It's lazy."

"It's not. And don't talk about your mother that way. If you really want to discuss this, fine, but then you'll have to change your tone. It's arrogant. Hubris killed the cat, you know."

"No, the cat had nine lives, which you, especially, should appreciate."

"And now you are just being rude. Good night," she says, and opens the door for me.

"Nana, I'm sorry. I was just kidding. I'm stressed out. That call from the lab was really bad!"

She pecks me on the cheek, and, before shutting the door, says, "You can hear them, by the way. Voices from the past. They are there if you want them. They speak to us."

"What? Don't talk like that. It makes me think you're crazy. And you are not crazy."

"I might be," she says, and grins.

I trudge down the hall. My body feels like one fat cramp. Jesus fuck. My friend at the lab? He says someone in Minnesota just got sick with superplague. They are short on details but long on gist: the man is gonna die pronto.

Five

Radbard begat Randver begat Sigurd Randversson begat Rag-nar Lodbrok, Bjorn Ironside, Ivar the Boneless, Sigurd Snake in the Eye, Halfdan White Shirt, Sigurd Schlangenaug, Orm Koenig, Erik der Gott Uppsala Koenig, and Knut the Soft, whose epithet I call my own.

What can be said of me? Knut delights in a hearty meal. The ground beef, sweet corn, mashed potato mash. Fit for a king. I am no king. These britches scythe into my groin and buttocks for I 'ave outgrown them, and skins are few. Wish I could drop pounds as well as me aitches.

But this is what we do. The dead eat shepherd's pie. Here I am joined by other members of the family, none of whom I like. There is a leprous pygmy-unfortunate who flings meat across the table with annoying brio. There is a woman whose clothes never dry. And a lad whose silverware I confiscated for sheer tedium of having to watch him prod his eyeballs. Fun, right? But then my kin are not much to speak of, either. Regardless, there is no escaping family, then or now. My experiences of the world are conjugate. And, as always, I am in many places and times at once.

It is midway through the ninth century. We are kings of the sea come to the Isle of Man from the south, round the butt of Essex and up the Mercian coast. The place is foul. It rains nonstop. The island is only thirteen miles wide, so you can traverse the land a few times daily. Even so, there are mountains and I am fat, so I never actually leave our coastal settlement. I can see land in three directions. There is no one to talk to. The Celts speak a language not even friends in Galloway understand. So mostly I sit alone. And I am lonely.

In the news: The Carolingian lands are chopped thrice, each ruled by sons of Pious. They have not done well. The Frisia is ours; Nantes is ours; the Elbe is open game. Apparently, my father has just returned from Paris with the Danegeld—seven thousand pounds—offered by Charles the Bald. Charles, you see, is a wussy puss. So are his brothers. Whereas the Viking expansion is frustrated by desertion, arson, greed, and suspicion, the Pious heirs are wussy. I can see that now. Language inimical to my era has given me new perspective. Back then we talked valor, truth, honor, loyalty, discipline, and fortitude. Now I just think: Wussies. If I am a soul reinstated, jive revamps my past.

But to have lived today! Well, I guess I'd miss the headlines. On the eighth June, the harrying of the heathen miserably destroyed God's church by rapine and murder. *Harrying of the heathen* would never make the cover of *Time* magazine. *Rapine*, either. No one likes high rhetoric anymore. And our traditions, such as they were, look silly today. I've noticed a sect called the Ring of the Troth that trains people to become Godwo/men who will preside over the true folk. There is also the Assembly of the Elder Troth that has designated March 28 a day of remembrance for my father. They find it funny that Ragnar, pagan bogeyman, should sack the Christian stronghold of Paris on Easter Sunday. To memorialize his achievements, they suggest you watch *The Vikings*, with Ernest Borgnine, compose a swan song, jot down ways to stay young, and cook a Nordic meal.

As if this were not insulting enough, I am instantiated in a woman who hosts pagan revival meetings in her living room. A woman who serves pigs in a blanket and lamb shank. The indignity is troubling. Especially since the pagan faith suffuses our lives with color and story. Our ethos is polychrome. And polytheism is the seat of art.

Among our gods, there are the Norns, in whose trinity time is measured: past, present, future. There is the rooster Vithofrir, who sits in the ash tree waiting to cue Ragnarook, the annihilation of all things. There is Jormungand, who lies coiled around the globe, tail in mouth, panting. Come the arch-winter, he will witness the sun's demise, the moon eaten, and the stuff of earth called to battle. Gods, giants, dwarfs, and men shall conduct a gorgeous slaughter that will empty the world of everything as we know it. Only two shall remain, Lif and Lifthraser, to start anew in the arable land. For meat they shall feed on morning dew, and from both shall man be reborn. So sayeth Hrofl Yngling on this spring night on Man. We are gathered about a flame, listening to song.

Fortune rends a family tree; cracks in the ice are frequent.

Dew is nerves of the earth, and petal skin, and woman's breath.

They say reembodiment of the soul is for the best. They say it proves the benevolence of God. It's not that humans are born unequal—some fated to misery while others succeed—but that each embodiment is but a rung on the ladder of growth. Some souls are more advanced than others, but only because they've been climbing longer. We are all possessed of latent gifts; our goal is to rouse our talents, one incarnation at a time. The handbook says the interval between carnal moments is about five hundred years, depending on how much information the spirit needs to assimilate post-corpus. Conceivably, you can tour the ether for millennia before reentry. This has its boons. There is much debauchery in the ether. Much cribbage, too.

First law of thermodynamics: Energy is conserved. It is neither created nor destroyed. It only changes forms. We do not know of anything in nature that violates this law, including the process of reincarnation. Nothing is lost. The imperishable soul alights on the brain until the brain is no more. Then it moves on to the next. Let me address myself to the skeptics: Do you say of a musician that he dies when his instrument fails? Or is it rather that this musician is compelled to find a new instrument? To play better and more passionately than ever before? What greater stimulus to ambition than the promise that the goals of which we dream, the nobility of spirit to which we aspire, the indwelling of gods and the radiance of their power, are but waiting to be discovered in the consciousness of man? Play the harp enough times, an angel you become.

This, at any rate, is what the handbook says.

My father's crew, returned from Paris, are detained at Bergen. A pestilence has felled half the seamen. Of the incident, it is written:

The buccaneers were struck down by divine judgment with either blindness or insanity.

In short: the rest of us have been stranded on Man for weeks. To pass the time, I have been reading a Viking romance, penned by a bouffant drag queen from Connecticut. She might not be a drag queen, but I like to speculate. She enjoys words like *tawny* and *buttocks*. Delayed gratification is her pleasure. Reeling from the terrors of night, her bosom heavy with milk, Thora plunged into the sea. Syntax is a marvel. And I admire a clause in the right hands. The opening-gambit clause. Who's reeling? Whose bosom? Thora. Thora Meaty Thighs.

It is not by chance that I like language and books and the oral tradition. Read up on us: In pagan mythology, he who is best with words also knows most about the hierarchy of the universe. Our poets are revered. We vaunt the most bloodthirsty among us, but it's really the learned who steal the show. In the sagas, it is told of men who spar with their wits, whose facility with language produces the right word at the right time, *Le mot juste*. Think about it: What conjures a spirit, the witch or the witchcraft? The latter of course, the incantation. I recently saw a movie about an orphaned child who finds a book of spells. The girl is a tomboy, red hair, pretty tough but hurting awful. At some point, she trots out a spell and, *booyah*, her Special Ops doll turns real. So now she has a friend *and* a bodyguard. In short, her life is saved. The girl cannot multiply in her head, but she can inspirit. All because of the right words in the right sequence. So yes, we love verse and we love poets.

In my circle, they call plague *pestilenti flatu,* which roughly means fatal anal breath. The gas of a dragon who can't digest. I find this rich with story, and many stories have there been. Certainly it's preferable to *gram-negative obligate pathogen,* from which good luck plumbing a saga. I'll take Ragnarook over zoonotic contagion any day. And so, of course, would Isifrid.

Posterity has yet to claim my Viking bones. They have found armbands in Anglesey and my brother at Repton. They may well find me. I was speared in the head thrice. Disemboweled and castrated. My kin buried me with a boar's tusk in lieu of my sex so that I might be whole for the trip to Valhalla. So this is Valhalla? Of course not. This is shepherd's pie with family.

My father's name was Ragnar Lodbrok, literally, Ragnar Shaggy Trews, because he wore goatskin breeches. So do I, but did I get Knut the Hirsute? Noooo, it's Knut the Soft for me. A sequence of words can change everything. I could have been a contender.

Six

Mrs. Monsen, thank you for having me over today."
"Call me Agneth."
"Mrs. Clark, it's a pleasure."
"Call me Isifrid."

Blech, pleasantries. We were sitting with a journalist who was profiling the family for a glossy magazine. No idea why we had agreed to this. Or rather, why Izzy had agreed on our behalf.

We were in the yellow room, seated across from the journalist, whose name was Alfred. He wanted to interview us en masse and then one by one. We were four generations of Norse women who orbited around the loss of Dad. Not much of an article topic, which turned out to be the point. Apparently, we'd been duped. Alfred was not interested in us, he wanted to know about the guy who died of superplague in Minnesota.

The guy died? Oh jeez, he knew about the guy. How'd he know about the guy?

"Ah," he said. The seat of the couch was so deep it broke well beyond the knee if you sat back. This made everyone look a little Alice in Wonderland. In particular, it made Alfred look like a dwarf. Also, he lacked for hair on the pate, which left what coverage he had horseshoeing around the sides.

"Ah," he said again. "It's being kept close to the vest."

I noticed he was missing a button on his shirt. And that he had the shakes. His teacup rattled against the saucer. I felt like telling him to ditch the saucer, only it was catching spillage from the cup.

"This is bad," Hannah said. "Really bad. Someone actually died?"

And suddenly Alfred looked bereft. And I felt for him. It must be hard having to straddle human feelings which are fear and grief, and reporter feelings which are, Yay, this is the best scoop ever!

He had cashew sacks beneath each eye, and lids whose cant suggested Asian pedigree, though really he was just old. I offered him a biscuit.

He told us the man died within nine hours of getting sick. A spiral the likes of which no one had ever seen. He'd complained of fever at midnight, was vomiting quarts of blood by dawn, and essentially had drained his own body as a tire lets air.

In secret, the CDC had dispatched several agents to the area, but none could determine how he'd gotten the superplague. Thus far, it was an isolated event, though the paramedics who answered the call, two nurses, and the man's wife were all put on antibiotics. Not that it would help, but just to feel like they tried.

"When did this happen?" I asked.

"Yesterday."

"This is bad," Hannah said.

Izzy came to life. "Can you stop saying that? We know it's bad. It's we're-all-going-to-die bad. You think saying that is helping any?"

Alfred put up his hands for calm. "I did not mean to alarm anyone. There might be an explanation besides worst-case scenario. Though I see you've already anticipated worst-case scenario." He was referring to Aggie's mask.

Hannah produced one from her backpack and started kneading it in her lap.

Isifrid covered her face. I bet she wanted to smoke real bad. I could imagine her departing for another room, but I couldn't see her mounting the chair to get her wings. Even a crackhead can't explain away that kind of behavior. But off she went. We had a view right into the kitchen. She said she needed the popcorn maker that's in the back, and who wanted popcorn? She even loaded the thing with kernels before excusing herself.

Alfred said he really needed this story, so could we get started with the background info? *Background info?* I felt like he was not appreciating the significance of the Minnesota Man. On the other hand, did I really need to be the one to scare the crap out of him?

He must have been eighty. I bet he wanted for bladder control. And he was mangling his cassette tape with a pencil, which spoke to the considerably worse problem of what happens when progress sloughs you off. Who still uses cassette tapes? If Alfred lost his job, he'd be qualified for nothing else.

Aggie removed her mask, ready to accommodate. Alfred said thanks because he had no idea what she was saying before. He asked about her past. She did not even hesitate, and said her life had two distinct parts, before cardiac surgery and after. She was certain she'd woken up in the hospital a different person from the one who came in.

"How do you mean?"

Even I wanted to know. I'd never heard this before.

"After they stopped my heart, something went wrong with the ventilator or blood pump, I'm not sure which. They say that technically I was dead for a couple minutes."

"But then you were fine?"

"I was different. It was 1950. Isifrid was about six. I had a romance with an American navy officer. We tried to elope to Mexico, but my husband found me. I don't know what I was thinking. I was not myself. And that's when I began to believe in reincarnation. Because it felt like a new soul had entered my body."

"Did you ever see the guy again?" This from Hannah, who was still kneading.

"I did. Once. At a V-day dinner in Paris at the American embassy. He was there with his wife, who was very pretty."

"Did you talk? Was it horrible?" This from me because what a story!

"He pretended not to know me and I did the same. But the look we exchanged . . ."

Alfred wanted to know if she ever told my grandfather. The answer was no. And her other children? Four dead, one a manners coach at a school for girls, and one a housewife in a suburb of Detroit.

Hannah was not satisfied with the close of this story. "Do you have regrets? Do you think what might have been if you'd stayed with the navy guy?"

But Aggie had replaced her mask, which meant she was done.

Just as well, since in came Isifrid. I believe she was dancing, which seemed to fit the yellow room. She asked Alfred to join her. Poor guy, I don't think he'd ever seen anyone on crack. He asked if she was all right. I nodded, thinking we had about six minutes before this got ugly. I suggested he attempt to interview her now. The maverick in Alfred had some pull, and up he went. Problem was, Izzy wouldn't quit the tango and Alfred was in no shape to prosecute the dance of love. And anyway, she'd mounted a chair that stood one.

I'd long felt that in these moments, Isifrid was the person she wanted to be. A little demagogue, a little Mussolini. The antsy fasci. She certainly has dictator pretensions and strut. Also a prominent chin that would have made a court sculptor blush. For Alfred, she was wearing breeches and riding boots, which complemented her posture: erect and formal. It was not often I really looked at her anymore. The woman in my head had been gone so long, I seemed to forget Mother didn't die with her. Surely no one would believe they were the same person. The woman in my head could open a beer bottle with her teeth. No chips or cracks. She'd leave the house with no makeup and get praised for it. A guy who made wigs for celebrities frequently petitioned for her thicket of hair, which she could wrap around her neck like a scarf. How long since I'd seen that woman? At least fifteen years. But I still missed her.

Alfred took notes, Izzy speechified. Said it took savvy to marshal your needs so that at least some could be met. He asked if I knew what she was talking about. I said I'd like to get her to her room within the next two minutes.

He returned to the couch. Moisture was beading along his forehead, which occurrence he'd foreseen, given the bounty of tissues that escaped his pocket the moment he reached for one. I saw that his shoelaces were different colors—one black, one brown. Perhaps he should try Hannah. I'd noticed that in the last couple days, she'd been gazing at mayhem the way some people stare at water. Mother's performance had not riled her in the least. The kneading was just a tic.

They began to talk.

"I turned twelve last month," she said. "For my birthday? My dad. How about you bring back my dad? Or should I just write Santa." Her contempt was so bald, it was jaw dropping.

"Yes, about your dad," Alfred said. "Did he ever talk to you about his work?"

"He was an *eraser*," she said, as if she'd like to erase him.

"I hear you've got quite a healthy respect for disease, yourself."

Hannah whined my name, which meant: Get me out of this.

"Would you like to show me your West Nile map?"

Okay, now she was riled. "How do you know about my map?" She looked from me to Aggie because Mother, per usual, was exempt.

Alfred smiled. He had his ways, his spies and moles.

"How is it only you seem to know about the man in Minnesota?" I said.

I got the same smile.

Isifrid chose to fold up in the fireplace. This one actually worked, which meant ash was getting all up her breeches. I didn't think anyone wore breeches these days. She was like one of the Four Horsemen.

The house phone rang. It had the most strident ring ever, as if to say: With every visitor comes an uproar.

"At last," Alfred said. "The photographer."

Seven

Eric is still my closest friend. This doesn't mean we talk but that whatever I do, I seem to be addressing myself to him. He is my interlocutor, my soundboard. When I shop, I buy clothing I know he'd like. If I go to the movies, we talk about our impressions in my head. Excepting drugs, I try to behave in a manner he'd endorse. It's funny how obsessive conduct turns acceptable the second you actually date the guy. Then no one thinks you're nuts. I'd argue that love accomplished is insanity next, but I do not have enough experience to know for sure.

When we first met, his affianced was working on a Fulbright in Berlin. Public art or something. They'd been engaged a year, and together for eight. To his credit, she was none too happy with the relationship, either. There were flings in Berlin. An urge to live in Berlin. Inability to discuss anything *but* Berlin. He went to visit. He slept on the couch.

We'd play video games in Chinatown. We'd busk on the Staten Island Ferry. Castanets and harmonica. He'd take two hundred photos of my elbow. His mother used to be an actress until liposuction gone wrong. His father ran a company that made pantyhose. That scar on his thumb came from trying to carve a turkey when he was nine. That scar under his chin he doesn't remember. Because he was engaged, mostly we talked. But it was only a matter of time. Pictures of Monique started to disappear from his apartment. One day I noticed her clothes in a box.

"Berlin bound," he said. "It's over."

And something about his stance, maybe the way his arms hung at his sides, the whole thing said: I'm ready.

Sex with a stranger is awkward. Friend sex is worse. I tried to remember everything he'd told me about encounters with other women. Not so into the testes. Has insensate nipples. Never been rimmed, but in an always-a-bridesmaid sort of way.

Antidepressants gave me dry mouth, so I had to be drinking liquids at all times. He had nothing in the fridge but orange juice with Lots of Pulp. I forgot that spermicide is a numbing agent, so when we took a break from sex and he ditched the condom, it was a bad scene for me. My tongue felt like sausage. And because I couldn't seem to taste anything, I could not sample my body before letting him at it. Plus I'd eaten asparagus for lunch. Only how not to seem prudish? Or self-denying?

He had trouble with my jeans. Button-fly. I had trouble with the juice. Lots of Pulp. Whole thing lasted half an hour.

But after! We culled animals from the swirl pattern on his ceiling. We talked about the election. How the country's going to shit. Five famous dead people we'd like to sleep with. I said William McKinley. He said Yul Brynner.

I said, "You're a nut."

He said, "And you're my buttercup."

I said, "Are you rhyming? Because rhyme is what guys who can't be intimate do to make fun of everything."

He said, "I love how you've got data on this. Buttercup."

I socked him in the arm. "Yul Brynner, huh? Is it the bald thing?"

"Do I look shallow? Of course not. It's those Vulcan ears and high cheekbones."

I laughed and touched my foot to his. "Let's just stay here awhile, okay? Let's just not move."

He turned to face me. "Where else would I want to go?"

We were ridiculous. A quality date was Play-Doh and curl-up time in his lap. It was the happiest I'd ever been.

That night we went to a free concert in the park. German lieder, Schumann. I know squat about opera, which might be why it sounded so good to me. We were sitting on a bald patch of lawn with a bottle of white between us. Someone had let loose a tie of balloons. A baby slept, a toddler slept, and all around came news from the stage, a melancholy so sweet it sidled up to you like a boy at the sixth-grade dance.

And here is what I have learned: the more touched you are, the sooner you break. I looked at Eric and I looked at me and knew for certain that I was alone on this earth, without purpose.

He caught my eye. "What's the matter? Why are you so pale?"

We did not have sex after that, but I slept in his bed every night. And every night I wept. He'd stroke my hair and promise it was okay, but I knew it wasn't. He'd say, "Can you talk to me about it? Can I help?" And I'd say no. "Can you see a doctor? I don't want to sound pat, but I hear exercise can make you feel better." And I'd say, "I know." Some nights he'd say I wasn't trying and that was the problem. Other nights he'd say nothing at all.

I was wearing him down. Surely he had not split from Monique for *this*. And therein lies the rub of depression. You can't just take a pill and make it better. You can't just *fix* it, which is what we all want for each other in the end. I was going to be unwell for the rest of my life.

But it's not like I had brain cancer. Or lupus. It's not like his friends were gonna judge him badly for abandoning his sick, drug-infested girlfriend. Far as they knew, I was fine.

We went on like this for a few months. We brought Kam into the fold. The three of us hung out: movies, parties, concerts.

One night Eric and I were having dinner at a restaurant in the theater district because theater was in our future. We were going to meet Kam and her boyfriend at the time. A guy was crooning at the piano. Our cheeseburgers were huge. We'd been talking about the florist for his last shoot. Or he'd been talking—I couldn't. Some days, the words just didn't come. But he was tired, needing much sleep and also, probably, me. Me when I could make myself reachable, which was not often. He carped at the waiter. He never did things like that, and I was startled. Then he carped at me. And next I knew, we were having the talk.

"There's just this thing in you," he was saying. "I don't know how to handle it. I guess I never did. But I thought, I thought that with me, after a while, you'd feel better."

"I know."

"If I can't help you, and you won't help you, how are we supposed to make this work? I don't see how to make this work."

He was so upset, I wanted only to comfort him.

"Can you stop that?" he said. He had never raised his voice to me before.

"I'm agreeing with you. I'm trying to make this easy. Why are you getting mad?"

"I don't know any other couples like us. Look at Kam! You think it's like this for her?"

I shook my head.

"It's no wonder you've had such a hard time getting people to love you back."

"Okay, that's just mean. And not true."

"You said it yourself! That guy you worked with? Okay, forget I said that. I'm sorry."

"I know. I'm sorry, too." And I was nodding because so far, he had not said anything I disagreed with.

"You give in so fast," he said. "Can't you defend yourself? Can't you say I'm wrong? Don't you have any self-esteem at all?"

I know now that I waited too long to respond. But I was dumbfounded. It sounded like he was asking me to say that I wasn't white or a girl, as if such things are just a matter of perception.

He sat back in his chair. "It's just, it's like you are more attached to being miserable than you are to being with me."

The breakup went on like that for another day or so. It was numbing. And he and Kam were a good team. I saw the romance between them eons before they did. By the time they noticed, I was upstate at rehab. A few months later, Kam showed up with flowers and news of the engagement. This was less numbing. I went on a rampage. Slept with the acupuncturist and woke up pricked from head to toe. I did not leave my house for a week. I dropped so much weight, it seemed the skin of my face might rip any second, so thin and taut was it against my bones.

I had not seen Eric since then and this was almost a year ago, which made his appearance at our door completely appalling.

So this was Alfred's photographer.

"Meet Eric Ludlow," he said, and I winced. I could have been Lucy Ludlow!

"Actually, we're old friends," Eric said, and nodded at me.

"Oh, good. Then we won't have to break the ice. It's hard being photographed by a stranger."

Hannah was amused. She may be twelve, but that doesn't mean innuendo is lost on her. Course, I couldn't tell who was giving off the vibe, me or him. He'd let his hair grow out. It was floppy, which I liked. I noticed razor burn on his neck, which meant the rest of that stubble was by design. I liked that, too. He was wearing Burberry pants that hugged his ass and a green T-shirt that said *spatula*.

"This is Kam's doing," he said, and began to unpack his gear. "I wasn't going to take the job but she wants to check up on you."

My shirt needed depilling. It gave me something to do. I picked and yanked and then there was a hole. Did I only imagine we were intimates? I think my judgment on the matter is sound. I have never conflated sex with love. How could I? Barring Eric, the two had yet to meet. Sex passes the time. Sex is orgasm and infection. It's someone between your legs while you read a book. It's hoping you don't use your teeth by accident. It's exploratory. A venture. It's mapping the body, yours and his. Is it fun? I guess. But so is white-water rafting. I prefer chess. I can't play chess, but I prefer it anyway. A tussle of minds. Empathy at work. Chess, in fact, might be love. Absent the whole demolish-your-opponent thing, it is love. And me and Eric, we had that. Banter that made us laugh for hours. Hours of solace just from being in the same room, doing a crossword, reading the paper. When you share your silence, you share everything. Now I was looking at the concentration on his face—setting up his *gear*—and thinking: How many other chances am I going to get? All doors are closing.

"I see Isifrid is about the same," he said. She'd moved from the fireplace to a corner of the room. She looked ferocious. "Should I—"

"No."

"Right."

He saluted Hannah. She snorted, but I could tell she liked it. That she liked him. Most kids do, especially the girls. They are as animals who can suss out a bad character ages before the rest of us.

"Whoa, Alfred," I said, and pulled him from the brink of Isifrid. I think he was squatting to hear her better.

Eric gave Aggie a kiss on the cheek, which jiggled. I hate to be repulsed by the natural process called aging, but I can't help it: I am repulsed.

They exchanged a few words. When he and I split, she took it badly. I'd explain what went wrong and she'd say, But I don't understand, you love him. I'd say, It's complicated. And she'd say, But you love him. This could go on for hours. Now that I have her sailor in mind, I guess I understand better.

"It's nice to see you," I ventured.

"You, too."

I was close to tears. I wanted to say many things, but come on, how futile. Under the circumstances, probably the best I could do was cry. And I wanted to cry. I wanted to cry so that he could see me cry because I am a woman of feeling, and sometimes all it takes is one feeling to revive another.

He turned on his heels to look at me. I do not hold up well under scrutiny, which means my face tends to lose shape pretty quick. It goes slack. I was ready for a face-lift by age three.

He smiled and said, "Okay, why don't you just stand over there next to Aggie."

I asked if it was okay to leave Mother out of the shot. Alfred said that rather defeated the purpose. I asked if we could arrange ourselves around her so that instead of looking strung out, she just looked down-to-earth.

"Maybe we should come back another time," Eric said.

But since Alfred was clearly never coming back, he nixed the idea.

I wanted to know more about the Minnesota Man. I demanded Alfred's e-mail address. He didn't have e-mail. I demanded his phone number. He relented. I took him aside.

"Alfred," I said. "Is it the same strain from my father's lab? If you're here, I'm guessing yes."

"I don't know."

"Bullshit."

"Really, I don't know. But whatever it is, it's deadly and no one has ever seen anything like it. So you do the math."

Throughout, Isifrid had been fairly quiet. I know she was wanting more crack. I know she was waiting for her rocks to dry. Can't boil an egg, but she can still make crack. It's that easy. All you need is baking soda, a pot, and a strainer. I never understood why crack didn't get fashionable. It's cheap, okay, but not if you make it yourself with premium cocaine. Maybe the laboratory part is too junkie for rich people. Or snorting is just more debonair. Needles get a bad rap. And freebase, that's out, though it used to be a tough call until Richard Pryor self-immolated in his kitchen, trying to react cocaine with ethyl alcohol. Guy sets himself on fire and he's black and forget it: freebase is for junkies.

The thing about crack, it hijacks the good in you. I am immured behind Alcatraz-like defenses, so Isifrid cannot get to me. But Hannah, I hated to see her so protected. It's good in the short run, she won't get hurt, but it also forebodes an indolence of spirit that conduces drug abuse. And I'll die if she turns into me.

Eric had us assume various poses and expressions. I always loved to watch him work because you just couldn't see what he saw until the film got developed. Not like there'd be any great art to be had from us. I was pretty sure no matter what Hannah did, she looked nonplussed. And that Aggie's eyes were insufficiently suggestive to compensate for what was lost behind the mask. And that Mother was dour. Dour at best. So it was up to me. But since I couldn't imagine Alfred writing that I am the pillar of strength in this family, I just felt exposed.

Eric said we were finished. Alfred said, Thank God. He was done hiding his contempt for us, he had gotten what he needed. I leaned against the wall as Eric packed up. How many times had I seen him do this? Tripods, screen, easel collapsed and in the duffel bag. Lenses in the bag, light in the bag.

There was not enough room in the elevator for Alfred, Eric, and gear. So Alfred went alone. By then, the rest of the family had retired. Eric seemed to notice this before I did. He was tapping his fingers against the doorframe. I should have probably just said bye, but I hated to foreclose on any opportunity to be loved. Because I figured maybe he could still love me. In some fashion. The elevator was almost here. I said, "Well, there's a story for the grandkids."

He shook his head. Laughed. "You're still a nut," he said. "Maybe that's what I'll tell Kam."

"You can tell her I'm fine."

He looked away, put his bag down, and I didn't even see it coming until he'd gotten me in an embrace so snug, it was breathless. The elevator opened. I think Eric said to keep in touch, but I couldn't know because Stanley was announcing great results from the lab and man was he hungry and did I see the snipers on the roof, some dignitary at the hotel across the street, and, as they traded places in the elevator, Hi, I'm Stanley, I'm Eric, oh.

Stanley pecked me on the forehead. I asked why he was laughing. He said it was because I looked like a child. And it was true; I got this a lot.

Eight

Now, Eunice, they said, you're not gonna die. Euuuuuuuuuuuu-nice, you're not gonna die! But they lied. So before Lucy was me, and before me were other kids like me. And now I don't listen to what people say. There's one adult here with a helmet and animal pants who keeps yelling that we're on a ladder. He doesn't spend much time with me—I think maybe he doesn't like me—but one time he explained how my ladder looks: Sal into Randall into Jack into Christina into Howard into me into Lucy. Six kids born dumb. I lasted the most, to when I was seven. At school, our teachers made us write poems so that other kids like us would not be alone. Everyone but Sal because he died before he could even talk. Oh yeah, and Christina, too, because she was blind.

A poem:

I am a failure to my dad.
I am a failure to my mom.
What if what I dream
is not their dream?
When God made me,
I wish he'd paid attention times three.

Sometimes dinner with the other people who keep coming back, it's fun. But mostly it's not. If I put burger on my mashed potato, it looks like a ski slope in summer and who wants to eat that. I wonder how it would look on my face. It's nice on my face. Lookit, my face!

My teachers said I was special and I guess that's true because I looked different from my brother and the kids at school, and I thought that was okay except for the people who made ugly faces when they saw me or the people who got upset because I guess they were scared.

Randall happened in 1927. He got polio when he was three, but since everyone was starving, it did not seem so bad, only he was starving with polio. He was sick a long time and Hoover was saying everyone should just laugh and then that big building in New York got lights at the top and Randall's mom was getting fifty cents a week and his dad was getting nothing at all and not so many babies were being made plus lots of adults were going to heaven and so when Randall got into Jack, he thought maybe the world had not ended after all.

Jack lasted until five. He could not get enough air to his brain, so he couldn't think very well or run around. He and his mom lived in Oahu on the base because the doctors were free since his dad was in the army. One time he got to sit in a fighter plane. He was four but had to be gated in so that he didn't do anything stupid while his mom was asleep. When the bombs came she held him tight and after, when everything was on fire and she was listening to the radio, Jack thought maybe this was the end of the world.

It's hard to come back. It's not really another chance because your parents and friends live someplace else and you can't talk and Lucy doesn't eat any of my favorite foods. And lots of times I want to play and she's just sleeping. She sleeps a lot. I don't think it's fair that she can get around without a wheelchair and her hearing is good and she can see fine and she knows left from right but still doesn't do much and is not any fun. I know Howard did better for Christina. She couldn't do letters for a tumor in her head, but Howard did lots of letters. See?

> Being dyslexic is okay, its the other stuff that makes it hard to tie my shoes and get to school and playing and dancing and sports.

I got old really fast. My bones broke. I lost all my hair. Kids at school called me Yoda. That made me feel bad, but my mom said I could make it feel good because Yoda has lots of powers and can do stuff with his mind. So I did stuff with my mind. My skin was like crepe paper. The whites of my eyes were cloudy. My feet were claws. When a really old monk came from Tibet to see me, we looked the same. The picture ran in the paper. I was tired a lot. And I never got to learn much except that when stuff hurt it was better to hide it because my mom would get sad and stay sad long after the hurt was gone.

They call it progeria. Rhymes with wisteria, which my mom says is a flower.

One time she didn't want me to see a movie where lots of people got sick and there's a man playing chess with a dead person. But I cried a lot so she let me. I asked if this could happen and she said yes but that it would not happen because this was a modern age and I thought that was weird but okay because I didn't want everyone to be scared and get the disease. I thought it was okay for me to die but I did not want her to get the disease. We talked more about it. She said that when I got to heaven I should make a bed for her because she'd come stay with me after a while. And that we'd come back together as new people but that she would still be my mom and I'd still be me only not old but more like the other kids. I guess I thought this was okay back then. Now not so much. I can't find her anywhere.

I wish it was true that when we are new we are actually new. That everyone's smart and has a good heart. But people are jerks and wishes don't work and I'm still the same and pain is still pain.

I don't feel good. These people are mean and shepherd's pie is gross. Why do I have to sit here? Mr. Animal Pants is a thousand years old. And he yells at me nonstop. How come I have to look like his grandpa? I'm just a kid. I'm just a kid! I want to start over. I want a sundae.

Nine

What I like about a twelve-step program is that you can put yourself in the presence of recovery and not be recovered at all. Not even close. Lotta people I know, they'll come to a meeting high. Or get high once they're there. Not that they ever get caught, but when a lady comes out of the john all itchy, all smiles, you know something's up. It's not the worst idea, really. No one is gonna give you grief, and in the event of overdose, everyone will know what to do. I've been hanging around the rooms for six years. I'll put together an hour, a day, a week clean, but that's about it. No one claps when I announce my day count anymore. They all know it won't last, which is a relief. I hate to be a disappointment.

Tonight it's powdered donuts in the basement of a church near Mother's place. I've come because I have nothing else to do and also because Agneth gave me the guilt. I hate the guilt. Dirty Ben's sitting in the first row. He gives me a hug, as do about five other people. I have come to tolerate these human moments because there's no avoiding them.

The guy who chairs the meeting has been in prison eight times. From him I have learned how to make a knife out of cotton. Also that quinine stops an eye twitch. He's got a Traumatizing Brain Injury. His name is Frank, and he's a sweetheart.

Tonight's speaker has a lisp. I think this is because he had a stroke, but it turns out he's just got a razor blade in his mouth, acquired for protection. If you look hard, you can see it glinting against his cheek. He's sharing on the first of the God steps, which are a doozy for the atheists among us, even though we are promised the steps are a spiritual undertaking that can exclude belief in God.

Despite how many meetings I've been to, I am so far from belief in a higher power that when the Blade talks about his HP it still takes me several minutes to realize he doesn't mean health care provider.

The Blade lives with his mom. He probably weighs about ninety pounds. Last night he jabbed the butt of a revolver in his eye and might have done it, only his mom slipped in the bathtub and broke her pelvis. At this he starts to cry. I'm glad we're not supposed to talk because how do you comfort someone over that? He says he is grateful to be clean today, and wipes his face with the back of his sleeve.

Comes time to open the floor, a lot of hands go up. I've known these people forever, it seems. The dancer in the rear lives alone and owes her landlord ten months' back rent. She claims incapacity to buy food though she will buy books. A lot of books. She tends to chop at the air with her hands. In Serbia, her parents were jailed for being enemies of the state. Her mother was murdered. She's been in New York for thirty years, but her accent is paramount.

Tonight she is saying she does not want to talk but that she has to talk. Her fist makes a thwack against the table. Someone's coffee is upset. A flurry of napkins and then she, too, is crying. Also, she is grateful to be clean today.

To my right is Odette. Her mother has Alzheimer's and arthritis, and is incarcerated in a welfare facility in the Bronx. It is not going well. Sometimes Odette finds her without underwear. She's been a Jehovah's Witness for thirty years, has been celibate for thirty years; only now, in her dementia, she is promiscuous. An eighty-year-old woman. She has intercourse with this doctor, that nurse, and likes to talk about it afterward. This is, possibly, the most horrible thing I have ever heard.

To my left is Phil, who wears an ascot. He's got two fangs tattooed on either side of his forehead, but it's the ascot that shocks me. He's not even gay, just twenty-two with a wife and kid. He's been doing coke since he was twelve. Now he's got a little over four months clean, which means apathy is on deck. First apathy, then complacency. Is that all there is? He has relapsed seven times. He does not want to use. He knows using is not the answer. But the alternative? There has to be more to recovery than just abstinence.

He wants to be rewired from the bottom up. I sympathize with this wholeheartedly.

Drew, Christine, Glenn, and Dave have their say. Then it's Mark. He's got diabetes and hep C and hypertension and a cold. He's got thin white hair and a comb-over. Seasonal rosacea. When he was drinking, he used to replace the antifreeze in his car with vodka so that when he had to take a drive with his wife, he could pull over periodically to check under the hood. She thought he was paranoid, and left him anyway.

Miles says his relationship with God is like two fat people in a boat. They keep bumping into each other and laughing.

Miles can't hear a thing, which means everyone within twenty blocks of this place can hear him.

There is talk of practicing these principles in all our affairs. There is talk of needing each other to stay clean. People around here tend to deploy the same phrases, which seems fascist after a while. Fascist in the way an orthodoxy will ply the language with bromides the rest of us are expected to use in lieu of original thought. Probably it's not as evil as that, but I do wonder at the numbing effect of using a prefab expression instead of coming up with your own.

From the back comes Allan, who runs a chop shop. Since I've known him, he's had nine kids, then seven, then four, and now it's down to one. Not that they died but that his lying tends to improve in degrees. Today his son has stage-four colon cancer, which means he probably had a biopsy that hasn't come back from the lab. Allan is saying that Let go, let God is the best thing he's ever been taught. Let God take my will. I am always wondering how people know the difference between their will and God's, but I keep this sort of inquiry to myself lest it sound contemptuous. It certainly smacks of the logic we are encouraged to dispatch when it comes to recovery. Allan is from Trinidad. I keep meaning to ask how a guy from Trinidad gets a name like Allan, but this, too, might sound contemptuous. In the rooms, I try to keep my mouth shut. Especially since people who've gotten high in the last twenty-four hours are asked to refrain from sharing. Even so, up goes my hand. Protocol suggests I respond to something in the Blade's share. Like I identified with it. And I guess I did, so I acknowledge kinship with the desire to blow your brains out. He nods, which means I'm free to say what's really on my mind. Something like how I just saw an exhibit at the museum about butterflies who are born without mouths and die within three days, and where is the humanity in that. Also that I don't know how to function without drugs. I just don't see the point.

The meeting goes on. No one mentions superplague, but then no one would. We are entirely too self-centered to let such matters upstage miseries of our own devising.

After, there is more chest-to-chest contact. I am thanked for sharing. My honesty is appreciated. I'm told to hang in there.

Dirty Ben follows me out. I am delighted to see he still smokes.

"Thanks for coming," he says.

"Sure."

"How are you? And don't say *fine*."

"Fine."

"That shit in Minnesota is crazy."

I nodded. News of the man's death leaked hours after Alfred left our apartment. The papers are calling it the First Strike, which is noticeably prognostic of a second. Since then, the skies have issued an Indian summer whose disposal of the forecast has given half the city a cold, of which 90 percent think a cold is the plague. I've already seen a commercial on TV sponsored by the CDC that features a guy in lab coat who basically calls a sneeze a sneeze before tussling with a bunch of kids with runny noses. The Minnesota Man's family is irate, suggesting that if the CDC were even a quarter as competent as they are insensitive, we would not be in this crisis, to which the CDC (a) balked at the word *crisis* and (b) pulled the ad.

I take a long breath of air, which is so thick I actually feel fatter for having taken it. I lean against the church, which does not help.

"It gets better," Ben says. "I know you don't believe me—I didn't believe it when I first came into the program—but it's true. Stick around long enough and it'll happen."

I sigh. You'd think that Ben, Ben of the daisy flip-flops and rainbow pubic hair, would produce something novel to say to me. But no. It's just the same advice, the same stories, and a promise that if you just *keep coming back*, it'll get better.

I don't feel sad, but my eyes are watering and the drops are falling and next I know, Ben's got his arms around me and is walking me home.

This is what happens when you start to mess with the hurt inside you. It starts talking back.

"You gonna be okay?" he says. We are at my building.

"I'm fine. G'night," I say, and kiss him on the cheek.

He grabs for my hand. "It's not the end of the world, you know."

"Actually, it is." I stand up straight because this is familiar territory. "You've seen the news. *Superplague*? It's like we're living in one of those blockbuster movies minus the part where I get laid in my shrink-wrap coverall. Bring in the pod people."

"It's just one guy," he says.

"For now. But it's Malthusian. We are growing beyond the world's ability to handle us."

"Maybe. I've been thinking about you guys especially, though."

"You and the rest of the world."

"How's Hannah dealing?"

"Poorly. I've got to find a way to help her."

"Coming to meetings is a start."

"She watches a sick amount of television. She's getting *urbane*. Says things like, Dyspepsia is the new Coke."

"She does not."

"She does. I don't know what to do. She's reptilian!"

"Oh, come on. She'll be okay. You'll see. Kids are tough."

"Uh-huh."

"Listen, I know it's not my business but for what it's worth I don't think your dad's to blame for what's happening."

"Yeah, well, someone is, which means we're all gonna die."

"That was gonna happen anyway."

"True enough." And what else is there to say? Nonspecific anxiety is just something you live with these days.

Ten

The interplay between principles of recovery and reincarnation is not lost on me. Both presume we can make different decisions based on lessons learned. Reincarnation, in particular, is a theory of progress that takes progress for granted. Not that you necessarily grow with every life, but that you *can* grow. It says: Even as you are reinstated with the essentials of character that screwed you up in your last life—after all, what is the soul if not the mainspring of our life's tragedies?—you can still make new choices this time around. The model is Pavlovian: Hand in the fire, it hurts; next time, recoil. But consider an alternative. What if the compulsion to thrust my hand in the fire is so great, it undoes the Pavlovian response? Either I think this time will be different, or I don't care about the outcome until it is upon me. Point is, if I could resist the fire, I wouldn't be me. Pursue this logic far enough and you get a stump speech for the death penalty. At the very least, life without parole. And this is where I get flummoxed. Because I believe people can change, can be redeemed. I just don't believe it can happen to me, at which point, if I were in rehab, someone would mention that I am not unique, not special, and that what's good for the goose, etc. They would talk about self-centered fear. That thinking you are irredeemable is the worst kind of egotism. I might ask, Well, how do I believe I can change? And they might say: Fake it till you make it. Or, my favorite: Pray. At which point, in rehab, I might bash my head against the wall. Because I always end up like a pretzel, and the only way to undo the mess is to knock myself out.

Eleven

Next week: we're two hours from Good-Time Living, and it's hot as fuck. The bus's AC doesn't work. A Milk Dud has just landed in my hair. I think it's been prechewed. This kid to my right, he's got a frosted Pop Tart stuck to his forehead. He's saying, Lookit, no hands! Someone from the back says, Shut up, Tart, which is what this kid will be called all the way through high school. The driver is about eighteen. He's wearing gold wire glasses with lenses big and square as a coaster, and a polo shirt. His collar is turned up. I bet he's got a stent in his neck for a congenital blood-in-the-brain disease. I bet he dies from it. I turn to Stanley and ask if he wants to play. He says, "Isn't there enough of that going around?" The game's about looking at strangers and predicting cause of death. This is fun at Dunkin' Donuts and museums, less so with a troop of fundamentalist Christian kids. I give Pop Tart deviated-septum surgery gone awry, and then fall into despair. So, apparently, does Stanley. He slumps low in his seat. The way he acts, you forget he's over fifty, though I don't know what conduct fifty mandates that the pressure of looming superplague can't retard.

The guy from Minnesota's wife has died. The paramedics who answered the call are in a lockdown unit of the hospital. Oddly, the nurses are fine.

Online: video that was never meant to be seen, but which everyone in the country has downloaded. Men in biohazard gear retreating to an armored van with the wife's body on a stretcher draped in vinyl sheeting. One of her arms escapes the tarp and hangs free. It is piebald from the elbow down and japanned in tar from the elbow up. Only it's not tar. It is simply what happens when your skin dies before you do.

Hannah has been refusing to go to school. "It's already October," she says. "We won't learn anything between now and June." The kids are ruining her life. They've been told to stay away because our dad let loose the plague. How's that for a schoolyard taunt? When I was a kid, the worst I got was a bra-snapping in the janitor's closet. Makes me want to beat the crap out of everyone she knows.

According to the news, there's been a run on gas masks, which has forced Aggie to acknowledge that her ICU bib is deficient.

The mayor has been asking for calm. The president has been asking for calm. We're looking at three incidents in a country of 300 million. Some people find it reassuring that the Minnesota Man juiced fruit for a living—that he wasn't a high-profile figure. Others that his everyman status is the worst part of it all. It's the difference between thinking that if you avoid monuments and tourist traps, you won't be on-site for the bomb, and knowing that the bomb could just as easily be in the slushy machine at your local Chuck E. Cheese.

On the bright side, we now know there's a guy in St. Paul who uncorked the superplague at a hippie juice bar, and what are the odds he doesn't get caught? There is rumor of a sister who wants to talk. Every outcast in Minnesota has been hauled to jail. Illegal searches have upturned seven pederasts, a steroids lab, and unsanitary conditions at the local dog pound.

In New York, it is starting to look different. I've seen a homeless guy try to seal his box with duct tape. Like he's just gonna sit tight while plague takes every third person on the street. SUVs packed with bottled water crowd the highways out of town. Diapers are in short supply. Mass transit, already a pesthole, is losing customers.

The Feds have finally admitted that the virus found in the Minnesota Man is the same strain that was taken from the lab. Officially, then, the superplague is out. On the other hand, the Feds are denying reports of a spread. I don't know why they bother. Absolutely no one believes them. Which is, for the most part, what this Family Day wants to address. Trust in government is at a nadir, so we'll just have to trust each other. Trust licks calamity—that's what today is all about.

At least this is what the girl behind us is saying to her seatmate, who could not care less. He's scratching his name into the window with one of those ice-pick math compasses. He's probably about ten, which means those buckteeth are for life. The girl turns her attention to us. She says her thermos cost three hundred dollars. It's a thermos *and* a boiler, she says. She's got a pear in her cooler. Also figs and prosciutto. I ask whatever happened to gorp. She gives me a toffee bonbon.

Stanley and I face forward. I take his hand and say, "You think Hannah's getting something from hanging out with these kids? I feel like she doesn't have enough friends, but these people?"

"Don't worry. I bet her crowd takes a different bus."

I look at the girl across the aisle and have to assume he's right. She's got a Blow Pop snug in her cheek. Her sneakers have neon lights built into the soles. I take an interest. She doesn't.

"My parents are coming in a cab," she says.

"That's nice."

"My parents say not to worry because only the poor people are going to get sick from superplague."

"That's awful."

"Are you poor?"

"No."

She smiles like there's been a victory here.

Hannah is glaring at me. Apparently, Blow Pop is a no-no. She's not liked by the other campers. I indicate confusion because what's not to like? Hannah rolls her eyes and marches down the aisle. Her breath is hot against my ear. "She's a one-seedliner," she says.

I see. Christian Identity is a fractured religion. They all hate each other, though together they hate the Jews. Half of Identity thinks the Jews are born of an actual union between Eve and Satan. The rest think it's just a metaphor.

First thing when we arrive is breakfast in the mess hall. It looks like a circus tent minus the fun. I notice the parents are congregated across the aisle. Hannah pokes me in the back, so I grab Stanley and head on over. We are served poached eggs on English muffins. Several parents have brought their own utensils. Stanley pops the entire muffin in his mouth. When asked which is his kid, he says: Geongowerwhere.

Consensus at the table is that we're not here to scare the kids about plague, but to start a dialogue about what to do if disaster strikes.

One guy produces an Excel spreadsheet and a laminated, wallet-sized card of phone numbers on one side and information about how to don a gas mask on the other. He says he made the cards for his kids, but brought extras for the table. I notice one of the phone numbers is for an airstrip, which means his master plan is to hit the family jet and bail. A woman across the table who's got her hair pinned up with knitting sticks says dryly, "I hardly think your jet plane can accommodate us all." The guy to her right says, "And anyway, how do you think you're going to *get* to the airfield? If there's an outbreak in the city, no one is going anywhere." "And further," someone adds, "those phone numbers are pointless. All the lines will go dead from overuse."

The man who distributed the cards retrieves them from the table without a word. You get the feeling he won't be participant for the rest of the day.

I notice several parents have come dressed in the finest outdoor gear, with fluorescent orange vests and khaki havelocks. One guy has a glow-in-the-dark GPS watch. His wife might be wearing a Navy Seal jumpsuit. By contrast, Stanley's in overalls and a base-ball jersey. I can see a sperm strip jutting from his pocket. Just in case the mood strikes on the Appalachian Trail? You can fit about three of him in those overalls, they are so huge. Three of him and me, which he's already suggested twice since this morning.

I try to ease the tension and say, "Look, I think we can all agree that there are no practical measures we can take to save our lives and that instead—"

"Excuse me?" says navy wife. "I don't want to hear that kind of talk. If you get within twenty feet of my son today—" She turns to her husband and to the others. "There's plenty we can do and plenty to teach our children. That's why we're here, right?"

Nodding, grunting, yes.

Her nostrils are so dilated, she could snort quarters.

A couple parents suggest I study the literature at the end of the table, pamphlets that say *Be ye separate and touch not the unclean thing*.

A counselor plays a few notes on a trumpet. The kids stand up like an army corps. I gather we are meant to do the same. The schedule is announced: two intergenerational activities and a lecture/performance. We are to play a trust game, rappel down a dam, and listen to the kids talk religion. I do not like heights and wonder if I can get special dispensation for being only half bound to Hannah by blood.

"Nice," Stanley says and shakes his head.

We are herded into a group and told to fall in line. I am instructed to hold on to the woman in front of me, who's wearing cream pumps and a skirt suit. As we march through the woods, her heels strafe the mud. I think this might be useful if we get lost. Stanley is wheezing and exhorting me to slow down. Like I have control of the line. The Navy Seal is on his ass.

We come out into a clearing and a couple hundred feet later, we're at the dam. I do not like the look of it. The kids are peering over the edge. I'd say we're about twenty floors up. At the bottom is a river and a landing. I can see two counselors sitting on the concrete, drinking bottled water.

Hannah says, "You're not gonna do this, right?"

"Are the other parents?"

She nods. "But you're not a parent."

"Look, I'm here for you. I'm doing it. Maybe they will let us go down together." I even believe this. With two hundred milligrams of Valium, I can do anything. After that, all I gotta do is stay awake.

The woman in pumps is the first up. Getting the crotch harness secured to her body is a chore. She cannot be safe and decent at the same time. Her son has his face in his hands. A couple girls pat him on the back.

The fun of rappelling is that you get to bounce from side to side. You take your time. Also, the crotch harness can feel pretty good. This lady in the pumps, though, she drops down like a stone. We all hear the thump as she lands on one of the counselors, who, in turn, can't unhook the carabiners from between her thighs. It's all looking rather lewd from up here. I half expect Stanley to dash off with his sperm stick.

A few kids make it down without incident. They do their parents proud, and the favor is returned. I am beginning to feel a little sleepy. It's nice. The leaves rustle in the wind and it sounds so tender, I marvel at how nature will share her pleasures with anyone.

Hannah is up next. She's wearing gloves to preempt rope burn. The counselor hooks her up. She is amenable to his touch. She even smiles at something he says. He helps her swing her legs over the rail. To my surprise, her hands are trembling. She is scared. I want her to look to me for support, but instead she just takes a deep breath and relaxes into an L position before lowering herself down the line. When she hits bottom, a few other girls give her a hug. Their voices sound lonely from up here, but mostly because I don't hear my own. Shouldn't I be down there congratulating my baby sister? Shouldn't we be working through this thing together?

There's only four of us left, me, Stanley, and the Navy Seal couple. Because we are assimilating, I am paired with the Seal while Stanley gets the husband. They rappel with ease. Stanley is even balletic.

I am glad to be going last because it's taken this long for the Valium to kick in. On the other hand, I am having trouble moving my limbs. I weigh a thousand pounds and I can't quite understand what's being said to me. The Valium twilight is like scuba diving. Like cupping your hands over your ears and hearing the surf. Like being a toddler whose sight lines don't extend above the ankle. It's like taking a dip in a vat of pudding. It's like being *made* of pudding. Remarkable how little anything matters when you are made of pudding.

The counselor who straps me in is kinda cute. I wonder about my hair. The trees are upside down, which has me baffled until the counselor rights my head. He's kinda cute. I want a tuna sandwich. He says I can have one later and now easy does it, that's right, just slide your leg over the rail, no, no, not over my arm, over the rail, you can let go now, let go, no, you need to let go of me now, I'm nineteen, yes, let go, that's it, yes, my mother tells me all the time, you're doing great, don't stop, why are you stopping, hello?

The concrete is hot to the touch, which is excellent given the spray from the waterfall. I feel like a pancake. And I am sleepy. I think I'll just stay here for a while. The surf can't rouse me. Not even the Navy Seal, who's prodding my side with a stick, who's shaking me and finally smacking me across the head. I open my eyes. I am flush with a dam, ten stories up, with legs adangle. I peel my check from the wall and look down. I am met by many angry faces, though I don't see Hannah's. The Navy Seal orders me back into the L.

Stanley says I slept for three minutes up there. That at first they thought I was paralyzed with fear, and tried to talk me down. Then someone proposed I'd had a heart attack. Navy Seal, who's versed in CPR and emergency aid, volunteered to go back up and get me.

We are exhausted. Mercifully, it's time for lunch. One girl tries to trade her roast beef for Hannah's pasta salad. Bad move. After all, mad cow is preventable. What insanity not to take precautions! And Hannah, she lets the girl have it. She explains everything. She says, "It goes like this: Sheep get scrapie. They claw themselves to death, but what's really happening is their brains have turned to cheese. In the meantime, farmers get the bright idea they can save money by recycling parts of the sheep no one would ever eat. It's called *rendering*. Take a brain, some kidneys, and spleen and turn it into meat and bone meal. The stuff is high in protein, which fattens up the cows. Only there's a problem because now you've got these vegan cows eating each other and the infected sheep." She pauses to let it settle in: If you eat that roast beef hero, then it's you eating the cow who ate the sheep whose brain is cheese. I know there's a song in that somewhere.

"Know what else?" Hannah says, sorta loud because the girl's covered her ears. "It took the FDA thirteen years after knowing all this to ban bone meal. Thirteen years! That's like, as old as you are."

I find myself nodding vigorously. People who get CJD, which is the human form of mad cow, lose one faculty after another. They forget their children's names. They forget their own names. They weep, they stray, they nap, they die. Thirteen years! I feel a protest march coming on, at least until the other girl unstops her ears long enough to say, "Shut up, Hannah. Everyone knows you're a liar. Like"—and here she points at me—"that girl is so totally *not* your housekeeper."

Stanley takes me out of earshot. Says, "I'm sure they were talking about someone else."

But I don't follow. These moments come at you so fast, sometimes you just can't keep up.

The counselor says it's time for the game of trust and sits us in a circle on the grass. Skirt Suit finds this awkward, so she's given a chair. The counselor asks for a volunteer to help demonstrate how the game works. One of the dads waves his arm. Because we are so many and the circle rather large, confessant and confessor need to speak through a bullhorn. This seems anathema to the intimacy of trust, but then what good is the exercise if no one can hear it?

The counselor sits the parent down opposite him. He says, through the bullhorn, "When I was a kid, I thought I was worse than everyone else." One of the moms claps her hand over her daughter's mouth, but it's too late; everyone heard her laugh. She is disqualified. The counselor gives the horn to the father in a way that suggests onus and ritual. I am still wondering if *Lord of the Flies* means anything to these people as he brings it to his lips and says, "I never won any trophies in school." Some people clap. And the trust game begins.

Hannah refuses to look at me. She probably thinks I'll make a scene come our turn, even though I am determined not to make a scene. My brain is cheese. I think I'll tell her I'm sorry.

Unexpectedly, Stanley joins us in the center. Most families have already left, which means we're not getting much attention. The game has gone on too long. People are restless.

Hannah takes the bullhorn. Mumbles something about being afraid the world is about to end, and throws the thing at me. Perhaps the horn makes a cracking sound against my chest because suddenly we are of interest. No one has sat near me since my nap on the dam and it's not like Stanley's making any friends, but now it's as if these people are at the movies and we're what's playing. I am supposed to say something but I can't think of what. I don't want to embarrass Hannah. I turn to Stanley like he's gonna help. He shrugs and says, "I killed my wife from driving drunk." My mouth drops open. Of all the things. I look at Hannah to check the damage, only she appears to be accepting condolences because with an uncle like that in the family, your life is tragic. Also, she seems to enjoy the attention. And the color in her cheeks, it's not from shame. I grab the bullhorn and clear my throat. With all eyes on me I say I worry I'm too messed up for romance because the guy I love married my oldest friend and it's not like the marriage is what messed me up but that I was messed up first, and probably they would not have married or even gotten together if not for that.

Midconfession I realize I'm not saying anything that couldn't be surmised from my conduct on the dam. Indeed, the group's reaction confirms it. Those coos people make when listening to poetry read aloud, these are not forthcoming. The camper who'd been rubbing Hannah's back removes her hand. The pitying looks turn away. Even Stanley seems uncomfortable.

The counselor decides we've had enough. Most of the parents have bonded with their children, mission accomplished.

I tell Stanley to go on ahead while I sit next to Hannah on the grass. She's plucking blades one by one. She's wearing denim shorts frayed at the hem. "On a scale of one to ten," I say, "how bad am I doing?"

"Four."

I perk up. "A four? Really?"

"No."

She looks at the tent, where the rest of camp is amassing for the performance. "I have to get ready," she says, and stands. I stand, too.

"Hannah, look. Probably we should talk about what's happening. Isn't that why you asked me to come? Are you scared? What can I do?"

My advances, though rare, are always met with contempt, so I am surprised when I don't get it. No, not surprised. Worried. So long as people think I'm useless, I can stay useless. Instead Hannah says, "I don't know. But maybe if the plague really does get to New York, you can be here? I guess that would be good."

"I've got rehab," I say. "But maybe—" I stop there because Hannah finishes for me.

"But maybe we can time the outbreak to suit your schedule? You are unbelievable."

I don't even try to detain her. I am too lowly for that. Because the fact is: now that rehab might recuse me from having to deal, it's starting to look good.

When I get to the tent, our group counselor asks me to sit in the back. He whispers and nods as if we're in on the same secret. And I suppose we are. He says he knows who my dad is, which makes me think maybe the other people don't. Hard to imagine, but then perhaps anonymity is what Hannah comes here for. He says, "You got any inside information for me? Like for those of us who don't have a private island, you got any advice?"

This kid looks about twenty. Blond hair cropped tight. Calf muscles and jugular vein prominent from most any angle.

"Not really," I say. "And anyway, you don't want to hear it."

He takes me aside, as if whatever I have to say will lose its value when overheard. "I do want to hear it. Tell me."

"You're hurting my arm."

"Oh, sorry. But look, I'm not like the rest of these people. I live with my dad, he's deaf; I support him and my younger brother, who's also deaf. It's a genetics thing. Probably my kid will be deaf, too. So you think with all this on my plate, I can deal with the fucking superplague? Did you see that woman who died? Did you see her *arm*? I'm going to throw up! You think this piece-of-shit loony camp pays well? You think when the time comes, my boss will find it in her heart to let me and my deaf family stay in her crypt?"

"You're still hurting my arm," I say. "But I'm sorry. I'm sorry about your family. I don't know what to tell you. Buy a gas mask, I guess. Buy three."

"You know how much they're going for now? A guy I know just spent a grand, and that's not even for one of the high-end masks. But look, I have a checklist here, maybe you can tell me if I'm missing anything?"

He hands me a printout of items to have on hand in case of

emergency: high-calorie foods like chocolate, peanut butter, beef jerky; flashlights and batteries; maps, money, tools (screwdriver, wrench, hammer); candles, whistle, butane, water; passport and driver's license; Bible and games (cards, dominos, Jenga). At the bottom are toiletries and first-aid items plus something about KY Jelly, which seems context sensitive.

I want to say I have no idea, but he seems so in need of reassurance that I tell him yes, it looks great, he's got all the bases covered.

"I bought an escape hood, too," he says hopefully. "Not as good as the respirator with Hycar rubber, dual-canister mount, poly lens, drinking tube, and mechanical speaking diaphragm, but it's something."

"How much is the fancy one?"

"I got a friend who can score three of 'em for under a grand."

I write him a check on the spot.

Stanley, who's been waiting for me, is nonplussed about having to sit in the rear. He says he never gets to sit in the front. I ask if he's five years old. "If I'm five, you're two."

Props onstage include a podium and a cardboard cloud stapled to a tree. Last I did this kind of thing, I had to read the Emancipation Proclamation dressed as Lincoln. I remember before the show I dipped my beard in pea soup by accident. I wonder if Hannah is nervous. If she has stage fright. I hope that by sitting in the back, we aren't sending the wrong message.

The trumpet player does his thing and the passion play begins. Hannah comes out in a purple bathrobe. I think she's playing a wizard. She says, "I know the blasphemy of them which say they are Jews, and are not, but are the synagogue of Satan." Hers is a mix of scripture and sermon, and what it lacks in coherence it makes up for with bile.

Next comes the Pop Tart to recite from John. When he's done he gives us an abstract of the reading, saying: "See how Yeshua doesn't say the reason the Jews are not of His sheep is because they are unbelievers, but that they are unbelievers because they are not of His sheep. Yeshua knows His sheep, and knows that the Jews are not of His sheep."

Stanley leans over to ask what's with all the sheep. I don't know but I imagine it's something bad because the parents are clapping and the parents are nuts. In fact, they clap for every reading that follows, and don't stop until camp president and pastor John Rhinestone takes the stage to tell us that one of the things they try to teach every Good-Time camper is that self-esteem and humility before God are not incompatible, but that when you forgo humility before God, you are in a world of trouble because God can punish, God *does* punish, just open your eyes and behold the superplague. His message is excruciating, and made worse when I see Hannah standing in the wings. She looks rapt. But in a peaceful sort of way. Like how I imagine you'd look in the glow of the alien ship when it finally comes for you. I do not begrudge her the feeling, but I wish she'd come upon it in some other fashion. She knows the science of plague better than most anyone. And yet because there's nothing that can stop it, and because no one in her family is of any comfort, she's done the reasonable thing of finding comfort elsewhere. Which is to say: Hannah appears to have cottoned to the idea that if you exterminate the Jews, all will be well.

I can't see the stage anymore because people have stood up. The lecture's not over, so I don't know what they are doing. But once I listen, I get a pretty good idea. They are being stoked. Because we are the lost tribes of Israel. Because the Jews masquerade as the chosen people, and rob us of our destiny. Because the Jews are not Israelites, *we* are Israelites. Scotland, England, Ireland, France, Germany, Austria, New Zealand, are all Nations of Israel. The United States is a Nation of Israel. Rise up to welcome God's government, and do as the Aryan Christ commands: Rid our nation of the mud races, for they have brought plague upon us.

A basket goes around while people empty their wallets. At the end of each row a camper passes out sign-up cards. This is the most civilized lynch mob ever.

By now Stanley is grateful we're close to the exit. I tell him to go find Hannah because we're leaving. He returns a couple minutes later, saying she won't come.

"I didn't say *ask* her."

"Then you go."

"Stanley. Come on."

But there's no need because Hannah has changed her mind. Says she's happy to take whatever abuse I am prepared to mete out.

Stanley says, "Jesus, that's horrible."

We head for the van home.

In the apartment, there's only Nana. She says Isifrid went out to sample a new caterer for Friday night, and how was Family Day?

Stanley says it was awful and what a bunch of freaks. I shrug. Hannah says I passed out on a dam.

"How is that even possible?" Aggie says.

"Well," I say, and try to explain. But I don't get far. She's watching that silent movie about love in Bora-Bora. This comes as a relief. It is one of the few entertainments we cherish together. I drop my bag and sit on the floor. Hannah throws herself on the couch. Stanley watches about three minutes, then says this movie's boring. He does not maintain this position long. Few things are worse than the hostile look of a woman, except, perhaps, three hostile looks, which is what he gets.

Aggie's gone misty-eyed. She always does, shortly after the start of part two. The young lovers are in hiding because the woman is supposed to be a sacred Virgin, and no man can know her love. Naturally, they are being pursued. Soon they will be caught and separated. But not before a snatch of happiness on this earth! They hold each other in a bamboo hut.

Hannah's nose has gone red. She rubs at her eyes like it's allergies. I am biting my forearm.

Moonbeams dapple the ocean. A breeze rouses pollen from the honeysuckle outside their door. The boy thinks he is blessed in all things. The girl has foreboding. They hold each other in a bamboo hut.

Agneth was married to the same man for forty-five years. But now that I know about her sailor, I can see why this movie slays her. Me, too. First time I watched it and saw that boy die chasing after his girl, it was like when you hold your breath for too long. The pain was visceral; I thought I was sick. And back then, I couldn't understand it. My reaction was not normal. I'd heard of girls who, jonesing for tears, will see the same movie over and over. Tears are relief, often ecstatic. To be moved is one of the great pleasures in life. But after *Tabu* I wasn't moved. I was demolished. I hurt so badly, and all because the one who got away is actually about the shell he leaves behind. It was prescient, really, that reaction. I hadn't even *met* Eric. But after we split, and I was about as hollow as you can get, I think I watched *Tabu* three times in a row.

. The boy goes out to dive for pearls. His body is lean and fit. In this still of night and bounty, he is the first man on earth. But back at the hut, things are bad. The keeper of the Virgin curse shows up to take the girl away. She does not protest. She boards his ship.

Aggie has gone through a box of tissues. She has resorted to her kimono. My sleeve is wet, I'm using Stanley's. As for Hannah, she is stifling the best she can.

The boy returns. The ship has already left port. He does not think, he does not hesitate. He plunges into the sea and swims. He almost catches up; he nearly gets her back. But the keeper cuts him off. And that's that. Under a summer moon, a boy drowns for love.

I am spent. The nap, the tears, the fomented anti-Semites, it's too much. I say I'm going to bed. Stanley protests. He wants to watch boxing. He wants me to stay up and watch boxing. He says, "I watched your stupid show." I wonder if he thinks we're a couple.

Hannah heads off to her room. Her face looks ready to blow. I bet she cries a monsoon in there.

I start to tell Aggie what they are saying at camp about superplague. I point out that just because fundamentalism has taken over the country is no reason to cede our every citizen to it. I ask if it wouldn't be good to get Hannah the hell out of there. Like maybe I should take her back with me to the chicken plant. Stanley says it's only October and what about school?

"Have you noticed she's not really going? We can school her. We can buy textbooks and stuff. Nate and Carmel homeschool and look at their kids. Model citizens."

"Levi's got those curls in his hair. He looks like a girl," Stanley says.

"Levi is seven. All seven-year-old boys look like girls."

"No they don't."

"Well, what do you know? Like you went to school."

"That's cold," Stanley says. "What's with you?"

Ugh. Poor Stanley. I pull him close and kiss his forehead. He says he'll come to bed with me, that it's okay about the boxing. He takes my hand. As we're leaving the room, I notice Aggie has not said a word in ages. She's been staring at the TV screen, which is frozen on a shot of the boy facedown in the water. I say, "Agneth, you in there?"

She is startled. Then she sighs, "I guess not," and fusses with the yarn on her lap.

Twelve

Such is the paradox: I have come back in Agneth, but I am still in the Gulf. I have endured her life and mine. I have even endured my comrades at dinner, the child with shriveled head and marble eyes. And throughout, I endure the body death. We reexperience the body death ad infinitum. I live in tautologies, though I call them rondos. I call them song. I was singing when I died. We all were. The Gulf of Finland was riddled with mines. The *Virona* went down with ease. We sang the "Internationale" and jumped overboard.

It is 1941. The sun has risen and set. From here, I can see Tallinn smoldering. An Estonian flag has gone up. Silly for the Russians to have thought the people of Tallinn would support them against the Nazis. Stupid of the high command to have ignored the German threat. Hundreds are dead. The volunteer brigades at Tallinn, most have never handled a weapon let alone fired one. Boys not sixteen years old were shot in the face. Our convoy was fifteen miles long. We met with torpedoes, artillery fire, air attack. Six thousand are dead. Fifty-three ships are lost. And yet this mine has kept me afloat while others drown.

What have I learned? Time will tell. They say it takes years to get over love. What drivel. It takes a lifetime. Or several. Possibly, it can't be done. Healing is unavoidable, but it is also without end.

My last few months in Norway were electric. What a time to be alive. We were a small country festered with ideas. Anarchosyndicalists. Socialists, fascists, Marxists, Trotskyites. We often shared the same house. Even the same bed. We fought, though it might have seemed otherwise: the Labor Party had been dominant since

1905. Strict neutrality was the platform. And about this there was no debate. Our concerns were national, and our biggest threat came from within. The Roma. The Roma people had everywhere put down foundations; the Roma intended to stay.

We used to hunt them down. We used to jail them in chastisement houses. We abducted Roma children and put them in orphanages. Assimilation was the plan. And then, thanks to Dr. Scharffenberger, sterilization. Persons who could not care for themselves were neutered. Persons who might pass on insanity or physical defect to their children were neutered. Some were lobotomized. It gave me no small satisfaction to see these methods carried out. The Roma threatened all that was pure and advanced in our culture. Science confirmed it. Their presence in Norway could only degrade our race.

Has anything changed? I hardly think so. Here at table, the trammels of capitalism are manifest in how the shepherd's pie is apportioned, and in whose hunger the knife and fork are wielded best. We do not ask: Who wants seconds? We say: Whosoever gets there first.

Leaders of men arise from homogeneity to express the collective will of the people. This is a staple of fascism, and I agree. But I was living with butchers. I knew not what to think. I still don't. Ethos is a funny thing. Live long enough and you've seen it all.

It was a time of intermingling. Wilhelm Reich was there. Sigund Heel and Wittgenstein. We stayed up late and made plans. Tracts were written. Fealties were sworn. In every heart a flower. At least until Held. My sweet Held. He was magnificent back then. I understood half of what he said, but it did not matter. He was haloed by the promise of rebirth. He might part the sea like Moses. When Walter spoke, you believed him. You'd follow him anywhere. And I did. I followed him here. I have read he suffered terribly.

At first I posed as a resistance nurse. I wore an H7 armband. I feigned loyalty to Haakon, who claimed to govern from England. The son of a union boss smuggled me into Finland. From there it was easy. Russian soldiers were returning home in droves. The Luga front was nearly collapsed. Leningrad was vulnerable. Passage to Tallinn was granted to most anyone able to fight. My plan was to fall back with the Russian Army all the way to Moscow. Barbarossa seemed unstoppable. In a few weeks' time, Hitler would march on Red Square while I tracked down Held. It was a crazy plan. He hardly cared for me.

In May 1940, what makes a German Trotskyite exile seek passage through Russia? Desperation. Britain and Sweden would soon negotiate peace with the Nazis. Held knew what would become of him. A journalist ideologue never fares well with a fascist. Or a Stalinist. We were certain he'd be killed, and so he was.

The circumstances of this war have everyone confused. Norway does not even know who she is at war with. That idiot Quisling continues to presume authority. Terboven is not much better. It seemed the Brits were to attack Norway under pretense of helping the Finns against Russia. It seemed the Germans were planning to occupy Norway under pretense of scooping the Brits. The armistice between Finland and the Soviet Union ruined both plans. And yet the fascists came anyway, followed by the Allies. The Allies left us to die. The fascists were no different.

I was three days in Tallinn before the Germans pushed through. The Russian defense was feeble, though they held out a month. Still, the collapse, when it came, was swift, and the evacuation was organized in haste. We were headed for Kronstadt. There was no way except by sea. The naval command knew the Gulf was heavily mined. To attempt passage was suicide.

I am a fascist socialist Freudian Trotskyite. I am a *völkisch* Bolshevik. A Strasserite. A third-positionist. I am Asatru. A eugenicist. I am dead. I am in love. My passions are rent and I know not my own mind.

Here in the Gulf is the wreckage of hope. Here is a life jacket. I have pursued a love and failed. They will drop the bomb in four. In the twentieth century, the experience of consciousness is bedlam, calamity, and woe.

Thirteen

Just what does it take to weaponize plague? I guess the hard part is having to create a strain that can linger in air. So long as it keeps in air, the rest is cake. How to spread it? Fill a lightbulb with the bacteria and drop it on a subway platform.

The Feds have tracked down everyone with access to Dad's lab. The result: nothing. The Feds have also detained nearly every radical in the country. Among casualties of the Patriot Act is due process, which has the ACLU looking more impotent than ever. And this is how it always starts, right? Some nut burns down the Reichstag, which gives Hitler grounds to purge house of those who would destroy us. Same went for Stalin. And Franco. Hard to decide what the plague will kill off first, us or our democracy. By contrast, extremists on the Right are doing just fine, and religion—the scary hate-your-neighbor kind—is experiencing a windfall. In my own home, no less. Tonight is Mother's Guido von List function, where there is talk about the Aryan ego and similitude with God and a drubbing of the Swarthy or else. What's frightening, besides the obvious, is the currency *or else* has these days. Or else what? Or else *superplague*. Every lobby has conscripted the disease as avenger and deterrent, both.

Our phones have been ringing nonstop. Mostly it's reporters. If all international flights to the United States are suspended, will we feel responsible? That or it's people responding to Stanley's ad. It's amazing how many women will sublet their wombs for a buck. He's setting up interviews. No clue what his criteria are or how, exactly, he plans to finance the thing. At least I'm not involved.

Wanda has called twice. In each message, she says the sentinel chickens are infected, but that she can't get anyone from the CDC on the line. Stupid plague, she mutters, and call me back. I decide to stop checking my voice mail from now on.

Because of the calls and letters and threats and *egging* of our building, Mother has requested police protection. She has not gotten it, which is too bad. The Guido von List people are scary as shit. They start off okay but once the ritual part of the night begins, scary as shit.

I remember the craziest thing about Waco and the fifty-day siege was the noise torture. I think the Alcohol, Tobacco, and Firearms people made Koresh and his lot listen to dying animals at full blast. Dental drills, bagpipes, and Nancy Sinatra. Nancy Sinatra! Apparently after a few days of this, a bunch of cows went nuts. I wonder how Nancy Sinatra took it. If things get too Jim Jones tonight, I'm gonna try Perry Como.

Mother has been having these parties for years. Cocktails, crudités, Brie. She has hired two bartenders and a waitress. Hannah is responsible for the coats. She is to pile them on Izzy's bed. When I was younger and this was my chore, I used to go through everyone's pockets. Once I stuck a note in some guy's camel coat that said *Let me out!*

On the topic of Mother's parties, Hannah and I are agreed: we hate them. Especially since our attendance is mandatory. We know all her friends and are expected to charm. Hannah is wearing a yellow dress with a bow at the back, white stockings, and patent leather shoes. No way was this her idea. In fact, only a geriatric would find this outfit suitable for a twelve-year-old. "Aggie?" I say. She nods.

The first guests to arrive are Suzanna and Oliver Lentz. He's tall, she's fat, they're German. The rest of the guests do not offer up much variety. Everyone is talking about superplague. Mother, who is a world-class hostess, knows how to sense a mood and work it. She taps a glass for silence. There are about two hundred people in the apartment.

"Friends," she says. "Welcome. For those who wish to stay for the organized part of the evening, it begins at nine. I know that's why most of you have come. In fact, I can't imagine anyone thinking of anything else."

Titters.

"My husband used to say that any press is good press. If he were here tonight, he might reconsider."

Titters.

"But really, I don't know anything more about it than you do. I married a man, not his life. So let us pray that Odin visits either a miracle on the sick or the bomb on Minnesota. Drink up!"

Cheers, laughter, exeunt.

Suzanna corners me by the cheese platter. She wants to know what I'm doing these days. I grew up with her son. We used to do horrible things to each other's genitalia.

"Soul searching," I say. "Taking a little time off before grad school."

"Grad school? How wonderful. Marcus just got his law degree. I am sure he'd love to hear from you."

Ever since I was young, parents have been trying to make me date their sons.

"You look wonderful," she says. "Grad school for what?"

"To work with children with learning disabilities."

"Oh, how wonderful."

And it sort of is. I just made it up, but it sounds good.

"Oliver," she yells, because the room is loud. "Lucy has just been telling me the most wonderful things."

I spot him and Hannah across the room. She is holding forth about Dad's simulation project, which is like applying a styptic to whatever dribbles of optimism were left these people before they got here. The project set a smallpox epidemic in motion: A thousand citizens were infected by aerosol clouds in three states. Role-play and real-time response were gauged. Given the government's limited supply of smallpox vaccine, three million people were infected, one million died, and interstate commerce was stopped. I remember Dad poring over the numbers. Was this scenario even possible? Yes. Yes it was. He was emphatic. Said the North Koreans definitely had the variola. That nine years before WHO announced the eradication of smallpox, the Russians were experimenting with an especially nasty strain they managed to aerosolize and send downwind, where a woman on a boat took in the fresh night air. The Aralsk outbreak, he said, proved how wily a hostile government can be. How brazen. And what can we do? Basically nothing. The smallpox vaccine is itself dangerous. And the virus, if twinned with human DNA, could easily outwit the vaccine, cf. the Jackson-Ramshaw paper on invincible mousepox. And anyway, what are the odds the government will inoculate with parity? They'll save themselves and the army while the rest of us drown in our own blood.

Oliver rushes over, happy for the chance to escape Hannah.

I excuse myself. This night requires many stimulants consumed at many intervals. Mother, apparently, has the same idea. Why doesn't anyone seem to notice that she's addicted to crack? Perhaps it's because none of the people in attendance tonight look that good, either. Lifts, tucks, nips, it's a chop shop in there. And the alcoholism is throughout. Even so, looking at her now, I wish she'd come to a meeting with me. Just to hear her talk. I still have no idea what could bring a woman so low, at least not a woman like her. She'd been beautiful, she'd been loved. She had money, a career, two children, friends.

I see she's putting on the whiteface. It's a talc-cream pâté she makes herself. Smoothes out the skin. And makes you look dead. Except this evening, she's flushed and excited, and she can slather all the pâté she wants, I still know something's up.

Aggie is in the next bathroom over. She's already put on her blue eye shadow and needs help with her cape. It cinches at the neck. Her blouse is black velour and the pants are black something. The belt is silver, so is the necklace. I wonder where's the mother ship. "Where's the mother ship?" I ask.

Izzy comes out in the same uniform, only her belt is bigger. "Shut up," she says. "Mingle."

Back in the living room are the diehards and initiates. Everyone else has left. A waitress is handing out capes. Some guests have brought their own. The newbies are given rhombus pins to wear at the heart. Really, I don't want to see this, but Mother insists. I say I've been to her Winter Nights blot eight bazillion times. She says, "No, no, tonight will be different from all other nights. Tonight we have purpose."

Isifrid corrals the *folk* into the black room. She actually calls it the black chamber after those buildings where twentieth-century

cryptanalysts did their work. Here the horrible effects of globaliza-
tion, imperialist Christianity, and the Zionist Occupation Government are stripped away, leaving bare the glorious shining of our
heathen ancestry. For me, the best thing in all this is ZOG. I never
tire of hearing people descry the ZOG Menace. But forget me. For
everyone else, the big thing is Theosophy, which says the world has
seven hierarchies and seven ur-races bound up in a cosmic spiral
that pursues enlightenment in cycles of birth, death, and rebirth.
Add a little pagan culture to the mix and you get Ariosophy, which
pairs the seven circles with Aryan preeminence. Then things get
tricky: According to Guido von List (whose *von* is assumed, mind
you), the seven ur-races correspond to the Viking Allfather Odin
and his sons, and to the offspring of four giants in the Norse sagas.
Somehow the Aryan or fifth race comes from Austria and does
pretty well until Christianity. Faced with extermination, the pa-
gans go underground. They encode their message in runes, lore, poetry, law, so that nowadays only a priest-king-scientist can restore
meaning to the faith. Somehow, no one at this party doubts Isifrid's
qualifications for the job.

The waitress appears with red wine. Aggie has a pewter goblet.
Hannah's got a mug and straw. I decide to stick with Scotch. Isifrid
takes her place at the lectern. The guests half-moon around her.
She waits for silence, then raises her arms.

Fourteen

She says, "Our forefathers laid claim to this land a thousand years ago. Bjarni Herjulfsson, Lief and Thórvald Erikson, Thórfinn Karlsefni, these were the first to see the shores of Vinland. Not Christopher Columbus and his ridiculous entourage, but Vikings. Vikings! Be not confused about what this means: the Aryan Norseman shall inherit the earth."

Then she toasts my dad, because he's dead. The rest of us toast my dad, same reason. There are paeans to lost relatives and famous people. A few toast themselves. This takes us through three rounds and nine bottles. Most of us are half in the bag. Hannah is shit-faced.

From beneath the lectern, Mother produces a rune set of twenty-four. I love the runes. Whereas the Roman alphabet is big on the curve—B, C, D, G, J, O, P, Q, R, S, U—the runes prefer a straight line. You see ᛁ a fair amount. Also ↑. Sometimes ᛚᛒᚦᛏᚡᚼᛊᛁᚡᛦᛏᛏᛚᚱᛊᚾᛚ. The alphabet or futhark, I guess (named for the first six characters: *fehu, uruz, thurisaz, ansuz, raidho, kenaz*), is pretty austere-looking, which makes you marvel at the extravagant arts that have grown around it. Each character has a phonetic value, *fff*, and a meaning, *cattle*. But each is also a metaphor, as in *cattle* means *wealth*. So if you roll them like dice and pick a few at random, they're gonna tell you a story. Hence magic, witchery, song.

Mother has been casting runes for years. She is much moved by the story of Odin, who, in order to gain knowledge of the runes, hung from the world tree Yggdrasil for nine days, impaled on his own spear. Mastery of the word is a quest for power. And Mother, she gets off on this.

"Guide my hand, guide my mind, guide my soul as I take these meanings into my life. What will tonight hold for us?"

She draws *ansuz, mannaz,* and *hagall,* which is supposed to give us an overview, course of action, and outcome. *Ansuz* is my favorite rune. It's about inspired speech. Oratory. The death rattle. Essentially any sound that communicates poignantly. *Mannaz* is the mortality rune. Man is but augmented earth. He comes, he goes. As for *hagall,* I don't know. It means hail. And something about change. But when Mother sees it, she looks upset. And a few of the guests turn away. So I guess it's bad.

She glosses over the *hagall* part of the cast and snaps her fingers. The waitress disappears into the kitchen and returns with a box. It looks like a crate those fancy stores use to ship pears at Christmas.

Mother smoothes her palm over the box. She bares teeth. "As you all know, a few years ago, the remains of our revered ancestor were found in the Columbia River."

Oh, Lord, not this again. The Kennewick Man, you've heard it before: Two kids find a skull in the river. They stash it in a bush and go fishing. Later they give it to police. Other bones are found, almost a complete skeleton. Turns out the thing is 9,200 years old.

Mention of the Kennewick Man in certain circles can start a fistfight. Several Native American tribes wanted to bury the bones according to their traditions. Under the Native Graves and Repatriation Act, any remains that predate Columbus are considered Native American. Thing is, the Kennewick Man didn't *look* Native American. He had Caucasoid features. You can imagine the maelstrom that followed. People were saying: Maybe ancestors of modern American Indians were not the first to see the New World. Maybe the first came from Scandinavia over the Bering land bridge. Maybe the first were forefather to the Vikings. The Vikings!

Archaeologists, scientists, the Indians, and Asatru Folk Assembly all claimed title to the KM. On the sly, a few tribes were allowed to perform rituals with the bones. The Asatru went nuts. Mother went nuts. They won a ceremony of their own. The legal battles were endless.

"The Kennewick Man," she says, "is a bridge back to the ascendancy of our culture. And until he is laid to rest, superplague will rage on."

Ah, yes, the *or else*. I saw it coming, but I feel stunned just the same. And Dad, if he's up there, is completely appalled. I look at the box and start to get a bad feeling.

Mother was instrumental in getting the Asatru access to the bones. She petitioned just about every government official in the country. Meantime, the court cases got more confusing and bilious. And the bones got trashed. Moved here, moved there. Never mind that the guys who found the skull stuffed it in a *bush* while they went fishing. I can just imagine their conversation. Dude, check out this skull.

Eventually there was DNA testing, which suggested the KM was related to the Southeast Asian people. The Asatru dropped their claim and Mother got depressed. I thought it was over, but no.

"Many have tried to refuse the Kennewick Man his homecoming. Many have stood in his way. But shall a blessed ancestor be denied? Shall his spirit never rest? The plague is a call to action!"

She opens the box. Everyone leans forward. And then back. Waaay back, except Hannah, who lurches for the bone. Wherever she waves it, people retreat like it's a torch. Or a gun.

My twelve-year-old sister is armed and drunk.

Mother ventures to talk her down. Since No Face, I never thought I'd hear *Just give me the bone* spoken in this household again. "Is it really nine thousand years old?!" Hannah says. "I bet I can hex people with this thing." The waving intensifies. Many guests have actually fled the room. I notice commotion at the front door. People are trying to get out. "Give me that," I say, and grab her ponytail. She frees the bone. It's a femur. And it puts me in mind to hex some people of my own.

Mother is angry. This is not how she intended the unveiling to pan out. I see Oliver Lentz helping his wife into her coat. "Wonderful party," she says. "But we really must be going." I start to feel bad for Isifrid and give her the bone. It's still intact, no harm done, but she flings it against the wall. I get the perverse idea that maybe we can grind up the pieces and snort the KM, but Aggie has already collected them in a dustbin.

Authorities lost shards of the KM's femur a few years ago. There was much scapegoating. The femur is important. Postmortem, it can help establish a person's size, fortitude, age, ethnic affinity, and composition. So it was pretty bad when it vanished. But since the hunt for the femur fragments availed nothing, the hunt was dropped. How in hell did Mother get one?

I sit on the floor next to her.

"Everyone gone?" she asks.

"How'd you get the bone?"

She shrugs, which means: You forget I am rich.

"You could go to jail."

"I could."

"Would you like that?"

"No."

Seems like a natural segue, so I ask if she's thought about her drug use lately because I am getting really worried about her. This lunacy with plague and the bone, come on. She slaps me across the face.

The shock makes its way down my whole body and back before I can speak.

"Was that really the Kennewick Man?"

"No. It's from that chimpanzee who died at the zoo. I just wanted to get some life in this house. It's so quiet all the time."

Hannah, who's been watching us from across the room, throws up in a garbage bag. Aggie complains of chest pain. When she complains again, I call 911.

Fifteen

Why can't I believe in a higher power? Even as Aggie nearly died—those few days at the hospital were touch and go—I did not pray. Fear is supposed to make converts of us all. Trench faith. But it didn't happen. And I was plenty scared. I gorged on fast food; I stabbed a bump's worth of Ketamine into my thigh and stayed in the hole for hours. I watched the Food Network. I wanted a donut. When I still wanted one by nightfall, I made for the church basement.

Because most meetings are held underground, recovery tends to have a certain smell. The Brothel Armpit. I imagine this benefits someone, maybe a gym coach.

Tonight's speaker is Jimmy. It's a full house. Dirty Ben's up front with a tower of Oreos on his knee. He offers me one. I've long thought Oreos are the doomsday cookie. They preach the triumph of evil, of darkness over light, and no amount of reversing the colors is gonna change that. I dial the cookie and expose the cream.

Ben asks how I am. I ask about Eric. He asks if we've thought about moving to a place where no one's heard of my dad. I say: Like bunghole Texas? I got it covered. He says this conversation is going nowhere.

Jimmy has someone read a pamphlet of questions. Have drugs ever landed you in jail? Have you tried to substitute one drug for another in an attempt to stop? Have your relations suffered as a result of drugs? I see other people nodding and find myself doing the same. Then I start to pose questions of my own. Do you think you'll die if you quit drugs? Do you think you *can* quit? Do you even want to quit?

This last one always gets me. I am ambivalent. I want to stop. I want to stop, later.

Jimmy is talking about Not Me. He says, "Not Me gets things done. Not Me drives the boat." This is his answer to the problem of God. There are forces out there greater than Jimmy, he doesn't know what they are or how they work, but it's enough for him to believe the sum totality of the universe resides elsewhere. I find this logic seductive. Not Me. I should try that.

"Just for today, Not Me has kept me clean. And a clean day is a successful day."

I wince. There always comes a moment in every person's share when it leaves me behind. Guy says, "I was miserable, I wanted to die," and I'm like yeah, yeah, "and then everything I am and believe went out the window and today I'm grateful." I don't mean to belittle the change—not at all. It's just that I don't get it. Not in practice. How does a self-hating suicide hopeful wind up thinking a clean day is a successful day? When did the bar drop so low? Or how did Jimmy come to believe that the bar, set thus, is high?

Ben gives me another Oreo. The cream center really is divine.

We put money in the collection basket. All I have is a ten. I wait for the basket to fill with singles, but I am nervous anyway. I am certain I'll shortchange the basket. Put in ten, take back eleven. Or that someone will think I'm doing that. I let the basket go by, which means now everyone thinks I'm cheap. Blah blah, no one is thinking about me at all, blah blah, I hate this.

There is mention of self-centered fear, addiction to television and pornography. One woman says her left breast is smaller than the right.

Mark waves his hand. He really wants to talk. And he wants to talk plague. He is flipping out. His neck is scarred from a bullet that passed through his esophagus; when he gets worked up, it turns purple. He is asking what's the point of sobriety when we're all gonna die. I think everyone is wishing he'd shut up. Denial is the only way to deal with this. The Minnesota Man, now dubbed the Primary, has caused six deaths not including his own. The entire hospital has been quarantined, though until today, no one has enforced it because no one wanted to be that close. Now they've got guys in moon suits manning every door. There is rumor of a Chinese takeout delivery boy who escaped. As a result, three Chinese neighborhoods have been targeted with hate crimes.

"I can't sleep," Mark says. "Everyone looks like a killer! A guy with a cold coughed in my face the other day. I nearly broke his neck." He stands up abruptly and says he needs some air.

We take a break. We speculate. Who is behind this? Could be Al-Qaeda, could be your mom. No one seems to have a clue, except the conspiracy theorists who think the government needed a pretext for more warmongering in the Middle East. Retaliation does presume the moral high ground. But retaliation for what? Used to be any affront to our principles would suffice. Operation Just Cause; Operation Restoring Democracy. These days, a principle offended just will not do. No one wants to die for a principle. But to vanquish a plague epidemic! Sign me up.

Aggie and I hashed it out at the hospital. She is of about six minds. Concedes it's possible the government helped facilitate 9/11 and now this plague thing, but also that even the most nefarious regime doesn't kill its own people at random. On the one hand, our government is too stupid. On the other, stupidity is just what's needed to bungle a plague spread so that instead of killing six, it kills six million. Most likely it's someone from within. A save-the-whales crusader. But with knowledge of aerosolized plague? So maybe it's a scientist. But what scientist would unleash deadly plague? So maybe it's a martyring scientist. But what sort of martyr works in secret? Where's the glory in that? So maybe it's Al-Qaeda after all.

The doctors said we were upsetting the other patients. One has pancreatitis, toxic shock, and adenoid cancer. Another's got renal failure. But it's the plague that gets them down.

We brought Aggie home three nights after the von List social. She's got blockages in two arteries and a bad valve. Surgery is out—she *is* eighty-four—which means we pin our hopes on blood thinners and diet.

I decide to share about her condition. Not because I think it will help, but maybe so that I can feel more a part of things. I have shredded a napkin to peas. There's about twenty people here, but the peas are my audience.

I say, "My grandmother might die soon. She believes in reincarnation, so I guess she's not too depressed. But I'm depressed. And I don't know how to deal with depression except by taking drugs."

Meanwhile, the subtext: I'm tired. Being a drug addict is the hardest job I have ever had. I should give up. I'm confused, I'm stuck, and I want. I want the person I love to love me back. I want to be a good member of society or, that failing, to not give a fuck. I want the courage to start from scratch in a place where I can walk outside and be happy. I want to not want any of these things because the instant I stop wanting is the instant I am free. I want a profession. I want a life.

"Also, at the end of a meeting the other day, someone told me to stop reading so much Kurt Vonnegut. What does that mean? I have no idea what that means. Thanks for letting me share."

After, me and Ben, Phil, and Fran go out for dessert. Fran used to be a hooker in Cleveland. When she was still a minor, her parents had her tubes tied. I'm certain this is illegal, but then God knows what goes down in Cleveland. Ever since that river caught fire, the jury's out, and frankly, I can think of few things more dissolute than a river so toxic it explodes.

The purpose of these outings, especially on a Friday night, is to recreate without drugs. To prove it can be done. We shuffle into a café and order two desserts each. This is vulgar in the extreme, but we are addicts, we cannot stop. Tonight we are destined for heartburn and nausea. I'm not even hungry.

Phil says his wife is pregnant again. The banter stops. Ben asks if he's okay for money. He's not. I ask if he's okay with having to be responsible for yet another person, isn't he afraid he'll just run out on his family, don't you need to love yourself before you can love a kid, and aren't you setting yourself up for disaster by presuming the wherewithal to raise a kid when you're really just a selfish and indolent junkie?

Fran's an ex-hooker, Dirty Ben has tried, repeatedly, to stab his mother, Phil admits to drinking his own cum, and yet somehow *I'm* the freak among us. Next person to ask if I'm okay gets the boot.

"You okay?" Fran says.

I thump my forehead against the table.

They decide to leave it at that. Fran has upturned the sugar dispenser over her cup. I have never seen anyone put that much sugar in her coffee. She catches me staring and taps her teeth. They are shockingly white. "All fake," she says, and winks. "Horrible to see Mark like that," she says. "I remember keeping it together after 9/11 until Dan Rather lost it on Letterman. Guy's supposed to be the strength of the nation. And there he was crying. Okay, so it wasn't during a newscast, but still. I wasn't afraid until that. And I wasn't afraid of *superplague* until Mark."

Dirty Ben takes the straw from his mouth. "What will we do, anyway? I mean, say this really does get out of hand, what are we supposed to do? Run away? Where?"

These questions are even worse than the fear. Because when you start posing practical questions to which there are no practical answers, you've lost your last recourse to sanity. So long as you're just hyperventilating, you can always get a grip and sort things out. But when you realize you *can't* sort things out, panic is all you got left. Panic qua religious fervor. Panic qua drug abuse.

"I'm gonna buy a mobile home," Fran says. "I'm gonna put a disco ball in there and drive."

Phil perks up. "I'm going to storm Alcatraz and make it my own. I hear the land out back is good for a vegetable or two."

"To hell with that," I say. "I'm gonna shoot, snort, and smoke every drug on the planet."

"Good point," Phil says.

The others agree, and for a second we are all lost to every addict's fantasy, the binge without consequence.

"Course, a mobile disco isn't bad, either," I say.

"Who said anything about a disco? Just the ball. All I want is the *ball*."

Outside, there's rain. Or slush. Unseasonably cold is what they're saying. I suppose the silver lining is that if it's this cold, the earth can't be warming at a pace likely to kill off mankind in a thousand years. If we don't die now, we can be safe in the knowledge that we won't die then.

Fran is headed uptown. Phil lives on the West Side. Ben and I will just have to hoof it together. We opt for the bus. The bus does not encourage talk, but unfortunately, the bus shelter does.

"I'm worried about you," he says.

"Why?"

He gives me a look that means: Even you can't be this stupid.

"Okay, I'm sorry. But I'm fine."

He turns away. I don't know when this started to happen, but it seems the more I try to spare people my unhappiness, the more exasperated they get.

We step into the street to look for the bus. Two seconds in the rain and we're drenched. "Are you getting out of the house?" he asks. "Are you seeing friends?"

Friends. What friends? I've been sleeping a lot. Should I tell him that? "Sure. I mean, sometimes. Movies and stuff."

"You're not really going back to the chicken place, are you?"

"Actually, I am. And I'm thinking of bringing Hannah."

This, it seems, is too much for him. "Are you kidding? Good luck with that," he says, and shakes his head because really, there's a limit to what you can do.

Sixteen

t's for you," Eric says, and gives the phone to Kam.

Three in the morning, and I am sad.

"Are you ever going to stop this?" Kam says. "Maybe we should have lunch. To talk it over." Her voice sounds a little Vivien Leigh, circa 1940, where she can be asking for toast and still mean: I'm dying!

Kam says she's going to hang up now. She might change her number. That she's still my friend, but really.

I ask if anyone has contacted her about Alfred's article. It won't come out for ages, but maybe Eric finagled a draft.

There is a long pause. "Is this what you called to say? Are these really the first words you want me to hear?" And then, "I don't want to talk about this right now. It's the middle of the night. I'm exhausted. If you want lunch, make an appointment with my assistant. I'll tell him to expect your call."

This is the nastiest Kam has been to date. I guess she read the article. Maybe the overzealous fact-checker got in her face. Maybe I shouldn't have mentioned her.

I have not seen the whole piece, but I have spoken to said fact-checker, in whose yen for truth I got a look. I said I could not verify without context; she faxed me a column. Kam's mention goes something like this: Lucy grew up with HSN mogul Anshu Yala-manchilli's daughter. The friends went to elementary and high school together. Kam's husband cut his teeth on Lucy. Lucy has no husband at all. Kam is a CEO, Lucy is not. Same past, two futures, one plague.

"Lucy, are you there? Oh for God's sake."

Eric gets on the line. Says he's taking the phone into the other room. I hear the fridge open. He says, "Luce, what are you doing?"

"I don't know."

"You are driving Kam crazy."

"I know."

"Is that the point?"

"I don't know."

"Well, what do you know?"

"I want to see you."

"Oh."

"Yeah."

"Will you stop calling in the middle of the night if I see you?"

"I'm sorry. You don't have to if you don't want to. Was just a thought."

"No, it's fine. But Kam—"

"Right, okay. Well, forget it. I just thought it'd be nice. To catch up or something."

"No, let's have lunch. It's no problem. When is good for you?"

This makes me laugh. "Well," I say, "between nothing in the morning and a date with nothing at four, I'm pretty flexible."

"I'll call you," he says. "G'night."

Seventeen

We had five interviews. Girls wanting to offer their uteri to Stanley. He made me sit through them all. Needed my input, he said. Dicey business. I skimmed a template contract between surrogate mother, egg and sperm donors. There were boxes to check if the egg donor was married or single, if the sperm donor was married or single, if the donors were wed to each other, if the donors were anonymous, if the surrogate was married, if all parties were of sound mind and over eighteen. Course, there was no box to check if the egg donor was dead. Or if the sperm donor was dead. Or if the sperm was to be extracted from a dead person. Apparently, this can be done. Fertility law is a nightmare. I asked Stanley if he needed his wife's consent to use her eggs postmortem. He said he had no idea. There was no mention of them in her will. I asked if he'd heard about that kid a few years back who was ruled Without Parent by a judge in California. Stranger sperm and egg unite in surrogate who delivers baby to couple that are divorced. Wife wants child support, husband refuses, and the court says the baby has no parents. Who would want to go through this?

Stanley, it seems. And he told me his story.

He and Sylvie met when they were teenagers doing summer penance at a roller rink in Pittsburgh. He worked the concession stand, she doled out the skates. It was 1970. They heard "Do the Funky Chicken" twenty times a day. They heard "Sex Machine" twenty times a day. Nachos were in, which had liquid cheese all up in Stanley's hair. Sylvie smelled of Lysol. A few legs were broken each month.

On break, they'd sit in the back and smoke cigarettes. He

wanted to go to college. So did she. He'd ask if she could afford college. She'd say no. Could he? Nope. Bottom line? They'd be working the Monongahela Rink-a-Dink for the rest of their lives.

When Sylvie's mother died, Stanley went to the funeral. Open casket, striking resemblance. When Stanley's brother died at Khe Sanh, Sylvie went to the wake. And to the after-wake. Stanley got drunk and said he had flat feet and if not for his flat feet, he could have been in Vietnam and died, too.

They'd work the weekend shift, and then the week. It was better to be with each other than anywhere else.

Stanley said his mother cried all the time. She took pills to sleep and pills to wake. His father had no say because his father was broke.

Sylvie said living with her aunt was martial law. Lights out at ten and none of that hippie music, you hear?

They went to the bank together. If they pooled their savings, they'd have just enough for a month's rent and a marriage license.

Best part of any day? One sleeping bag, two beloveds.

Midspring, they were headed for the rink. They were asking for a raise.

You go first. No you. Her teeth were red from a Starburst. His Rink-a-Dink cap was askew. You go first. No you. There was laughter. And a candy passed from her lips to his.

Outside the office, he cleared his throat. She curtsied. If they did not get a raise, they could not have this baby.

She kissed him on the cheek. He went first.

After, she said, What happened?

He took her by the hand and marched them out of the building.

What happened? she said.

Nothing. We'll find other jobs. *Better* jobs.

Stanley, you're hurting me. Just stop and tell me what happened.

At home, he said he was going out. Don't stay up.

She unzipped their sleeping bag and asked him to stay.

He was not at the bar down the street or the next one over, though he had been to both. She waited by the phone. And waited some more. She called her aunt, who said, Sweet Jesus.

When Stanley got in, she asked what happened.

He was drunk. Said, Let's name the baby Felix. I always liked that name.

Stanley, I'm going to make an appointment. Aunt Claire said she'd pay for it.

She was on a stool, he on the floor. He wept into a leg of her jeans. We were fired, he said.

But why?

I don't know.

In every marriage, the one lie.

Next morning, he found her cornered on the bathroom floor. He said he would file for unemployment. She said she'd lost the baby. How do you mean? I don't know. In the toilet. Should they go to the hospital? No. Was she okay? Yes. We'll have another, he said. We'll get settled and secure and we'll have another. I promise.

I ask did Sylvie ever find out what happened at the rink. He says, "She knew that night. A girl who worked concession with me called the house."

"So she knew?"

"She knew."

Stanley owed the Rink-a-Dink three thousand dollars. Three K's worth of liquor. He had thought no one would notice. With ten bottles of Jack under the bar, who would miss one? Or even two? Someone had ratted him out and because that cheap tramp of a shoe clerk was his girl, the boss had fired them both.

I ask why Sylvie never left him.

"She was my life," he says. "I wouldn't let her."

"How many times did she try to get pregnant after that?"

"Four. Four miscarriages. One in the seventh month."

"Oh, God."

I flip through the résumés of women coming to see us. The load of having to help Stanley vet a surrogate just got huge.

First one in the door: Natalie Threadgold, twenty-seven. Married with one child. A daughter. Hails from Virginia, lives in Midtown, works a perfume counter at Macy's. She takes a seat. Declines a drink.

Stanley says, "So, tell me a little about yourself. I see from your letter that you have a full life."

Natalie's glasses are convex. Don't think I've ever seen that before. Her eyeballs look stuffed.

"It's not as full as it used to be," she says. "Just got sacked. Downsizing, I guess."

The glasses come off, her eyeballs retract. I find myself squinting in sympathy.

Stanley offers her nuts from a crystal bowl. She extends her arm and gently begins to probe the air until she hits glass.

"But it says you only just started."

She nods in his direction.

I ask if she wears her glasses to work. She says, "No, of course not, why would I?"

"Contacts?"

"No."

Stanley asks about her husband, who is an entrepreneur. Does he make money? Does he take good care of her? Is he good with the whole alien baby in the sack part?

She says yes, only with an air of having taken offense.

Stanley gets up. "And why do you want to do this?"

She blinks and orients her face in his general direction. "Your ad was sweet. I lost my first husband and always wonder if only we'd had a child."

"What else?" I say.

"Ten thousand dollars and health insurance for me and my family. If the superplague hits New York, I want to be covered."

I point out the false economy of seeking health care to fund treatment for a disease that has no cure.

She retrieves her glasses and this time when her eyeballs swell, they have the disconcerting affect of a woman with powers.

Stanley says we'll call her, and thanks for coming. One down, four to go.

———

Ella Norcross, thirty-three, professional surrogate. Has birthed four to date. One more and she can make a down payment on the boat. The SS *Freedom*, because that's what she'll have. She has come with letters of reference from previous employers and a character assessment from the president of the American Dental Association.

Stanley has her out of there in ten minutes. "Too smooth," he says.

I gather he's hatching standards as we go.

By the third interview, I am whupped. Can I sit this one out? No. As it happens, the interview is pretty quick. Sabrina Roy, twenty-six, versed in current events and, No, I'm not here about the baby, I'm actually studying journalism at Columbia, my thesis project is about a pair of seven-year-olds suffering from massive anxiety who, from my vantage, represent a generation of children for whom tension, nerves, ulcers are the new ADD, so part of my project is to interview people, people like you, who live in, how should I put it, a nexus of anxiety, to ask how they manage and what advice they can impart.

I smile hugely, thinking: Agneth, you are but a servant's quarter away. I tell Sabrina that my nana blossoms with advice, and would she come with me. Sabrina says she wants to be a foreign correspondent one day, so why not. I hardly think the unease of following me into the bowels of our apartment trains for the Afghan-shanty trip, but why argue. As is, Agneth opens her door looking a touch warlord (mask and robe), and every bit a teacher of men. I shut the door on them and return to Stanley, who's been en-sorcelled by candidate number four. Victoria Olivetti. Thirty-five, never married, no children. She's wearing black leather gloves. The diamonds round her neck could put us all through college. Her pumps are two-tone.

Stanley says, "So, if you like, if it's okay, please tell me a little about yourself."

"I live alone in a Park Avenue penthouse. I am independently wealthy, I want for nothing."

"Nothing?"

"I am bored. I'd like to write a book."

"About being a surrogate?" I say.

"No, about Iran-Contra."

Is this deadpan? It's not. Stanley offers her nuts from the crystal bowl. The bowl is becoming a litmus of sorts. She draws a macadamia. Gloves and all.

I suggest being pregnant can tax the brain. Morning sickness can last for months.

She asks about Stanley. What does he do? What did his wife do? She is the first to probe his bio. He seems delighted.

"A traveler," he says. "Been all over the country."

His vocation? Pluckhouse supervisor at ZOG Kosher Chicken.

"ZOG?"

"Zalman Ofer Guildenstein. A father-and-son team."

Victoria asks him to stand up and turn around. She asks me to stand up and turn around. I say I'm not involved. She says, "Then never mind."

Watching her pluck macadamia nuts from the bowl has me questioning her character. Sort of like how at every bonfire, there are those who toast their marshmallows with concern and those who just combust the skin and pare. I am of the latter school. I imagine Victoria is not.

"We are offering four thousand dollars," Stanley says. That *we* is noticeable. Also, he's skimmed a grand off the top.

Victoria nods. I think she's had lard injected into her lips.

Do we have a contract drawn up? No, we have not gotten that far. Do we have a lawyer? No, we have not gotten that far. These questions percolate with a goal in mind, I just can't tell what.

She says she will call us with her decision. And even as I sense voodoo mind trick, I am also worried about my outfit. Is this skirt too casual? Did I impress?

Stanley says he looks forward to hearing from her and thanks for her time.

After, we sit across from each other with heads in hand. I don't think she liked me, he says. Me, either. I should have given Wanda as a reference. Yeah.

It occurs to me that perhaps Victoria has a Baby M thing in

mind, but I'm too demoralized to give it much thought. This does not bode well for the experience of our last interviewee. I don't read her résumé. I do not care. When the bell rings, I tell Stanley to get it, only Hannah gets there first. It is her friend Indra, with mother in tow.

Indra has the misfortune of growing in spurts. She is always feet shorter or taller than everyone else in her class. These days she is taller. And her hands, they are huge. I never saw such big hands in my life.

"Come on," Hannah says, taking her arm.

They make for Hannah's room. As per, I can hear the lock click from here.

Indra's mom continues to stand in the foyer. Am I to invite her in? "I'm Connie," she says. "You don't remember me."

Oh, but I do. My memory is shot, but when a woman rips through Family Field Day, having swallowed a wasp and screaming murder, it tends to stick out. How do you swallow a wasp? You get overweight, attempt the potato-sack race anyway, and pant. I think I even saw the wasp fly down her throat.

Stanley has come up behind me. "You're Connie?" he says, and looks from me to her to me to her résumé.

"You're here about the baby?" I say.

She nods. "Indra told me about it. I had her when I was eighteen, I'm still in good shape."

Stanley is flabbergasted. And so am I. Hannah actually shares with her friends what goes on in this house? Why would Connie Denton want to surrogate a child? I wonder if Indra knows about Isifrid and the crack. I wonder if *Connie* knows about the crack.

"Have a seat," Stanley says. "Would you like something to drink? We'll be right back." He puts his hand on the small of my back and nudges me out the room.

"What do we do?" he says.

"It's weird, right? She doesn't need the money. She has a child already. Probably this won't do much for her social standing."

"Seltzer?" he says loudly. "Or orange juice?" He turns on the faucet and whispers. "Yeah, fine, but what do we do?"

"What do you mean? Interview her, I guess."

Stanley looks at me like I might be retarded. Then his face relaxes. "Okay, ha ha, but seriously."

I wait for more.

"Are you kidding?" he says. "Don't you notice anything *weird* about her?"

"The lazy eye? You're gonna rule her out because of a lazy eye? That's obscene."

He ushers me to the other end of the room. "Notice anything about her skin?"

"No."

"Are you blind? She's black!"

"She's coffee."

"Whatever!"

We return to the living room with a tray of drinks.

Stanley fidgets with a cocktail napkin. "So tell us a little about yourself," he says.

I interject. "Actually, don't bother. We've already chosen someone else."

"Is it the lazy eye? I'll just be carrying the baby, not passing on my DNA. Besides, I don't think lazy eyes are inherited."

Stanley looks incredulous. "Hey, I didn't even notice you had a lazy eye! How 'bout that."

"Is it that you're spooked? Because a lot of people are spooked by the lazy eye."

"Mrs. Denton," I say.

"Call me Connie."

"Connie," I say. "Does Indra ever talk to you about Hannah?"

"Of course. They are best friends."

"Do you have any reason to believe Hannah is mean to her or treats her badly?"

"Of course not. What's this about?"

Stanley so welcomes this digression, he prolongs it. "What Lucy is trying to say is—"

"My sister spent the summer with psychotic fundamentalists exhorted by the Aryan Christ to exterminate the mud people. I think it might have turned her head a little."

"The mud people?"

"The Jews," Stanley says. "And I guess black people, too." He looks to me for confirmation.

Connie stands up. "Are you saying that sweet little twelve-year-old girl is a bigot?"

Stanley nods aggressively.

"I wouldn't go that far," I say. "I'm just worried."

"Indra told me you people were a mess. We're leaving. Indra!"

Stanley rushes to get her coat. Indra arrives with a tub of sour-cream-and-chive dip. I think she's been ladling the stuff with her thumb.

"We're going," Connie says. "Get your things."

"Mrs. Denton," I say. "There's no reason to overreact. Hannah doesn't have too many friends."

"Small wonder," she says, and punches the elevator button. "Indra!"

Hannah shows up red-faced. Whatever's happened here, she knows it's my fault.

Stanley says, "Thanks for coming. We'll be in touch." He shuts the door, his relief is palpable. "*Phew,*" he says. "Man."

Meantime, Hannah is about to snap. I say Connie wasn't a good fit for surrogacy, she didn't take it well. I say it's not so bad, I'm sure Indra will be back tomorrow. I say I'm sorry, but Hannah should not have told them about the ad in the first place. I say she is always screwing up this kind of thing, why was she always screwing up?

"Hey, go easy," Stanley says.

Aggie appears with Sabrina in tow, Sabrina who's got a leather-bound pocket notebook and, I notice, a Bic pen she's chewed halfway down the barrel.

"What's going on in here?" Aggie says. "I bet the whole building can hear this."

Probably right. When a preadolescent girl screams that she hates you, even the dead roll over. Best way to estrange a loved one? Kill off her only friend.

"You want to know what's going on? I'll tell you. I'm going to hell, that's what's going on."

Sabrina looks at Agneth, who nods by way of encouragement, like this is Sabrina's chance to try out what she's learned, which she promptly does. She says, "Actually, it seems you are coming back. I saw the family tree. So even if you *do* go to hell, it will be a short stay."

"Get out of here," I say. "For God's sake."

Agneth apologizes on my behalf. We all watch in silence as Sabrina puts on her coat and quickly gives Aggie her number. After she's left, I try to feel relieved. As if Sabrina were the real evil here.

Agneth says, "What did you do to Hannah? I'm sorry, but it's hard to feel bad for you. Don't you notice that Hannah suffers for everything this family does?"

Loretta, our cook, rings the dinner bell. Stanley takes a pass. Aggie says she wants to call Sabrina because there's just so much more to explain and the girl seemed willing to learn. I feel a stirring of jealousy and say, "I'm willing to learn!"

Aggie rolls her eyes and asks me to read off the phone number. I consider lying. I do not lie, but it takes restraint.

So now Sabrina knows more about my sister than I do. Hannah, the flagellant; I, child.

Eighteen

Hannah, the frail. I, flagellant. Of the two of us, the flagellant rules. Just think what I have been through. Suffering? They hardly know.

In the year of the Lord 1348, it was like this:

> Whoso will through our penance go
> Let him restore what he's taken away,

whose hopes for respite are death, whose spirits are flayed, whose souls are lost, in these where sighs the end of all things, for they who are too many,

> Solace of the wretched, pray for us.
> Medicine of the sick, pray for us.
> Mother Most Sad, the passion of Christ is stoked against us.

We are descended of the Camaldolese and the Cluniacs, the Servites and the Dominicans. The Disciplinati di Gesù Cristo are the dawn wherefore hope survives.

> Now let us all lift up our hands
> And pray to God this death to a vert.

This horror is unsustainable. I don't know that I can go on. My chest is given to welts and boils that do not heal. I refuse women, I refuse to bathe. My flesh is bludgeoned for the sake of the Lord. My blood is spilt for the sake of the Lord. I do not speak, I only sing. And yet my sufferance is nothing. The plague can claim a man in fourteen hours. Others linger for several days, blood scum around their lips, feces down their legs, swellings like gourds that burble the Devil's work, the bruisings and mottled skin, the weeping and hysteria, the stench, this rancid breath of excreta, rot, sweat, and vomit that collects in a slime that paves every road, the keening children who take with them unto death their parents, servants, siblings, and everyone who has touched their clothes or spared a moment's compassion to behold them and pray; nay, every stranger who so much as passes the house; Lord of all, deliver us from this torture.

Hour by hour, carts drone through the streets, interring the dead five deep. The plague flag snaps in the wind. Last rites are dispatched with haste, and few receive the obsequies they deserve. Madmen are amok. Some say even we are amok. But consider. Venice and Genoa are locked in struggle. Simony mars the papal court. All around is calamity and strife, and yet Clement VI frowns on our conduct. He reviles the apostolic mendicants who are the Disciplinati. We are laymen whose penance claims miracles, which behavior threatens the provenance of oblates and priests. Wherefore shall we desist? Our work has only begun.

In the year of the Lord 1348, can we be found of Him pure and without fault? Ten thousand passings this last fortnight. In the year of the Lord 1348, are we without defect? Mark the dreadful splendor of His wrath. None among us can abide the day of His coming, much less the blanketing hail of His displeasure.

It is no coincidence that there made its appearance the pestilence in April, whence He who was foretold was expired by they who rejected Him. Sayeth the Son of Man: "But those mine enemies, which would not have me reign over them, bring them hither, and slay them before me." Should we disobey? Should we vaunt our will and expect mercy? The Jews comport themselves as swine and exist by way of debauchery. They are Christ killers who must be made rid of, else more of this punishment, which none will survive. I have seen it with mine own eyes.

In the year of the Lord 1316, it rained without end. The rain pelted the land like spikes. Fields were scalped of soil so that it seemed one walked across the earth's core. Houses were collapsed and soused. Cattle were butchered, then horses, dogs, cats. It is told of men who ate one another. In 1316, when the crops failed and hunger seized rich and poor alike, my mother wrested manure from a beggar who died crying while she fed me this vile meat. I watched my father lie down in a thick of mud until his body turned to stone and was swallowed by the pitch. Everywhere were limbs jutting from the rising tide like driftwood. Day by day, we huddled, naked, under leafless boughs and stared at the livid skies, hoping for respite. Our hair grew out, we were all bone, and the rain continued. Some fell prey to a fate worse than starvation: Saint Anthony's fire, in which one's limbs are as if seared by flame, and in which after much writhing and agony, these limbs rot and fall off. Others fell to a disease of the bowel in which one is unable to relieve oneself until suffocated from the inside by one's own excrement. Others went blind and others still were ceded to rash, fever, delirium. And yet these tribulations were but presage of worse should the Jews be kept unmolested among us. There followed the conjunction of Jupiter, Saturn, and Mars three years ere now, which was regarded by Jean de Murs as augury of sedition, disease, and unspeakable mortality. Did we listen? Did we vanquish His enemies until none survived? In the year of the Lord 1348, we persist in sin and dereliction.

In the northeast, the Jews are plunged in barrels and thrown into the river. Elsewhere, they are cast into great bonfires whose smoke is as a beacon for Christians at a loss for means with which to ward off plague. When put to the question, many of the Jews have confessed to poisoning the air, though no one such confessant has escaped retribution by death. But it is not enough.

Fear and rumor throng to mind with every tiding from the west. In this our early spring the skies are clement and the crops are well. No matter. Pisa and Livorno are stricken. Genoa has ceased to trumpet her glory. Here in Pistoia, the pestilence claims near five hundred a day. Crowds are forbidden. Those who have left town are barred from return. Al be these measures well intentioned, they do little to assuage the terror of we who are quarantined. To be sure, the pestilence aggrieves most he whom it spares day after day. Some have taken to flight, abandoning neighbor and kin, *amori proximi* of no more virtue than *amori bovis*, often less. Among those who remain, whom contagion disposes to reform, there are sufficient voluptuaries to people a village. Healthy persons shut their windows to the south, where vapors are dense and foul. They say pediculous humors and flyborne air are culprits of plague, so the townsmen make a pyre of flowers and brush, attar and spikenard, by way of purging the air of offense. Fig, apple, bol armeniac, venesection—all are thought to forfend plague, though none has proven itself capable. If such be the case, and our dead swear it, whence resist we who live by example? Arise, by the honor of pure martyrdom! Rend thy skin for that the people be absolved their sins by The Anointed. Pray with us, for the Disciplinati are trustees of spirit, an office shared with finer souls consecrated in this wise. Recall Saint Sebastian, who triumphed over that which would kill him, Apollo's wrath unloosed but the arrows of plague overcome. Recall Saint Rocco, whose breath cleanses the sick of what agony rains down for his Lord's sport and vengeance. Indeed, there are eighteen patron saints whom the afflicted beseech, though none so glorious as our Lady, who gathers unto her breast and shields with open arms.

When time allows and my will is mine own, I am possessed of the thought that our most iconic arrows are for love and pestilence. The plague of dark, the disease of noon, Eros and Apollo flex their bows and from them quivers the same tip.

I have read that in our appeals to the Mother Most Sad, in her mercy and intercession, are the origins of modern drama. We seek refuge in her calm, she responds, and stories are made. I have read that in our ex-votos are permutations of art for the people. We commission the image, offer it up, and because we are true, He will reward us. I have read, even, that with reference to our burning of the Jews there were committed pogroms and holocaust for the propitiation of Christ by the folk, but that such employment, glorious in design, has little reward in this life. *Condemnant quod non intellegunt*, they condemn because they do not understand.

I am fortunate to have seen our worship studied, though the

advancing of science counterclaims the cause of our torment. *Rattus rattus*, they say. *X. cheopis. Y. pestis, Pulex irritans*. The flea that swells of one blood made of two, of three, and four—to this we owe the demise of twenty-five million people? Three alive for every one departed? The flea feeds on diseased blood that never acquits his stomach. Thus he is always hungry and always choking for why his body cannot intake more blood, blood festered with plague bacilli that he vomits into each new bite, the flesh of my kin: mother, brothers, aunt. On this sequence, it is said, we are to blame the near collapse of mankind.

In this afterlife, I have had many years to reflect and discourse with others whose ethics dispute mine own. I do not think it has been the most salutary disposal of my time. Across the table, a leprous child eats with passion unfettered. What sort of humble condition is this? In the year of the Lord 2002, He does not say: Seat you well and gorge of the pie I gave you. He says: Deny yourself and I will sustain you.

But who will listen? There is a woman among us who drowns. Who drowns and prays to men of the earth. Men of *ideas*. I have attempted dialogue:

What expedient is agitprop against the terrors of God arrayed against us?

You are a stupid votive, and the apparatchik army will not be conned by word of salvation.

Are you acquainted with the Might who avenges consort with false idols?

Your mortified flesh and bubbling stool are killing my appetite.

It is told that the virtue of these lives on earth be to grow up into Him in all things, always to covet advancement of feeling, to seek out knowledge of Him in every experience for to accomplish the nova of spirit that is promised, and for eternity to bear the sheen of His resplendence. Still, the current of progress moves slowly. What will be for us? I fear the instant demise of fellow feeling during the plague. Parents who cast their sick out into the street. Parents who killed their sick for fear of contagion. The woman who drowns ascribes this inhumanity to the survival instinct, which is paramount and irreproachable. If the one you love is soon to perish, should you, too, cede yourself to death to provide only a few days' comfort? Consider of what good you will have deprived the world with your absence. A reasonable argument against which there is little to say except that in my time without body and constraint, I have come to see that when love be the end of all things, only then can we rejoice in this our year of annihilation.

Nineteen

With an hour to go before Eric, I was attempting outfits. When it comes to outfits, I lack for taste. History bears this out. The one chance I got with the principal's assistant—dinner at a local café—I wore for the purpose of seduction black leggings and a white sleeveless shirt. Only the shirt was more girdle than shirt; and my breasts were prominent like eaves. I remember draping a green cardigan over my shoulders in prep-school fashion, as if to conceal the eaves, but not really. I remember tying another cardigan around my waist as if to conceal the ass, but not really. Calvin was thirty-five; I was sixteen. After dinner, he kissed me good night on the forehead, and I went home to cry. I cried for a year, and my wardrobe went baggy. Suitors were not forthcoming. I had erred in the other direction and perhaps allowed the appearance of sloth to boost whatever suspicions men had about me in bed—that I was drowsy and absent taut genitalia owing to the libertine sport of my youth. I was always worrying about the relative tautness of my genitalia and questioning my lovers about them to bad effect. I guess *Am I tight?* only sounds hot the first or second time you ask.

For my lunch with Eric, I was vetting options that might have struck me as absurd the day before. Like earrings. Pink lipstick. My colors are dead leaf, hazel, and biscuit, which means anything not brown is a risk. In the brown family I tend to include gray, black, and olive, which delimit the spectrum of my closet, and walnut, which is the only color to hit my face. Walnut blush. Eye shadow. I look like a tree every time I leave the house.

Naturally, then, pink lips were impossible. Likewise the earrings. There's no jewelry to match a dog collar. Maybe the collar had to go. In the end I settled on leggings and a white sleeveless shirt that cut above my belly button. I was twenty pounds lighter than in high school; the eaves, the ass: no longer a problem.

December in New York. With sweater, vest, bomber jacket, hat, scarf, gloves, I was still freezing. The avenues were adorned with cheer, with Christmas perennials holly and pine. Every year I wait for the giant wreath above Fifth Avenue to snap loose and gird our shoppers as in a Lifesaver or donut. I feel this way because holiday decor is coercive and annoying, not to mention nervy. It's the city's way of saying fuck you to its homeless. Sorry, we're only budgeting for lightbulbs and ribbon this year. Perhaps the theory is that pretty trees attract tourists and tourists mean revenue. But for what? More trees, of course.

Such thoughts carried me for several blocks until I decided there's nothing worse than a drug addict with opinions, at which point my white sleeveless girdle started to feel stupid and this vagina-pink nail polish was a bad idea and my God, I really do walk like a man, I should make better use of my hips, Jesus my hips are fat, I should donate them to a shelter or sell them on eBay, and, while I'm at it, maybe I needed mitten clips, a new wallet, and a spanking because on eBay you can buy a spanking for fifty bucks.

I had chosen a dessert place for us to meet. You could order lunch, but the place was all about dessert. It pitched to a rich clientele of eight-year-olds. I figured if things got bad at my table, Eric and I could always delight in the relief of having made it past age eight.

Curdle was gathered in the joints of my mouth. My eyes had secreted a lubricant turned crusty at the seams. This happens when I am nervous. I get leakage. I am always dreaming of leakage, though I do not see what relevance it has to my life. In any case, it was nothing a fragrance-free baby wipe couldn't handle. I had overapplied perfume for fear of underapplying. I smelled of industry, which was carried out by the antiseptic lozenge on my tongue, excess deodorant, lotion, and chamomile hair product. When I got to the café, industry collided with the distinct aroma of kids and cake. It is the smell of birthday parties before you were old enough to realize that when gaiety is compulsory—as on birthdays or New Year's—it is frequently the worst night of your life.

Eric was in a corner, flanked by a table of two girls and a table of eight. Me included, this made eleven girls to his one boy. In the war of the sexes, I felt we were evenly matched. He was wearing the same clothes I saw him in last. A few months had gone by, but for all I knew, he wore the same thing every day. Some girls might find this unappetizing. But I liked it. It sprang terms of endearment to my lips. I used to call him Pajama Head.

He made some crack about my layers piled on the seat next to him. Maybe if I'd chosen a warmer top, I wouldn't need the pile. I smiled, but the girdle said, See?

He had already ordered a milk shake. I ordered same and wiped at my lips for dread of curdle.

"So what are you working on?" I said, and the girdle went, LAME! Worst opening ever.

"Just some stuff. Nothing exciting."

"Can I see?" He'd brought a zipper case of photos.

"Nah, I just have this because I'm going to see a potential client later."

I thought: What the hell, he'd show them to some stranger and not me? But then: Well maybe he's afraid I won't like them. Maybe he cares what I think! Or: Maybe he just wants this lunch to be as sterile as possible. His wedding ring was hard to miss. A big silver thing, almost like a napkin holder.

"Come on," I said. "I want to see."

Unexpectedly, this produced a reason to sit next to him. Of course, if our legs touched and he inched away from the contact, I'd weep.

He flipped through the portfolio like a Rolodex. I slowed him down. Asked questions. He'd done a series at the unclaimed luggage depot in Alabama. Largest place of its kind, and everything is for sale. A lump of wedding dresses high as my shoulder. A coffin. Dentures jammed in a laundry bag and biting the mesh. The photos were lovely. Eric said the proliferation of loss was less about product than story. A woman loses her wedding dress—before or after the ceremony? What becomes of a bride whose dress vanishes on her wedding day? What becomes of a marriage inaugurated in attire that runs away?

As Eric spoke, every part of him seemed to come loose. His hair mutinied. His crewneck sank. I remembered that great red-fleck birthmark just above his nipple, haloed by skin paler than his natural color.

"But what about the relief?" I said. "Like: There go all my possessions and hey, I feel lighter."

"There's probably some of that involved, sure. And without the trauma that comes with a tornado or hurricane, when you lose everything."

Was this poignant? Was he referring to something else? My experience is that men are the least subtle creatures on earth, so probably no.

"What's this one?" I pointed at what appeared to be a bowl of eyeballs.

"Eyeballs."

"From toys and stuff?"

"Yep."

"But who loses just the eyeballs? Wouldn't you have lost the whole thing?"

He nodded.

"So wait. There's a bowl of eyeballs and across the hall there's a bunch of dolls and stuffed animals with gaping sockets? You're saying that the people who run the depot chop the stock to up the price? Why would a blind Cabbage Patch kid and eyeball sell for more than the kid whole?"

"Because a pervert will pay a lot more for a face with sockets than a little girl whose toys come secondhand."

"That is vile."

He grinned hugely and flipped the page to a double-spread photo. Eight stuffed bears propped upright against a wall like construction workers on break, each gazing at the camera with pits black as a well. The sight was so dreadful, I laughed. I laughed for at least two minutes. And the pleasure centers in my brain rejoiced.

"Glad you approve," he said. "Kam hates it."

"Oh, she's just worried about the kid you'll have."

Funny how mention of a kid can bring you up short. Even the ones who live in your head. He closed the portfolio. "And you? You think you want children someday? In all this madness?"

"What?"

"Children. You thought about it?"

"Sure. Of course. But it takes two, you know."

I had been doing fine until then. I had been feeling fine, and then, suddenly, not. I'm sure my face went vagina pink. I looked down at my napkin. He flagged the waiter and said to me, "Well, sure. But that will work itself out. And anyway, we didn't come here to talk about that."

"Why did we come here?"

"I don't know. Because you asked."

We'd already had cheeseburgers. The check was en route. How much lingering could I expect once we'd paid up?

He tossed a credit card on the table. The green Amex of yore that almost no one still has.

"Let me," I said, recalling the cash I'd taken from Mother's purse. Who's thirty and still sneaks cash from her mom?

"Lucy," he said. The sound of it was tender. He cared. He cared! I sat up knowing the look I gave him was all sparkle and light.

"Lucy, I'm worried. About you, I mean. We both are."

But that *both*, it was like taking it in the face with a nail gun.

"I'm okay, Eric."

"You are not. An *okay* person does not call her oldest friend at three in the morning every night."

"What makes you think I'm calling *her*?"

"Lucy, stop."

The obvious question here was: How much dignity did I have left to rally? Every unrequited love depletes your store of pride, which is unfortunate because pride will usually outlast hope, self-regard, and all that other good stuff ravaged by the love gone wrong.

"I'm kidding," I said. "Jeez."

"Are you going to meetings? Are you seeing a therapist?"

I welcomed this line of inquiry because it reeled me back from despair. I was too annoyed to despair. Say your boyfriend does something horrible and when you react, he asks if you're still going to therapy. As if you are the problem! I felt like smacking him. If he'd just love me the way he was supposed to, everything would be fine.

"I'm doing what I have to do," I said.

He stared me down. He knew I was lying, which was the most unhappy thing to have happened at this lunch so far. How many people know you well enough always to know when you're lying? I wanted so much to put hands on his skin. No, for him to put hands on mine. How was I going to experience the rest of my life alone? When the plague got here, and it would, who would I have to hole up with? Whose life would I have to fear for the most? In a calamity, the body forgets everything but love. That fight you had the night before, your hideous divorce, the ten years since you last spoke—who cares? When the bomb drops, your first thought is: How can I get to him? But for me, I'd have no one. No one to curl up and die with. The thought left me breathless.

"Like what?" he said. "What are you doing?"

"I'm taking Hannah upstate. There's a little school near the plant or maybe she can get homeschooled with some of the other kids. I think it's too hard for her here." He was shaking his head. "Look, it's got to be an improvement. It certainly couldn't be worse." But he was still shaking, so I said, "What?"

"Ben says you're going back to rehab."

I nodded. "Texas. I hear they have antelope."

"So your idea is to bring Hannah upstate and then leave her there with a bunch of Orthodox chicken farmers while you're in Texas?"

Crest, fallen. I wanted to go home.

"I'm sorry," he said. "This is so not my business."

Okay, so we had officially reached the point where everything he said was excruciating. If he'd just love me the way he was supposed to, it could be his business!

"I won't get another chance with Hannah for a while," I said. "I don't know how long I'll be away. This is the best I can come up with. I have to do something."

"Is that what this lunch is about?" he said. "I'll still be here when you get back. We both will."

The need for him to stop talking had suddenly become the most important thing in my life. Just stop talking. I was ready to beg. It crossed my mind that I might even lose my lunch if he didn't.

Outside, he walked with me a few blocks. The wind chafed my

skin. My nose watered. More leakage. We held our arms close and hunkered down. This was less a jaunt than a mission.

"I hate this city in the winter," he said. "Stupid Christmas lights."

I threw my head back. Driblets like rain fell from my eyes. It was also very cold.

Twenty

For the trip back to ZOG Chicken, we take Mother's SUV. Hannah, who is pleased to be fleeing the reach of classmates and media, has still insisted we bring her Young Einstein Chemistry set, desktop computer, and Euwin the Brew Bear, who makes porridge and soup and chili and grog with a wood paddle that's Velcroed to his chest. I've often seen Hannah make short work of Euwin with the paddle, which makes me question the wisdom of his designers.

I am driving. Stanley's in the passenger seat, venting about the surrogates. Why couldn't he find a good surrogate?

"You only interviewed five. Didn't you get like a thousand letters?"

"Yeah, but those were the most promising."

Hannah says he should just grow his own baby at home. That probably there's a do-it-yourself uterus for sale online.

I look in the rearview mirror. Her impassivity, it's starting to seem permanent.

Stanley says Fertility at Will is not that expensive. That he pays about two hundred a month to keep Sylvie's eggs frozen. I wonder where he gets the money, but then recall he has zero expenses besides liquor and chew.

"It's easy, too," he says. "Doesn't hurt at all. Only downside is having to take some fertility drugs for a while, just to produce a lot of eggs for extraction."

Hannah says I can always use my eggs to cultivate low-level titer viremia.

"What the hell is that? And when did we start talking about *my* eggs? My eggs are going nowhere."

"I think that's the point," Stanley says.

Hannah: It means just enough virus to trigger an immune response.

Stanley: You're not getting any younger. Why don't you think about it?

H: Maybe your eggs could give us a cure for AIDS.

S: This way, if you get married at forty, your eggs will still be thirty!

H: Or that horrible disease where kids look a thousand years old by age ten. Your eggs could test-run gene therapy for progeria.

S: I have some literature with me, if you're interested.

H: Though I guess some people might be offended. If you can't abort your embryo, I guess you probably can't give it AIDS, either.

This goes on for about three hours.

When we arrive, Hannah makes for the sentinel sheds even though the surveillance program is done for the winter. Also, it's too cold for mosquitoes, migration is over, the chickens who tested positive for West Nile in the fall are dead, and the rest are back in the coop. No one is certain why the alarms triggered by the sentinel chickens did not amount to an outbreak. Possibly because mosquito control is pretty good these days, or that the escape of superplague preempted articles and TV spots about West Nile. How much disease is a news organization supposed to cover? It'd get boring. Ratings could drop.

I follow her to the sheds, which are actually cages under tarp. Not much room to maneuver in there. Not much sunlight, either.

"I don't want to be here," I say. "It's mean. Not two months old and you're getting bled from the wing."

"Actually, they get bled from the heart."

She says this with pleasure. Some girls like lip liner, others are just morbid. Morbid girls who also like lip liner are Alice Cooper.

I suggest we unpack the car. She says no way is she sleeping in my guesthouse hovel and anyway, Stanley already invited her to his place. I've yet to spend a winter out in my barn, but I agree it is not ideal. On the other hand, Stanley lives in a trailer home, how is that an improvement? She says at least his doors shut.

When we get there, he's barbecuing outside. Snow up to his ass, and he's barbecuing. Catfish burgers.

I've never been in the trailer, and it's bigger than I expect. Full-size bed, lean-to privy, trundle couch, kitchen and round table. Photos on the wall, of him and Sylvie, I presume. *Presume* because he is unrecognizable—maybe thirty years old with Hitler mustache—and she, my God, she looks like a girl who rides horses bareback through the prairie. Flaxen hair and all that. She is seated on his knee, gazing into the camera with conviction—that *I'm going to climb every mountain* look you see in ads for antidepressants.

I tell Hannah her stuff is not going to fit in the trailer and maybe we can leave the chemistry set in my barn.

"And freeze the unction? You wish."

When Hannah talks disease and I have no clue what she's saying, I don't think it's because I am obtuse in all matters emotional and humane. Whenever she says anything else, I feel like a brick.

"Don't say *unction* around me. You're twelve. It's freaking me out."

"Yeah, and I live for your pleasure."

"Soup's on," Stanley says. He's steamed his glasses. The catfish burgers look more fish than burger, which is to say there are gills in my patty.

We hear someone outside. Instinct: it's Wanda Deckman. Instinct: whack her with a frying pan.

"Door's open!" Stanley yells. It is indeed Wanda. Wanda looking pissed.

"Well, well," she says, and rubs her hands because it's brutal out there. "Could smell the catfish for miles."

"Want some? I got enough for another burger or two."

Stanley does not appear to notice he's about to lose his job. Or that he's already lost his job and simply needs to be told.

Wanda looks the three of us over. "Who's this one?" she says. "What's the ransom?"

"My sister," I say.

"Half-sister," says Hannah.

Wanda cups her mouth. "Wow, how you've grown!"

Mother and Wanda have the sort of friendship that thrives on no contact. Would that all my relations worked out so well.

"I guess I'll have a burger," she says, and waits for one of us to get up. Apparently, we're conducting a threesome of rocks, scissors, paper, only it's whoever has the nastiest look wins. I offer Wanda my chair. Hannah might be sitting there for the rest of her life.

"So," Stanley says. "How have things been getting on without us? Place fall apart?"

He really is amazing.

"Actually, it's running better than ever."

"Well, never fear," he says. "We'll be back on the job tomorrow."

"It's only been three months," she says. "I should just welcome you back!"

I wonder if it's time to start kissing ass. But Stanley has a better idea. He says, "Hannah is going to be with us for a little bit. Things are pretty rough at school these days."

Wanda looks out the window. It has begun to snow. Not one of those White Christmas snows but a forbidding tundra of Siberia snow where you stagger through the drift with finger pops and hypothermia.

"*Brrr*," Wanda says, and I know she's staying the night. Also that we're not fired. It's Hanukkah, after all. I can't remember if Hanukkah is the fasting one or the flight-from-Egypt one, but either way, I bet mercy is a part of it.

Stanley suggests hot cocoa all around. It's not clear what our sleeping arrangements will be, but camaraderie via cocoa might solve everything. That or a bottle of Scotch. Can you spike cocoa with Scotch? What about rum? There's got to be a liqueur that goes with cocoa. Sure enough, Stanley produces a flagon of crème de something. It's actually a flagon, which means he's either dumped six bottles in there or, shudder, he's made it himself.

"You'll like this," he says to Hannah. "I made it myself."

"With an online kit?"

He nods. The rapport between them is getting creepy.

The flagon comes down from his lips, leaving a milky froth behind. I pour some in my cup. It smells noxious. Wanda says she'll stick with cocoa. Hannah is more intrepid. I try to encourage temperance, but without much heart. A person who cannot heed her own advice does not diminish the quality of the advice, but so what, you still feel like a jerk.

If you don't stir the crème de, it congeals. I spoon out a chunk and wait for it to dry. Crème de crack, I think, miserably.

Stanley decides there's not enough cocoa to go around, so he opts out. Under guise of self-sacrifice, he's just given himself permission to have a beer.

Hannah curls up on a papasan cushion under the table. It looks like a dog bed. We can hear the wind lash the trailer, which rocks from side to side. The windows are crusted in rime. I scratch at the frost with my fingernail.

"What'll it be?" Wanda says. "Cards? You got a TV?"

"I get some of the local stations. But the picture's bad."

"I'll take my chances."

I trot back to join her. *Family Feud* is next, after a commercial break. The spot is for a pharmaceutical company. It has a scientist talking about how hard it is to find a new drug that works *and* is safe for humans, but he has to try because bacteria develop resistance. And he wants props for this. For his company's quest to find new drugs. This makes me ill. Half the reason bacteria develop resistance is that antibiotics are overprescribed. The drug companies lobby the doctors, fete the doctors, until their drug gets into every bloodstream in America. What's worse, they glad-hand farmers and the FDA to ensure their product hits livestock. When chickens get the drug, their bacteria mutate to survive the attack. Upshot: people who get food poisoning now have no recourse to antibiotics because none of them still works.

"Turn this shit off," I say.

"Beg pardon?"

Blood boiling. In 1977, Congress buries a motion to curb antibiotic use in agriculture, citing lack of definitive evidence that such use undermines the benefits for humans. 1982, scientists match drug-resistant bacteria in a human with the drug-resistant bacteria in the livestock. Congress demurs. And the FDA wimps out. 1988, a new fluoroquinolone antibiotic reaches the market. It's a hit. A miracle! So naturally, the Netherlands, Denmark, Britain, and the United States approve it for veterinary use. Three years later, FQresistant salmonella is up by 1.4 percent. By the time Congress actually revokes the licensing of FQs to livestock, the damage is done. Bayer company flips out, and hastens a PR campaign like the commercial I just saw.

I make for the door, thinking I've had enough of this trailer. Close quarters are for prostitutes in Manila. As reward for my attitude, I get wind in the face like a switch.

"Oh, look," Wanda says, motioning to the TV, "here's three Chinese women in leotards singing in, well I guess it's Chinese. Oh, never mind, I got Schneerson."

I roll my eyes. Being at ZOG Chicken, it's Schneerson this, Schneerson that. The man has been dead eight years, but he's still the most influential rabbi in the Hasidic community. I often see him in wallet-sized photos hung from rearview mirrors or baby carriages. Up here it's mostly Lubavitcher Jews, who are fairly progressive for their kind. And though Wanda's not a Hasid, she's still much moved by anything Schneerson has to say, which is usually that ours is the last generation of exile and the first of redemption. That we are living in a uniquely messianic age. Thing is, he'd been saying this for a while and now he's dead, so when does an age stop?

Wanda turns off the TV. She looks forlorn. I join her on the bed. She's seeming less my ogre boss than a middle-aged woman with no reason to live.

"I'm beginning to understand you," she says.

Oh, no. But it's too late and there's no place to hide. Maybe if I just don't respond.

"I mean," she says, "I see you destroying your body and moping around with zero enthusiasm and I think: What's with this girl? There's so much to be grateful for."

If I burrow under the covers, will she stop? Stanley is at the other end of the trailer. I try to look at him so hard, it will draw him to my side. But he just catches my eye and waves like, Look how big my trailer is!

"But now," Wanda says, "now I'm starting to see it different. I guess it's all this business about superplague. I can't help but think it's going to get me. I don't have much money saved in the bank so I can't just fly to Paris for a last hurrah. The one person I loved I never got to tell. So really, there's nothing I can manage today that

I always wanted to do before I die. And just thinking about that, it gives you perspective, you know?"

Is she asking me for drugs? Because if she wants drugs, she should just say so.

"What I'm saying is"—and here she puts her hand on mine—"what I mean is, you're not alone."

I look past her out the window. In the distance, I can see lights from neighboring houses, which go out as if by agreement.

"Blackout," I say.

Stanley comes to look as the wind takes a break. Our generator might be the only sound for miles.

Twenty-one

In the ten days we've been here, Hannah has alienated four children, two moms, and one rabbi. That girl who fly-papered her neck and forehead for the unveiling of ZOG Chicken's new conveyor with the intent to subvert proceedings but with the effect of upgrading them—Hannah called her gay for not having an opinion about Stanley's ass. The girl who pelts feed at the suits from Kroger, Hannah called her gay for having too many opinions about me. School is Stanley failing to coax her into the little building each morning. Home is me watching her rip pages from *When Zachary Beaver Came to Town*. I have begun canvassing moms at the plant to see what their kids are reading, just to keep Hannah on par. Kathleen, who works in legal, said her thirteen-year-old went nuts for *The Face on the Milk Carton*, which is about a lactose-intolerant girl who, in thrall to dairy addiction, reaches for the very carton bearing her likeness, which suggests, in all probability, that she was kidnapped as a toddler. I imagine the degree of wish fulfillment advanced by this novel has girls all over America going wonky. Certainly Hannah would love to think she'd been kidnapped—that her real family is living in a hot-air balloon traversing the skies of Malaysia. Yesterday, I found her editing with black marker a page from the YA novel *Rat Boys: A Dating Experience*. The premise? Girls needing prom dates abracadabra rats into prom dates, only Hannah does not like the word *date*, so she's swapped it out for the considerably more topical *death*. Girls needing prom death turn rats into prom death.

The decision was easy: Hannah needs to work.

So today, we work. I've put her on the incubator task force; when the chicks hatch, she transfers them to the nursery. It always amazes me to see the eggs crack within minutes or hours of each other. Nature's clock, which operates even in the most unnatural of settings. Eggs in a crate, crates stacked forty high in what amounts to an oven. The best part of incubator duty is handling the chicks, who come out bewildered and all fuzz—as if the fuzz were meant to communicate a state of mind. The worst part of incubator duty is knowing these little guys will die at the hands of a rabbi who can sever sixty necks in sixty seconds.

As for me, I'm back on the evisceration team. I gather this is Wanda's idea of the doghouse. Or maybe she thinks that instead of abandoning what I can't do, I should try. Used to be I'd reach into a bird like you might a black sack at the magic show—fish around and see what you get. Rectal canal good, breast meat bad. No one knew how I kept coming out with breast meat, the chicken corpus is not like a squid, but, you know, leave it to me. Sharon advised I let the viscera reveal itself. No need to rape the cavity. I did my best.

She asks what I'm doing for New Year's, which is tonight. The Jewish New Year started months ago, but such is the tyranny of the Christian calendar. Naturally, I don't much like New Year's. In order from earliest to most recent, I have spent the last five like this: with people from boarding school at an unofficial reunion near school grounds watching the ball drop on TV; at some party having sex with some guy while watching the ball drop on TV; watching the ball drop on TV with syringe in tryst with a vein that showed itself, miraculously, just before midnight; at a rehab where we watched the ball drop with the sound off because Mandy was made psychotic by the din of any crowd; and finally, last year, in a network of lies disported to make all my friends think I was spending the night with other friends so that I could actually spend the night alone, watching the ball drop on TV.

"Watching the ball drop," I say.

"Oh no, you can't do that. That ball is evil. Bob Barker is evil."

I think she means Dick Clark.

"Dick, Bob, whatever. They dye their hair, they are evil."

"I didn't realize you felt so strongly about it."

"Well, I do. Come to my house. We're playing Twister."

I reach into a bird and pull out what looks like a flaccid balloon the length of my arm ending in a knob's worth of gut.

"Stop right there!" Sharon yells. "That's perfect."

We break for lunch.

Joe's brought a thermos of chicken soup. Am I the only one to find this vile? I am. The talk is about layoffs. The talk is always about layoffs. Joe's got only himself to support, so he thinks he'll get it first. Like ZOG Chicken gives a dime about his personal life. I say more likely me and Stanley get the boot. Joe says, rather bitterly, that I got Wanda eating out my ass. Rachel says, Really, Joe, not in front of the kid.

Hannah wants out of the afternoon's labors. Says this is yeomen's work and that our cook's shit tastes better than this lunch. Rachel's mouth drops open. Sharon's too. I feel inclined to excuse Hannah's temperament, but what am I supposed to say? That our mom's a crackhead, give the girl a break? If I know Wanda, the entire staff knows our story, anyway. On good days, I think discretion keeps them from asking questions. But mostly I think it's disgust.

"Do you like Twister?" Sharon ventures.

"I like Twister," Stanley says, which makes us all laugh. As if Stanley can even get his arms above sea level.

"Then come on over," Sharon says. "We'll ring in the New Year like a pile of puppies."

I look from one face to another and think, These are my colleagues, this is my sister, this is my lover. I get up and go out the back, through the parking lot and into the fields. On either side a mountain range, the Allegheny and Appalachian, and everywhere else: snow. I start to feel majestic, like an elk, maybe. Just taking it in.

Next I start to feel droopy and just a little stupid. My tracks in the snow are fascinating. I catch sight of a snowman in the lot and address myself to him. I have seen that movie where a boy's dead father reincarnates in a snowman who will melt unless repaired to higher ground; where father and son bond on the hockey rink of love; where an earnest snowman can save the day. I wept through the entire thing. Why can't my dad come back?

Aggie saw the movie with me. She was agnostic on the matter

of whether one could actually reincarnate in a snowman, so we suspended disbelief and celebrated the principle: We keep coming back until we get it right. I said but doesn't the promise of a million chances recommend sloth? Why bother now if we can just fix it later? She said it's not all that fun having to come back and suffer anew, and that the sooner you get it right, the sooner you can rest with God. Right, God. Every discussion ends in God.

Me and the snowman were the same height. I'd skipped lunch, which made his face all the more appetizing. Raisins, prunes, carrot. Then again, on the off chance he really was my dad, this was probably not the way I wanted to initiate contact. I produced a haiku.

Snowman who art Dad
Get me the hell out of here
Life unbearable.

Sharon was calling my name. Break's over. I trudged back to the rec room, through sterilization, and into my antiseptic white apron, white gloves, and white shower cap. Whatever I'd learned before lunch was long forgotten. I was tossing entrails all over the floor. Tossing and listing, because it was getting hard to stand up.

Rachel said, "Are you high again? Oh, come on."

Sharon said, "Stop slurring, I can't understand a word."

The conveyor whizzed past. Soft focus made everyone look like a tampon.

In Wanda's office it was something like: Don't bring her in here, she's covered in guts. And Hannah, who was making a beaded necklace in the corner, saying: Gross.

They took off my gown, gloves, and cap.

From the couch I said, "What're you making, Hannah? It's pretty. You're so good at this stuff. Hey, it's beads! I love beads!"

"Drop dead, Lucy."

But wait! I'm an elk! Just taking it in!

The phone woke me. Wanda answered. Since it gets dark at four, it could have been four, it could have been eight. It was eight. She covered the mouthpiece and said, "It's Sharon. Wants to know if you're still coming tonight." I nodded.

She hung up. "Want some tortellini? I made it yesterday."

"What are you still doing here?"

"Waiting for you."

"Oh."

She made a decent tortellini. I said thanks. Where was Hannah?

"Over at Sharon's. Stanley, too. And Joe and Rachel."

I sat up. "Look, about before, I'm sorry. It won't happen again. I mean it this time. It won't. I've been trying to cut down. I just got, well I just messed up a little."

"How right you are. Because guess what? We finally got a bed for you. Tomorrow a.m., you're getting on a bus. Your grandmother and I made all the arrangements."

"Oh, great. First day of the new year. Is that supposed to mean something? I'm supposed to turn over a new leaf? Resolutions are idiotic."

Wanda smiled and said, "I'm very pleased. This is the best thing for you right now."

I asked if she knew anything about the place.

She said, "It's in Texas."

I said I knew that, but could she tell me more.

She said, "It's in Texas."

We took her truck to Sharon's. She'd fried the clutch so bad, we couldn't get out of first gear.

"Your driving's making me sick," I said.

"Vomit in this car and you are dead."

We could see Sharon's five minutes before we got there. She had a glowing Santa on the lawn. Candy-cane torchlights. Mylar bows on every post. When we opened her door, it jingle-belled.

You're here, look who's here! She offered up two goblets of nog and some pinecone earrings. Everyone was wearing them, it seemed. Over her shoulder, I saw people I did not know sitting around a fire. Who are these people? "The brass," Wanda said, and arranged her face into a smile. The brass are the men who run ZOG Chicken, and their wives. They were eating fruitcake.

Sharon took our coats. "The gang's over there," she said, and pointed to a room opposite the brass. "But I'm trying to get them to mingle."

Wanda said, "No problem," and cozied up to the dowager brass whose deceased had founded the plant.

I made for the gang. They were crowded around the TV, which had me relieved. I am a little superstitious about the ball. Still, there were three hours to go, so why the focus?

I was told to shush. If I hadn't been so drained of the where-withal to interest myself in other people, I might have gauged the tone of the room sooner. As is, it took a few seconds to realize we were watching the TV with horror. It was an emergency news flash: The superplague had hit California. It had not traveled from Minnesota, this was a new outbreak. The nation's lunatic had struck again. Four people were dead.

My first thought was rehab, thank God I'm going to rehab. My second thought was to suppress the first.

Hannah was hugging her knees in a corner. I figured now was the time to mention I'd be letting her down first thing tomorrow. Plague's a comin', I'm a goin'.

I managed to get her in my shadow before she stood and made for the other side of the room.

The screen split into a quartet of coverage from the White House, the CDC's headquarters, the Pentagon, and the biocontainment facility where the four victims and their families were being held. We watched a series of speeches asking for calm. We listened to scientists admit the situation was grave. We saw footage of the moon men zipping across Carmel and Big Sur, rounding up anyone who might have come into contact with the victims. Consensus among the experts: If this gets to Los Angeles, we are doomed.

I held up my glass. "Nog, anyone?"

Rachel turned off the TV.

We heard laughter from the brass and envied it. Ten minutes ago, we were laughing, too.

Joe said, "I thought maybe it was over because they nailed it in Minnesota."

"They got lucky," Hannah said.

"It can't last," Rachel added. "Not so long as that nut's still out there. Can you imagine? One man could kill off half the world."

"How do you know it's just one man? Maybe it's organized. Like the Black Panthers."

For a moment, we all eyed each other suspiciously, which harbingered worse if plague hit Pennsylvania. Every man for himself.

Sharon burst through the door. She was a little drunk. Why the long faces? It's New Year's!

Without discussion, we were agreed not to spoil everyone else's night. There was nothing to be done. In fact, I almost wished the press would start vectoring the news as per the North Koreans, where so long as you're hidden, who cares if you're starving. Because really, what is the point? We can't protect ourselves, there's nowhere to run. Okay, so maybe some of us will finally begin to live each day as if it were our last. But as Wanda said, most of us can't finance our dreams, last day or not.

"Well, come on!" Sharon said. "We're setting up Twister."

We filed out of the room like men off the plank.

Twister for adults is made for reunion weekends in the log cabin, just you and your five best friends from college graduated twenty years ago today, look at our paths divergent, and yet here we are with a bottle of Chardonnay, six wounded hearts, and a slipped disc. The one with the disc gets bedridden. The others cancel the river raft. Tempers flare, resentments will out. There is inadvisable sex between two. There are tears in the chamomile. Convalescence, hangover, s'mores. If only half as much happens tonight, it will bring the tramontane of Pennsylvania to their knees.

Because we are new to each other, Sharon has issued name cards. Linda and Kathleen. Deirdre, Noah, Lonna, Donna. We are like the ZOG family singers. Rachel shakes out the Twister mat and secures it to the floor with paperweights. Doug Guildenstein, homosexual son of dead founder brass, mans the spinner. He has a bad knee. He sits on the couch with legs crossed, spinner handy, Merlot on deck. He's wearing dress socks and penny loafers. Sharon seems alarmed by the prospect of brass v. yeomen, so she divides us up herself. She makes like she's assessing our skills and choosing accordingly. Half of us find this funny, mostly the brass. The eldest has an umlaut in her name. Urüla. No clue how you end up with a name like Urüla or whence the umlaut, but Joe says she's from New York, which apparently explains it.

Urüla wants to captain our team. She's got a vision. The youngest and most limber among us should go last. Seems reasonable enough, only the first trial asks Sal to make like a starfish and hold it. He does not last three seconds. He's nearing seventy. He is an accountant.

Urüla revisits her game plan. We are asked to huddle. I am beginning to wonder if she didn't use to be one of those Eastern Bloc gymnastics coaches.

Stanley and Wanda take to the mat. She's on all fours, he rides her like a pony. Half of us find this funny, mostly the yeomen. Doug trades his Merlot for brandy. Watching him fondle that snifter puts me in mind of *Masterpiece Theatre*. He looks ready to impart wisdom. And when he calls out a new position, it sounds Shakespearean. Poor Doug, he was meant for better things. Had he not gambled away his share of ZOG stock, he might have financed a regional theater dedicated to the lost works of.

I am told to squat and loop my arm around Wanda's knee. Ah, the much touted indignity of Twister. I loop, Joe straddles, Kathleen assumes a yoga pose that seems unfair. She's had training. I bet she can give herself head.

Comes Hannah's turn, the game gets ugly. Doug sends her to the other side of the mat, but somehow she's able to hook her foot around my ankle and effect a collapse that slams me into an elbow and splits my chin.

"Foul!" cries Urüla. "That's a foul!"

Doug reminds Urüla that there are no fouls in Twister. Shylock could not have said it better. The game takes a break. My chin trails blood across the mat. I wonder if premonitions of blood account for the mat's fabric, easily cleaned with sponge and water.

Stanley ministers to my chin, which is more flap than chin. Two flaps, really. Must be some dry skin on Joe's elbow, dry like a rotary blade. Stanley cannot stanch the blood, so he has me lean way back in my chair. I can see up his nose. If his teeth were terrible, it'd be like a dental appointment. My dentist, anyway, has ugly mouth. I figure in the way shrinks want to help you because they're crazy, dentists have the ugly mouth.

Hannah peers into my chin.

"How's the movie?" I ask.

"You'll need stitches. But probably I can sew you up for now."

"Why does that not excite me?"

"What if I used black string? What if I rounded you up some painkillers?"

Stanley says, "No way. It'll get infected. Plus, you're twelve." He looks at me. "She's twelve!"

"Well, what would you suggest? No way we're getting to an ER in this weather."

"Does it hurt?"

"Not if I get painkillers."

"We could tape it?"

Hannah rolls her eyes. "You think Scotch tape is a better idea than sewing it shut? You're a retard."

Sharon comes in to check on me. Takes one look at the gash and says, "*Ewwww.*"

Does she have disinfectant? No, but she has vodka. All those who think vodka's as good as hydrogen peroxide, say aye. It's a split vote.

Doug's snifter avails itself. Fits my chin perfectly. I dip and howl because fuck it hurts. Sharon produces Percocet and Advil. First easy choice I've had all day. Hannah cuts strips of cheesecloth left over from turkey dinner. She dresses my chin, tapes the cloth to my cheeks and secures the bandage by looping the rest of the cloth up over my head, much like a football player's chin guard, only I look postsurgery, and those guys look hot.

"Crisis averted!" Sharon says.

But Twister is done.

Rachel slinks off to a corner. A few of us notice her whispering into her cell phone, which has the unfortunate effect of wooing the rest of us to our cell phones for similar calls—friends in California, friends in the know, doctors, therapists, the bank.

In three seconds, the party's turned into that scene immediately after the verdict comes down when reporters disperse to call in the lede.

"What's going on here?" Sharon says. She's got a baize table spread in one hand and a bucket of plastic chips in the other. Her tone is accusing, though this has more to do with the success of her party than anything else.

Phones are returned to pockets. Joe makes a show of *turning his off*. Others follow suit.

"Poker?" she says. "Who doesn't love poker?"

The suggestion is met with enthusiasm that dies out in shame. After all, Doug is among us. Doug who gambled away his share of ZOG Chicken.

I wander into a back room, a child's room, it seems. Hatch marks extend up the wall at intervals, charting a little person's growth. Between April and September of last year, the kid had a spurt.

I have marks like this on the inside of my closet door at Izzy's. Months in which growth was not in the offing are annotated with caveats like: *wore bad-luck shoes*. The door's logic arraigns fate with maturing intensity until one April, showing a failure to grow for six months contiguous, the caveat reads: *have bad-luck life*.

I stretch out on the bottom of the bunk bed and regard clippings taped to the underside of the top. Rock stars I do not recognize. Teen heartthrob actor I recognize all too well. The name *Johnny* cut from various headlines. I gather this kid, a girl it seems, loves Johnny. Well, good for her. Good for them both. Love is good. Crushes are good. Mine have never been good, but who am I to cull from my experience a judgment on the aggregate?

From the other room: Charades? Monopoly?

I look at my watch. An hour to go. There's a small TV on the desk, which I turn on to check the progress of mayhem at Times Square. But all I get is Dick Clark musing on the dialectic before our very eyes, the unfettering of joy come the New Year vis-à-vis the unfettering of terror the rest of us are experiencing since his telecast has been interrupted fifty times by news from the plague front where six have now perished alongside the decency of Californians jostling for supplies at Ace hardware.

Stanley walks in and covers his eyes. "Turn it off! I can't watch."

"What's happening out there?"

He shrugs. "Looks like your chin stopped bleeding."

I twirl my finger in the air. "Did you hear I'm going to rehab tomorrow?"

"Yes. That's good."

I sit up, furious. "So you want me to go?"

"Oh, grow up, Lucy."

I slump back into his chest. "Why's it good again?"

He sighs. "It's going to be fine, you'll see."

"Hey, look," I say, pointing at a board game. "There's Sorry. Let's play Sorry."

My spirits rally with the thought. I love this game, whose goal is to get all your pieces to the finish line, but whose pleasure is to screw as many of your opponents as possible along the way. It's a game of alliances and betrayal. You can team up with a player to retard a third, then stab your teammate in the back. And you are encouraged to apologize for it. How many board games actually thrive on sarcasm? And how many players have been known to cut loose with a rapacity that belies good character? I bet this game chips away at ZOG solidarity. I bet the executive board dissolves next week. "Let's play!" I say, and grab Stanley's arm.

"Sorry? That game's for ten-year-olds."

And like that I start to cry.

"Oh, honey, I didn't mean it. We can play Sorry."

I dump my head in a pillow. I say I hate rehab, that I'm scared of the plague, that this heartache is unsustainable—I miss Eric so much, I have no one to talk to—but the sobs are censoring and Stanley gets none of it.

"Is it your chin? Does it hurt?"

He strokes my hair, which makes me cry all the more.

"I know, baby," he says. "I know. It's gonna be okay. Let's get you some nog."

It is nearing midnight. Group talk has devolved into accounts of everyone's happiest moment. Or top five. But because we are drunk, nostalgia quickly cedes to gloom. Five happy moments. Some of us have to dig deep to produce three. And even then, they are so far in the past as to offer no comfort.

Rachel lifts her glass. "To the year of living dangerously," she says.

The brass hear, hear. The yeomen nod.

"I saw that movie," Noah says. "There was some little Asian lady in it, right?"

"To the year of happy moments!" Sharon says.

Grunts all around.

"To the year of sex!" Doug says.

We glance at his mother, but she's ten sheets to the wind.

"To sex on the pool table!" Rachel shouts.

Kathleen stands and raises her glass. "To sex with yourself," she says gravely.

I knew it!

By now, everyone is laughing. Even Hannah, though she's still sore about the thread.

I put up my hands and wait for quiet. I want to toast something I've had just once. And I want to honor the inexperience that makes me think it can't last. I raise my glass and notice I've been drinking rum, which is foul. "To sex with the one you love," I say, and drain the last of it.

My toast is met with appreciation until Hannah lets out a snort and with it, a wad of gum. Her laughter is picked up by Linda, who, between gasps, says, "I'm sorry, that was very sweet, it's just that you standing there in that bandage and—" She gets no further.

Just as well, since here comes the countdown. Sharon is determined to use her watch, despite Kathleen's thrusting her GPS timepiece in Sharon's face. With a minute to go, the brass gather around Kathleen while the rest of us stick with Sharon. This is her worst nightmare. Our countdown is symbolic of the class divide that scuttles ambitions like peace on earth. Our countdown is syncopated. The brass hug and kiss a whole five seconds before we do.

"Well, that settles it," I say. "My year is ruined."

Stanley takes my hand and leads me back to the kid's room. He staggers. I tuck him into the lower bunk and curl up next to him.

"Want to hear something?" he says.

"Yes, anything."

"A few months ago I started sneaking into that farm across the road. I'd go with a couple six-packs. First few nights I was just sitting on the fence, watching the cows. But after a while, I got to putting some beer in the trough. Just so I wouldn't have to drink alone."

I put my arm around his waist. He smiles, but the hurt on his face is awful.

"Look, Stanley, if I have to go away, someone's gotta look after Hannah. I don't want her going back to Isifrid's." There is a pause. "Okay, forget that. What I'm saying is, you're a good man and also, can you look after Hannah?"

"That's a lot to ask," he says.

"See? You already know enough to know it's a responsibility."

"And that's supposed to be an accomplishment?"

I don't know what to say. You try to bolster a man's self-esteem and all he does is depress your own.

"I need to sleep," he says, and rolls on his side.

I listened to him breathe. I might have stayed with him all night, but Wanda peeked in the room and motioned for me to come out. She was holding her cell phone. She looked undone.

"Lucy, sit," she said. "Sit next to Hannah," who I couldn't believe was still awake. Her eyes stared at Wanda, but who knew to what effect.

Wanda sighed. "I just got off the phone with your mother. This is rotten timing, I'm so sorry, but your grandmother, she passed away tonight. Isifrid wants you both to come home tomorrow."

I said, "But she was fine when we left."

Hannah put out her hand, as if for a shake. "Thank you," she said. "Thank you for telling us."

Wanda and I exchanged a look that meant: Something is very

wrong with this child. Only her look had the advantage of passing into something else, as when you rubberneck on the highway. Mine stayed put, as when you're the one whose car got wrecked.

Wanda shut the door behind her. After that, the room was still but for the dribble of little fists on my chest.

Twenty-two

First thing back, I got my chin replaced. The wound was infected; the skin was flayed. The plastic surgeon tried to sell me new lips and nostrils. End-of-the-year special, I presumed. I asked if he could give me a metal plate to bilk airport security. He said I needed to waive my rights in case I died on the operating table. This was my first surgery and though I did not fear death, I did fear waking up in the middle, unable to open my eyes or communicate, but entirely aware of the pain. I'd heard of this happening. The doc said the chances were slim, and when I protested he said, Look, just be glad you don't have *superplague*. And to think only a few months ago, this could have been funny.

I wanted to wear my dog collar to surgery, but they said no. I had not taken it off in five years. And it showed. The grommets had stained my neck green, the green of bumps and bruises, so that my head looked sewn on, or as if I'd been strangled.

Stanley was waiting for me in recovery. When I came to, he said I looked like a blowfish, so swollen was my face. At home, Hannah agreed. And the cook, she suggested gumbo. Gumbo could fix anything.

There's no joy in convalescence now that TV has turned into the scariest thing on earth. Round-the-clock reports on Superplague: A Nation in Crisis. Unwittingly, soap star Claire Anderson is just about to seduce her brother when, wham, the show gets preempted. Daytime drama has blue balls. As for the nighttime stuff, the networks have yanked any show about doctors, cops, or espionage. CBS has gone the Bambi route. NBC has sponsored focus groups to see if soft-core will allay tension or depress the crap out of us. ABC has hired several trampy-looking women to deliver the bad news as they see fit. As for Fox, they have decided to downplay the outbreak lest anyone turn against the government as a result. The anchors, however, have taken to wearing U.S. flag ties, presumably to rally their viewership against them outsiders, whoever they are. When did wearing the flag start to mean fundamentalism and xenophobia? After 9/11, I wore a flag pin, but I was embarrassed. I wanted it to say: I love my country despite most everything. But what it really said was: Kill the A-rabs, kill 'em all! And while you're at it, have a beer.

To my mind, panic is understudied for something so destructive and ubiquitous. I mean, your average fight-or-flight theory polarizes emotion with no regard for the stuff in between. What of the people whose panic results in apathy? I'll just stay here until I die. Or the panic that stampedes an electronics store when the grocery is just blocks away? The mind scrambling for purchase. Indecision or madness. Flee to the suburbs or flee this life. Stay and help; stay and help no one. I can think of few feelings that disperse in such antimony.

Me, I've been comatose. I think we're all going to die, yes, but I have been spared the pupal experience of having my thoughts convert into fear and fear into unpredictable bowel movements and clammy skin. Instead, I just sit around watching the footage from out West.

The quarantine has actually turned Northern California into the world's largest jail. Unemployment has dropped because of all the work a quarantine requires. To lock down even a single county, you need one hell of a border patrol. Just think how many roads lead out of town. The National Guard can barely manage. And people are enraged. How dare the government confine them to this death trap! The Berkeley underground developed overnight. In the hippie splendor of Santa Cruz, there's a black market for guns. Everyone wants out. The guys who run Mexicans into Texas are in hot demand. Bounty hunters in Washington State are in hot demand. Number one crime in California: hospital break-ins. The prize? An oxygen tank. Snatch it from a dying guy's bedside if you have to. With tank and mask, you never have to breathe the air again. No air, no superplague. Across the country, police guard hospitals like Fort Knox.

The moon men have left the area. They fear for their suits. Anyone might kill them for a suit. And when the National Guard is not chasing border crossers, they are defending their gear.

Here in New York, we say: But only twelve have died, what's the big deal? Because surely we'd behave better. Meantime, middle-of-nowhere real estate is experiencing its first boom ever. Thirty miles to the nearest store? We'll take it. In New York, we feign calm and make our plans in secret. But you can sense the fear. A new crease in the face. That extra bit of energy it takes to perform duties once rote, now cavalier. Taking the subway, eating out, movies, the gym. I think I prefer the mania out West because this repression, it eats away at your sanity, slow and painful.

Aggie's memorial is tomorrow; today is the probate lawyer. Rehab's been postponed indefinitely, which leaves me at the vanguard of coping theory, where most anything's a go. If it helps you deal, it's a go.

Isifrid wants to know what I'm wearing to church. She's been on the phone for days, inviting friends, buying flowers. I don't think she's been hopped up on crack, which means this is just the stamina of grief deferred.

"Doesn't matter," I say. "No one will notice anything besides my chin."

"Don't be a pill, Lucy. And if you wear that dog collar, well, I don't know. I'll think of something."

"Like there's anything worse than rehab."

"I can think of something worse."

"What's that?"

"If I came with you."

I break into a smile. My mother, she's still got sass. I say I'll wear a black skirt suit, no collar.

"And Hannah, will you make sure she's dressed right, too?"

"I don't think she's talking to me."

"Is she talking to Loretta?"

I nod. Everyone talks to the cook, it's protocol.

"Then put her in charge. And go on, I have things to do."

I find Gumbo in the wine closet. I can't seem to call her any-thing but her last meal. She does not appreciate this. I tap her on the shoulder, we have words. She says Hannah's not talking to her. I say, "What the fuck, Gumbo? You're like Switzerland around here."

"Come again?"

"Never mind."

By the time we have to go to the lawyer's, Mother is herky-jerky, which happens to a body denied its drug. She does not want to go. I don't want to go. We have not seen Quinty since Dad died. I imagine doing probate for an entire family is like working a dog pound. You just watch 'em go down and try not to get attached. But Quinty, he's got sangfroid. On the phone, he said we both had to be there, which means Aggie probably left me something. Maybe she had land in Norway no one knows about.

Mother has booked Raymond for the day. He is her favorite driver. He comes with limo and service cap. He's got a brassard and fatigues. When we are in his car, people think we're diplomats.

Outside our building, he opens the limo door and stands at at-tention. Mother returns the salute. I clap him on the shoulder and say, "Howdy, Ray." He is impossible to break. He's like those guards in front of Buckingham Palace.

While Mother sees to our drinks, I tap the partition. Raymond's eyes appear in the rearview. I lean forward and drape my arms over the lip.

"So what's the word, Ray? Seen any good movies lately?"

"No, ma'am."

"That movie about the girl killers is supposed to be good."

"I wouldn't know, ma'am."

"And that rapper movie. That white rapper guy."

"Yes, ma'am."

The window comes up between us.

"Sherry?" Mother says.

"Blech."

"Only a boob says blech to sherry."

"Blech."

"Did Loretta talk to Hannah?"

"No. They're not talking."

Mother sighs and says, "You know your nana was probably her best hope."

"Mine, too."

She pats my hand. I love how resigned we are to failing Hannah. How drugs have foreclosed on denial so that we can't even pretend to believe in ourselves. Nana's been gone only two weeks, but I feel her absence acutely.

Mother says it's going to be a long winter. Then she loses an earring. The rear of this limo is so big, it accommodates two women on all fours. The shag is dense and the diamond small. I turn on a reading light. The beam hits Mother from behind and my God: she looks like someone replaced her skin with Saran Wrap, and pulled tight.

We bump heads. I say, "Oh, forget this. You've got eighteen thousand diamond earrings."

From the speakers comes Raymond asking if he can be of service. Mother relates our problem. He pulls over. Allow me. Mother and I get out. He holds an umbrella over our heads and escorts us to the warmth of a deli. Then he retrieves something from his trunk, which turns out to be goggles. Like, night-*vision* goggles.

I turn to Mother and say, "Okay, this guy is nuts."

"He rather is. But your father gave me those earrings."

The deli smells of bacon fat. I buy some gum. Raymond returns with goggles on brow, earring in hand.

Mother makes to kiss him on the cheek, and he flinches. He actually flinches. I hope she didn't notice. To be the one horror that makes Raymond flinch.

Outside Quinty's office we're both too scared to go in. Once probate's done, there's no way to arrest the passing. Isifrid slinks off to a bathroom, hiding behind her bladder the way only a crackhead can. This leaves me with the secretary, who's even frostier than her boss.

When Mother returns, she seems disappointed to find me still there. Like I'd break ice with Quinty alone.

"Well, go on," she says, and holds the door open.

But if I go first, she's gonna bolt. And bolt she does. Her heels clatter down the hall like marbles.

Quinty says, "Welcome, nice to see you again. Wish it were under more pleasant circumstances."

Is there a school for this stuff? Or a book of phrases?

Quinty's one giant pouch. His cheeks hang from his bones like sacks on a rack. Beneath each eye, tear bags that slosh about with every jerk of his head. He reminds me a bit of No Face minus the big baby muffinhead appeal.

His chair wheezes. Of the two left, I choose a black task and lower it so I am eye level with a picture of Quinty, Jr., and Jr., Jr., who's nine.

"Where is your mother? This won't take long."

We hear her chatting up the secretary. Talk about your wrong tree. She gets out three words before the secretary buzzes her in.

Quinty kisses her on both cheeks. She settles in a lounge chair and stores her feet under her lap. "Blisters," she says. I nod. Her shoes narrow in tips sharp as a dart.

"Cigarette?" Quinty opens a box on his desk. He's got those colored ones with gold filters, and an electric ashtray to eat up the smoke. Mother produces a silver holder with rhinestone barrel. I don't think anyone has used one of those since 1950. Mother thinks the farther she holds the cigarette from her lungs, the longer she'll enjoy it before feeling ill. She's allergic to tobacco.

I take note of the bathroom abutting the office, just in case.

Quinty hands out two copies of Aggie's will and props his elbows on the desk. "Take your time," he says. I fold mine and rest it in my lap. Isifrid asks me to hold on to hers, as well.

Quinty looks surprised. I return the look. We're supposed to read the will here and make sense of it? I ask if he'll summarize.

"Very well. As you probably know, Agneth did not have much by way of possessions. She also did not have a pension or independent funds."

Mother is nodding—or rocking, actually—so I suggest she go freshen up. Quinty and I sit in silence, waiting. Unfortunately, he decides to acknowledge her dry heaving whereas I am content to talk sports.

"Lucy," he says, "I do not wish to pry, but your mother is not looking well. Not well at all. I trust she's been to a doctor who's monitoring the treatment?"

For a second I think Quinty might suspect Mother has plague. But then this is absurd. There's no time to look bad with plague; you just get it and die.

"What do you mean?" I say.

"Lucy, it's okay. When did she start chemo?"

I sit back in my chair. Quinty thinks Mother has cancer?

I suggest we stick with Agneth.

He pares dead skin from the cuticle region of his thumb. Whereas death is just part of the job, dying has Quinty upset. "Your father and I were good friends," he says. "Obviously I can't do anything about this plague fiasco, but I do know a lot of doctors. And I am owed many favors."

What can this mean? Isifrid's got money. Maybe he knows of drugs as yet unavailable to the public. Or maybe he just gets free scrips. Whoa, free scrips. I love these words, they are like the brakes on a lawless train. I can't keep a telephone number in my head for three seconds, but I've got genius when it comes to the free scrips. Also, it doesn't take much for the evil in me to well up fast.

"That's kind of you," I say. "The cancer's pretty advanced, we're doing all we can."

"Is there anything I can do?"

"No, but thank you. Actually—no, no that's all right. Let's finish up with the will."

He leans forward. He's about to get avuncular, I know it. I think: Please don't get avuncular, please please please.

"Listen, Lucy. I know things have been hard on you—"

Crap.

"—and that having to take care of your mom can't be helping. So let *me* help."

Double crap.

"It's okay, you know, to ask for help."

It turns out the only thing worse than conning a guy is conning a *nice* guy. Before, when I wanted nothing, he was all pouch and breeze, but now that I'm gunning for the free scrip, he's Mr. Goodheart. I wish Mother would come out of the bathroom and put an end to this. Because otherwise I will not stop. I will exploit Quinty's good heart until he cashes in every favor he's got.

"Well, there is one thing," I say.

And that's that. Quinty will produce a scrip for Oxy that will last me weeks.

We agree to keep this between us. Mother returns. Quinty offers her some bottled water, which she waves off in martyr fashion.

"Okay," he says. "As I mentioned, Agneth did not have any assets. She's left her jewelry to Hannah and her private papers to you, Lucy."

I flip through the itemized part of the will and see a blurb about an elaborate family tree rendered on posterboard, and a compendium of biographical sketches leather-bound with capeskin and boasting a charcoal frontispiece of the port in Bergen, Norway.

Mother's reading over my shoulder and shaking her head. "She left you the tree. Oh, Agneth."

If this is loss slamming Isifrid head-on, it's all about the collateral damage: she's chuckling about the hoot that was my grandmother while I feel so choked up it's as if clumps of lung tissue are ramping up my throat.

"Lastly," Quinty says, "Agneth made a request. She wished to be cremated. She left no other instructions but one. It's about you, Lucy."

Mother says she needs to go home, so if there's nothing else—

I say I'll be there in a minute. I'm glad for the chance to hammer things out with Quinty, especially now that Aggie's death has me choking on lung tissue. Whereas the capricious, hand-of-fate death romping through California has the country in an uproar, it's the natural passing of an old woman that has me wrecked. Never to see this person again? Ever to sorrow the loss? I understand none of it.

Mercifully, Quinty will have the scrip for me next week. He does not even ask why I can't get it from Mother's doctor. If he did, I'd say she's too proud to ask, that she does not want to appear weak. This wouldn't hold water with anyone but a good man like Quinty. I sigh and wonder if I can get to the Oxy before self-disgust gets me.

"Lucy," he says, "I should add that Agneth requested you, specifically, to release her ashes."

I am so giddy about the scrips, I've stopped paying attention. "Any place in particular? I can do that, sure."

"She didn't say, only that you do it with a man named Eric, a friend of yours, I gather."

Attention restored. I belt out a laugh, it can't be helped. When that's over, I think: Huh. And then: No. Because what can this mean? It means that for all her talk of reincarnation, Agneth was not above wanting to live her dreams through me. I think of her sailor and hope she comes back a nurse who pursues love undeterred. But in the meantime, she can pursue vicariously and—but I stop there, as a gathering of real loneliness accosts my heart. A more likely explanation for Aggie's request? She was not so much trying to live through me as trying to get me to live, period.

I thank Quinty for his time and also, wink wink. But there's no joy in it. I have been robbed of the special buoyancy of knowing drugs are in my future. Mother's in the waiting room, with a *National Geographic*. A picture of hippos has her rapt. They are splayed in mud, cheek to cheek. The mud pit's huge, plenty of room, but the hippos like it snug. She is explaining as much to the secretary, who's actually into it.

Downstairs, Raymond's with a cop whose plans to ticket are dashed. He's an army man, himself. They have an understanding.

In the car, Isifrid asks what Quinty said. I suspect she will not like it. That she'll feel slighted.

"I'm supposed to spread her ashes," I say. "With Eric."

She cocks her head. "Who the hell's Eric?"

I hate being reminded that my mother knows nothing about me. Equally, I hate knowing it's my fault.

"That photographer. Remember? He came with Alfred."

"That feminine-looking boy?"

I beam and say, "That's the one."

"Why? What a strange thing to ask."

"I don't know. She liked him, I guess."

Her eyes narrow, which means: uh-oh. She can smell a lie for miles. Not because she's savvy, but because she's paranoid. When you think everything's a lie, you're bound to hit on a few. Thing is, while she can spot a lie, she's got no sense for the truth.

"I don't think so," she says. "I think you just don't want me to come. I think you're making this up! I can call Quinty, you know. I'm not stupid."

Eyes narrowed to eyes darting. Any second, she will fashion out of Aggie's request a conspiracy to deprive her of crack.

I decide to shut her down fast, and say, "If you call Quinty, you can forget about your stash at home."

Amazing how a face pale as cream can still go snow white. She turns away from me and hugs her knees. Discussion over.

Twenty-three

Aggie's memorial woos a crowd. People I don't remember, but who remember me. Friends of the family is what I think they're called.

I spot two women who were in Mother's avocation class. One runs a lucrative rice pudding business. She wears a fur muff. Two has yet to get her product off the ground. She has patented a nail-polish jar in which the brush splays when pressed on the bottom, ensuring no polish goes to waste.

I am to stand at the mouth of the nave and greet. Hannah has been banished to a corner pew for sporting Converse high-tops with white socks that bloom at the ankle. She's wearing a black skirt, I don't see what's the big deal.

Friends of the Family three, four, and five I recognize from the Kennewick event. Three is a CEO at Maybelline. He's got a tie clip and cane. Four looks just back from Honolulu. I'd wager his tan lines cut at the groin because it's always the old guys who insist on swim briefs. As for five, I think he's a scientist, which makes his show at the Asatru *blot* a little weird.

Six, seven, eight, nineteen, forty, forty-five, ninety. Ninety-seven's in a wheelchair, so I am spared. I am a kissing post. I'm like the girl in the booth with the added grievance of grief.

Oh, good, here comes Wanda, lips on deck. She takes me by the sleeve and strays us to a corner. I don't think I've ever seen her in a dress.

"I just saw your mother," she says. "Why didn't you tell me?"

This could mean anything. Best course: silence.

"How bad is it? It looks bad. Oh, Lucy, you should have told me."

Is it possible Wanda thinks Mother has cancer, too? Best course: silence.

"No wonder you and Hannah are in such bad shape. No offense, but come on, you're almost family. Okay, you don't want to talk about it. Bad timing, I know. But look, if there's anything I can do. I suppose I could try talking to her—no, that won't work. Your mother is a mule. I remember she once wanted these boots—boy were they ugly—but she wanted them and bought them, and then decided to wear them every day for a year, no matter the season or outfit. It'd be ninety degrees out, and she'd be wearing her boots with the sheepskin liner. Most ridiculous thing I ever saw."

Wanda's nearly lost to the memory, which gives me a chance to escape. I begin to inch away, smiling and nodding like I'm back there with her and the clompers, and gosh the fun we had, but no, her hand latches onto me, frog to fly.

"The point is, I want to help. What with your father's passing and everything in the news and now Agneth and you taking this big step, going back to rehab, it's just a lot to deal with."

"Wanda, what are you talking about? Speak your mind."

"I'm talking about your mother. She's on drugs."

Sweet fancy Moses, someone noticed. I give her a giant hug. Maybe now the burden of helping Isifrid can fall to someone who knows how to do it.

She says, "It's all right," and rubs my back. "We'll talk later. I know, I know."

Postclutch, I am wobbly. One tends to forget how a hug steals your balance. Or that when you hug, it's like you've turned in your balance unwittingly. I lean against whatever's closest, which happens to be Oliver Lentz. He takes me by the arm. Hard to tell if he's holding me up or just saying hi. Oliver is a bowling pin, his proportions are sad. Actually, he's worse than a bowling pin, but why niggle. I can smell Scotch on his breath. And his face, much like the cherry atop a sundae, is all sweat.

He is just saying how much he admired Agneth when his son, Marcus, shows up. I can hardly believe it. In school, Marcus was

Gumby. Shapely and soft. Loafers, argyle, turtlenecks. If not for a manly-man name like Marcus, I would not have pegged him for a guy. But now! Now he's this lanky homosexual with sparkle lips and enough goop in his hair to grease a trough. I bet his parents are appalled. I bet they stopped sending those family-photo holiday cards. I bet they suffer.

"Marcus?" He looks right past me.

When we were kids, we used to kill the lights, hide under a couch, and grab Aggie's calves as she walked by. Scared the kimono right off her. We used to call her on the phone from my room and say we were friends of mine and did Aggie know I was missing? Then we'd hide under the couch and grab at her ankles. This could go on for hours. I have not seen Marcus since we were thirteen.

"Lucy?" he says. "I would never have recognized you."

"Likewise. You're so—"

"Gay?"

"Hot. I was gonna say hot."

"Well, thanks. I'm really sorry about Agneth. We had some good times with her."

"That we did. So have I really changed that much?"

He shrugs. Gay, yes. Smooth, no. He says I've *matured*.

Well, then. I stand tall and exert my breasts. Comes a time in every girl's life when she requisitions her honor. Too bad this isn't it.

"Good to see you, Marcus. Thanks for coming."

He leans forward. Air *bisous*, on both sides.

In the presbytery, Mother has arranged a large painting of Aggie composed at one of her parties by a renowned artist whose story— amputee turned pimp turned bum turned religious—hits theaters next month. I try to take in the crowd when a little man catches my eye. He shuffles as he walks, his feet pronate. Knock-knees are his bane. This depresses me no end, largely because the shuffle posits decline, he wasn't always this way, which thought hastens adjunct ideas that steepen the decline—say, that he was a CFO *and* dressage champ three years running, and look at him now. I watch him take a seat. An usher hands him a program, which he folds and puts into his breast pocket. His clothes need a wash. I doubt he was invited. Some people feast on death, and I am okay with that. Maybe the little man tramps from one memorial to the next. Maybe the only food he gets is the transubstantiation, which is pretty cool if you're hungry *and* a Catholic. I don't even know whether they do the Eucharist at a memorial. Do the Eucharist? Is that like do the hustle? I am the most contemptuous person ever.

The little man piles his coat next to him. He retrieves the program and runs his finger along the frame of Aggie's photo, a candid of her at age thirty. She's wearing her hair in a bun, except for a rogue lock that hangs off the side of her face, which makes her look significantly more reckless than if she had spikes. Reminds me of this noir movie where the Deadly Female walks into a guy's room and it's so pristine that when she rumples the nap of his carpet with her shoe, it portends havoc better than if she'd shot up the place. So that's Aggie, her rogue lock, and the little man.

Everyone's been seated, which means I have a clear view of the door when Eric walks in. I knew he'd be here but still. Just the sight of him reduces me to the basics. I need food, water, shelter, Eric. I'd like to crawl under his shirt and stay there. I'd like to pitch a cot under his shirt and *live* there. And this is how I know I'm ruined. Because if I'm fantasizing, anyway, it should be about sex. Or, okay, since I'm a *girl*, walks on the beach. At the very least, cuddling.

He says hi.

I say hi.

Stalemate.

We haven't seen each other since lunch. And I've been good. Have not called them at three a.m., have not stalked him at work. Have not obsessed except for your basic obsessing, which is much like your heart at rest. It's still *beating*.

I say, "Thanks for coming."

He says, "Of course. Kam couldn't make it, but sends her condolences."

Nods all around, followed by the shoulder squeeze. Most ambiguous gesture ever.

Stanley has saved me a spot between him and Mother. The effluvium of mourning seems concentrated in her perfume—lilac, gladiolus, honeysuckle. By contrast, I smell like Hubba-Bubba, never mind that I tossed my gum ages ago. Or that I was caught midspit by Colleen Hathaway, who stimulates Mother's deep tissue twice a week. So embarrassing. The list of people I can never see again grows daily.

Eric is a few rows back. He's wearing a suit of pieces filched from other suits—pants, vest, jacket, bow tie. Bow tie!

Isifrid has asked a number of her friends to speak for the family. Agneth lived with us for years, everyone knew her. There is talk of heroics—she was an autodidact—of fortitude and altruism. There is talk of reincarnation. Sigrid Hoffman reads some Old Icelandic poetry, which I love. The way the stanzas work, they are always dropping the other shoe at the last moment. This simulates a unique sound in nature, which I also love. I guess it's a thunk. Maybe a thud.

> So I learned when I sat in the reeds,
> Hoping to have my desire:
> Lovely was the flesh of that fair girl,
> But nothing I hoped for happened.

Thud.

> Foolish is he who frets at night,
> And lies awake to worry:
> A weary man when morning comes,
> He finds all as bad as before.

Thud.

> Two wooden stakes stood on the plain,
> On them I hung my clothes:
> Draped in linen, they looked well born,
> But naked, I was a nobody.

I imagine the last lines of these poems, in their condemnation, function better when spoken aloud, as per the oral tradition in which they were conceived. Too bad the written word has supplanted the oral tradition. Sometimes I think that if not for the addicts in recovery, there'd be no oral tradition at all. I mean, story is the fulcrum of recovery, the biggest part of the program by far.

Stanley pinches my leg. I worry I'd fallen asleep, only it's not me, but Mother. So I pinch her leg and think we could get a relay going since the guy next to her could probably use a fillip. And the lady next to him, she's not looking too vital, either. I bet we could snake this game all the way to the back of the church. I bet—but then I realize Stanley's been looking at me and I am ashamed. Some people can accord their behavior with context. They can arrange their feelings like the spray on a casket. I do not excel in this department. Worse, it's not that I'll be at a funeral and laugh because it's funny. I'll just laugh. And maybe, from strain of withholding laughter, I will get aroused. And maybe, from horror of arousal, I will get a headache that hurts so bad, I'll end up crying anyway.

Bottom line: I loved Agneth and with her death accrues just one more reason to follow suit.

It takes Dag Bersvendsen three minutes to mount the stage. Polio nailed him at twenty, and now he's got age to contend with. Not sure if someone should help him and if so, who? An usher? Me? Each step accomplished lets out some tension from the room. By the time I decide to help, he's made it. Made it insofar as he hasn't passed out. Reaching the mike is another story. An usher brings him a footstool. But how's he gonna get on it? This is awful.

Dag and Mother grew up on the same block in Bergen. They were lovers and then they were engaged and then he got polio and she split. How to develop a million-dollar company selling hats on the streets in Bergen? How to do so with a crippled beau? You don't. You come to America and make trilbies. You get some guy to wear your trilby in the season's blockbuster, and for the attendant photo shoot. You furnish your sidesweep with quills and orchids. You sell your millinery to the Queen of England.

Most important, you keep your lovers close. So Dag, he runs the international division of Mother's company. Rides it like a woman. Without mercy. Think those crutches with the arm cuff hold him back? Think he won't mount that footstool? Think again!

He asks for a moment of silence. For Agneth Monsen and her family. For the plague victims out West. And while we're at it, for the entire country since at this point, nothing short of prayer can save us.

The memorial closes with Bach. Something from an oratorio. It bellows through the church, whose acoustics distill the tin from every voice. Treacle, treble, not much difference when you're blue. We stand. I have never understood traditions that straddle events opposed to each other, like how at a wedding *and* a memorial, you don't get up until the family does. Whence this premium on family? And who thinks the tradition does a family good? Display is torture. I've just wept my eyeballs to soup, look at me! Or, in my case and thus worse, I have not wept at all, I am frigid, behold the face of dispassion!

Raymond is waiting by the double doors. Light at the end of the tunnel Raymond. Mother rushes to his side. Get me out of here, is what she's thinking. Only reason I know is that I'm thinking the same thing. Unfortunately, the task of seeing everyone out falls to me, especially since Raymond, in special-ops fashion, has kidnapped Mother under cover of nothing, and *still* no one saw them go. Others MIA include Wanda, Stanley, and Hannah. Haven't seen her since *naked, I was a nobody*, when she was huddled on the floor, knees drawn, head down. I could have tipped her over with a nudge of the toe.

I check out the spot and find evidence to suggest she was just here. Opened bottle of soda, effervescent. Marble warm to touch. If Converse, then tread, which muddies around the reliquary sealed in glass. I find her on the lee side, biting her thumb.

"Aggie would have hated the memorial," she says.

"I know."

"Think she's really out there someplace?"

"God, I hope so."

"Why?"

"I don't know. When you believe in something so much, I think you should be right. Or at least never have to find out you spent your life being wrong."

"I heard Wanda say you were going to Texas. Do you have to?" The look on her face is like when the Death Star disables its shield just long enough to get blasted to shit.

"Afraid so. I have no say in these things."

Star rearmed. "How long?"

"Month? Not sure. But I'll be back as soon as I can."

"Uh-huh."

"Hannah, stop that. It's true. You think I want to be going just now?"

She presses her forehead to the glass, but since now is not the time to upend the reliquary, I suggest we leave. Also, I can't summon the wherewithal to continue charading with my baby sister.

She looks up. "And help Loretta with the squab kebobs? I hate our life."

"Oh, come on. Wouldn't want to miss the speeches. Remember the guy at Mel's engagement who read a poem about not slapping your wife? I hope he's there."

Hannah's face brightens, and I realize that party was the last time we had fun together.

"Remember the Kraut?" she says. "The guy with the bubble head?"

I nod. "But can you not call him a Kraut? I've been meaning to talk to you about this kind of thing."

She snorts. "It's just summer camp."

"It's for terrorists!"

"Shut up. You know Indra's not allowed to talk to me anymore, thanks to you."

"Still?"

She gives me the evil eye. Eyes. I follow her down the center aisle. We are the only ones left, excepting church staff. One guy gives me a DVD of the memorial—that was quick—while the others sweep the floor. Amazing how fast service flowers shed their petals.

At the apartment, people are talking in low voices. Jumbo Prawn looks frantic. She has prepared for fifty; we are ninety. Already we're out of deviled eggs and sturgeon caviar; the black olive tapenade Brie toast can't come out of the oven fast enough; and the wonton sampler, forget it. I pocket a handful of bourbon pecans for later, and send Hannah to lay claim to at least one squab kebob. But she has her own plans. She's traded her skirt for garb that keeps with the Converse. If Mother sees her in those jeans with the hundred-dollar fade, she will have a fit.

Stanley appears by my side.

"Thanks for waiting for me," I say. "Got real fun back there after you left."

"And miss a ride with Raymond? The man has nunchucks in the glove compartment."

"He does not."

"Yeah, but he *could*."

I take a long look at Stanley. He didn't use to be like this. I think the change is for the better, but in no universe does this mean I'm right.

He's got a glass of Pinot in each hand, and a couple bottles on the mantel. We sit in a loveseat. I tell him to make like a lump and stare out at the room so that together, in our bleakness, we will appear remote and forbidding. Then again, the strategy presumes tact, that our guests have it, which they don't. There's a man coming our way. Says: "May I?"

Stanley nods and invites the guy to take his seat. I've got blur vision, mostly by choice. But one hates to be impolite. I turn my head and focus. It's the little man from the memorial. Seems pleasant enough.

"I'm Dan."

"Lucy."

Pause.

"You're Lucy?"

Nod. Nod again. This is awkward. I say whatever comes to mind next. "Hate to be frank, but you are incredibly little. I mean, I saw you in the church, which, now that I think about it, is weird since you don't exactly stand out."

"I'm Dan."

I look around to see if anyone finds this as odd as I do. Who *is* this guy?

"Who are you?"

"Dan."

"Right. Lucy. Bourbon pecan?"

"Thanks, no."

We both sit forward and clasp our hands, me because what's to talk about, him because his feet won't reach the floor otherwise.

Still, I decide to try. I go: "Lovely to see you. Lovely services."

He puts in hearing aids, which explains a lot. "So you're Lucy?"

"Yep. You?"

"A friend of your grandmother's."

"Agneth had friends?"

"Friends might be overstating it. We were close once."

Addicts do not like to feel surprised, which is just as well since drugs so deaden your sensitivities you can barely register the brass tacks, say: I have to pee, or: My skin's on fire. So the little man, I take it in stride and assess. He is little, I got that part. He shuffles as he walks. He is married. Skin manifold and pale. Beard long enough for curlers. And eyes, these blue eyes so recessed and bright, they spangle.

I say: "The navy man, right?"

He nods. Says it was a long time ago. That he read about Aggie's death in the paper. "But," he adds, "I've kept tabs on her over the years. And I saw her recently, just a couple weeks ago, in fact."

Okay, now I am surprised. So maybe it's not the surprise I dislike, but having to accept that other people know things I don't.

"You saw her? Where?"

"She came to my place."

"What did she want?"

"To see me."

"Yeah, but she must have said something."

He shakes his head. "I took her to lunch. We tried to catch up on fifty years in half an hour. She was so beautiful, you know, when we first met."

I uncork one of Stanley's bottles. "Wine?"

"No, but thank you. Bad liver."

"So what happened between you two, anyway? Aggie mentioned it once, a couple months ago, but her account was kinda sparse."

He takes a cigar out of a Ziploc in his pocket. It's been chewed halfway down the trunk. I ask if he's gonna light that. He says no, his wife can't stand the smell, and fits it in the hinge of his lips, passing it from one side of his mouth to the other. I notice tobacco slop in his beard.

"It's a simple story," he says. "As simple as it gets. I wanted to marry her. We tried, but life got in the way. It always does, it seems."

"Aggie said she saw your wife once."

"Yes. My wife is a wonderful woman. We celebrate forty-nine years together next month."

"Did you ever tell her? About Agneth?"

He looks at me and smiles, and just now I can see why Aggie loved him. "No," he says. "There are some things best kept secret."

"I see."

Another smile, wry and ageist. It says I have a lot to learn, but with such warmth that I cannot be offended. I can, however, be made depressed. I take a sip of wine, and think: Prattle. Prattle will get me out of this. I do not want to be having this conversation. I do not want to hear about compromise and settling and resignation. "Lovely services," I say.

He looks at me with the wry smile.

"I should probably go mingle," I say.

Smile bares teeth.

"Want to meet my sister?"

"I do, indeed."

We find her in the pink room talking to Colleen Hathaway. Hannah tends to elevate her voice when excited, which is why I can hear her say, "No, it's worse than that, this strain can live in air, you can get it just from walking to the store. No, you don't have to be around someone who's already sick. No, this kind of plague can't be cured, it moves so fast by the time you realize you have it, you're dead."

Colleen slinks off to the self-serve bar.

"Hannah, meet Dan. Dan, Hannah. Dan is Agneth's navy guy."

Hannah says: "Whoa." And then: "The *navy* navy guy? From Mexico?"

"A pleasure," says Dan.

They are the same height.

"Whoa," says Hannah. "I imagined you—"

"Taller, yes. We've covered that."

I like the way he says *we* and am amazed, as I often am by language as power, at the way a simple pronoun can upend a relationship.

Hannah, on the other hand, does not like the results. If we're a *we*, then she's a *she*.

"What else did you cover?"

I say, "Oh, just the marrow of every artistic enterprise since the caveman."

No response.

"That they didn't get married because life got in the way. And that Aggie went to see him a couple weeks ago, first time in fifty years."

"Whoa."

"Yeah."

"Drink?"

"No, thanks. Bad liver."

"Okay," says Hannah. And: "Nice services."

I shake my head and say. "Forget it, it doesn't work."

Our trio moves to a corner. Decor for the room includes three six-foot paintings of fat people on roller skates. Fat people with tapered limbs, limbs like twigs, which could never sustain all that fat in the real world.

Hannah's looking at Dan, trying to make something of the alternate life Aggie could have had. Or maybe that's just what I'm doing and Hannah is thinking Barbie. No, hantavirus. Nope, it's Aggie. She says: "So do you regret what happened?"

Dan appears to have been waiting for this question. He's certainly rehearsed his response.

"Regret's complicated," he says. "Especially as you get older. I have a lovely wife and three children. Grandchildren, too. When I see them, it validates my life. The life I built after your grandmother returned to the life she already had. I do not regret any of these things, I cherish them."

Hannah is not satisfied. She looks stricken. And so do I. *Moving on* is a horrible process. Accepting your lot. We have now lost our father and our grandmother, but we will move on. All the truisms about loss will show themselves worthy: We won't forget, but we will cope. We will ask loss to tell us what matters. We will say: I want knowledge only of God's will for me and the strength to carry it out, what will be will be, I cannot rue a life so long as God has planned it for me. We will come to terms with the good and the bad, and find peace in the offing.

Hannah says, "But you loved her, right? Don't you ever think about what could have been?"

"I'll tell you in a minute."

We follow him to the foyer, where he retrieves his coat from the spillover rack. In his plaid ivy cap he looks like a cabbie, circa 1974. *Sanford and Son.* He buttons up his coat to the neck and up-turns the collar.

He extends his hand and the instant I touch it, I don't want him to leave. Don't leave!

"Your grandmother knew she was dying, you know. That's why she came."

Don't leave!

He puts his other hand atop mine and looks at Hannah. "You're probably too young," he says, "but I'll say it anyway. Regret is irrelevant."

Hannah is near tears. "But then why did she go see you?"

The elevator opens. He's got his hand on the button.

"To say goodbye."

"Did she?"

Again with the smile and then: "Not really."

Door closes. Hannah turns on me in a rage. "What the hell was that? What did he mean?"

She slumps to the floor, crying. Can't even make it to her room. Some of the guests look away. No one thinks to get Mother, which is for the best.

I squat. Probably I should put my arms around her, but I know she'll just slough me off. We are sitting in the doorway like earthquake survivors, foot to foot, sole to sole.

"I like those Converse," I say.

Snuffles. "Thanks."

"I'm sorry I brought him over. I wasn't thinking."

She wipes her nose on her sleeve. "It's okay."

"Want a tissue?"

I go to the guest bathroom, stocked with twenty rolls of toilet paper. Mother fears poverty, which, in her mind, is best represented by abrasive paper or no paper at all. One of the cabinets in the pantry is all Charmin.

By the time I get back, Hannah's gone. Off to her room.

I could smack that guy Dan. You can never say goodbye to your best love, even if you're dying—*that's* the moral here?

.I look about the room for Eric. The postmortem has thinned out. I spot him, Stanley, and Wanda, milling by the cheese.

Twenty-four

No one has to tell me, I know: my heart stopped. I was in the park, on a bench, feeding the pigeons. I do not know why people of advanced age—women in particular—like to feed pigeons. Or why most old ladies look the same. Our coats cinch above the waist with a fabric belt; our breasts are saddlebags. Many my age have not stood upright since 1990. You make peace with the decline of your body long before you'd like. In turn, you settle into pastimes of no appeal. So there I was, pinching dough from a street pretzel. The birds, as birds do, were in a scrum. They had little regard for me, which was fine. It meant I should be on my way. I uncrossed my ankles and made ready to stand. Who could have imagined what trials are standing, sitting, climbing, walking, come eighty-four? I once heard a writer say that though it's hard to get characters to perform basic functions without feeling like a jackass, it must be done. As he put it, "Even Proust had to open the window." So consider me, who actually *can't* open a window unaided. I thought the limbo between incarnations was a time to reflect, but how can I think with this pain in my arm? My chest is so tight, it's freeze-dried.

I was halfway off the bench when a young boy barreled through the flock. He wore ski pants that hampered the progress of his legs so that he'd barrel, fall, and barrel again. I lost momentum on the way up. I covered my face and head. Mayhem is the sound of wings flapping.

They say we are doomed to reexperience the body death ad infinitum. I will never leave this bench. And my heart, it will rear and stop, and stop anew.

In winter, the cold lacquers your face and hands. It's what I re-member most from the early days of my marriage. Erlend and I met one year into the occupation of Norway. We had poverty and jazz in common. Jazz could colonize your body like a drug so that nights spent listening to the phonograph were nights that kept the war at bay. Teddy Wilson and Roy Eldridge. We might not have eaten in two days, but get those guys to play and we'd *move*. We'd move when movement was impossible, fifteen deep in a boiler room with zero clearance if you stood. After the war, you could tell collabora-tor from rebel by posture alone. The spine will bend as needed, though the change is permanent.

For myself and Erlend, there was pregnancy and marriage. We were in the resistance, teamwork was key; when the pregnancy failed, the marriage didn't. Benny Goodman held us tight. We knew, of course, that we'd been left behind. While the Nazis sat tight, jazz had outgrown swing, it was something else now. We said, Soon as the war is over. Our favorite refrain.

Quisling banned the radio. And the word *swing*. Jazz clubs shut down. Public dancing was out. By 1943, the jazz scene was so re-pressed, none thought it could survive.

When Isifrid came in '44, I swore she would be the last. The nausea made me crazy. The swell in my joints locked a bangle around my wrist so that it had to be cut off. I was hungry all the time. But then this child. This little creature! Erlend sat by my bed and peered into her face. I looked from him to her and back. We had done this together? I decided to love my husband.

As a country, Norway emerged from the occupation relatively unharmed. Bloodshed had been minimal, our cities were intact. But the hatred of the postwar period! You'd think the Nazis had killed every woman and child in Bergen. We were a lynch mob waiting to happen. It was not enough to execute Quisling or jail his cabinet. Every other Norwegian had been a traitor. Every other Norwegian. Maybe. Few were spared accusation. If the butcher skimped on a flank, perhaps he'd been seen at a certain club with a certain official. We looked on each other with suspicion and fear. This was no place for jazz—jazz, which is freedom, jazz, which is art. Our musicians went to Sweden. And for the rest of us, it be-came: If only we lived in Sweden. We read *Estrad* and *Orkesterjour-*

nalen, and we yearned. We listened to Charlie Parker on Voice of America, and we yearned. We caught up with the rest of the world. Isolation had failed us terribly, it was time to mingle. The government pooled resources with Italy, Belgium, Luxembourg, and France. Even Germany got involved. We began to import music. We were Erlend, Isifrid, Berget, Linnea, Petra, Gerd, and myself.

I laundered clothes for the rectory. Erlend worked on the docks. Money was scarce and we were too many, but the war was over, it wouldn't do to complain. The girls slept on habits piled knee high. My knuckles were split and chapped. Erlend would come home smelling of brine. If he ever got three days' leave, it would take as long to rub out the smell. At night we collapsed into each other. By morning we were like marionettes in a box, tangled in sleep, apart onstage. Because that's what it was, this life we had: a performance at odds with the people we were inside. Erlend was good with his hands, he could whittle a chess set out of planks from our floor. He would have liked to spend his days in a small shop, educing figures from oak or marble. Instead he was up at four to shuttle clams and cod from boat to warehouse to plane to Asia. Our sea is the world's larder. Redfish, ling, and pout. The Ministry of Fisheries had its work cut out for it. And so did Erlend. The physical labor tried his strength but the mental strain was worse. To begin each day knowing you will make no effort to change the path you're on, that you will subordinate your dreams to whatever provides for you and yours. Wake up like this enough and you resile, back to when no one knew you, to when you were alone, because to be seen for what you have become is too much.

I was no better. I wanted to go to school for medicine. The resistance was more about morale than combat, but whenever one of ours got hurt, no matter how cursory the wound, he usually died from lack of professional care. Hospitals were out of the question. Most of our doctors had been conscripted or kidnapped. Think *Dr. Zhivago*, it was like that. I knew how to disinfect and bandage, but to save a life, it never happened. I'd say: After the war, I will study. And after the war, I'd say: When Isifrid is grown. Then I took sick, my heart was not right. Back then, cardiac surgery was larval at best. I volunteered for the Vineberg operation, in which, I think, you take an artery and reroute it to the heart so that it looks something like a waterslide that feeds a pool. No one took Vineberg seriously and neither did I, but I was dying and cared little for the odds.

When I recovered, I began to read *Zhivago* in earnest. Passages from the book circulated among us samizdat-like. We didn't get the novel until '57 like everyone else, but excerpts had been floating around for years. So here was this doctor conducting one of the great love stories, and here was I, with suds and vestment. I thought of the heroics that awaited accomplishment in the field. I thought of the liberties that attend any pursuit of science; you can learn as you please and discover by chance. I did not think of my children. Even less about Erlend. We hardly spoke because there was nothing to say. I was suffused with need for a different life.

Daniel's ship came to port in Bergen the summer we lost Linnea to bronchial pneumonia run amok. I recall the timing because on his ship were samples of oxytetracycline, which could have saved her life. I remember pacing the dock for hours, petitioning the captain and anyone else who ventured on shore. But it was useless. They either had no idea what I was talking about or shrugged it off because bureaucracy isn't worth fighting unless the fight is your own.

Linnea was only two years old. Erlend was crushed. I was crushed, though I also managed to have the frightful thought that one less mouth to feed was one step closer to escape. I began to look on the other children as punishment. Berget and Gerd were four, Isifrid six. Petra was one. Such is the burden of the firstborn; Isifrid cared for the others when I could not, which was often. I paced the docks and feared for my children even as I wished them away. What was happening to me? Every day felt like an experience of loss. As if my head and heart were seeping, and I a husk where once a life. Friends blamed the surgery, and said it would pass. But I knew better.

How many nights did I sit with Daniel before noticing myself? I had skin and blood, a cut on my thumb. My heartbeat was audible. My cheeks could blush. He was stationed in Bergen for three months. We met his second day in, and it was as if his gaze made things visible to me. Sunset in Bergen, had it happened before? Boathouses reflected in the harbor when the light is just so. The way water moves over cobblestone in runnels. My nails, which were flecked white for lack of calcium. The many shades of blond in my hair.

I'd come to the wharf every day at five. He was never late. We'd sit on a bench and talk jazz. He'd seen Dizzy Gillespie play. Louis Armstrong. He said in the States it was easy. And that there was nothing better than tapping your feet to the music you love.

We left in the middle of the night. I kissed my girls and packed my things. It was mad, this furlough, not to mention cruel. But I was crazed. I did not even leave a note.

Was this what they call true love? I don't know. Was it rapture? Was I happy? I'm still unsure about the relevance of these questions. I never much cared for what I felt, just that I felt at all. And for those months with Daniel, I felt everything. I missed my children. I missed Erlend. Foreplay roused sensation between my legs. Gooseflesh was my response. I laughed at the movies. I went to night school. When Daniel said I was beautiful, my eyes produced water.

By the time Erlend tracked me down, I was ready to go home. My children needed their mother. Had he not found me, I might have married Daniel and returned home anyway. Poor Erlend. When I got back to Bergen, he was waiting for me on the couch. He looked wretched. The place was a swamp. The girls were at school, but I could well imagine the condition they were in. He got on his knees and clasped me about the waist. Later he said it was the first time he'd felt anything in ages. Later still he said he'd treat the new baby as if it were his own. I looked at him and I looked at me, and I decided to love my husband.

He was true to his word. When my child with Daniel died two years later, Erlend shut down completely. By then, I was due with Karen and could not work. Isifrid had to take up the slack. She was enterprising, thank God. The others would not have survived childhood without her.

When the new baby came, taking care of her and Erlend was not much different. They'd both stare out into the world with limited understanding. For Karen, this was a source of frustration. For Erlend, it was mercy. They never knew each other.

Days spent washing clothes, I'd think: Daniel. Mostly I felt nostalgic. Our time together seemed more like an era than an affair. The year after him, the world was different. It was the year of annihilation. I'd come to life and then destroyed, one by one, every thought and feeling that was not germane to my responsibilities at home. I put on blinkers. I soldiered on.

Isifrid sent us money each month. She paid for Erlend's care and hired a nurse to live with us. He'd had a stroke, which incapacitated his left side. I read to him and watched television. I was not lonely, per se, but anxious. I was waiting for him to die.

After, I told Isifrid I wanted to move to Paris. She rented me a flat, no questions asked. I lived in the Marais for five years. I read the phone book. In my purse, a map on which I'd charted the location of Daniel's boat, wherever it went. Navy vessels were not hard to track. So even as we'd been parted for years and years, I always knew where he was. And when he retired, I knew he was in France.

What were my intentions, I still don't know. But after I saw him at the embassy, after the sight of him gusted through my body, I understood I no longer had the fortitude to sustain the experience of him in my life. It would kill me, I was sure. I told Isifrid I wanted to move to New York. She made up my room. I knew little about her business or her life, just that she'd married a man of science, which was good.

Despite what I know of the afterlife, I don't think science and spirituality are opposed. Quite the opposite. For instance, while there is no reason to accept intelligent design in lieu of the big bang, there is every reason to embrace reincarnation as the means by which our lives have purpose. Just knowing you'll be back is reason to prepare. I wanted to see Daniel the moment I realized I was dying. If it hastened the hour, so be it. At the very least, when I came back for another go, I would be armed with knowledge of what it means to pursue love until the end.

We ate club sandwiches. His hands shook. I think he missed every other word out of my mouth. I looked at him and I looked at me. And it was the first I'd felt anything in a long time.

Twenty-five

Every gathering has a core guest who thinks she can't possibly outstay her welcome. Tonight we have three: Wanda, Eric, Marcus. The talk is about *Tabu*, which is still in the DVD player. Now that flat-screen TVs double as wall art, a silent movie can turn into ambience real fast. I am decided to watch it again once everyone leaves. I feel like I have new information to unload on my experience of it. Because the thing about love in Bora-Bora—the movie, that is—it mobilizes all this *Golden Bough* stuff to inveigh against the System, which affects the natives and white folk alike. We've got these lovers, primitives, who are denied each other by force of law. She's gotta preserve her virginity for the gods, he's gotta buzz off. The couple flee to an island governed by the White Man, who exploits their naïveté. The boy falls into debt. The girl drinks champagne. Inter-island politics regard the pair as chattel. The boy discovers graft. The girl gets mettle. And the movie, it says the hydra of convention will nail you one way or the other. Lop off the first head with a bribe and a second pops up, saying blah blah ritual, blah blah virgin. I imagine the hydra allegorizes a whole bunch of things besides convention. Like: Betray your vows only to confront the specter of your four little girls back home in Norway. Take up in your beloved's hat company only to discover she's married someone else. Snatch your beloved from his fiancée only to watch him marry your best friend.

I sidle up to Eric and Marcus, who are staring at the screen. "This part kills me," Eric says, just as the boy takes a last look at the ship escaping with his adored.

"Wait, but he *drowns?*" Marcus says. "Why can't he just swim back? Oh, never mind. It's a metaphor. I'm stupid."

"You're not stupid," I say. "It is a metaphor, but maybe not the way you think. Not: I can't live without the love of my life, but: I should die now so that I can reexperience this death by heartbreak and learn from it. That's what Agneth would say, anyway."

Eric looks at me funny. Like my good sense is on the lam and what is this twaddle?

I raise my glass and toast Aggie. I am not certain when I switched to gin, but I think it was a good move.

"To Agneth," Marcus says, though he hardly sounds committed. I'm not even sure why he is still here. Perhaps because we shared our adolescence and there's a camaraderie there you can't erase. Alternately, given the way he's ogling Eric, I'd say camaraderie be damned.

Mother and Wanda are gathered around the coffee table. We convene. Mother asks Jumbo Prawn to join us because she's been on her feet for hours. Wanda has her shoes off. Eric starts telling Marcus about an abandoned missile site he saw for sale on eBay for three mill. It's got an 1,800-gallon septic tank and a two-story silo underground.

Marcus says it'd make a splendid getaway spa. I suggest a night-club. Wanda thinks an amusement park could be good. Isifrid says: Sepulcher.

And with that, we are reminded of the dolor that brought us together. All but Marcus, who just looks lost.

Often, at the close of a recovery meeting, as we make a circle and join hands, I'll note the odds of these people finding each other in this group; our sundry pasts and principles; the entropy that collides addicts like so many molecules. It's nice, that moment. Less nice is when it happens in your own home. Mother, Marcus, Wanda; Stanley, me, Eric, Jumbo Prawn. Not even a rock band would have us grouped together.

Unexpectedly, Wanda stands up. Puts her hands together and says, "Now Izzy, I know today has been hard—hard on everyone—but it's no coincidence you find us all here."

I have no clue what she's on about, but Stanley's shaking his head, saying, "No, Wanda, this is not the time."

Sometimes I forget they've been working together for twenty-some years, that Wanda has tried to *intervene* for Stanley at least twice, that she relishes the opportunity and does not take no for an answer. But really, what sort of opportunity is this?

Isifrid nods, bleakly. She's wearing a pillbox hat and weeping crepe pulled back over her head. She obviously has no idea to what she's just consented. But Wanda will take what she can. She continues: "We're not here to judge you, we just want to help."

Oh, this is bad. It is what I think it is, and it is bad.

Wanda looks at Marcus. "And where do you think you're off to?" He's made a run for it. If only he kept going. As is, she brings him up short and he returns to his seat.

"I, uh, I'm just a friend of Lucy's. Probably I shouldn't be here."

"Are not!" I say, because for a second the association seems risky.

He looks at me, like: Huh?

I've heard this kind of drollery can mitigate a bad situation, but I don't see how. The awkwardness of our group is excruciating.

Stanley takes Wanda by the elbow and leads her across the room. They have words. Words within earshot. They go like this: I know you mean well, but this is really not the time. Or the place. Don't embarrass her in front of strangers. And this: Did I ask your opinion?

Stanley returns to the couch.

Their exchange reminds me of that Pink Panther movie where Inspector Clouseau's valet-lunatic keeps ambushing him at the wrong time. Like the once a century Clouseau gets a woman in bed, here comes that wily tai kwan do butler. It's heartbreaking, really. Thing is, Clouseau keeps saying: This is not the time, this is not the time, when, in fact, this is never the time. Even when he finally says it's the time, it's not the time, as they are at a crowded restaurant, and the butler's in drag. Probably my favorite line in all of cinema: *Beware of Japanese waitress bearing fortune cookie.* So maybe Wanda's got a point. If no time is the right time, then this time is as good as any.

She resumes like a cassette that's been rewound too far. She says: "We're not here to judge you, we just want to help."

Jumbo Prawn pleads kitchen duty. Wanda shuts her down.

I see Eric nod. Nod to what?

Wanda: "We are here as your loved ones who love *you*. And out of love, we want you to go get help."

Marcus looks ready to raise his hand, like: Um, Ms. Deckman, can I go to the bathroom?

Wanda: "Are you listening, Izz? This is serious. This could be your last chance."

And the thing is, she's right. My mother might actually be dying.

Eric, who hasn't said a word since the missile base, tosses his hands in the air. Gets up. Walks around the room with head tilted back, arms skyward. I think this gesture means: Why, God, *why?* but I'm not sure. He addresses the ceiling as if we were not here. He says: "What's wrong with these people? Why am I here with these people? How did I get involved with these people?"

On the one hand, I'm glad he feels sufficiently at home for theatrics. On the other, I'm beginning to doubt how well he'll take Aggie's request to spread her ashes with me.

On the whole, though, we are glad for a diversion. If you can call it that, since the rhetoricals are getting more specific, less: Why am I on this planet, more: What's the fucking point of rehab when we're all going to die?

Wanda: Oh, not that again. An epidemic is no excuse to go hog wild. You're just like one of those looters who'll take advantage of any situation to get new Rollerblades. And besides, we are not all going to die.

Stanley: Did you watch the news today? Every channel but Fox says it's gotten out of California.

Marcus: Can we not talk about this? I can't talk about this!

Eric: Everyone's saying Malthusian this, Malthusian that. But I don't think that's what's going on here. Forget survival of the fittest. Forget restoring the ecological accord between flower and fauna. This plague thing, it's the universe telling us to say: Fuck it. Just bear with me here. In times of crisis, people turn barbaric. They rely on instincts, which are primal. And what I'm saying is that the way we are now, the way we live, it antagonizes the primal. Shuts it up. That's what we spend all our conscious time doing— suppressing the primal. And because we do it so well, Nature has to intervene. So she gives us a plague and says: Now see how well you do, you enlightened and elevated people with your Constitution and your laws, your rehabs and your jails, your strength and insipid pretensions to the moral high ground.

Marcus says, rather quietly: In sum, fuck it?

Eric: That's right! You got it.

Meantime, Wanda has sat down. Intervention on hold.

I say, "So lemme get this straight. Because Nature presents us with a challenge that solicits our baser instincts, she's advising us to fuck it all? To just say, Screw it? What if she's saying: I challenge you and in so doing give you the chance to rise above yourself, to face extinction and to prevail, knowing you stayed true to the principles one thousand years of culture have bored into your brain?"

"Pardon me," says Isifrid, which is a shocker. This whole thing started with her, but who can remember that far back? She sips a cup of tea. Says: "All this talk of Nature is well and good, but very much beside the point."

She sounds so commanding, no one presses her for more except Jumbo Prawn, who's looking really tired of all this shit, and says, "And you are an authority because . . . ?"

I laugh. Thus far, the epidemic is not making people barbaric so much as nasty.

Wanda steps in. "What she means is that your discussion is not practical."

"No," says Mother. "What I mean is that there's some asshole out there poisoning everyone. Not Nature, not God, not Odin."

Marcus says who's Odin?

"A Norse god, you idiot." This from me because if there's gonna be nastiness, I'm in.

Stanley looks at his watch and yawns hugely. Well, would you look at the time.

Wanda has a you've won the battle, not the war look about her that means she'll be back tomorrow. Marcus already has his coat on. Jumbo Prawn is collecting glasses. Only person to make no attempt at the door is Eric.

Twenty-six

You couldn't ignore it: The plague had breached quarantine and was heading southeast. Eric and I watched the news late into the night. Fifteen people had busted through a checkpoint in Sacramento. They were armed and possibly infected, you couldn't know for at least a day or two. The National Guard was ordered to shoot first, question later. The escapees were three families and their children. The children put a face on things. Their pictures were arrayed along highways like pennants at the dealership. You saw them at bus depots and train stations. You got the feeling that every hunter in America was loading his gun.

We were in the yellow room on parallel couches. It was where you went to think in twos. I used to find Mother and Dad in here all the time. You'd lie down and have a catch with whatever food availed itself, usually an orange or a peanut. Tonight we had an orange. The volley is meditative, really, the back and forth. So is the counting.

Eric said, "So are you scared?"

"Yes and no. I can't seem to accept this is actually happening."

"Me, either. Sixty-three."

"I might never accept it until it's in this house."

"You're going to stay here?"

"Aren't you? I haven't really thought about it."

"You should start. Sixty-eight."

"Well, where are you going to go?"

"Kam's parents still have the house. I bet you could come. If it came to that."

The thing about the volley, you're not supposed to take your eye off the orange. This is the only way you can converse freely. As soon as you make eye contact, it's all over.

He sat up. "What? It's not that crazy under the circumstances. All your life you've lived like a child."

"You used to like that about me."

"I used to like a lot of things."

"What else?"

He laughed. I could make a game out of anything. "Let's see. I used to like those winter gloves where if it got really cold, they turned colors."

"Not colors. Didn't they have pictures or something? Like at three below you'd see a Gobot?"

"Don't remember. Also, Buddy Schimelhorn used to steal mine the first day it snowed."

"Ah, Buddy Schimelhorn, where are you now."

"He runs a day camp. Buddy's Wood."

"He does not."

"Nope, it's true."

I returned to the volley position. "That is absurd. Seventy."

"Seventy-one."

Stanley came through the swing door. "What's doing here?"

I said, "You're looking at it."

"Count me in."

He positioned a chair at the foot of the couches so that we made a U.

"Nice work today," Eric said. "About what's her name. Wanda?"

"Can you imagine?" I said. "Trying to have a spontaneous intervention? At a wake? Something's not right about that woman."

"She meant well," Stanley said.

I snorted. Seems like there's always someone around to make you feel schmucky no matter what you say.

"In that case, why not ask *her* to surrogate?"

"Surrogate for what?" Eric said. "Ninety."

"Long story," I said.

"Ninety-three."

"My wife passed away, but froze her eggs."

"Oh. I'm sorry."

"Are you and your wife planning on kids?"

"Stanley!" I nailed him in the chest. The orange, dented, retired at a hundred.

"Okay," he said, standing up. "Guess that's my cue."

We watched him leave.

Eric said, "Are you dating that guy?"

"I wouldn't call it that, no."

"Uh-huh."

I took another orange from the bowl. This one was smaller, more aerodynamic.

"You know," I said, "your to hell with everything theory is worrisome."

"Why?"

"Because it's licensed anarchy."

"It's not. It's carpe diem."

"I don't see you doing anything differently," I said. The bitterness in my voice was impossible to ignore. But he ignored it anyway.

"Six. What's the world record with this?"

"Seven hundred. Me and Hannah, day after my dad died."

"I hear you're going back to rehab. That's good you know. I'm proud of you."

"Am I being patronized?"

"You are impossible."

Eye contact.

"I should be going."

I nodded. Like Marcus, it was, in fact, unclear why he was still at my house. A part of me had hope, which another part snuffed out. In the last couple months I had learned that to love a married man also means wanting to protect him from wrecking his life because of you.

"Kam's in Italy," he said. "Else she would have come."

The hope flared up anew. Look at me, here I am, hello!

"She's producing a fashion shoot at the opera house in Milan."

He said this with pride, which seemed charming until it wasn't. Proud of me for rehab, proud of Kam for her life.

"She's trying to get a lot done because she might be taking a leave in a few months."

"Yeah, well, we all might be taking a leave in a few months."

"Right."

"Listen," I said. "I'm sorry about the phone calls. I was, I dunno, in bad shape for a while there."

"Things are better now?"

I shrugged. "I'm trying. I go to Texas next week. Maybe I'll intercept the plague and do everyone a favor."

"Call me from out there, okay?"

I walked him to the door and thanked him for coming.

"Of course."

"Aggie appreciates it. She's up there, you know."

"Right."

The elevator was on its way. "She asked me to disperse her ashes."

"Really?"

"She asked if you'd do it with me."

He looked skeptical, which made me feel pathetic. And then *more* pathetic. Because the fact was, I loved this person. I was trying, always, to do the right thing, but I loved this person and did not know how to feel otherwise. Also, this was not the farewell I had in mind. More like a kiss that veers right at the last moment.

"No, really. I swear. Why would I make that up?"

"No, no, I believe you. When?"

"When I get back. Good night."

I made to shut the door.

"Lucy, come on. I believe you. It's fine."

"Get home safe," I said, and pecked him on the cheek.

The elevator took him away. I put my ear to the door and listened for it to open eight floors below. I had the stupid idea that if I listened long enough, he'd come back.

After, I checked myself the way you might post–car crash: are you hurt, where and how bad? But it was nothing major, just the nicks and dents your body sustains daily.

Stanley was in my room lying in bed with hands clasped beneath his head.

"What a day," I said. "Move over?"

I put my ear to his chest, then his stomach. I could hear his dinner having a party.

"I've been thinking," he said. Oh, boy. "Maybe I could stay here while you're in Texas?"

"And do what?"

"I don't know."

"Well, it's fine with me. But I don't really call the shots."

"The other thing I was thinking—" Oh, boy. "Maybe you should take your mother with you."

I jerked away from him so fast, you'd think he was sewage. "Are you *kidding*? Me and her in the middle of the desert?!"

"You and your mother in rehab, yes."

"And Hannah?"

"I'll be here."

"Oh, I get it. Ditch me and Izzy and you get the run of the place. Nice, Stanley. Nice try."

"She's dying, you know."

I drooped. "She might not be."

"She needs you. And I think she wants to go."

"She *told* you that?"

"In a way. But anyone can tell she needs you."

"I don't think I can get clean under those circumstances."

He looked me square in the face. "You don't think you can get clean period."

He made a good point. I tried to burrow under his shirt. "What's wrong with me? How can you stand me?"

He sat up on his elbows. "I see through you is all."

I burrowed deeper.

"I'm starting to worry, Luce. People are actually dying from plague. Like many people, not just here and there."

"I know."

"So you have to come back and be here with me."

"I know."

He lay back down and pulled my face from under his shirt. "I have a question for you. And be serious. If the plague really does get here, will you be sorry to die? I mean for real. No jokes."

I smiled. There were few things I liked better than to contemplate my own death. "I don't want to die in agony, if that's what you mean. And I don't want to leave Hannah. But I don't know. I guess I want both. I want to die, but still be here. Like when I fantasize about it, it's not a Tom Sawyer thing where I want to see everyone mourn me and say how great I was. Frankly, who'd even say that? It's more like I want to experience the relief of not being alive, but I can't do that unless I'm alive."

Stanley laughed. "That's one hell of a problem."

I laughed. "Don't I know it."

"I read somewhere that you're not supposed to die without being a little happy first."

"Okay, the bathroom stall is not a source of wisdom you can share with me."

But by then, of course, we had stopped laughing. And I was ready to go.

Twenty-seven

Texas is *brown*. Wherever you look. Not like bouquets of oak and chocolate, not like a brown *bonanza*, just a deployment of tones, each more drab than the next. Out the airplane, it's acres of brown and dead stuff. Trees and brush. Here at the airport, it's brown plus kids with guns. Army kids in oatmeal vests. I try to give them a wide berth, though they are everywhere. Now that a toddler bearing plague is the nation's public enemy number one, I am feeling more threatened by men with guns than ever. Kids with guns, I'm not so sure. Likely they are worse. Surely in Texas, they are worse. I have prejudices about the South that embarrass me, but not so much that I want to give them up.

We head to the baggage claim, and I try to keep a low profile. Turns out by *try* I mean *fail*. I am with Mother after all. I still can't believe she wanted to come. I can't believe I asked. We are booked for a whole month and already she's annoying. That cadet on his cell phone? He doesn't want to talk to her. Likewise the soldier kid humping his duffel. I grab her arm and say, "Stop it."

We were supposed to be met at the gate by a counselor from Bluebonnet, but I don't see him. Just as well since right off the plane, Mother split for the bathroom, where I know she's rubbing coke. Couldn't even wait to parse a line. I imagine the logic is that if anyone opens her stall, they'll find her with fingers between her legs, which just isn't so weird in a bathroom stall. I've done that before, the mucous membrane thing, because the twinning of drugs and orgasm is good.

Experience has just borne out the following rumor: It's ten times easier to fly with coke than grass. Pop it in a compact and be on

your way. Overnight the rest to a local P.O. Mother's going to rehab, but with zero interest in the rehab part. I think she just got
scared at the exact moment I was leaving, and by the time she
recommitted herself to a life of soul-sapping malaise and suicidal
ideation, it was too late; we were here.

I am, perhaps, no less ambivalent. I came willingly enough,
though I don't have much interest in the rehab part, either. Well,
some interest, which, in terms of things I want to accomplish before
I die, values rehab alongside sky diving and children.

We spot our counselor eating a Nutter Butter sandwich cookie
and browsing the magazine rack at a newsstand. His name is
Robert, and he's not helping with our luggage. He does mention a
town car. And that there's plenty of bottled water for the trip. I
have brought one suitcase, Mother has four. Mine is mostly filled
with her stuff.

Robert's town car is more like a flatbed with room in the cab for
two, three if you squeeze.

Mother says, "You're kidding, yes?"

He says no. Also: something something short a car, something
something mother daughter cozy.

I opt to sit in the truck bed. Texas sky, open road, no problem.
And in fact, it's no problem. So that I don't fly overboard, I get on
my back and splay legs. Besides the cow-patty stench of whatever
normally gets freighted back here, it's fine. Especially the wind,
which is so loud and ambient, it seems to take up residency in my
head and crowd out all my thoughts.

We get to Bluebonnet in three hours. It looks like a single-story
roadside motel, only there's no road for fifty miles in any direction.
Even the road we take is not much of a road. More like a gravel
drive that veers off the highway and ends in a cul-de-sac. When we
arrive, a woman in tailored slacks suit, gray-green, is waiting for us
outside. She's got a clipboard. Her heels kick up dust that cottons
to the hem of her pants. I'm unclear why you'd wear a suit in the
desert, but then Aggie did say we'd be among a diverse and affluent
clientele who probably respond better to Versace than chaps.

The clipboard's name is Susan. She's been assigned to our case.
Our case? Like there's only one? Because, I tell her, we are definitely two.

"Actually," she says, "here at Bluebonnet we put a premium on family and think team recovery, especially in the family, works quite well. Don't worry."

She has gathered half her hair into a ponytail trussed with a ruby barrette. This gives her the appearance of a cheerleader circa 1950 or a prostitute circa now. The way she's looking at me, though, I get the sense I'm not stealing any hearts, either. I ask Mother to confirm. She says I look like a tornado blew through my grill.

We all get in a van and head farther into the desert, where, lo and behold, there's another roadside motel, U-shaped around an empty swimming pool qua terrarium qua morgue. Like those turtles will ever get out.

Susan says, "You are in adjoining rooms, F-10 and 11. You'll find a binder with a schedule. Here are the keys. For now, just wash up and we'll see you at dinner."

Off goes the buggy, which leaves me and Mother stranded. In the desert.

We part. My room's the size of a luxury Port-o-Potty. Maybe two. It lacks for amenities. No clock radio. The bedside lamp needs a bulb. Water trickles from the faucet, the drain's got a rust aureole. On the plus side, there's sconce lighting above my bed, frosted glass. Wall-to-wall carpeting, ochre pile. There's rehab literature in every drawer. The pages are thumbed and soft. I have dread of literature as public facility because I am always thinking someone has ejaculated into the pages. So far, though, I have yet to meet with this problem.

Mother opens the door that connects our rooms. She looks panicked. "There's no TV," she says. "What am I supposed to do without a TV?"

"I don't know. Sober up, maybe?"

She slams the door, which appears to lock from her side only.

I call Eric and get his voice mail. I say: Everything's going *just fine*. Then I draw the curtains. Under guise of creating an atmosphere of recovery, this view—desert, desert, mountain, desert—simply deters escape. I'd be parched and sunstroked within ten minutes out there.

On closer inspection, my bed, a single, turns out to be an air mattress on a box frame. I wonder if this is because bedsprings make for a nice weapon. Then I remember we're not in jail, so what the hell? The duvet cover is burlap. The walls are self-adhering strips of floral laminate. Shelf liner, perhaps. No way is this place for the rich and famous. Aggie was duped. I can see how it happened, like maybe Susan is the house shill who's got the desert pitch down. She's certainly not your average recovery bear. She's too suave. Maybe she used to be one of those tony escort girls whose death by stretch mark brought her here. Maybe she has actorly ambitions to restore a star and land the part. Probably, though, she's just a decent woman with a shitty job.

Thus far, we've yet to be frisked. Our bags are untouched and my supply is safe. But I hardly feel calm. I'm sure they've got people who ransack the rooms while we're in group. And I'm sure someone is going to feel me up shortly. This means stashing *and* carrying are risky. Used to be I could peg the staffer of loose morals in about a day or so, but now—and maybe age is to blame—I'm too lazy. Can't be bothered to make deals or even to investigate an alternative. Mother, on the other hand, has all the energy in the world. She has crawled out her window and is stabbing the earth with a rock. She could have walked around to the back of the building, but I think the window egress gives her a sense of transgression, which might be the only excitement we get for days.

I procure a rock of my own and kneel by her side. There is a chain-gang feel to our labors that gets demolished when she drops her compact of blow into the hole. From rehabs past, I have thongs designed for the purpose of drug trafficking. The one I got on now has a ribbon sewn along the ass in which to store pills like a string of beads. It's not even uncomfortable, kinda nice in fact. But never mind. All but thongs go in the hole. Unfortunately, Mother is not having it. She says, "Get your own hole," and begins to remove my stuff. She does this with the umbrage of siblings who divide their room in half.

I watch her for a minute, then start a hole of my own.

There is no way I can stay here for a month. I will go crazy, I know it.

The binder says we eat at eight in the morning, dine at six, and spend the interim in group after group, with a break for lunch. We have two hours until the buggy comes. There is little else to do but read the literature or nap. I can hear Mother in the other room cursing because her cell phone has no signal. Click goes the lock, and in she comes, beelining for my phone, which I have already buried because personal amenities like phones and iPods are forbidden, unbeknownst to Mother, who's actually gone her entire life without aid of a rehab facility, God bless her.

She rifles through my shoulder bag in such a way as to conceal her efforts, like part of the fun here, this greedy forage through my belongings, is doing it in secret.

"Who do you have to call, anyway?"

"No one. I just like to have it around."

"Use the phone in your room."

She looks at me like I am thick, thick. "There are no phones."

I quiz the room and see she's right. "Oh, jeez. Well, my phone's in the hole. And I'm not getting it."

"Where's your hole?"

"Oh, so now you wanna share holes. Tough shit."

"I've got codeine in the other room." She says this like it's tempting.

"Child's play."

"Lortab?"

I am thinking of Quinty's scrip, which I filled yesterday. OxyNorm, quick-release capsules. A hundred twenty for a month. It's not enough, but it will help. I just might get through Bluebonnet alive.

"I cannot be bribed," I say. "Ginger chew?"

There's a knock at the door. It is Robert. He looks effete in those cowboy boots and CHiPs sunglasses. I didn't think it was possible to look effete in cowboy boots unless that's all you're wearing. He seems about twenty-two and none too pleased to be here.

"I'm Robert. We met before."

"I'm a drug addict, not a retard," I say. "Ginger chew?"

He's got a clipboard of his own and appears to be scanning it for permission to accept the chew.

We're standing in a circle. I got my hands in my back pockets, and am rocking on my heels. My years in rehab outnumber his, ten to one. I suppose he needs a little help.

"History?" I say. "Do you need to take a history?"

"Ah right. Yes. Thank you. Please, sit down." He swipes his fingers through his hair to preserve a side part that's so fixed in the declension of his head, the swipe can only be a tic.

Mother and I poise on the edge of the mattress. It wheezes. Robert takes the wicker chair in the corner. We get through the preliminaries, no problem. Comes time for the details, forget it.

"How would you characterize the extent of your drug use? Mild? Moderate? Excessive?"

Mother says, "I dabble."

I say, "I dabble even less."

She turns to me, aghast. "What are you talking about? You are a zombie. You stagger around the apartment like the undead. You sleep twenty of every twenty-four hours. You slur!"

I look at Robert. My gaze is steady and, I think, reassuring. "I dabble," I say.

"Your booking agent said you're here for downers. Is that correct?"

Mother laughs. "Her booking agent?"

I laugh, too. The more I think of Agneth, the more incredible she seems. Posing as my booking agent. Posing to impress a rehab that is itself posing as a celebrity sanctum.

"That's what I got here," he says, tapping the clipboard with his pen. Followed by the swipe. So the swipe is nerves. I see. If we ever get to playing poker, I got him nailed.

I shake my head with the thought. Robert looks from me to Izzy and back. I am beginning to feel sorry for him. This might be his second day on the job. Given the condition of his hands—soft and manicured—I'm thinking ranch intern just wasn't his beat. Oilman, neither.

"How would you quantify *dabble?*" he asks Mother.

I step in. "Good question. It's like when they say a pinch of salt in a recipe for Cornish Christmas puddin'—who knows what that means?"

Robert continues to stare at Mother.

"I don't know," she says. "Ask her."

"Why thank you. Robert, my mother has a hard-core crack addiction. I'd say she binges at least once a week, will substitute most any drug if need be, and can blow through your salary's worth of coke in an hour."

He checks off several boxes, says, "Okay, good," and flips to the next page. Swipe.

Mother empties two sugar packets in her mouth. Then she opens them along the seams and licks the inside. At home, decorum rules, but here in the desert—

Robert says to me, "And about how much Valium do you take a day?"

"I don't know. Am I supposed to know? I just keep taking them until they work."

"Are they blue, yellow, or white?"

"Blue."

"And are you taking anything else regularly?"

"What's regularly?"

"At least once a day."

"Oh, of course. OxyContin, Vicodin, Celebrex, *Lortab*," which I say for Mother's benefit, "Talwin, though it sucks, Demerol, and, uh, Dexatrim."

Mother says, "Dexatrim! That stuff's bad for you."

Robert says, "You take all that every day?"

I blush. This is a kind of pride. "I mix and match."

"Do you have a history of eating disorders?"

"No. I'm not fat so long as I take my Dexatrim."

He nods, writes it down. He's already got three pages of notes. I feel like the notes are bad, like we made a bad impression, and now it's on file.

"Want some iced tea?" I ask. "I can make it in the bathroom, brought my own mix and everything."

He says private foodstuffs are not allowed and would I please hand them over.

I make like he's kidding, which might get him embarrassed enough about the rules to forget this one. Instead he takes a plastic grocery bag from his pocket and holds it open. In go my Country Time tubs of peach iced tea mix, a snack bag of Cheetos, and several packages of Wasa crispbread.

"And the chews?" he says.

Mother gasps derisively. "Not the chews!"

I shake my head and say, "You know, Robert, you do not exactly redound to my well-being."

He makes a note of something, then excuses himself, says we will reconvene after dinner.

"Reconvene? With you? How enchanting," Mother says.

But Robert is done. We are well afield of whatever he's been told to expect, and now I have regrets. I say I'm sorry, and that we're not so bad. He jams his thumbs in the demipockets of his jeans and says, "No big whup. Liza Minnelli, Judy what's her face—I heard of family situations like this."

Judy what's her face? Good God. I slam the door behind him. "What a jerk," I say. "I hate this place."

Mother gets on her bed, prostrate, with hands folded under her chin. I adopt the same position and in this way, we can see each other without having to leave our rooms.

"Don't be obnoxious. He seemed nice."

"That's because he didn't confiscate your drugs."

"*Shhhh.*"

I roll over onto my back. There's gum on the ceiling. And an eraser impaled on the crests of impasto paint. I am just thinking about what I can add to the collage when from outside comes the blare of a horn that won't quit.

I watch Mother toss a velour wrap around her shoulders. I'm still waiting for the day she takes flight in one of those things. Or *we* take flight, since I forgot to pack a sweater and now have to sport a wrap of my own. She offers me something black. So, black it is.

"Come, dear," she says. "It's time for *group.*"

Twenty-eight

In the cafeteria, one of the counselors had his son over for the day. Kid was about one, not too keen on strangers. He was wearing red sweats and bomber jacket. His dad, Bruce, was more Lumberjack, in thermal shirt and beanie. He was prancing around the tables with the kid on his hip. It was our second day there. I'd made no overtures to the other inmates, who, it turned out, were women. A women's rehab. Mother took it worse than me. She hates women. As a result, we were sitting alone, which was not allowed. The dad, Bruce, came over. Plunked his kid on the table. And the kid, he was adorable, so fat you couldn't find his joints. Bruce, it turned out, didn't give a shit about us and our isolation, he just wanted to hang out with his son. I did not take it well. The kid said, "Qwhy," which had Bruce praising him to the moon. Never mind that I was actually crying or that Bruce was there to counsel me.

I stared ahead, and had my thoughts. I want a child! I want a husband with low-rider jeans, a thermal, beanie, and half a day's growth of beard! I want a baby!

The bell rang. Bruce stood and said, "Hang in there, Lucy." Then he waved his son's hand and went, "Say bye-bye!"

I waved back. But it was more like farewell. Farewell from the *Achille Lauro*. Farewell with love. Mother took my sleeve and said, "Snap out of it."

We went to *group*. We wore our capes.

Inside, we were seven, but since two of the women were called Dee, it took some of the pressure off. I can never remember people's names and I think it's because I do not listen when they introduce themselves. I figure I'm not going to see this person again, only I do, inevitably I do, at which point I realize that I never know how to evaluate incoming information. It's like how in school you were always wondering if this was going to be on the test. Your teacher could be telling you about segregation and the KKK, but if it wasn't gonna be on the test, let 'em hang.

Our group leader was Susan, which had me wondering about whether this place had any disposable income. Everyone seemed to have six jobs. I'm pretty sure I saw the cook doling out meds in the infirmary. Susan had traded her suit for gymwear, which meant she probably taught the four o'clock yoga class, as well. Her hair, however, was still secured in that barrette. So either the clip was a crutch or doubled as a shank for when the ladies got raw.

We were in a library whose offerings were Julia Child, *The Grapes of Wrath*, and self-help workbooks that ranged from Buddhist to neocon. The carpet was tan sisal, the chairs industrial plastic. We sat in a circle. Did anyone have a topic they wanted to discuss? All hands up. A topic related to addiction? Hands down. Susan looked distressed. "Should I remind you that we are here to recover? I am authorized to suspend radio privileges, you know. We need to stay focused."

Radio? Izzy and I didn't have a radio. I sensed a hierarchy and raised my hand. I gathered that here at Bluebonnet, news of the outside world trickled in slowly, if at all, but if some were getting it, all should get it.

Susan said the radio was in the lounge adjoining the cafeteria, as described in the welcome packet in my room.

I said, "Who decides what station?"

She said, "Don't be tedious."

We left it there. I was starting to like Susan a whole lot.

Hand up. "Cecilia, yes."

We all turned to Cecilia. Could she possibly be as old as she looked? Who goes to rehab at eighty-five? She cleared her throat. Her head was so sunk into her chest, you forgot she even had a throat. "I think," she said, "about what you said yesterday, I think superplague is more relevant than you made it out to be. We are here to recuperate hope, yes? To think our lives are worth living? Isn't the threat of holocaust germane to these efforts? Isn't it adolescent, even irresponsible, to pretend it's not? We are, after all, in the line of fire."

I asked what did she mean. Last I heard, a few people had escaped California. Cecilia pawed deep in her satchel to produce an article she'd clipped from the newspaper about a local manufacturer of body bags and mortuary garments scrambling to fill a giant order from the governor's office.

I understood the point here, but got distracted by the idea of the mortuary garment. Vinyl hoods, booties, and gloves for when your parts sever ties with the rest of you. I expect these are useful in countries that favor machete death—the Congo, for instance—but is there really enough demand in the U.S. to warrant mass production? Of mortuary garments?

"The order was confidential," Cecilia said. "But now that the story leaked, the governor insists it's just a routine precaution. What hooey. They ordered thousands of bags because they expect thousands will die."

Everyone looked at Cecilia like: Who made you God?

Another hand up. "Gale, yes."

"I just want to point out, also, that our new guests, as you called them"—and here she looked at us—"Isabelle and Lucy? That they are pretty connected to the plague thing, I've seen them on TV, not that I give a rat's ass because if I did, I'd be feeling way more alive than I do, but since you keep telling us to hide nothing and speak our minds, I thought I'd bring everyone else up to speed."

So much for anonymity. I watched a caterpillar traverse the sisal. I tried to keep my head down and not notice Mother's arm, flung up high and waving.

"Isifrid, okay, but then we will be moving on to a topic of my choice."

"Thank you, Susan." She sounded like a reporter on scene. "If there is to be a holocaust, even if initiated by a man of singular evil, it is for the express purpose of hastening Ragnarook, the End, to which I have been looking forward my entire life and about which I will brook no criticism in these my last weeks or hours, the most solacing time for a person whose soul is promised return in the new world—redolent, glorious, happy."

Dees one and two conferred, lip to ear, until they had consensus, which seemed to be amusement, for they smiled at Mother and crossed legs, followed by one, who sang into the floor lyrics from an Eagles song in which there is much wooo-hooing for fear of the succubus who turns your skin red. Witchy woman. Ha.

Penelope, who'd yet to say a word, opened her mouth wide, wider than any mouth should open, and laughed in raspy heaves, all while slapping her thigh and plugging her tracheotomy tube with a finger.

Susan asked for quiet. She suggested we move on. And that we talk about the obsession to use. The whys of our drug addiction. We started with Gale, who looked midforties, pale and thin. Orange. Orange hair that came down in sheets, and whose tint intensified the pallor of her face, which was drawn into a tight frown so that all her features appeared to taper and aim for a spot somewhere just past her nose.

She sat forward and braced her elbows on her knees, chin in hand. "Oh, I don't know. I guess I started on crank because that's what the other drivers did to stay awake. Trucking is a lonely job, especially for a woman, so at least I wanted to be making good money, which meant making good time and all that. Problem was, at some point I got really into my truck. I was cleaning it all the time. I dismantled the engine at least once a week. And the driving, the way it got the engine dirty, it started to make me crazy. So I'd take more crank to stay up even longer so I could clean the engine. Eventually, I spent more time cleaning than driving, and I lost my job and went into production for myself."

Here she held up her left hand, which I had not noticed before, but which was bandaged in gauze so that it looked like a giant Q-tip.

"And that's all she wrote, I guess."

Susan said, "Okay, Gale, but do you know why you continued to take methamphetamine after you stopped driving? Seems like you didn't have to keep long hours anymore."

"Oh for God's sakes," I said. "Because she was addicted. Don't you need a degree or something?"

"Thank you, Lucy. We'll get to you shortly."

Gale zipped up her sweatshirt and shoved the Q-tip in her pocket. "I don't know," she said. "I felt too depressed without it. A year before I got canned, when I got back from a run to Sonoma County, my husband was gone. No note, nothing. I'd only been away two weeks. I thought we were happy. Turns out he split with a hooker. Can you believe it? A hooker who wants out meets a man who's ready to save anyone so long as she's got pussy to spare."

"Well piss on him," said Dee one.

Penelope: wheezing.

Cecilia, in drawl: "You said it."

"But mostly, I felt alone. I've always felt alone. I mean when you think about it, what kind of woman wants to be a trucker? I never really had a community, friends I felt comfortable around. And I think my husband just got off on the whole thing. Probably thought this heifer redhead would boss him around and cuff his nuts to the bedpost. I wasn't always this thin, you know. Anyway, I started producing my own stuff because I was too shy to go to the clubs, and when I was high and feeling like I could do anything, I forgot I was out to cop. I burned my fingers down to the bone and had to get them amputated. After that, it got too hard to work the lab. And the guys at the bars and stuff, they didn't really want to fuck a woman with this horrible stump. So I started covering it up with gauze, but I guess it doesn't make much difference. I have the virus now. And I'm on so many drugs for that plus antidepressants to help withdrawal, I feel like I'm in some horrible creature's mouth."

Susan nodded, said thanks, and immediately passed us on to Cecilia, the logic being that the accrual of miserable anecdotes beats a slow pondering of each, for the one results in overflow and horror while the other is a term paper.

Cecilia wore a straw hat pulled low, which served no discernible purpose except to shield her eyes from view so that she might be looking at you or out the window, who could say. I was surprised Susan let her wear it in group, but then the woman was eighty-five and how much clout can a yoga teacher–cum–clipboard muster on a day's notice? Cecilia was saying she'd gotten the hat yesterday and that it was her first happiness since coming to this pit, selected by majority rule among her grandchildren, 75 percent of whom said Bluebonnet was the shit, in contrast to the 15 percent who wanted an old folks' home in Key West and the remaining 10 who were too bound up in addictions of their own to vote, but whose proxy (illegally appointed, FYI) thought Bluebonnet was actually a kind of butter and that if they could do butter and recovery in the same place—wait, did the patients *make* the butter, like prisoner widgets?—the world was a marvel and the proxy just a kid, so, sure, whatever, majority rules.

"My husband and I have been retired for ten years," she said. "And we did it right. We sold our house in Maine and bought a motor home. Not one of those low-class campers, mind you, but a luxury motor coach. There's an entire community out there of retirees who travel the States like this. It's quite civilized. Seven-foot ceilings, marble-tiled floors, Ralph Lauren bedding, custom-built cabinets, a quad slide-out for more galley space when we parked—we had it all. Dennis taught me to drive the coach and with practice, I did it well. Oh, it was so much fun. The places we went. But then, after a while, I still don't know what happened. We were visiting a campsite up in Amarillo. Dennis had been talking about it for months, this restaurant where they gave you a free seventy-two-ounce steak if you could eat it within one hour. Dennis said the world record was a little over nine minutes. Can you imagine? Nine minutes to eat a steak the size of a puppy? I told Dennis it'd be like eating a puppy. I had gone to Radcliffe as an undergraduate; I had studied nutrition. He was a land developer from Kansas. We were not exactly bred from the same stock."

I caught Dee two looking at her watch. It was impossible to run out of time in group because we'd always pick up where we left off, but this was of no consolation to Dee, who needed to talk very badly. Meantime, Cecilia had grown quiet. I thought she was reflecting on the acid flare-up Dennis had mistaken for a heart attack, during which flare-up he had panicked and veered off the road, losing two of the three ounces of hide he'd put down, and pitching Cecilia's beloved feline, Tina, against the windshield with such force that she stuck there, in the radial crack, like a hunter's kill mounted for show. But it was not that. Rather, Cecilia had lost her train of thought, not to mention cognizance of her whereabouts, time of year, and the happenstance of her outfit—this straw hat, Nike trainers, and knee-high sheers.

I looked at the others, trying to gauge the degree to which I should be alarmed. But then a bunch of drug addicts are not the best measure of cool under fire, so I looked to Susan, whose expression ciphered marvelously whatever ran through her head, whether Cecilia couldn't remember her name or began to zig heil.

We moved on to Dee one, which seemed to provide Dee two with some relief. Her turn was only a single Dee away.

Susan said, "Don't be shy, Dee. You've done this before. They won't seem like newcomers once you've shared. That is the beauty of sharing, it makes you fast friends. You may not want new friends, but this is beside the point."

Dee had actually said nothing, which meant Susan was conducting this conversation on her own. She was starting to puddle in those sweat pants and hoodie. Sinking low in her chair, losing shape. I bet this job killed her before the year was out.

"Go on," she said. "We're listening."

I thought Dee two might pop a gland for how she was squirming in her seat. Dee one, at last, took a breath and started. "My story's boring," she said. "That's the problem. I went and broke my arm, got set up with a rod they put in there, took some painkillers, and I liked them. But I never did crank or nothing."

"Do not compare," Susan said. "Identify."

I smiled. In every recovery group there's always at least one person who does not think she's addict enough to belong there. This is either a source of pride or self-disgust, though in both cases it is by way of rejecting help.

"Well, all right, but I'm not sure what to say. I been here a week and I still don't know what to say. Painkillers just made me feel less miserable. My daddy abused me all his life until the Lord saw it right to take him away. My stepmother's part hobo, so she took to wandering from place to place and I didn't see her after I was nine. I moved in with a cousin who must have been raised with Daddy because he touched me, too. I never did tell anyone when the time mattered. I never did get pregnant either, which was a blessing until I got married because if you can't bear children with the man who's agreed to take care of you, you aren't worth much."

She leaned back and began to tug on her earlobe. I noticed it was ripped from pierce to rim, like someone had yanked on her earring until it gave. She had brown tinsel hair streaked with gray that parted in the middle and gathered in a ball atop her head. Her face was chiseled and gaunt, but it didn't look natural, as if masculinity was just a defensive measure she had worn so long, it took.

"My husband put me down, said he was gonna leave me for a woman with life between her legs. I said I understood, I wouldn't stop him. Only he didn't leave. He just impregnated someone else and when the baby was born he brought her to our house and said we was going to raise her. From then on, I hardly existed. It was Martha this and Martha that. I could tell from looking at her she belonged to the hairdresser in town, no one else had those blue eyes, and the hairdresser, she just upped and left one day, which was fine with me. We were a family and it was good. I even told John as much, when we were lying in bed, because it had been so long since we were intimate and I figured now that we had Martha it wouldn't disturb him, my infertility, so I got to messing around with him but it was no use. I decided a barren woman cannot rouse a man no more than a wart, so I gave it up. We were a family, like I said. Anyway, next night I had gone to bed early, which might account for why I woke up round midnight because there was no other sound in the house, not even John breathing next to me, which made sense since he wasn't even in bed. I didn't think to call after him, I just tiptoed down the hall and as I did, all the memories from when I was a girl came back at me so violent that when I found John with Martha, and his hand was cupped over her mouth, and her little nightgown was drawn up her chest, I took the first thing I could find and next I know we were tussling and I was biting and clawing and then we struck through the banister and fell off the landing. I heard a terrible crack and didn't much care if it was me or him, except for Martha was screaming from her bed and I had to do something about it.

"By the time John was in the earth and I got my arm fixed, the courts had taken Martha, saying she wasn't mine to begin with, and, I don't know, I guess she's with her mother or in foster care, they wouldn't tell me. Back at home, there was nothing to do, so I took my painkillers and slept and I found I liked the sleep and that I could save money on food if I slept through meals, and if I hadn't been busted by my aunt stealing from the pouch under her mattress, I'd probably still be on that floor, with the shanks that was our banister, sleeping peacefully."

Susan said, "Does that mean you miss the drugs?"

Dee said, "Does the Pope shit?"

In the two seconds that followed, I realized I'd begun to feel very bad. These were not nice stories. These people were on their last legs. If they did not get clean here, probably they would die. Meantime, I had to pee. All of a sudden. I was even starting to feel incontinent. Overflow and horror is right. I glanced at Susan, whose carriage was like wet socks on the line. I nodded, glad for this moment of camaraderie because it's stupid to vilify the counselor just because you feel bad. She stood and said, "I think now is a good time to break for lunch. Be back here in forty-five."

Dee two was ready to blow. And her impatience was catching. There wasn't enough time to get back to my hole for replenishing, which meant I would have to deal on my own. Mother, of course, was worse. She had her nasty face on, which meant she not only thought everyone was on the verge of doing her harm, she also imagined they had done so already. I took her arm and made for the cafeteria.

We ate mac and cheese. We sat at our private table and this time we were not disturbed. People recognized that look on Mother's face because they'd had it, too.

I said, "Pretty hard-core, those women."

Grunt.

"Warnings, I guess."

She stabbed at her macaroni with a fork, trying to load each tine full.

"Not that our experiences can't claim the same heartache and degradation."

Grunt.

"Or that every drug addict's story doesn't reduce to the principle of take for the ache. I mean, here we are in the middle of nowhere though we might as well be in the city for how different it is. Maybe it's like how you hear the same music played all over the world. Even in Uzbekistan, you can probably catch Madonna or Bono. Possibly this has everything to do with the hegemony of the

West but I think it's more like what that gay guy said in those Harvard lectures, how when you call out to your mom, no matter what language, you always cry out the same two notes, likewise when one kid teases another—*nyeah, nyeah*—it's always the same music, so that even as diversity abounds in our universe, we continue to abuse the same refrain. Take for the ache, you know?"

She looked up from her bowl. "We are the world, we are the children."

"Oh, shut up."

Grunt.

It was time to go back.

During lunch, Susan had raked all her hair into the clip and gelled the migrant pieces around her ears. She was drawn up so tight, you could strop knives where once was her face. She looked like a performer at the start of Act II, where the lead seems restored to fire after the exertions of Act I, though the effects are cosmetic. Any second, she was gonna look ten times the wasted rehab Samaritan she had been before.

Cecilia raised her hand. She'd traded the hat for a headscarf, which tied under her chin. I wondered if her room was in the main building and not out in the barracks. The scarf complemented her overall frailty so that when she began to address us as her students, as if she were our teacher, you just wanted to indulge her any way you could. Unless you were Susan, for whom hallucination came at the expense of the group, or Dee two, who'd had just about enough. She turned on Cecilia like she might slap her and said, "You've had your turn, kindly be quiet."

Cecilia brought her hand to her mouth as if perhaps she'd let out a little belch and said, "Oh, dear." Her eyes darted across the room. "Oh, dear."

Gale squatted at Cecilia's knee and said, "Don't mind her, Ms. Broome. She's having a bad day and you are still the best teacher we ever had."

At this, Cecilia relaxed and patted her shoulder. Gale returned to her seat but not before shooting Dee two a look of such hatred, I thought I'd wither just from being in the vicinity.

Dee one, who sat next to me, leaned over. I guess I looked bewildered. She said, "It's not Alzheimer's. She's gone batty because of the tranqs and sleeping pills. I guess if you're old and take too much of that stuff, you go demented. Sad, right? She's got insomnia."

I nodded, though *sad* hardly covered it.

Susan said, "Okay, Deirdre, you've got the floor."

Deirdre?

Dee one picked up on my thoughts there, too. "She's Deirdre, I'm Dee-Ann."

This was the most confusing rehab ever.

"Thank you," said Dee two. "I'm glad the *why* of drug use is today's topic because I struggle with this a lot. My therapist says I need to get to know myself, that I should go about it the same way as if I were making a new friend. So I'm supposed to put to myself lots of basic questions. 'Why did you use drugs?' is usually at the top of my list."

She was wearing makeup. Pink lipstick that did nothing for the teak-and-olive color scheme of her face. She wore novelty earrings—miniature mugs—and a gold fish around her neck because she was a Pisces. I could not imagine what she and Dee one had in common aside from a diminishing sobriquet, but it seemed they were for each other what left is to right. She crossed her legs at the ankle and sat erect with hands folded in her lap. I was thinking a Sears photographer would have had a field day with her.

She blew the bangs out of her eyes. The sheen of her forehead was near reflective. I imagined her skin felt like putty, sorta wet and cool. She was taking deep breaths by way of preparation for her share, which was so long coming, we were primed for it.

"Oh, I can't," said Dee two.

Cecilia got to her feet and said, "You had better start talking right now, you can't just leave us hanging out to dry, how many consolations do you think we get in this horrible place?"

Gale attempted to coax her back to her chair, but as she only had success with Cecilia gone mad, she was told to buzz off by Cecilia sober.

Susan appeared to have turned the group over to self-rule. As if from self-rule comes esprit de corps and not anarchy. She put her hand up for quiet. Everyone looked at Dee two, who was, she swore, ready.

"Okay, okay. Let's see. I want to preface all this by saying I grew up in a loving family, that I had no complaints as a child, and wanted for nothing. So my, my habit, it's absolutely my fault. Nothing triggered it. It's maybe even inexplicable, which is what I was saying before. I don't know. My husband and I have two sons, they are both grown now, one's at Ohio State and the other's at Tufts. Our house was always full of their friends. There was always lots of noise and activity and I was proud, you know, that my house was where people came to be social, that people felt comfortable there. My husband and I were like second parents to a lot of these kids. And when there was trouble, they came to us. Don't think I didn't hold a hand or two at the abortion clinic."

She paused to search Dee one's face for approval because you could never know whom the word *abortion* was going to set off. But it was fine, she got the nod.

"Dick and I, we thought after the kids left we'd sell our house and move to Seattle, where my mother lived. She was getting on in years. And we didn't really see the point in keeping such a big house for just the two of us. Dick would go to the office and suddenly the house would get so quiet. It had always been quiet during the day, but this was different. Maybe because the quiet wasn't an interlude. Anyway, we kept talking about Seattle and looking at houses online and talking to brokers about selling our own house, but somehow, I don't know, the months went by. Dick was busier than ever at work—he had a class action suit against Ford—and I hardly saw him. Most nights I ate alone in front of the TV. But then it was Christmas vacation and Jack and Michael were home. They'd come with a few friends each. And it was like old times. You should have seen these boys. Full of life. With them in the house, I started pulling my hair back again. And wearing more color because Jack said I looked too Romanian in my gray flannels. Dick was so tired from work, he didn't much enjoy the visit. He couldn't take time off, so he was more like a guest than the guests were. He'd come home at one in the morning and find us sitting around the kitchen table, playing poker. The boys would be going through six-packs of beer faster than I could finish a single White Russian. I must have lost three thousand dollars."

She took a sip of water. I noticed her hands shaking in her lap. You got the feeling this story was about to go south.

"On their last night home, I got a little frantic. I had not realized how lonely I was until I had company. I didn't want them to leave. It was irrational, but I was afraid. The house was so big, you heard things. Anyway, that last night we sat around a fire in the living room and roasted marshmallows. I was always trying to take my cues from the boys so as not to overstay my welcome. I was just the mom, after all. But they seemed content to have me there, especially when they were high. Just pot, I thought it was fine. That night my sons were both super tired, and they turned in. Their friends did the same, except Todd, who helped me clean up. I was wearing a robe cinched at the waist. I remember this because it kept opening when I walked. I cleared the ashtrays and tossed the beer bottles, and started to dust. I couldn't stop moving. If I kept moving, the night would not end and I would not be alone. Todd said I looked a little anxious and did I want some grass. My heart was pounding so fast, I thought it would split. He sat me down. He took my wrist and just, I guess he just took over. We smoked joint after joint because it wasn't working for me. Then it did. I remember laughing a lot. And him saying I had a beautiful smile. And me feeling all warm inside, and the next thing he's cupping his hand around my breast. Mind you, I had seen *The Graduate*. I knew this was Mrs. Robinson. But I didn't stop him. I just slid really low on the couch and let him part my legs. He was kissing my stomach and moving down my body and I knew what he was about to do, but I didn't stop him. Dick wasn't keen on that sort of thing and neither was I. But I had smoked some pot for the first time and I was afraid to be alone and Todd had his mouth on me and there was nothing that was going to stop it. And I swear, I had never felt anything better, it was a sensation I could not explain, but which was, I guess, that thing you heard about. I nearly pulled out his hair. I was like some animal. After, I hardly knew what to do. I heard him finish himself off in the bathroom. I wrapped my robe tight, but my legs were jelly and I could not get up.

"The next day, the boys left and as soon as Dick went to work, I went to the public high school to ask about how to buy pot and then to the library to read up on *orgasm*, and then home, where I used the computer to buy things that promised to reproduce the sensation I had with Todd. By the end of the week, I had a large bag of marijuana and a collection of toys that cost four hundred dollars. I smoked and I smoked and I used the toys and all that happened was that I bruised myself and slept a lot. Eventually, once I was too sore to carry on, I gave up on that part of it and just smoked. Every night, then every day and night, then all the time. Eventually Dick found out and said he would leave me if I didn't stop, he had a reputation to keep. So here I am."

Susan said thanks. And that the *why* of Dee's drug abuse was maybe not so hard to figure out. I stood to stretch my legs. Also, I had to go. One more miserable story and I'd strangle someone. I pleaded indigestion. Susan said I could go rest in the infirmary, which was just a room where the nurse-cook, when not nursing or cooking, did crosswords. I told Mother I'd see her later. Grunt. I headed for the infirmary, then walked right past it. It'd be a thirty-minute walk through the desert to get to our barracks, but I figured it was worth it. I didn't quite get the purpose of having to mire myself in so much dismal story. Then again, I was feeling for these people, feeling in general, which, they say, is a door opened. Every feeling a new door.

Twenty-nine

My heels are cracked. By the time I reach our barracks, it feels like I'm soled in thorns. Noticeably, someone has been in my room. It pleases me to think of the intern rifling through my drawers and coming up empty. At least I will have succeeded at something.

While I am still lucid, I recoup my phone, which I am now hiding from Mother in the bathroom. There is voice mail from Eric and a text message from Stanley. Eric says things I cannot understand, except for *USAir* and *come home*. I listen again and again but cannot glean from the static anything that telegraphs subtext. Does he need me? Why? The message is long as song—there is loop and riff—and so adieu, wireless network provider, may the apocalypse befall you and everyone who works for you and their children, too. I listen once more but cannot gauge his tone, which failure has me feeling irate and insane.

I check Stanley's text. It says: *SP in TX, get out now*, which has the dual effect of scaring me about plague but relaxing me about Eric. I want to be missed, I do, very very very very badly do I want to be missed, I want to be loved by this person so furiously that it is often the only thing that animates my day—I want this, but no. Not given what's real in our lives. In *his* life, whose joys are nascent and fragile, and born of things that do not include me.

I release three pills from the tube in my thong, and from my bag retrieve a portable TV, which the underappreciated, trespassing intern should have taken but didn't. The reception is crap, plus I worry Mother might barge in, so I keep the sound down, with one ear trained on the happenings outside, which, far as I can tell, are nothing. I manage to get a Western, a classic in which manifest destiny rationalizes the way John Wayne and pioneer consorts depredate Native American culture. Only some other station keeps cutting in and it's like the flashes from New Year's Eve all over again. There's been more death, this time in New Mexico. An elementary school teacher who lived alone not one hundred miles from here and who apparently had the presence of mind to photograph herself as she got sick. What better way to protest the government's response to plague than to put a face on it? It was like those photos of the battle of Antietam taken before the carnage was swept away. No one in the North had a clue what the Civil War was really like—all that death and gore—until these photographs went on display at a snappy gallery in New York City.

A note on-screen cautions that the following images may be disturbing. In the first, the woman wears a dashiki. She is a practitioner of Eastern religions. She is vibrant and without brassiere. I bet she grew her own marijuana. In the next photo, she is in bed. Gone is the dashiki. And the brio. And all her clothes. The network has fogged over her nipples and pubic hair, as if these are the body parts whose exposure cannot be survived. Her cheeks are tinted sea kelp owing to the depletion of oxygen in her blood. She has a bolus on her neck, which is actually a lymph node swollen with bacteria. Her fingertips are livid in gangrene. There is blood sputum dribbled down her chin.

I look at my own hands and shudder. The avarice with which disease troops through your blood just doesn't cohere with the upshot, which is a body slick and foul, dense like mud, with limbs hard and black as a truncheon. It is so vile as to seem unreal. There is rape and arson and murder and war, but you'd never know it from the way light stalks the trees at dawn.

I turn up the volume. Apparently, two of the plague bandits—that's what we're calling them now—were spotted in West Texas. I do the math: incubation period is about two to four days, which means if they were able to transmit plague, they should be dead themselves. Only they are not dead. And they are close to Bluebonnet. I start to listen more intently, despite John Wayne's redmeat inflection crosscutting with the Asian reporter for KSAT News. Molly Ning is saying we have reason to believe the *bandits* might well be the first asymptomatic hosts. The two anchors do not understand. She elaborates. "They are like grenades only they detonate every time they come into contact with another person, and scientists cannot say how long they will remain contagious." The anchors are silent because the news is staggering—because anyone could have the plague and not know it. And so a new moniker is born: shadowplague. Holy Christ.

I take the batteries out of the TV and throw them in the toilet. I cannot sustain fear. Fear makes me crazy. The only reason I even wanted to come here was to plane fear. To level the terrain of emotion so that nothing trips me up on the path to sobriety. I head for the back window on the balls of my feet and look out to make sure the coast is clear. This is why I do not notice our holes have been violated until I'm already out the window and sitting in the brush. Our holes! Violated! Then I look down the length of the building and notice several such excavations. I can't believe the underappreciated, frangible intern found my drugs. Mother's drugs! I wonder if he works on commission. I wonder if he skims off the top. The intern! How dare he!

I haul ass through the window and race for the drawer, where I left one of my thongs. I can feel the panic creeping up my neck. The odds that plague finds its way here, to this idiot rehab, are very slim. We will be fine. We'll be fine!

I open the drawer, grab thong—no pills. Holy Christ.

I call Eric back, only this time I do not sound so charming. I say I know the *bandits* are in Texas. That I hate this place. I want to go home. I'm scared.

Then I consider calling Hannah. I get as far as punching our number before giving up. If I call, I might start to cry about the intern who stole my drugs. At the very least, I need to hide how little progress I am making. Besides, plague is not in New York, I have no duties there.

The air mattress sneezes under my weight. It's almost a whoop. I hug the burlap throw to my chest and say, "Fuck, fuck."

And then it gets worse. Outside there are coyotes and snakes, cottontail rabbits and armadillos—a whole mess of wildlife I never want to encounter, but which certainly does not include the species responsible for the susurrus I hear, coming close. I've hardly taken any pills, so it can't be I am imagining things. If there are Martians outside my window, well, okay, I am always wanting to make new friends.

Since I am the dumb broad who always gets knocked off first in every horror movie, I step outside with little but a branch to protect me. The sun sets early in winter and the darkness is like pawing through squid ink. My heels burn and I'm not especially graceful, so I stumble and make a ruckus. The whispering stops. I look left, I look right, nothing.

With my luck, the *bandits* are hiding in some bush, waiting to exhale.

The druggie buggy wends up the road. Its headlights mean I won't get slaughtered by whatever's out there. The relief is nice, but quickly displaced by fear of Mother when she finds her hole's been spoiled.

She flounces into my room and collapses in an armchair. "I'm exhausted," she says. "But here, I brought you some dinner rolls."

She might as well have a marsupial pouch for how many rolls turn up in her lap.

"Uh, thanks. I take it I didn't miss much in group?"

"No. Just the woman with the tracheotomy tube. She's a heroin addict. She started *after* throat cancer. Oh, and Susan made off with the radio. The news is too disheartening. So now we are totally cut off. Excuse me."

She retreats to the other room. Politesse always strikes her at the weirdest moments. I'm sitting tense because any second she's gonna look out the window. And the shriek will be awful. I plug my ears, get braced. This lasts for a minute or so. I start to get alarmed. If she's not shrieking, she must be dead. I knock on the connecting door, then let myself in. Well, would you look at that. Mother is doing lines off the dresser.

"Where'd you get that?"

"How stupid do you think I am? A place like this, they always find your hole. Mine was just a decoy."

"Gimme some."

"I think not."

"Give it!"

She relents. I do a line and spread out on her bed. Ten, nine, eight, and things start looking good. I get to believing I can clean up over the next few weeks. That I can lick this thing. Shadow-plague, how absurd, I will go home and start over.

Mother gets in bed next to me. "See that?" she says, and points to the ceiling, whose impasto, like what's in my room, renders the ocean during a storm—capping waves and all that.

"It's ugly, yeah. I could do better."

"No, but you see it?"

"What?"

I stand so that my face is only a few inches from the ceiling. And there it is, written in pencil: *This is not the appex of our lives.*

"You write this?"

"*Apex* with two *p*'s?"

I start jumping on the bed, shouting, *This is not the apex of our lives!*

Mother gets to her feet. "Let's take a walk. I want to walk."

Outside, the moon's on the wane, which leaves the sky flecked with stars. We can see the milk of the Milky Way. I pull off my shoes. And my clothes. The air rips through my hair because I am running.

Being nude in the desert black is not like skinny-dipping, with its uterine appeal. It's more like, Look at me and my kingdom; my chest is percussive, the animals heed me.

I circle Mother at top speed. I have an unflagging spirit and stores of energy that nothing can deplete. When's the last I felt so happy? My options are unlimited. I will get clean. I will feel joy.

I attempt a cartwheel and come down hard on a rock whose edge jabs at the rim of my kneecap. When I stand, the cap feels wobbly, like it's come loose. And I start to laugh, thinking, I have entropic kneecap disease!

"Did you hear that?" Mother says, and grabs my arm.

"How's my knee? It's okay. Thanks for asking."

"*Shhh*, listen."

It's the same sound I heard before only this time I think maybe it's angels come down to love me because I am impassible. My knee is healed. My heart is healed. God asks me to tend the rain.

"I'm getting the fuck out of here," Mother says, and hightails it to her room.

I start skipping to my Lou when the shriek I forgot about snakes through each ear and collides in my head. I race back, if only to shut her up. The sound is so painful, I am ready to smother her face with a pillow.

I vault the window with insufficient regard for my naked body. Tomorrow, I will be one giant lesion with entropic kneecap disease. The shriek continues to ring in my ears, so it takes a few seconds to notice it's stopped. Stopped a while ago. I open the door to her room. She waves and says, "Hey, Luce." And the people next to her—a young couple, *strangers*—look away like I'm the odd duck here.

I reach for a bathrobe hanging from Mother's door. The pattern is green and reticulate—I am foliage from the knee up.

"Yeah, hi," I say. "So who are you people?"

Mother frowns. "Don't be rude, Lucy. This is J.C. and Samantha."

"And Luke," Samantha says, patting her stomach, which is distended. "You can call me Sam." She looks about eighteen. They are both seated on Mother's bed, leaning against the wall. Around her shoulders is a varsity jacket. He's got pomade in his hair. I am waiting for Eisenhower to peek through our keyhole.

"Uh-huh. Well, welcome. What brings you to a rehab in the middle of nowhere? This can't be part of your high school curriculum."

Mother smacks my leg. "God, you are so rude." And then, to the prom teens, "Don't mind her at all."

Sam's a brunette stippled blond. She's wearing a paisley headband that recedes her hair enough to expose a dime of skin above her cheekbone, color plum.

J.C. takes her hand and says, "We were looking for a place to wait things out. Someplace safe for the baby." He nods in the direction of two backpacks stashed under the desk.

"To wait what out?"

They exchange a look like: Indulge the junkie, be patient.

Mother says, "The plague, sweetheart. The escapees—"

"Bandits."

"The *bandits* are in Texas."

"Somewhere in the desert," Sam adds. "I got scared. We don't have any family."

J.C. brings her hand to his lips. "I kept telling her not to watch TV, but she insisted. Has to know everything." He says this with a smile, with pride, despite the unfortunate consequence of her fear turned flight.

"So you came here to *hide?*"

Sam nods and rubs at the mark on her face with the heel of her palm. "Did you see the woman who just died?"

J.C., who bites his nails, obviously wants to liberate Sam from neuroses of her own. He says, "Don't do that, honey," and returns her hand to his. And then, to me, "Sam got upset about the photos. I can't believe they showed that on TV."

I pinch my eyes shut, trying not to recall the woman, which is like trying to forget your own name.

Mother says, wistfully, "Thank God I missed it."

I tell them about my TV and the lustral experience of having drowned the batteries.

Mother says, "Are you nuts?" and dashes for the toilet, calling me names along the way.

Sam suggests it might be better for us to stay abreast.

J.C. says, "In any case, we figured Bluebonnet was pretty remote and not likely to take in people who don't have, um, a reservation. Plus you got a cook and a nurse and stuff."

Mother is asking if she's going to get electrocuted from wet batteries in a portable TV. Sam says she's got a blow-dryer, if that would help.

"Do you realize this is a rehab?" I say. "I wouldn't bring my unborn baby to a rehab for anything."

"Good thing you're not *pregnant*," Sam says, and turns away. J.C. strokes her hair. Mother shakes her head like I am the most heartless creature on earth.

Yeah, good thing I'm not pregnant. I sit down and think how much easier everything seems when you have a partner.

"Are people really panicking out there?" I ask.

J.C. says yes. And that it's getting a little hairy because everyone is trying to find a place to hunker down where the plague bandits won't go, which means the ranchers have turned border patrol because they don't want anyone seeking refuge with them.

At this point, Sam attempts to withdraw J.C.'s thumbnail from the vise of his front teeth. The gesture is met with rebellion, and he slaps her hand away. She looks stricken. By way of apology, he locks his fingers in his lap.

Mother says, "But they are only two people. We're in a state of lockdown because of two people? You can't even hide in the desert. Just look at it out there. I can probably see all the way to Mexico."

I shake my head and roll out mitosis theory to explain how one person infects three who infect six and nine and nine million and how of them maybe none dies or everyone dies or just some die, so as far as we know, half of Texas is carrying already.

Sam says nothing. J.C.'s retracting the cuticle on his index and stripping the catch. Mother retires to the bathroom to cut lines.

"They shooting people?"

I say this sarcastically, but the response is dead serious.

"Not yet."

"Oh, Jesus. This is insanity."

Mother reappears, leaning against the doorframe with one arm skyward. I think she might be posing.

Sam asks me if she's okay.

"Not really, no."

"What's wrong?"

I laugh. J.C. pinches her arm. "It's not really our business," he says.

"No, it's fine. She's a crackhead."

Sam says, "Nuh-uh. I thought crackheads were black. And lived in the slums."

"Not this one," I say.

"And she's your mother? You're a mother-daughter team in re-hab? I think that's sweet."

I nod. "*And* we're for hire. You know, kids' birthday parties. Bar mitzvahs."

Sam says, "That's awful," and hugs her stomach as if to protect the baby from my aura. I look away. Plague is imminent, but in the meantime let's defend against my self-contempt, which is so viru-lent, it smites the unborn.

"So lemme get this straight," I say. "You want to stay in our rooms indefinitely and we should, like, bring you food and stuff?"

"That would be great," J.C. says.

"We don't have family," Sam adds, as if I missed it before. As if the salience of being alone rationalizes everything.

"Except Luke here," J.C. says, and pats her belly. I notice the smile between them and it depresses me no end. My life really does suck. No, wait. Life is fine, I suck. I'll never be like this couple. When I was eighteen, I was already fixated on subway tracks, how I'd like to sit on the tracks and wait. I could never throw myself before a speeding train, but surely I could wait for one to come along.

Mother is lolling her head against the wall.

Sam wants to know if she's dangerous. I say only if she runs out of drugs. J.C. asks the obvious question and I say, "Well, look, you can't just clean up because someone sends you to rehab."

"My dad was a drinker for years until he found God," Sam says. "After that, he'd start and end every day with the Lord's Prayer."

J.C. has clearly heard this story before. He looks out the window and I notice he's got ears like coins jutting from his head. I have never seen ears so independent of skull. I wonder if he has extraordinary hearing.

I suggest we turn in. J.C. and Sam opt to sleep in my room. I make a crib of burlap for them on the floor. Amazing how fast an incredible situation becomes rote. All you need is a toothbrush or hand towel. I wonder if it was like that for the people hiding Anne Frank. I turn off the light. J.C. and Sam spoon. He puts his palm on her stomach and says good night to them both.

Thirty

Next day, Mother was a wreck. She'd been snorting coke all night to compensate for lack of crack. She was also upset the prom teens had slept in my room, not hers. She said, "I found them first, you know." As codicil to why she was depressed, she mentioned last night's rune casting, which ended with *uruz*: weakness, sickness, death.

I am on the benzodiazepine wean, which means I'm pissy all day, too. I should be grateful there even is a wean—courtesy the cook-nurse—else I might have a seizure and bite off my own tongue. I'm not into that at all. I'd be like Lavinia in *Titus Andronicus*, minus someone to avenge the rape of my loins. As is, cook-nurse metes out pills, humbles dose, and no one loses a tongue, whose cognate, apropos nothing, is an octopus arm, which, now that I know, has me creeped out about my own tongue, but newly enthused about everyone else's.

We went to breakfast. My scrambled eggs looked like moon rocks. I pocketed some honey buns for J.C. and Sam, a dented orange, and a tub of peach jelly. Mother rolled her eyes. "The girl needs *nutrition*," she said, and scooped her eggs into a napkin.

Two women I didn't know joined our table. Mother was so busy purloining the ham she forgot to put on her shun-me face. The women were Margaret and Sandra. They were in their forties, maybe, it was hard to say. Most addicts verge on decrepitude well ahead of schedule, so it's wise to strip five to ten years off the gloss. They had been here nine months. One kicked horse tranquilizer. The other, coke. When they shook my hand, it felt disingenuous, like when your mobster buddy gives you a hug just before you get whacked. Also, they were of some dense matter, both of them. Like Polish charwomen. All gam and cankle, which portmanteau I learned at my last rehab because of the Olympic weight-lifter lady who came in lacking for the appearance of connective hubs between, well, calf and ankle. I guess she had forists, too.

Margaret and Sandra asked our names and clean dates. Mother said, "What's that?" I said, "I'm in detox." They nodded. I began to detect mutual simulacra in their hairstyles, as if each were trying to copy the other, but failing. They wore it short and packed, though Margaret's came at her face like some unruly bush while Sandra's attempted to quit her skull like men overboard. They were both gray at the roots.

Margaret said she was staying in F-7, which was not too far from me, so if I ever wanted to stop by. Sandra said, "Me, too." Turns out they were sisters. Sisters in rehab. I guess Susan wasn't kidding when she said Bluebonnet prized family.

We tarried at breakfast. Today was Mother's turn to share at group, and I didn't think I could stand it. Also, the rehab sisters were fun. Of chief interest to them both was the money they'd saved by being clean. It was earmarked for plastic surgery—farewell dewlap for Margaret, snip and lift for Sandra. I never thought of clean-time money as a *kind* of money, but then I had never had it, so what did I know.

Margaret checked her watch and groaned. They were expected in town as part of the resocializing program, which got them jobs at the dollar store. Margaret cashiered. Sandra made announcements over a PA. The druggie buggy was idling outside. The driver, Dan, who'd had to wake up at four a.m. just to get here on time, was probably working out a pension-to-nuisance ratio, and figuring this job was not worth it.

The ladies stood, and only then did I notice their aprons, vertical mint candy-cane stripes, and that plastic surgery was probably a good call for them both.

Margaret asked if we were going back to our rooms anytime soon.

"After *group*," I said.

They exchanged a look. All these women and their looks.

"Listen," Sandra said, and sat back down.

I felt a secret coming on. So did Mother. She looked almost in-terested. We all four leaned in, making a tent of heads.

Margaret produced a bag of food shanghaied from the kitchen. Mostly staples. Roughage in a can. Dried fruit. She said, "Any chance you can bring this to my room?"

Mother sat back, disappointed. "You got a bunny or some-thing?"

I socked her in the arm. These were our new friends. You can't offend new friends in rehab. It is a bit like jail in that regard. There are factions. And smugglers. And a chain of command.

As if reading my thoughts, Mother said, "Don't be ridiculous."

Margaret asked us back into the huddle. "Have you been able to follow the news at all since getting here?"

My jaw dropped. "You can't be serious. You have refugees, too?"

"*Too?*" Sandra said.

Mother nodded. "We have a couple stashed in *her* room."

She said this like my room had spores.

"Who's in your place?" I asked.

"We have five, if you can believe it. Single mom, her father, and her three kids."

"This is totally insane," I said. "Is this really happening? We are turning into Hotel Rwanda. And all because there are a few people running around Texas who may or may not have plague?"

"Superplague," Margaret said.

"Shadowplague," Sandra added. And then, "We didn't make the rules. And if I were out there, I might be doing the same thing."

Out there. I couldn't believe that's what she was calling it. In recovery, *out there* is where people relapse. *Out there* is a horror. It is everything we hope to leave behind. The cretinous things we do to score drugs, finance drugs, hide drugs. I can't even name all the people I've raked over. The lies I've told. Getting clean is not about leaching Xanax from your blood; it's about getting the hell out of *out there*. Only now, the phrase had taken on a whole new meaning. Now, *out there* was just a place where everyone lived and behaved like us, minus the stigma. They might say: I am simply protecting my family. Or: I will screw you over a thousand times if it means protecting myself. How long before the prom teens or the family in F-7 disbanded? How long before survival trounced compassion?

Out there was getting closer by the second.

I took the bag. Margaret said she'd be by later to talk, she wanted to talk to me. I said, Fine, sure. We headed off to group. Mother was flagging. Breathing hard. She was all bone by now. She could fit into clothes I wore when I was ten. Clothes I *did* wear, because she's a pack rat. Nothing worse than seeing your mother in a Care Bear shirt so tight her clavicle juts from the arc of a rainbow.

We had not walked three minutes before she stopped. "I can't make it," she said, and clammed up against the wall. I stood her upright and took her hand.

"My stomach hurts," she said.

"You can have some water in the library."

"I don't feel well."

"Come on, Izz."

I dragged her alongside the sack of provisions for the refugees, who were beginning to feel less alien, more mirror image. I was disgusted, of course, but then I was only projecting what the future held for them. Maybe they would prove me wrong. Maybe they would stick together.

We were first in the room. This meant we could sit where we pleased, which was by the window. There were shrubs to admire—for instance, the creosote bush. Or lechuguilla, which looks like a nosegay of spikes. And, of course, tumbleweed, the brier of wanderlust. I love any plant whose chief enterprise is peregrination *and* empire. About 250,000 seeds per plant, dispersed by principle of the wheel. I saw one big as a sheep the other day. And here's what gives me comfort: no matter what you are doing or what is happening in the world, there is, someplace, a tumbleweed ambling down the road.

Mother languished in her chair. She looked like a snowman on the first warm day. I kneaded her shoulders. I said, "You can beat this thing if you want. We're already here. Maybe I can even help." But she just shook her head and, with a rearing of the lips, expelled into a napkin a clot of black cream hewn to the armature of her lungs.

The others came in piecemeal. Cecilia was having a bad day.

She kept asking for her parasol because no jaunt through the park is complete without a parasol. Gale sat her down. Possibly an Electra complex was at work in Gale, retarding her loyalties; she'd fare better with the Dees, whose binary cried out for a third. They came in next and sat opposite each other. Unclear if this was for the purpose of sight lines or enmity. I could not imagine they'd had a fight. Oops, they'd had a fight. Dee one's rage came out in a muttering designed to solicit comment: Are you okay? What's wrong? Dee two just stared at her thumb. Penelope dropped anchor next to me, said, "Want to see something?" and proceeded to sock, unsock her trach tube and drone with mouth wide, the effect being the syncopated hum of, I don't know, Hiawatha. Susan came in last, which meant overtime at the staff meeting. She appeared underslept. Or unslept, given the pulp beneath her eyes.

She settled in and turned to Mother. "Now, Isifrid. We are here to help you. But you've got to help us, too."

I nearly threw up my hands, with relief or anger, I could not say. Happy someone was getting in her face, but upset it would not work. It never worked. Isifrid was unmanageable. Also, if it did work, what was wrong with the way I did it? These freshmen were going to succeed with my mother? How galling.

Susan went on. "We are all here trying to recover. This is supposed to be a safe environment. That you continue to take drugs on the premises hurts our efforts. And makes things dangerous for everyone else. So will you let us help you? Say yes, and we can all move on."

Mother could barely keep her head up, but she looked sorry. Susan nodded, and in came two women security guards to pat Izzy down. I could not believe it. They confiscated her compact. A pillbox. A dummy twist of lipstick. And throughout, Izzy said nothing.

After the guards left, Susan said, "Obviously, we have been back to your room."

I sat up. J.C. and Sam! Mother's equivalent was to raise her eyes.

"Now look. We can't stop you from getting stuff here, you will always find a way. But if you are caught again, we will have to ask you to leave."

I thought Mother might slide off her chair. I had never seen her so bad off.

Susan said, "It's your turn to share, Isifrid. You can talk about what just happened, if you want."

Mother rallied enough to say she felt sick. And then, amazingly, came the tears. "I don't want to break the rules. But there's just something in my head that drives me the wrong way."

She was heaving now, and I was terrified. I had never known her to melt down in all her years of abuse. It is possible I just wasn't looking. Or that I wasn't there. But more likely, Isifrid was bottoming out.

"Can we stop this?" I said. "Is this really helping?"

But Susan ignored me with such authority, it gave me the impression she'd seen this a million times.

Isifrid composed herself. Slightly. "You took away all my cocaine," and she wiped at her nose. "You can't just do that to a person."

She was dissolving. She was three years old. And she wailed. "Nobody loves me. You notice how there are no men here? No men? I don't have anyone to love me. Why did they leave?" She had moved into a crash-landing pose, tilted forward, and then was off the chair entirely, squatting with arms wrapped tight around her head. "Come back to me. Please come back. I wish I could die." They? Why did they leave? I had no idea what she was talking about. "You get used to a way of life, you can't just stop. No one has ever been there for me. And why should they. I'm a terrible mom." She was panting now, mewling and bawling, but the words were out. "Can't you see? My babies hate me."

I was not learning anything new about my mother except that she couldn't hold on. She was giving up. I wanted to pray for her. But of course I could not pray. Pray to what? If God were out there, he'd know the duplicity of my heart.

I got down on the floor and pulled her in close. She balled my shirt in her mouth and wept silently into the fabric.

An attendant from the infirmary finally showed up. Crack addicts have no recourse to a compensatory drug like methadone. Their minds crave the drug more than their bodies. But I didn't care. I was ready to give her whatever she wanted, just to make it stop. "Can't you give her a sedative at least? Something to knock her out?"

"Calm down," Susan said. "There is no reason to shout."

The attendant was three times Isifrid in girth and hulk. When they left the room single file, I lost sight of Izzy altogether.

"Don't worry," Susan continued. "They are going to give her fluids and something to eat."

But I was still trembling. When did it get so bad? Susan asked if I wanted to share. I did not. She said she really wished I would. Dee two said, "Oh, go on," like I was stalled on the diving board. What was there to say that I had not said before?

"I can't make myself believe in God. And because of that, I can't pray for my own mother. That and I'll never be able to stop drugs."

Gale went, "Who you been talking to?"

Dee one said, "Hooey."

Susan told me to continue.

I said, "I bet that sounds like just another excuse. But it's not. If I don't believe in a power greater than myself, then I obviously think there's nothing out there to help me but me, and *me* is unacceptable. So . . . that's all I got."

"Would anyone like to comment?"

I felt a heaviness come on, lethargy and grief, because Susan just looked so bored, the others were burnt out, and this was my seventh rehab.

Dee two raised her hand. "I think, maybe, the thing is not to take everything so literally. All you have to do is remove yourself from the center of the universe, and you've already made a step toward conceding a higher power."

Dee one said, "Horseshit. You don't need God, you don't need anything."

They glared.

"Why can't I have faith?" I was actually asking Susan. "What's so wrong with me that I can't have faith?"

Cecilia raised her hand. "You have faith," she said. "Just not in things eternal."

The group adjourned. I was leaving the room when Susan took

me by the arm. I felt conscious of my sack of refugee food, and tried to hide it behind my legs. Still, I felt pleased, like I was being singled out after class because mine was the noteworthy cause that had recommitted Susan to the sacrifices she made for us.

"I want to talk to you about something. This morning, when your mother's room was being cleaned, we found two people asleep in your bed."

"How Goldilocks," I said, but I thought she might slap me.

"I'm sure you know visitors are not allowed, especially now."

She took me even farther away from the door and began to whisper. "We are very lucky to be here right now. We are very . . . *protected.*"

"What did you do?"

"Nothing. No one wanted to go near them."

"What do you mean? Because they might have plague? You can't be serious."

"Superplague. Lucy, listen to me. You can't be accepting strangers into the center, though I suppose it's moot at this point. Today we set up a perimeter with electric fencing. No one gets in."

"And no one gets out?"

"Don't be silly. This isn't a death camp. If you want to leave, leave. You'll just have to leave on foot."

"What about the people in town today?" I was thinking of Margaret and Sandra.

"They won't be coming back."

"Has everyone in this place lost it? Or is it just you. It's not just you, is it. Everyone's got a gun now, right? And there's a brawl in the pantry over the last hunk of bread."

Susan gasped slightly, as if her water had just broken, and ran for the cafeteria.

This was madness.

Thirty-one

J.C. and Sam were distraught. I found them on my bed, re-hashing. They'd had a faceoff with Bluebonnet staff, which was more like people backing away slowly, and a row with the refugees in F-7, in which voices were raised and covers blown. J.C. was saying, "The whole *point* of coming here was to avoid stuff like this." And Sam saying, "Don't upset the baby." Who were these people? "Who are you people?" This seemed to bring them up short. But really, what did I expect them to say? They were lovers who wanted to make it.

"Don't worry," I said. "There's a perimeter out there now. Like a fence. Just think of it as the DMZ."

Blank faces.

"The Berlin Wall. Great Wall of China. We've got a threshold now. We're as good as any nation-state. *No outsiders*."

J.C. said, "Are you making fun of us?"

"What? No. I'm just being, I'm just being stupid."

They were grateful for their honey buns and ham. I said, "Don't think badly of me, but I've got to go bring this food to the family in 7."

Resignation.

The family in 7 was subdued. Latest news: Cases of plague in Arizona, New Mexico, Texas. Illinois, Indiana, Ohio. Vermont and Florida. Inexplicable distribution pattern. Degree of contagion unknown. Possibly, plague bandits were apportioning disease at random. Possibly, victims were treated before lethal effervescence downed everyone in sight. Maybe the highly patriotic American was releasing plague in measured doses all over the country. Maybe, in breeding new virus from the ur-strain, some potency was lost. No one knows anything. Speculation is rampant.

I introduced myself. First time anyone was relieved to find out I was a junkie. If junkie, then inmate; if inmate, plague-free. They were grateful for the food. They worried about Margaret and Sandra. They'd been in town, exposed. What if they came back?

There was Larry, the grandfather, who'd been three years old during the influenza debacle of 1918. He struck me as the sort of old man who is always trying to make relevant his experiences of yore, and for whom the plague came as a welcome reprise of them—the sight of his father and uncle dead, his elder brother, too, victim to an epidemic that took 200,000 Americans in one month.

There was his daughter, Jill, and the kids: two teens, one toddler. I found them arranged around the bed, playing a board game like Life, but not quite. All but the toddler were entranced by the fate of their avatars as they coursed through the game to the end. In times of crisis, I guess auguries are found wherever you look.

Of the teens, there was a boy in the swan song of puberty and a girl whose friends the boy probably jerked off to at night. His shorts hung well below the knee, his T-shirt well past the elbow, which excess concealed the distinctions of obesity but not the condition itself. By contrast, his sister chose to articulate her fat in vestments that hugged the body—stretch jeans and tank—which, for their bravado, made her seem even more diffident than her brother. I did not know where to look, so I settled on the toddler, who kept one fist in her mouth and the other pounding the bed so that avatars Jill and Larry flew off the board with annoying frequency. In sum, they were a family like any other, whose opted recourse to preservation was here.

The game ended. Boy teen had been remanded to wolves in a district that did not fall under the king's purview, he was shit outta luck. Girl teen and Jill settled for indentured servitude on the outskirts of town. Larry ascended to the throne. In lieu of having to listen to him discourse on influenza—When I was a boy—the family trained its attention on me. It was not unbidden. I'd been clucking my tongue and shredding napkins. I'd been saying: Any day now. The family was resolute in all things, including focus. So now they were focused on me.

I said I didn't much see the point in them hiding. The staff had already busted the prom teens, to no effect. Likely everyone had heard them arguing. And anyway, what good from secrecy? The boy teen agreed. He thought the best way to secure the property was simply to take charge of it. Girl teen thought he'd seen too many Commando movies. Jill demurred, said, "Becky, don't talk to your brother that way."

"What do you mean 'secure the property'?"

Here was Larry's chance. He had huge lips, lips like two slugs in a bunk, so that when he spoke, you could not see in his mouth at all. Maybe this was for the best. "In 1918, we shut down every public gathering in the country. Parades, ball games, shows. Nothing was too drastic. And we still lost everyone."

He seemed to relish these memories of a time when life was precious for its transience, when men of science ceased to prate about medicine, when men of the cloth ceased to prate about God, when questions outnumbered answers and the country was ripe for growth, even as so many of its people died.

"What I mean," said boy teen, "is that we need to get a system in place. Being here in the boonies only makes sense if we can make sure no one else gets in."

"That's why there's the fence," said Jill.

"And the guards," said Becky.

I smacked my head. "Oh, great, now we have guards?"

Becky seized her tank top and plucked it from a wedge of fat around her waist. "Saw them myself. A sorry bunch. Guys who work here, I guess."

Boy teen was unimpressed. "It's not enough. Where does the food come from? So long as food gets delivered, there's a breach."

Larry was nodding. "In 1918, there was no place to run. Not like in the fourteenth century, where half of Florence spirited away to villas in the country. Everything comes back. It's painful, but I guess that's how it goes."

"Can we grow our own food?" Jill ventured.

I cocked my head. How does a woman handle three kids and a father near dotage without having any common sense?

At this point, there was a disturbance outside the door followed by what sounded like a coconut smack against the wall. On instinct everyone went silent. Boy teen killed the lights. I looked out the peephole just as J.C. came bursting through the door. I was going to have a lump the size of Texas on my forehead. He was panting and flushed.

"What happened to you?" I said. "Where's Sam?"

At mention of her name, he looked panicked, like he'd forgotten. And in fact he had. "Shit, we have to get her." He turned from one face to another, looking for a volunteer. He tugged at my sleeve. He really wasn't a day over nineteen. "I, I can't go back out there," he said. "Sam's in your room, can't you just get her?"

The toddler seemed to pick up on J.C.'s anguish, as toddlers do, and began to wail. Becky, with unsettling dexterity, removed her wristband and shoved it in the baby's mouth. Jill said, "Becky!" but then yielded to compromise, in which she replaced band with bottle. The effect was nearly as good.

"Can't go out there why?" boy teen said. "What's out there?"

I snapped at him. "Look, boy teen, this is not Dungeons and Dragons."

"Did you just call me *boy teen?*"

I was suddenly conscious of how little authority I had here. The situation, whose stakes I did not as yet understand, was getting away from me. Where was my mother? I wanted to call Eric. What if anarchy had overtaken New York? I stood up straight. "Fine, I'll go get her. If you hear a scream, Roswell is no lie."

Blank stares.

I let myself out. Soon as I shut the door, I pressed my back against the wall and listened hard. My stomach was a loony bin, and the desert the darkest place on earth. So as not to attract strangers at night, the staff had killed all the courtyard lights. I couldn't see shit. My room was four doors down, so I began to count knobs, never leaving the safety of the wall. I did not get far. I stepped in something wet and phlegmy. The sensation was so gross I forgot how to walk and fell over. The landing was soft. I felt a button imprint my cheek, hair graze my lips, and I flew off the thing, reeling until within touch of F-7, whose door I banged on repeatedly, saying, It's me, it's Lucy, let me in, and fearing, somehow, for my life.

J.C. looked right past me. "Where's Sam?"

My hands were shaking, and I glared at the dark print my shoe had made on the carpet. Becky followed my stare and gasped. Jill was in the bathroom, nursing. Boy teen, *Christopher*, could not contain his fear or enthusiasm, which were here commingled. He asked if it was blood.

Larry shook his head. "Oh, boy," he said, like: Here we go again.

"What is that out there?" I said, trying to imbue my voice with calm and, perhaps, the kind of ferocity that commands respect.

At this, J.C. fell apart. "I don't know. I didn't mean to. He wouldn't let go."

So that thing I fell on was human. This ruled out nine out of ten possibilities I had in mind. Unfortunately, the tenth was no consolation.

"What happened?" Becky asked. "Is—is he dead?"

"Oh, God," I said, because I had not even checked. All that blood, how could he be alive?

"You have to go out there and check," I said.

"I'm not going out there," he said. "No way."

Jill walked in with the baby strapped to her chest. She took one look at us and returned to the bathroom.

"I'll go," Larry said. "I been to war."

He could barely stand unaided. I said I'd go with him. This time, we left the door open so as to make use of the light. It was a man all right. Fallen to the concrete. His blood stained the wall. I gathered he'd hit his head with some force and slipped to the ground. The wall was unfinished plaster, runnels and peaks. I imagined his head snagging on the way down, and my stomach lurched. Larry squatted next to the body. No pulse. I watched over his shoulder, leaning in, but just barely. The only dead body I had ever seen was my father's, but I can't say I really looked. Before that, there had been an open-casket viewing of my aunt Petra, but since her car had slammed into a divider that catapulted her out the windshield and down the pavement for several feet, it hardly seemed credible that the unblemished figure in the casket was her or even human.

We walked back to F-7.

J.C. was standing just inside the door. "Where's Sam?"

"The man's dead," I said. "Please tell me it was an accident. We have to call the cops."

"No way," Christopher said. "They could be infected."

Even Larry seemed to agree.

I brought my palm to the lump on my head, which had, I imagined, the compass of a Ping-Pong ball.

J.C. stared at his hands, front and back, mesmerized by what he had done. "He came out of nowhere. I was just taking a walk, and there he was. He looked insane. Said he lived on a ranch not too far from here with his blind uncle, but that his uncle complained of fever and a sore throat and that he'd been to town just days before, in fine health. So the guy just split. Left his uncle to die. Town was too far away and he knew about this place, so he came here. He'd been walking for a day and a half, at night, too. He was hungry. He needed water. But he just looked so sick and crazy, I only wanted to get away from him. I was covering my mouth and trying to get away, but he grabbed my shirt and wouldn't let go! So I shoved him."

"You shoved him," I said.

Becky asked if a dead person could still give us superplague.

Good question. If you got it from people coughing, sneezing, or breathing on you, it stood to reason that the dead could not transmit. On the other hand, I had no idea. I wished Aggie were still alive. She would know. So would Hannah, in fact. Mother and I had to get back to her.

"No idea," I said. "Though I guess we'll find out."

"Great," Becky said. "I didn't even want to come to this place. There was a party tonight. I could have been at the party."

"Like you had a date," Christopher said.

"Shut up."

"What are we going to do?" J.C. said. "My wife is pregnant!"

"We?" Becky said. And then, "Oh my God. How do we know he didn't give it to *you?*"

She backed away from him. I couldn't help it, I did too.

"Oh, come on," he said. "I covered my mouth. I wasn't with him for more than two minutes. He probably didn't even have it!"

J.C. was getting frantic.

Larry just shook his head. I felt bad for him, having to watch history repeat itself. It should not happen in the same lifetime. At the very least, you're supposed to die and come back first.

"I'm calling the police," I said. "Someone has got to keep a level head."

This meant, of course, having to retrieve my cell phone of the shoddy reception, which meant having to step over the unknown man, who had left his blind uncle to die. Probably the uncle would not have died if his nephew had just stuck around. Probably he was still not dead. I hope he called someone. But what if he didn't have a phone? Everyone has a phone. But what if he didn't? What happened if this sick blind man was withering away, starving to death, or, I don't know, eaten by coyotes! I had to call the police.

Once my eyes adjusted to the dark, I could make out his shape. The glint of his pupils. Absolutely vacant. I guess I was supposed to close his lids, but no way was I touching a dead man. I tried using a stick to turn out his pockets, maybe to give a relative his belongings. Then I noticed a ring on his finger. He was married. Strangely, this seemed to humanize him enough so that I could take his hand and free the ring. It came off easily. His hands were stiff. Despite the stare, his face wore evidence of panic, jaw clenched, brow furrowed, lips sealed. I wondered if this was how my father looked when they laid him out. If the anxiety that ended in suicide dwelled on his face long after he had released himself from it.

I sat there for what felt like a long time. From a distance came the sounds of a train slicing through the night. The backs of my legs chilled against the concrete. My ass was going numb. I was aware of these sensations the way you might notice a traffic jam on your walk home. Bully for them, but who cares. I was tired. And something about the fatigue, the dead man, this place—it got me thinking in a way I tend to reject, which is to say, in a way that substantiates an interest in things philosophical and thus lifesaving. Me and the dead guy were just two bodies in the desert. On principle, I had little care for the body, which negligence felt like a strategy toward enlightenment. By contrast, here was a man who'd do anything to *protect* his body, and in whose will began abasement. Something like kenosis, when Christ abandons the form of God for the corporeal. Say we are all born in the form of spirit, what then if you assert the body? Me and this guy, we had totally different ideas about how to deal. But I didn't know whose was better. The choice seemed to ride on whether we resurrect or reincarnate, though neither option yields to the proposal that with each generation, we only die, die again, die better.

I shook my head. In this madhouse-once-rehab, getting clean seemed like the least pressing business of all.

I stood, failing to note the man's hand still in mine. It fell from my grip with a thud.

In my room: Sam, Margaret, Sandra. I was not surprised. The sisters were hardy and resourceful. An electrified fence manned by a Bluebonnet intern was not going to deter their homecoming. I found them talking birth rites. Could Sam have her baby underwater and call it a baptism, too? The celerity with which she had taken to the sisters, how she had settled herself between them with zero discomfort, made me suspect she had lacked for women all her life.

I flung myself in a chair with floral-print cushion, which actually kept with the hodgepodge furnishings doled throughout the rehab.

"Look what the cat dragged in," said Margaret. "You're a sight."

"So are you. How'd you get back here, anyway?"

"Ingenuity," said Sandra.

"Cutoff switch," said Margaret. "And a couple guys looking the wrong way."

I told Sam her husband was adamant she join him in 7. She seemed not to have noticed his absence. Or that they were married. Clearly, she did not want to leave the embrasure that was the sisters wise. But I wanted her out. As she left, I counted down from three. When the scream came, Margaret leapt to her feet and made for the door, but I put up my hand and shook my head. "J.C. will tell her."

"Tell her what?"

And out it came. They were appalled, of course. Equally by the *accident* as by the refugees' horror of their return from town. As for calling the police, they were none too sure this was a good idea. If the rehab shut down, what would become of them? Of us? By now, word of the death and the refugees, the bandits and cavalry at neighboring farms, had likely spread throughout the rehab. Our mandate had grown twofold: help the junkie, avoid everyone else. It would be bad news if junkie and outsider joined forces. To what end? So some asshole could get a proper burial while the rest of us got evicted, jailed, or deathly ill?

I went for my phone, which I'd hidden under the mattress. Battery dead. I went for my charger, which I'd also hidden under the mattress. No charger. This fucking rehab! Now even if I wanted to call the cops, I'd have to go to the office and use a landline, which meant having to encounter staff, which seemed ill advised under the circumstances.

"So what are we supposed to do?" I said.

"Wait it out. Go to group. Get clean."

"Are you kidding? What about the food? The boy teen—Christopher—was saying so long as food gets brought here by truck, we're at risk."

Margaret laughed. "That's a bit extreme, don't you think?"

Was I being mocked? Who knew, at this point, what was prudent and what was extreme? Minutes ago, I thought it was crazy, too, but here I was, parroting the latest.

"She's just teasing," Sandra said. "We've been thinking about the food."

I was not even relieved. "And?"

"We're working on it."

There came a silence among us, in which all retreated to thought, ostensibly to solve our communal problem. But I was elsewhere, studying the carriage of both women and marveling at how little each registered anxiety or distress. At least not the kind to which I was accustomed, to which I attributed 90 percent of my drug use: I can't deal, I need to get high. Despite everything that had happened in the last three hours, I rarely left contemplating drugs. How to acquire drugs. How to acquire and hoard and take drugs. It was like the thrum outside the shrink's office. The fan in the background. I simply assumed the same held for every addict, recovered or not.

Sandra had rolled up her pants and lobbed a shank over the arm of my desk chair. She was so much beef, the shank looked edible. Same for Margaret. Her body was impressing a caesura in my mattress, right down the middle. She had her elbows propped, chin in hand. Nothing could touch these women. Nothing at all.

I asked how they did it.

Margaret looked me in the eye. What she lacked in anxiety she made up for with compassion. "It's like this, honey. You can have everything or you can have drugs."

I shook my head. I'd heard this before. "That's not true. It's just not true! Without drugs, everything is the same as before, only I have no way to cope."

Sandra said, "I know you don't believe us. I didn't believe it when I came in, either."

And there it was again, the language of in and out. It seemed like such an artificial threshold, like the fence between us and the plague bandits. As if some vector rat couldn't just as easily bypass the fence and kill us all. Like one day you are a fucked-up drug addict and the next you're seeing God. I knew I was being cynical. But this kind of talk drove me crazy.

"No one comes in brimming with optimism and love," Margaret said.

I smacked my forehead. "Shut up, okay? Just stop saying that stuff. Why does everyone say the same thing? The same words! The same expressions! Does everyone just quote from the same book? I can be here, I can be three thousand miles away and you can be sure someone's gonna say, How'd you do that? One day at a time. Or: I need you people for me to stay clean. Or: Let go, let God. Turn it over. Don't think. Fake it till you make it. Does anyone even stop to think what these phrases mean or do you all just toss this shit out like robots?" I was getting so angry, I could almost see my brain wallow in the blood rushing up there. How dare these people have hope for me. "How do you know?" I yelled. "How do you know it'll get better? Because it's worked for everyone else who *works their program hard*? Because I'm not special? Because *meeting makers make it*? How do you know? And why do you care?"

By now I was crying. I'd drawn up my legs and pressed my mouth into the flesh of my knee. If I thought there was more out there for me than dispiriting snippets of anti-innuendo with a married man I loved, maybe I'd let Eric go. If I thought there was more out there than nodding out whenever possible for dread of having to experience my life, maybe I'd give up pills. If I believed in God, maybe he'd help. All things consequent on me. It was infuriating, but then this rage was just terror in disguise. There couldn't be anything good out there for me. I could not believe it. It pained me to believe it for fear of being wrong. Or worse, for fear of being right.

Margaret drew the blinds. It was after seven a.m., but the sun had only just crested above the horizon; the color was scumbled, muted and sleepy.

I blinked as the silhouette of a tree gave way to twigs and branch. All things refined in the glare of dawn. And to think it only took a minute.

I looked at Margaret and Sandra, and opened my mouth to speak. No need, they knew I was sorry. We left my room to see about the dead man. But he was gone, absconded to a better place, or, more likely, to F-7.

We stood over the site of his death, unsure how to mark the spot but certain we should. A death that goes unnoticed seemed to forfeit more than just custom. Also, if this was going to be it for me, if superplague was going to stampede through Bluebonnet, who knew how many chances were left to be decent?

"Maybe say a prayer?" I suggested. "I feel bad for him."

"Why?" Sandra said. "He sounds like an asshole."

"But somebody loved him," Margaret said.

"Probably he can hear you," I said. "Spirits, reincarnation, all that stuff. In fact, if my grandmother were here, she'd say we can even hear *him*."

"Good," Margaret said, and then, hollering at the sky, "Somebody loved you!"

Sandra nudged her affectionately. Smiles all around. Laughter, too.

Thirty-two

Oh, for the love of Christ. Me, dead, *again*. Travis goes down *again*, at a women's rehab, no less. If we're supposed to learn from our past lives, how come I haven't learned shit? It's a Hegel thing, isn't it. We learn from history that we never learn anything from history. So be it, I am collateral damage four times over. I am the world's concession to panic. Panic irradiates.

Before Travis, I'd been on this earth three times. Let me recap, I have nothing else to do. Life one, let's call it Unreason of the Masses. It went like this: Turn-of-the-century Denver, and I am a busy woman. Just moved into a Foursquare with eaves and dentils. I have always been partial to a good molding. Harold and I were just finalizing bylaws for the Denver Teachers' Club. It was, essentially, a union. We did good work, and we worked hard. But who doesn't crave a respite? Back then, film was a nascent technology. Edison had lost the AC-DC war of attrition; Westinghouse made him a fool. Edison's talking dolls had even flopped. He was, in a word, passé. Who knew he'd reinvent himself with the birth of film? And who knew I'd be queuing for tickets to see evidence of our nation in bloom? *Travel*. It was all about travel back then, at a time when many feared for the nation's self-regard absent a new frontier to conquer. The high-powered locomotive solved that. Every stride made by Union Pacific was cause to consider, with the solemn regard advancement must always inspire, the path of the nation toward greatness.

Harold and I sat in the front row of the theater next to a couple ranked in our circle as the best accessory to the neighborhood in years. They were Easterners. They had voted McKinley. The lights dimmed. The first film was an advert for Admiral Cigarettes. Quite charming, really. The next was of seminary girls—a rambunctious sextet, pillow-fighting in a dorm—in whose behavior the matron finds cause to intervene, which prompts one of the girls to seek refuge under a bed, only to suffer the ignominy of being retrieved by her ankles. I found the characterization outré, responsive, as it was, to the ubiquity of pornography in my day, as much in the news as in the home. Nevertheless, I was much riled and, perhaps, not of best mind come the beginning of strip three. Five men pounding the rails of a train track at the foot of a hillside. Two porters wielding kerchiefs to signal a train just around the bend. I remember the noise in the theater was boisterous, owing to the phonographic sound effects that accompanied the projection. The train whistling. The timbre ever strident as the vehicle neared.

Our new Eastern friends sat to my left. Elsa, the lady of the pair, clutched my forearm as the train came into view. What magnificence. My heart thrilled to every churn of the wheel.

There is, to the best of my knowledge, an unconditioned reflex of the brain known as the *looming* response. As an image shrinks or grows, it can trigger a reaction, often violent and without prelude. Something in the retina addles our perception so that an enlarging object appears proximate, more so the larger it gets. The response might be layover from more primitive times; it certainly has little value today, which is why, in most people, it is suppressed. Unless, say, you are a woman with what are called "untrained cognitive habits," who does not frequent the moving pictures, whose imagination knows not the *whoosh* of a train as it speeds by, in sum an Easterner named Elsa for whom the Black Diamond Express, traveling at seventy miles per hour, rounding the bend, and heading straight for us, initiates panic—a flinch, a cry, a rousing from her chair, a race to the nearest exit—and in whose palsied state arms push when they are to pull, whose fear grows confirmation that the exit is locked, who rushes to the next exit, though her path be obstructed by those of the opinion that there is actually a fire in the building, a gunman in the building, and by at least one audience member, née Louise, née Travis, whose hem is snared underfoot, whose hem is deadly for its robustness, whose hem takes her down so that Louise hits the ground and, for her fall, is winged straight to heaven.

Panic. It's all about panic. If I didn't learn it that first time, surely I got it the second. I must have, no? No.

Life two, let's call it Unreason of the Masses. We had in our midst a man-eating tigress that marauded across Champawat like she owned the place. Seem funny? Not so much. Funny were the white men with their safari suits and E. M. Forster. I know it took a Jim Corbett to vanquish our tiger, but only because it's easier to gun a thing down than to whisper in its ear.

It was 1907, at a time when, for me, there was no better gift than the forest. Ours was dense. Very beautiful, where every species of animal made his home. The trick was to stand still, then the animals left you alone. I did not even fear the man-eating tigress, though she had killed more than 430 people by the time someone saw her just outside our village. I remember it was a beautiful day. Many peaks of the Himalayas were visible—Nanda Devi, Trishul, Panchchuli—I never tired of the sight. And the sky. Such a wonderful blue.

I took a nap. When I awoke, the sun was set. I adjusted immediately, for I was used to work at night, and there she was. So graceful. I think my eyes even watered for her beauty. Three of my family were just down the road—older brother, sister, uncle. I noticed the tiger before they did, but she was many feet away. Even so, my brother was the first to run. Then the others. They ran and screamed and roused the villagers from their meals. Pandemonium set in. No one bothered to see if the tiger gave chase. I am told many were hurt in the process. And the tiger, she had never seen a spectacle more terrifying. What was she to do? I would have done the same. She ran. In her shock, she made to flee the village. To get back to her cubs. What did she want with these maniacs? She was just taking a stroll through the day. But the maniacs, they got her thinking danger was afoot. So off she went with a mind to butchering whatever lay in her path. As it so happened, I was in her path. After, what do you think was left of me? A lock of hair, a trail of tears.

Do these stories exalt our best faculties? Do these deaths speak to the sagacity of mankind as it's evolved over time? Nope, they sure don't. In fact, I even seem to regress with each trial on earth. It's not right. But what do I know. There's a sweaty Viking up here who says it's better not to think too much about it. And a sociopath who keeps beating the crap out of himself. There's also an old lady and—Good Lord, what the hell is that? Some kind of elf the rest are calling Tard. Want to hear what they're saying?

Tard: I look even older than *Agneth?* Why? How is that possible? Hell is other people.

Viking: Look, she's *way* better than the politico. If I had to see her drowning for one more second, I swear.

Masochist bloody-mess man: A catechumen! Come sit with me. Better yet, kneel with me! On your knees!

Old lady in kimono: What pleasure to see the tenets of my life so validated.

I've been in this game long enough to know the more you did in life, the longer you gotta putz around up here, assimilating. That's why after my third stint, I was here for maybe half an hour tops. I mean, how much was I supposed to learn in seventeen years on earth? I was just a boy in the suburbs stuffed with lust for the rock phenomenon known as The Who. Of my friends, I was the only one who didn't drop acid, smoke weed, fuck boys, fuck girls, fuck boys who were girls, take it in the ass from John Weismann's black Lab, who was way into ass; I had no interests, thoughts, or feelings to spare outside the parameters of infatuation with the rock phenomenon known as The Who. They had me entirely. Take my life, my soul, you are the four pillars of my universe, I have prayed and prayed and now it's happened, you are pledged to revisit the bunghole that is Ohio, and I will be there, in the front row of the Riverfront Coliseum, because I HAVE FAITH IN SOMETHING BIGGER, and, unlike my parents, my teachers, my friends, you *understand:* My heart is steeped in melancholia, too. It is 1979. I'm not going to college, and my dad wants to get me a job at his bank. Says if I want, he'll keep the Oldsmobile for when I save up enough money to buy it. Do I want that? Do I want anything? I don't know myself. So yeah, I could give it a go here. Or, OR, I could skip town after the Coliseum and follow you guys to Buffalo. And back to Cleveland. Then Pontiac. Chicago, Philly, D.C. I hear New

Haven's a pit, but I'll go! After that, London. And Vienna. And Essen, wherever the hell that is.

I know exactly what you're gonna play at the Coliseum. Or mostly, because of the improv stuff. "Substitute," "I Can't Explain," "Baba O'Riley," "The Punk and the Godfather," "Boris the Spider," "My Wife," "Sister Disco," "Behind Blue Eyes," "Music Must Change," "Drowned," "Who Are You," "5:15," "Pinball Wizard," "See Me, Feel Me," "Long Live Rock," "My Generation," "I Can See For Miles," "Sparks," "Won't Get Fooled Again," "Magic Bus." The set is kickass. And I'm going to go nuts when I hear "Drowned."

Okay, look: Your Schecter gives me a hard-on.

I got a ticket to Buffalo and my gear's in a locker at the station. I been outside the Coliseum since nine. It's fucking cold. But no one cares. There must be five thousand people behind me. The line travels all the way down the ramp to the wharf, where it looks more carnival than queue. The river's got ice floes, though it's so foggy, you can hardly make them out. Guy next to me has a bong. Guy next to him's reading a biography of Camus. This was all well and good at five, but now it's almost seven and the doors are still closed. Temperature's dropped at least ten degrees. Guy with the bong's out of grass. Guy with the Camus has set it ablaze to keep warm. Everyone likes this idea and soon enough there's a bonfire going. Someone has a boombox and next we're doing "5:15" call-and-response style. And "Long Live Rock." "Long Live Rock" fifty minutes before show time. You can feed on the energy. And you can see how friendships born in waiting are dissolving fast. You only have to inch your foot forward to declare war. It is festival seating, first come first serve.

Forty minutes to go. Why the fuck aren't the doors open? We're on the west side, but what's happening on the east? Maybe the doors over there are open and we're getting screwed. I will kill myself if I don't get to the front row. People are starting to get aggressive. We hear glass shatter, which makes everyone a little crazy. Did someone just break into the Coliseum? I can feel the buildup, the pressure of eight thousand at my back. There's maybe fifty guys ahead of me, I can take them.

At thirty minutes to go, someone swears he hears music. No one thinks they're still sound checking, but then what's with the music? The word spreads: They've started the show. A surge jams me against a woman up front, and I am actually lifted off my feet. Over the crowd I see two security guards heading for the west gate, and I make a break for it. Forget the slalom, I start climbing over people, and my footholds are whatever I can find—an arm, a shoulder, a knee. I fight my way forward with the intensity of the moment when a life is cut short, that moment which disturbs nature, for the young are to inherit the earth, but which disturbance invigorates like a drug so that I am able to surf atop the crowd and make it to the door first, just as it opens. The joy in my heart is Pyrrhic, stunning, and the instant I double over from the burn is when the mass of eight thousand breaks over me.

There are two ways to suffocate. Either you are denied air, or the air in your lungs is forced out, the way a child might stomp on his water wings until they are but two pupal sacs. I went down under a thousand feet. Two thousand. I have the imprint of so many lives on my skin.

Since then, I've learned a few things. Like: Stampede as phenomenon comprises multiple elements, among them herd mentality, the fight-or-flight response, and the architectural dogma of the space assigned to crowd control. The right combination will always result in fatal pressure, which can overrun brick, even steel. In mathematical models of escape panic, you get "interaction forces" that are almost sexy: *counteracting body compression*; *sliding friction*. And this makes sense since panic and lust distill to the same brew, which is energy. A surge of energy. Ever wonder why asphyxiation makes you come really hard? It's not magic, you know.

Also, escape panic is a contagion that apes the behavior of any pandemic except for its origin. Even a disease born of man usually results from a mutated gene. But escape panic is simply an expression of instinct that keeps with the Darwinian model of survival. As he put it, we, as enlightened creatures, still have no right to expect immunity from the evils consequent on the struggle for existence. At some point, the rush for seats becomes a struggle to live and in that struggle, you might as well be fighting with aliens, such is your regard for their well-being. Walter Cronkite, referring to the stampede, called us a "drug-crazed mob of kids," but then perhaps Cronkite is not quite as in touch with humanity, or Darwin, as he purports.

When Roger Daltrey heard the news, he cried. And the next night's show in Buffalo, it was for us. For me. I had the best seat in the house. They sang "Young Man Blues" and "How Can You Do It Alone." You really got the feeling they were asking us in earnest, not rhetorical at all, so for what it's worth, I didn't do it alone. In life, it was all isolation and I never understood how one day passed into the next with me still in it, but for the trespass to the other side, it was like they were carrying me over. My own experiences, to which I had zero access in life, came forward to show me how it's done.

Even so, where is the progress in this? I keep *dying* for God's sake. And I'm pissed off. This last time, I did everything right. Life four, let's call it Unreason of the Kid. Me and my uncle living on the ranch together, where is the harm in that? Poor guy had four children of his own to raise, but still went and took me in after my dad passed and my mom did, too. Over the years, the others got degrees and fanned out across the globe, but I stuck around. Uncle Bill wasn't much for talk, but I got from him what I needed to know. Even from just watching him live life as a blind man, didn't piss and moan about his sight being gone, or all the things he couldn't do. He toughed it out. The ranch got lonely some nights and sure, I thought about the girls in town and wouldn't it be nice, but I wasn't gonna leave my uncle. Not for anything. Then this plague thing hits and people start to act a little crazy. Me and Bill decide to sit tight and go about our way, head into town maybe once a week to get supplies. This last week I took him to the bakery because he was having a keening for pecan rolls, while I loaded up on the basics.

The truck was acting funny, which I did not like. But then it'd acted funny before. Anything happened, I'd just take a horse into town and get whatever part I needed. That night, when Bill took sick, I didn't think much of it. But then his fever got high. He had the shakes. I'd read my bit on superplague and knew if he had it, he'd die within twenty-four hours if I couldn't get him something, and even if I could, he'd probably die just the same. I figured if he'd already passed it on, well, we'd both of us die anyway, so it'd be best to get help. He seemed pretty sure on death, though, and before I left, he asked me to take his wedding ring. It fit just perfect. For a second I was put off by wearing another man's wedding ring, but then it made me feel like we were all bound up in the same love, what difference who you pledge it to.

I went out back. Course the damn truck chose that night to go bust with the timing belt. And wouldn't you know I'd find the stable door unhinged and the stalls empty. Bill was going down fast, so I grabbed a canteen and decided to hoof it. No doubt I'd hitch a lift on the way. Only there was no one on the road. It was the deadest I had ever seen. Best choice was to make for the rehab and hope I didn't pass out from dehydration along the way.

When I got there, I was so happy. Strange about the electrified fence, but I didn't make too much of it. Felt like my mouth and throat were thick with baby powder. I just wanted some water and a phone. In the courtyard, I saw a kid and made right for him. I think I even waved, in a friendly-like way. The place was for women, I guessed him a counselor. So I'm waving and maybe dragging ass a little, but the kid, he panics. Turns his back on me and runs. But by now, I've got all my hope and desire bound up with this asshole, I can't give him up. Next I know, I'm running after him. I try to explain. But I might as well have been speaking in Arab because the kid was all terror, and I had never seen anything like it. But now here's the thing that strikes me in retrospect, I *had* seen it before, and I knew that look on his face. I knew his problem, and in that instant I knew everyone else in the rehab had it, too. *Escape panic.* I should have just shot myself right then and saved him the trouble. Instead he gets a jolt of survival energy and, whack, my brains are splattered all over the wall, which is jagged and none too pleasant to have all mixed up in your stuff.

Time's different out here. I've already had a chance to read up on herd mentality and a fact sheet about infectious disease published by a company that specializes in herd mentality. Obviously, the two bed down together. The madding crowd—they're hungry, they're sick, they're furious. Want to be scared shitless? Here's what just got leafleted all over New York City:

BE PREPARED: A PLAGUE PRIMER

If a 30% attack rate, understand what this means:

30% of your family. 30% of doctors. 30% of emergency staff. 30% of bank tellers. 30% of drivers. 30% of police officers.

Add to that the number of people withdrawing from society to protect themselves and their loved ones.

In sum: Rely on no one to help; take precautions now! Do not be complacent about your own resilience! Be *self-sufficient*!

MODEL 1: Plague is transmitted via contact with infected person and/or his belongings.
PROPHYLACTIC: Wash frequently.
ASSUMPTIONS: Water is available, soap is available, towels are available, towels are clean, detergent to launder towels is available, water for laundry is available, paper towels are an alternative, paper towels are available, paper towels are sterile, paper towels can be disposed of safely, etc., etc. *Plan ahead.*

MODEL 2: Plague is transmitted via breath.
PROPHYLACTIC: Use gas mask.
ASSUMPTIONS: Gas masks are available. Gas masks are effective. Use handkerchiefs. Handkerchiefs are available. Handkerchiefs are effective. Use tissues. Tissues are available. Tissues are effective. Etc., etc. *Plan ahead.*

Etc., etc. We have a people's-watch nonprofit to thank for this. Flyers have clogged up every drain in the city, the debris is worse than your average ticker-tape parade, and this nonprofit, with best intentions, has the nerve to add, oh and by the way:

In regard to all of the foregoing, panic-buying is not recommended.

Ho Ho very funny, ha ha it is to laugh.

Thirty-three

When Alfred's article about the women of plague hit stands, it sold out immediately. Eric faxed me the piece, though I already had a copy pilfered from the dollar store by Margaret, who still snuck into town and back on occasion. It was six pages long, spliced with photos whose accruals of light and shadow seemed to bully out of frame evidence that we looked awful. Mother's prying bones turned avant-garde. The rotunda of Aggie's body, once silly, now majestic. Even I looked okay, like the autumnal coloring of my face and hair had been commissioned by L.L.Bean to invoke home, hearth, and cocoa on a chilly day. This was Eric's doing, of course. He could wrest beauty from anything. For Hannah, though, I'm not certain what he was after. The gap in her front teeth, symbolic of the adolescent ordeal the world over, it was almost cherubic. Likewise her C-curve bangs and freckle spread. But the eyes—globes of pea green in which pupils sapped tight—they seemed to allege hatred as the sustaining emotion of her life.

The article mentioned me and Mother and Agneth, several times of course, but it was really about Hannah. How one nation's duress could be sourced to a little girl keen on pneumatic plague. There was Hannah saying, "Dad didn't even *want* to study plague." There was Hannah saying, "It was my idea." And she was right. Dad might well have studied malaria otherwise. But her persistence, it probably delighted him in some regard. His nine-year-old in pigtails fixed on the most tenacious slate-wiper in history.

I read the piece and decided I had to go home immediately. Only it was too late. I'd heard something about leaflets dropped from a helicopter that had seized New York with a pell-mell disregard for the law, for instance, people were breaking into the low-budge clothing depot Old Navy. Stanley said it was too dangerous, I had to stay put. We spoke every few days. I'd use an office landline to call him and Eric, but since there were always people waiting for the phone, I'd save Hannah for next time. Or the time after that. Whenever I'd ask about her, the news was so upsetting, I didn't want to know more. Stanley would say they didn't talk much and she wasn't home much. That he assumed she was still back in school, but could not say for sure.

I asked about surrogacy. He said people were not in the mood to have babies, theirs or anyone else's. Plus can you imagine having to get plague in your ninth month? Horrible.

He asked about me. I said I was alive. And Mother? Less so. She'd been off drugs for several weeks, but her health showed no correlate improvement. Hers was the most unwilling detoxification ever.

Eric corroborated Stanley's account of life in New York. Said he and Kam were trying to rent a car to get the hell out of there, but that there were no rentals left. Also, her parents had forbidden them to use the house upstate, they were saving it for themselves. He was thinking of stealing a car. How did you steal a car? I said there were cars left to steal? He said not really. I told him I'd been weaning for a whole month. He said, "That's fantastic." I asked if he could help with Hannah. He said he wouldn't know where to begin.

We savaged Alfred's article. How dare he allow a young girl to take the blame. How dare he make of her flagellating a spectacle. We also noted how little he'd written about my dad. As if in the way conflicts outgrow their putative cause—like anyone gave a shit about Archduke Ferdinand once the war started—the superplague had left him behind. If Dad had gleaned a vaccine or remedy from his work, and if an inimical government or highly patriotic American had devised and unleashed a strain of his own, the country would have been inured and my dad a hero. Instead, he'd become paterfamilias to the hybrid identity of America in a time of plague, part vigilante, part soccer mom. We were assimilating new concerns into old routines. And for every problem, teamwork.

Apparently, our rehab qua embattlement had attracted notice.

Eric heard mention of it on a Sunday morning talk show about the country under siege. If these were really our last months on earth, how were people dealing? What was the country doing? I could just hear McLaughlin now—Predictions: Koresh or kibbutz, Pat Buchanan?

We were thirty drug addicts and seven refugees (eight if you included Sam's baby, which seemed okay since she was getting huge), Susan and five other staff members who lived on the premises. This made forty-four. Forty-four people in a self-managed domicile whose remove gave us a chance.

We had devised a system. And because we were in rehab, there were certain principles on hand, most notably: in every problem are the conditions of its undoing. This is why addicts are often thanking God for their addiction: in the disease are tools not only for handling it, but for learning from it, too. It is the same argument that favors growing biological weapons for study and the same that holds smallpox samples in reserve. It takes a pox to fight a pox. It takes a deadly strain of plague to articulate a cure. And in some cases, not just a cure but a cure-all.

Dees one and two had solved the food situation. If we absorbed IGA branch manager Tom Watson's gambling debts, he'd arrange for a weekly drop of groceries to an abandoned warehouse. In this way, no human contact and enough time for plague droplets, if extant, to self-destruct before pickup. Next came the task of precincts inviolate. The electric fence was fine, but we needed people on the line equipped to deter trespass. People who could aggress the deadly interloper with more than just rage. Cecilia and Gale were on it.

When you log as much mileage on the road as Gale, you acquire friends divers and seditious. Among her favorites were two Cubans she had smuggled into Florida a couple years back for Elián González activity. Now she was calling in the favor and next you knew, the Cubans had procured for Bluebonnet a crate of Taser M-18s. Cecilia's job was to sell us on the Tasers. Who'd say no to an old lady? Who would *doubt* an old lady? She said they were like BB guns. *Christopher*, who was at that meeting, launched out of his chair. Said, "Are you cracked? The M-18 could bring down Godzilla." You couldn't know if Cecilia was genuinely surprised because you couldn't tell which Cecilia was there. But Gale was miffed. She had assumed the perimeter jobs would lose cachet if they meant having to strut an arm of the militia. She was mistaken. There was a rush on the crate. And after, a lecture about use and care, which only the people in front could understand and then only just, since in addition to the trach tube, Penelope had a cold. Something something electromuscular disruption. Darts, wire, fifty thousand volts. Central nervous system disabled. Muscles contracting unbidden, intruders rendered fetal and paralyzed on the ground for ten seconds. When asked, Penelope said, "Of course I have a problem with this. Should be *twenty* seconds." When asked, Gale said, "It's not like you're *killing* the guy, just telling him to back off. The Taser is really a self-defense weapon. Like a stun gun. But more fun. Hey, I like that: More fun than a stun gun."

At first, the perimeter jobs seemed to act on the volunteers the way junior ROTC works on the high school kids. They had responsibilities to discharge. Guns to discharge. Our safety was in their hands. This one woman, Monica, I'd seen her come in a month ago. Maybe a few days after me and Mother. What a mess. A nurse had brought her, and they'd just gotten off a plane from Chicago. Monica was dope sick and lolling on the floor. Occasionally, she shrieked. "I can't be dope sick! I can't be sick! I can't stand it!" The admitting intern stood over her with a clipboard and tried to get answers. Age, weight, allergies, and was she experiencing any withdrawal symptoms? The courtyard smelled like vomit for days.

Weeks later and Monica was the first to get hands on a Taser. A month before she could not look you in the eye and now there she was, standing tall and issuing orders to her unit. It's true, we had units. And Monica was team leader. She prosecuted her duties with gusto. She reminded me of the Navy Seal woman at Hannah's day camp, which got me thinking about the ass-whupping female in general and the last horror film I'd seen, one of these werewolf v. vampire things in which the battle for global supremacy is entirely physical. The thinkers die first, and the spoils—such as they are— always go to the species that can effect the most lurid method of snuffing the enemy. The added appeal of this movie, however, was the presence of an ass-whupping female, whose prototype has been in vogue for years. She is hot, she is prehensile, a smattering of blood always complements her skin tone. The AWF might well be analogue to the bra burners of the sixties, but you have to wonder if she's advancing or retarding their work. Come Halloween, I'm not looking to ape Eleanor Roosevelt, I've got the delectable Catwoman in mind. In fact, I have Catwoman in mind even when it's *not* Halloween, which is to confess ambitions that demean my gender for the simple reason that a girl in latex will always beat a girl in chambers. In short, Monica was looking good.

After a while, though, when no one came around to disturb the peace, patrol started to get demoralized. There was nothing to do out there on the perimeter at night. And under the welkin of desert America, whose brights number in the millions, if you're just out there doing fuckall, you're bound to end up wanting drugs. What purpose the stunning landscape if not to incite drug lust? Monica began skimping on her shift and eventually stopped going altogether. The others followed suit. I worried they'd start zapping each other for sport. I worried that principles of recovery were not going to take.

The dead man's name was Travis. He had a wallet, IDs, a library card, even a ticket stub for a Who concert just last year in Dallas. He was in the system. Probably he had friends. So why hadn't anyone come looking for him? I found this three times more disturbing than his death or even the circumstances of his burial, assuming burial is what had happened that night, though you couldn't rule out desert pyre or, I suppose, carrion under the Joshua tree.

Everyone tried to make like it never happened, and to blend in, the logic being that if you just went about your business, the plague would not notice you. J.C. and Sam folded themselves into Bluebonnet without incident. They worked the kitchen. Turns out J.C. made a good bulk chef. Could not cook for five, but give him fifty and he was tops. Larry and brood picked up chores here and there, laundry, cleaning, handymanery. Actually, just the brood; Larry was too busy holding court or playing Ping-Pong. You had to see this guy play Ping-Pong. Couldn't hold a cup steady—Parkinson's or arthritis, who's to say—but get a paddle in his hand and out came this shark with relevant accoutrements in tow, stuff like charm, zeal, and *smooth talk*. He'd don his Panama hat and stump for the hard bat. The new rackets and thick foam, they corrupted the integrity of the game. Nope, it was the hard bat or nothing. He beat Dee's ass. Dee one, whose much touted facility with topspin was belied 21–2. He beat Susan, J.C., and even aspiring batsman, flesh of his flesh, young Christopher. Gale, whose finger stump aggrandized the talents of her good hand, still floundered at about 7–19. Only Monica gave him trouble, Monica whose aspirations were irreclaimable—smash the ball, kill the ball—so that even as she'd miss nine slams out of ten, the ones she hit could pop your eye out. After battle with her, Larry would call it quits, hang his hat, and start in on an encomium for days past. Anyone caught listening could be stuck there for hours.

What I'm saying is: Life went on. I tried not to worry about Hannah. I tried to focus on recovery and to prepare for what would happen once I left.

We went to group every day. Margaret and Sandra, who'd obviously quit their resocializing jobs at the dollar store, joined us. My benzo wean was almost over. I didn't feel much different, but people said I looked better. And had stopped slurring. I do not recall ever having *slurred*, but then I don't recall my twenties, either. I began to entertain the possibility that being clean was a good idea, but more in the way you might consider existentialism a good idea. Still, I was entertaining. Toying with. Flirting, even. And I guess this was progress.

One morning, there was a new person speaking at group. Not new to Bluebonnet, just new to me. A former patient turned staff. Clean for seven years. I started listening to her share about halfway in. She said, "You can have drugs or you can have everything." Nods all around. "See, it's like this. My life has never been better. We're all but jailed in this place and it pretty much seems like the world's coming to an end, but you know what? My life has never been better. And I have you people to thank for that. I have my higher power to thank for that. When I first started coming to the rooms, I was a wreck. No hope whatsoever. The pain of just being alive was unbearable. But you told me to keep coming and you loved me. No matter how many times I relapsed, and there were plenty, I was always welcome. No one had ever hugged me before the program. Not a single person. But even if you people weren't actually hugging me, it felt like you were. Does that make sense?

Being here with you is like being cradled all the time. The other thing you said, you said I should pray. That when you pray, it doesn't change God, it changes you. I didn't understand that. But I was so desperate to change my life, I would try anything I was told. You said show up, I showed up. You said make coffee, I made coffee. And somewhere along the way, the program got me. Sometimes it gets you way before you get it. Today I work on my attitude all the time. I still have trouble giving myself a break. I still have trouble letting go. It's an ongoing process. But it's worth it. It is so worth it. So thanks, that's all I have today."

Then she made for the food. It always amazes me, the way people can serve up their guts and five seconds later eat a donut. It makes the inner life seem sort of banal and proletarian, which has the painful effect of minimizing your problems, even as it helps you to manage them.

After, I asked how she got to praying without belief. She said, "I just did." I asked for more. She said, "Just drop a pencil on the floor and while you're on your knees picking it up, stay there." I said I'd heard that before. She said: "So?"

I walked away. The truth was, I'd heard every single sentence in her share before. She had not said one original thing. Not one. And then I thought, So? And I had no answer. And I felt confused. And maybe a little happy.

A few hours later, I was in bed considering all the things I wanted to do when I got home, assuming I could get home. First on my list: Hannah. I'd spend more time with her. When I'm not high, I'm actually sort of fun. Our relations would be strained at first but kid rage is assailable. Next I'd see about volunteering for a special-ed school. Not sure whence my growing interest in retarded children, but there it was. So long as I am clean, I'm actually good with kids. As for Eric, I'd start to nurture the healthy parts of the love between us because, after all, he was my closest friend.

I turned on my side. And here's what I saw: me among the peonies, all optimism and light, and, tiding over the nearest peak, an army of drooling sadists come to brain my idyll and beat me to death. In this scenario, I have nothing but a parasol to fend them off. It is absurd. I smile because it's so absurd. Even so, I parry a swine or two before going down. But once I'm going, I go down hard. And it looks like this: I can't work with retarded kids. *I'm* retarded. Or whatever they call it, *challenged*. My sister despises me with unflagging singleness of mind. If I attempt to make things right, she'll probably forgive me seconds before I let her down anew. And Eric. What's to nurture? He doesn't love me. I am hateful. I am hideous.

The sadists have an answer for everything. Why am I so unhappy? Because you suck. Why can't I crawl out of this pit? You don't deserve to. If I *did* crawl out, would that be okay? Question is moot. Why am I scared to find out? Question is moot. Why am I so scared of my life? Because it's about to kill you. Are other people as scared of *their* lives? No. What if my life continues in this fashion? You'll die. Can I deal with that? Asked and answered. Why does hoping for anything seem appalling? Because it's futile. Is it because I am so childish that I think hoping and not getting is worse than not hoping at all? Question impenetrable, move on. How come re Travis, instead of feeling sad, I feel *jealous*? Because if you were dead, you would suffer no more.

I palm my ears to shut these people out. It does not work.

I think: So? So what? and land on the floor, on my knees.

Hands steepled, throat cleared. But now what? Do I look at the ceiling or the carpet? Do I talk out loud or say it in my head? Is it okay to slouch like this? I start to whisper the Lord's Prayer because it's the one I know. But I don't get far, the hypocrisy is excruciating. The last thing I want is to mock prayer. And what else can you call my efforts but mockery? But then I think about the other addicts who swear it's okay to pray from a condition of doubt, and hope they are right. I try again. I say: God, if you're out there, you know I don't believe in you but that I'm trying to pray anyhow because people here say it will help me and I need help really bad. It seems hideous to be asking for help, like I'm one of these bad-weather friends, and I can't even begin to describe how incredibly stupid I feel, but I've run out of other options and I'm trying to save my life. I don't want to die, but I also can't live like this. Still, I'm not all that committed. I don't have faith that faking faith in you is gonna help anything. I mean, I believe in forces greater than me. Stuff like physics and love. But what do these forces have to do with my life? I not only have to believe in you, or something like you, but I have to believe that you, as you, actually want to bother with me. Impossible. Look, maybe this is selfish—I *know* it's selfish—but can't you just show me something? Can't you just suffuse me with conviction? A lot of people here say we are born with you inside, and that if we can't find you later on, we're just not looking in the right place. Other people say we can evict you from our hearts without meaning to. I don't know if either is true, but I'm doing my part; I'm looking. And if you've been here before, I'm asking you to come back. Just come back, okay?

I ask again, a few times, until maybe the Lord's Prayer makes just a little more sense to me than it did ten minutes ago. Thy kingdom come. Thy will be done.

zzy, you have to eat."

"I wish you wouldn't call me that."

"If I call you Mother, will you eat?"

She looked away. I'd been coming to be with her in the infirmary for two weeks, and every visit was the same. I think she was trying to starve herself to death. Bluebonnet had medical supplies, including IV nutritional bags, but Mother was not exactly begging for a line in. And what were they supposed to do, tie her down and find a vein? As it turns out: yes. In a more salubrious atmosphere, Bluebonnet would have palmed her off on a mental facility whose charter included the right to restrain and force-feed. But since no one would leave the compound, and since no one was permitted in, they revised their mandate daily. I wonder what would have happened had someone taken ill, not with plague but cancer. What then? I know what then. I don't want to know, but I know.

"Mom," I said. "Why are you doing this? The worst part's over. You've been clean for almost two months."

"We've been in this shithole for two months?"

I nodded. "Six weeks."

"When can we go home?"

"Soon as Stanley gives us the okay."

"Since when is Stanley the arbiter of our plans? And what's he still doing in my house?"

"Taking care of your daughter?"

"Go away."

"Listen, Izzy—Mom—I was thinking that even if I go home, you should probably stay here."

She wiggled her hands, which was about as much movement as the restraints allowed. I glanced at the IV bag, near empty. "It's not punishment, you know. And you did come here voluntarily."

"I do not know what I was thinking."

"Yeah, but I do. You wanted help. Now you are getting it."

"You can't leave me here. I'm not senile or insane. You have no power of attorney. I don't even know why these people listen to you. I can't believe I'm in restraints!"

I did not want her to start screaming like last time so I said, "Mom, I'm sorry. But I can't just let you die. And the only reason you can't put up a decent fight is that you're too weak because you don't eat. Just eat and be normal and we can get the hell out of here."

"Be normal," she said, despondent.

"Mom, honestly, why did you come down here? No one forced you."

"Maybe I wanted to spend time with you."

"Okay, that's just low."

We watched the IV bag dimple and collapse for lack of fluid.

She said, "So what's happening in the world? Do I even want to know?"

"The space shuttle blew up. And in brighter news, no reports of plague in twelve days."

"What happened to the shuttle?"

"Not sure. It exploded on reentry."

"How awful."

"Yeah. But isn't it weird how when seven people die in the shuttle it's a national tragedy, but when seven die in a pileup on the freeway, no one gives a shit?"

"That's because when you go out to space, you're representing the country. You're like a diplomat."

"Yeah, but only if you meet someone."

"How odd about the plague. I wonder what that lunatic is doing. And why he still hasn't been caught."

"No one wants to get a false sense of security about it, but then I think people are ready to jump at any chance to get rid of this anxiety. At least in this place, we don't have to worry about the *bubo*."

"The bubo is ridiculous. No modern disease should give you a bubo. Certainly not a gurgling bubo. But I thought pneumonic plague skips the bubo."

"Oh, right. I guess that's true."

"Can you believe Aggie chose this place for you? I've been thinking about that."

"I'm sure she didn't realize what it was like."

"I miss her, you know."

"Me, too."

"We didn't have much of a relationship. But she was my mother." I understood she was trying to tell me something and stayed quiet. "Lucy, can I ask you a question?"

"Oh boy."

"Is everything okay with you?"

My mouth sorta fell open. "Tell me you're kidding. You did not just ask me that!"

"What? Why are you laughing?"

Just then cook-nurse came in to replace the bag. She was tough. And big. You could probably conceal a small otter between her breasts.

It was my cue to leave. I stood and pecked my mother on the forehead. "You're amazing," I said. "They broke the mold and all that."

She sat up. "Not according to your nana!"

I smiled. "Okay, Knut. I'll see you later."

"Lucy, wait. I'll eat, okay? Just get us out of here. I'll eat."

"Roger that."

I checked my watch. I still had ten minutes before I was supposed to pray—I'd put myself on a schedule, thinking I do better with a schedule—when I heard a car pull up, a Taser blast, and a whole lotta cursing thereafter.

Thirty-five

The sight of these two men—one fetal with voltage charging through his body, the other blind and searching him out—and of the squad car bedecked with lights on top, bottom, end to end, it was as a juggernaut headed straight for our way of life at Bluebonnet.

Since I was the first to get there, I had the unfortunate experience of seeing the blind man—Travis's uncle, I presumed—grope for Penelope and, in so doing, molest her trach tube with fingers immured in cow patty. Penelope, whose history I still didn't know, was frisking herself in a panic. She was wearing a vest with all manner of pocket—mesh, recondite—in which, somewhere, an extra cartridge. She'd already shot up the state trooper—he was just regaining command of his body—and now she was gunning for the uncle.

I intervened. Said, "What are you doing?"

She gave me a wild look. I thought she might even zap me, which, from the gist of things, was exceedingly unpleasant.

The uncle had withdrawn to the backseat of the car and covered his head for protection. I didn't get a good look at him except to note his height, maybe five feet tops. Also worth noting: he was not dead of superplague.

I helped the trooper up. This was private property and the Taser, though savage, is not considered a firearm, nor is it illegal to carry and deploy. So what we had here was not so much a legal situation as a bereaved uncle looking for his nephew who had died and whose body had vanished and whose passing was not reported, so, okay, we were dealing with a legal situation and it was bad. On the other hand, I was relieved to see someone take an interest in Travis. Maybe he was divorced, maybe his wife had left him, but the uncle, he was alive and well and looking.

The trooper was unseasoned, though I don't know that any number of years on the force can prepare you for the Taser.

"What in holy hell was that?" he said. He was wearing one of those ranger hats with a wide brim so that eyes and nose were occluded in shade. He had also drawn his gun. Not that he was pointing it anywhere, just scratching his thigh with the barrel. If he'd been a girl, this could be hot. As is, it was embarrassing, like he had a rash that just couldn't wait.

"It's like a stun gun," I said. "Penelope here probably thought you were aiming to burglarize the place."

I grinned. Like a jackass. Like I imagine a Southern girl grins just before she gets knocked up. This habit of getting local—of trying to *talk* local—it had to go. Especially since it always came off obnoxious, like I was razzing the trooper, when if I was going to razz him, it'd be for the fruit in his crotch because no way could a guy look so huge, even in trooper pants, which, to be fair, hug the body like riding tights.

He shook his body like a dog out of water and retrieved a notebook from his back pocket. He was all business now. Said he was looking for Travis, who'd disappeared on such and such, had we seen him and so on.

I took the manner in which he comported himself and the fact that he had come at all as a sign that things were returning to normal *out there*—that if you had the wherewithal to police a rehab, you were no longer consumed with the imminent extinction of the race. The old laws were pertinent again. And what we had done here, under duress, was going to seem unconscionable. If only the uncle had showed up last week. All's fair in love and plague— people would have understood that. Instead, J.C. and whoever helped him were going to be pilloried. Theirs would be made to stand in for monstrosities committed all over the country; and when they went down, it would be so that the rest of us could go on.

Penelope had recovered herself and begun to flutter about the trooper, apologizing. I suddenly felt terrible for her. Because of the trach, she could not *inflect*. I'm so sorry, I want a bagel—everything she said came out uniform. How do the animatronic make love? The trooper waved her off.

Meantime, the uncle sat still in the rear of the car, face turned to us. He wore boots and plaid, but no sunglasses, which gave him a voodoo look I did not like. His lids were drawn halfway; his eyes were overcast, and they seemed to dawdle in their sockets, from one side to the other. I was staring at him with the idea that if I stared hard enough, he'd regain his sight.

"So you haven't seen him?" said the trooper to Penelope. She had not. And in fact, it was true.

The trooper seemed satisfied. I guess he figured Penelope was answering for us both. Clearly he did not want to broach the rehab. But the uncle goaded him on. It was the first I'd heard his voice. Feeble and sad. "Please," he said. "He's the only family I have."

We drew back as the car headed up the driveway. The dust eddied behind them, adding to the genie effect of their having appeared to threaten whatever self-esteem I'd managed to acquire in the last two months.

"Well, that was horrible," Penelope said.

"Yes, it was."

"You know they'll find out what happened."

"Of course. I should have said something, though. That poor old man. I can't believe I didn't say anything. Or call anyone."

"His nephew sounds like a jerk. Just leaving him there, thinking he had plague."

"That's what J.C. said, but can we really know anything about other people's motives?"

"No. But you can know your own. And that's a start."

"I guess I didn't say anything because I don't like to get implicated in other people's business."

"That's just fancy talk for being afraid."

"Afraid of what?"

"Of showing up for your life, which for most people means loving and being loved. And all the hard stuff in between."

We'd been traveling in the car's wake and could see it parked by the front door. I turned to look at Penelope's face, streaked from forehead to chin with rivulets and hairline seams, and found the drone of her voice stirred me to grief.

"I bet you've heard that before," she said.

I nodded and wiped eyes.

"I guess that's how it goes," she added. "You know: my story got me here but yours keeps me here. We rehash what we know and what we've been taught, hoping to get it right."

I nodded again.

"It can happen," she said. "With all the craziness of the last couple months, I think anything can happen."

We hurried up. By the time I made it back to my room, the clank of spade to rock to earth was the loudest sound in the desert. They had found Travis.

Thirty-six

It's one thing to get clean, quite another to stay that way. Sort of like how anyone can float in outer space, but return him to earth and good luck. In my case, reentry seemed like a particularly bad idea. There were matters to be handled. People to be handled. Stanley and Hannah. Wanda. Eric and the inconvenience of wanting to blow my brains out whenever I thought of him. Agneth and her ashes. I derived zero pleasure from thinking ahead, so naturally I thought ahead. My life seemed to require of me a fortitude I did not have, only now I'd get to experience the deficit awake. Yay. Yay, I'd say to Margaret and Sandra, who'd just frown and go: Fine, get high, that'll fix *everything*. And so another day. We could not recluse forever.

Stanley had begun to lobby for our return. New York was safe enough, could he book our flights? Mother had grown three pounds, and I was still on the wean. What could I say? I gave him the go. Meantime, Bluebonnet had lost half its keep. The business with Travis undid what confidence a lot of people had in the place, and the news spread fast. It was grim being there; we left pretty fast ourselves. We left like hoboes. Didn't say goodbye, didn't take our stuff, just walked out and hitched. Two rides: man-with-a-van Dan and John Shirley, cook. I hated goodbyes—fanfare in general—and used the relief of having escaped it to tame the anxiety of going home. It worked for about an hour. By the time we were on the plane, I was a mess. The travel industry had nearly gone under for lack of business, and yet there we were, among a hundred passengers in a confined space. A little over a month had passed since the last report of plague. One month and people revive their old habits? The fear that plundered Old Navy could evaporate so quickly? I didn't believe it. This was fear on hiatus. Fear that would return, indignant at having been displaced and more intense as a result.

Mother was staring out the window. We were well above the clouds, which looked like bedding. I asked about her plans.

"I don't know. I'd like to have another blot this month."

I threw back some peanuts.

"You really believe in that stuff? Odin and Thor and all that?"

"You're asking me now? After all these years? The truth is, I don't know. When your father started spending all his time in the lab, it gave me something to do."

"Really? So Asatru is a diversion?"

"I wouldn't call it that. It gives me comfort."

"What, Ragnarook? That end-of-the-world stuff actually calms you down?"

She nodded. "But only because I like the idea of starting anew. 'After the war, only two shall remain. For meat they will feed on morning dew, and from both shall man be reborn.' Beautiful, no?"

I nodded. "Would you like to be one of them, you think? One of the last? Or I guess the first?"

"No. I'm too old. But I like the idea of it just the same."

"Me, too, I think."

She bared a peanut fallen in her lap and posed a question of her own. I still could not acclimate to her being lucid and communicative, so whatever she said caught me by surprise. She wanted to know what gave me comfort.

I shook my head. "I have no idea anymore."

"What did it use to be?"

"I don't know. No Face, probably. Painkillers."

"That's dispiriting."

"You're telling me. Are you going to keep eating once we get home?"

"Yes."

"Are you going to stay off the drugs?"

"I don't know. I'm going to try. It just gets so lonely in that apartment."

I put my hand on hers and said, "But how lonely can it be with me there?" I had meant this to sound funny, to satirize what small consolation this was, but it came out awful, and my heart sank.

Raymond was waiting for us at the gate. "Mrs. Clark. Ms. Clark." We followed him to the garage.

In the car, I watched people in other cars. I looked at billboards for new movies. An ad for the lottery, now $24 million. Everything looked as it had before Bluebonnet, which gave me the disconcerting sensation that after all I'd been through, I was not going to behold my life with new eyes. Also that life in New York had a way of soldiering on.

I asked Raymond what he'd been up to the last few weeks. He said he'd used his vacation time to help the National Guard enforce the quarantine in California, and then joined a bounty hunt for the fleas. I asked if that's what the pros were calling them now, *the fleas*, and what was wrong with *plague bandit*? He had no response. The fleas. How clever. I could just see a national map with pushpin bugs for every sighting.

"I haven't heard anything about those people in a while. Did you get 'em?"

"They are still at large," he said, grimly.

"You realize if they're still alive, they can't have plague? The people who were asymptomatic, it turns out their incubation period was just really long."

"Your sister has reason to believe that some among us are genuinely immune."

"Hannah? You've been talking to Hannah? And passing on what she says? That's crazy."

The glass partition began to rise.

"Oh, leave him alone," Mother said. "You know how Hannah likes to talk."

I sat back in my seat. "What if she's not okay? What if we get home and she's just not okay?"

"Lucy, you can't just start caring and expect everyone else to sympathize."

"I always cared."

Mother did not even bother to reply. I dribbled my head against the window.

"You only just got rid of the last bump," she said. "Stop that."

I noticed a clot of powder base on her cheekbone, and thumbed it over.

"Mom," I said. "I *always* cared."

She asked Raymond to turn up the radio. It was on the hour, news time. A crocodile was making waves in a Jersey family's pool. The health of fish tissue in the Mississippi was at an all-time low. James Watson said in public that being stupid was an inherited disorder and should be arrested with gene therapy.

I turned to Isifrid and said, "Okay, I don't like this at all. Being back. Things just can't be like how they were before. All petty and meaningless. Fish tissue in the Delta? Come on."

"Not me. I like it just fine. Drink?" and she poured herself some sherry.

"You're not supposed to drink."

"The day sherry is crack, I will have died and gone to heaven." She drank her glass and poured another.

When we arrived, there was no one at home, just a note on the door saying Stanley had gone out to eat and Hannah was at Indra Denton's. At least that friendship got patched.

Mother withdrew to her quarters. I had learned enough to know that I could not keep her from drug use and that if two months at Bluebonnet had not deranged her will, I wasn't going to do it in ten minutes. Still, I knocked on her door. Prayer was a few hours away, but I asked all the same if maybe He could spare her.

The shower went on, a toilet flushed. I headed for my room. The bed was unmade and one of Stanley's undershirts was strewn across the pillow. I guess he'd been sleeping there, which was nice. Nice until I made for the kitchen, from where, I realized, Stanley was just trying to sleep as far away as possible. Everything there was fine except the sink, in which a lubricant thick as chowder drizzled down glassware and dishes piled high. Who could live like this? I'd been out of rehab not eight hours and already I was starting to see Bluebonnet through a scrim of nostalgia.

I retreated to my bed. I think I'd been hoping for a welcome-back party. As if Hannah and Stanley, Eric, too, would be eating crudités in the blue room under a banner that saluted my achievement. There might be gifts. Something felicitous rendered in needlepoint by my sister, who'd have discovered in my absence a hobby that affirms life. At the very least, a cake with my name on it. Maybe a card.

I turned on the TV and began to surf through our six hundred channels. On 527 I found a movie about transsexual kung-fu exiles incarcerated in a hippodrome tripping through space and headed for the Hole of Sisyphus. A family favorite.

I called Eric. Voice mail. Said I was home, the place was a landfill and that I wanted to set up a time for Agneth.

Then I made my bed. I felt restless and afraid to feel restless and afraid to feel afraid and then just afraid to feel at all because feelings incite drug use. I returned eyes to the transsexuals. They were versed in martial arts. They were spiked with estrogen. Still, it would be another hour before the movie got good. I traipsed down the hall. Put an ear to Mother's door. Sounds of shower and excitable kung-fu transsexual, let's call her Elbow Toast, ruing her fate.

I paced the hallway. Picked at my nails. And finally resorted to an old standby: the despoiling of Mother's walk-in closet. Closets, because Mother had five, of which three retained vestures from the sixties and seventies, e.g., neon hip-huggers of combustible fabric and trim. I've heard it said these pants can ignite a dryer and ruin your life. I loved them. On occasion I even tried to fit into them, under the illusion that radical changes were happening to my body or her wardrobe. This visit, though, I didn't bother, just flung them at a column of drawers in which handkerchiefs and belts fashioned from skins you never thought could make a belt—porpoise, for instance—and a shoe box. I hadn't been through the drawers in several months, but I think I'd remember a shoe box. Naturally I had to open it. And naturally, it was crammed with secrets. Letters from Dag Bersvendsen, fiancé of yore. The only surprise was that Isifrid had kept them. And that she'd obviously been going through them recently. I thought back to her meltdown at Bluebonnet and began to piece it together. I could not read Norwegian, but the marrow of his subject was evident in the hearts he'd drawn in the margin. A man who draws hearts. The letters were dated 1970 and one from

2002. 2002? The handwriting was not much changed, but there were no hearts. Just a couple lines and his initial, D. I sat down on the carpet. What were the odds that Dag, who never married, had continued to love my mother all these years? Even as she had become monstrous in her addictions and self-disgust? I was just about to return the box to the drawer when I noticed a small envelope, small like what you'd find in a bouquet of flowers, taped to the inside. On the front, my dad's cursive, addressed to Mother.

I opened it without hesitation. It was dated 1992, shortly after Hannah came to live with us. It said two things. *Izz, I'm sorry.* And underneath: *Go back to him.*

I flipped it over, thinking there had to be more. But no. I returned the card to its envelope and the box to the drawer. I was waiting for some kind of response. Like my head would spit out a feeling as if from one of those mixing chambers at a lottery draw. I wanted, at the very least, to be curious. If my mother had a secret life, maybe I could forgive the one she led in front of us. But it wasn't happening. What the letters and note suggested about her inexorable and doomed attachment to Dag Bersvendsen was so horrible, no sooner was it exposed than it ran away. There was no thinking about it. None whatsoever.

I returned to my bed. The kung-fu exiles had just cleared the lip of the Hole of Sisyphus and were wondering just what sort of trouble they were in. This was my favorite part. The hippodrome had to progress through a gas membrane so toxic it nearly killed everyone on board. But they made it. And they rejoiced. Thing is, what now? The Hole of Sisyphus is bleak, goes nowhere. So they think: Oh, crap, our fate is to peruse this hole for eternity. All faces stricken. All hands on deck for debriefing by ship captain. He's just about to say there might be other life-forms in the hole, that cross-breeding is not so bad, when the power goes out and, wham, they are headed again for the Hole of Sisyphus! And the toxic membrane! No one wants to endure this. But they do, at which point the sous-captain produces a book of Greek mythology three thousand years old, from which he reads aloud. The camera pans from one crew member to the next as they realize this is their punishment, to traverse that fucking membrane for eternity. I've seen this movie eight times and yet I always find this hilarious. Duh, Sisyphus. Duh, homophobic allegory. And, now that I think about it: Duh, reincarnation allegory, too.

"But why?" shrieks killer she-male nine, let's call her Yang Yuehai. "We're the same as everyone else!"

I rolled onto my back and eyed the crown molding in my room. Crown molding is tacky. My bedroom was tacky. Maybe I should paint it black. Maybe I needed a do-it-yourself ambition to keep me occupied for the rest of my life.

Stanley knocked on my door. Thank God. I guess he wasn't expecting the welcome because when I barreled into his chest, he caromed off the wall. "I've missed you, too," he said, and kissed my ear.

I stepped back to have a look. So long as Stanley was still Stanley, everything would be fine.

I led him to my bed because this was where we had our best talks. He kicked off his boots and settled in. I was relieved and also alarmed to feel nothing by way of interest pressed against me. Maybe I looked awful. Maybe he was sleeping with someone else.

"Where's Hannah?" I asked.

"Didn't you see my note? She's at Indra's."

"When is she coming back?"

He hesitated just long enough. "Oh no," I said, and shot out of bed and into her room. Empty. Or empty of everything that mattered. The West Nile map. Her chemistry set. Books, clothes. I glanced at some notebooks stacked on the desk and grabbed the top one, feeling like I had to acquire something of hers before it vanished.

I returned to my room and very quietly got back under the covers.

"She's been staying there awhile," he said. "I didn't think it would do you any good to know. And besides, have you seen what the rest of the house looks like? This is no place for a kid."

"But I'm here now," I said, pleading, essentially, for Stanley to believe I could make things well between me and my sister.

"She's a little afraid of you, I think."

"That's great, Stanley. You should have told me she moved out. I would have come home sooner. Did she know I was coming home?"

He looked at me with such pity, I had to turn away.

"I should go talk to her. Maybe take Isifrid, because she's cleaned up some. You think I should go talk to her?"

He stroked my hair and said, "Sure. I bet she'd like that."

I opened the notebook. I skimmed. "Oh, this is horrible," I said. "Listen to this, it's from her journal."

"You took her journal? You shouldn't do that."

"No, no, it was this thing she started doing. Like a chronicle. Stories from her life or something. Just listen."

I read highlights out loud.

If there was no superplague, my biggest problem would be the dance. Two of the most unpopular boys like me. The first is George. It seems to me he is very confused. He only cares for himself. Maybe he is running away from himself. Then there is Adam. He is chubby and rude. Sometimes I feel sorry for him, nobody likes him, but I guess he deserves it.

"Oh, Jesus," Stanley said. "You forget how awful it is being twelve."

"*Shhh*. It gets worse."

There is one student who does everything right. Charles is his name. He always dresses fine, he never complains. It is funny that I think he has the most complex problems of all. He is an overachiever. He pushes himself too hard and so do his parents. He always has to be Mr. Perfect. He is probably going to kill himself.

I put the notebook down. Stanley said, "No, no, don't look like that. This is good. She's just a normal girl. This is how girls think."

"How do you know?"

"Did you think like that when you were twelve?"

"No."

"My point exactly."

I snorted.

Michele likes Mark and has already asked him to the dance. He is sick-minded but in a way so is everybody. He has frenched and he has given girls hickeys. He is cool. I have a date for the dance but I am not satisfied with it. His name is Carlos. He was the first boy to ask a girl for the dance. I said yes because I was afraid that I might not have a date. Well, now I'm stuck.

At this I laughed. "It's kind of dramatic, actually. I wonder what happens next!"

Stanley grabbed at the notebook. "I want to read! My turn!"

But then there was a pause. "Well?" I said.

"Oh, never mind. She starts talking about algebra."

He tried to close the notebook, but I took it back.

I wish I had a brother to be a father figure in place of my dad. There is Lucy, of course, but she's a baby. She's also never home. She tries to pretend like she wants to be home with me, but I see through it.

"Oh my God," I said.

"Come on, she's just a kid. She doesn't really mean it."

But I started to cry. "She hates me. How am I supposed to take care of her?"

Stanley drew me to him with such calm I realized there *was* something different about him. He wasn't drinking. I blinked through tears and said, "What have you been doing these past couple months? I never even asked."

"Not much. I finally stopped looking for a surrogate. It was a crazy idea, anyway."

I sat up. "It was not. It was a beautiful idea. And I don't think you should give up."

"I can't raise a child."

"You can."

"Plus I've been thinking. What if I want to do it for the wrong reasons? What if I just want to bring our child into the world out of guilt? My drinking ruined Sylvie's life, it *took* her life. Do you see what I'm saying?"

"Yes. But it's also possible you want to bring into being evidence that you loved and were loved. And that's good. What's a life worth if you don't have that?"

He sighed heavily. "I don't know. Maybe I just want a family."

"Me, too."

"It's good to have you back," he said.

"Did you stop drinking?"

"Trying."

"Really? How long?"

"Couple weeks."

"You astonish me. How has it been?"

"Awful."

I rolled onto his stomach and lost my face in his neck. "Proud of you," I said.

After a few minutes he asked if we should check on Isifrid.

I said no. I knew exactly what we would find. And it could wait. I was having trouble enough with the day's disclosures. All I felt, lying there with Stanley, was a vague affinity with the space shuttle whose failed reentry was a cautionary tale, and the thing I had feared most about leaving rehab. Not so much you can't go home again, as you could die trying.

Thirty-seven

An hour later, I was back in a basement, sitting among my peers, who were delighted to see me. Actually delighted. I did not shirk human contact, I returned embraces as they were given. In attendance were the regulars—Phil, Allan, Fran, and the Blade—a couple people I didn't know, and Odette, who was talking about her mother. Her mother, I gathered, had died while I was away. And Odette was saying how painful these last few months had been, not for her mother but for herself. "Every night I'd pray to keep her health," she said. "But it was a lie. I knew it and God knew it. I was praying so hard and loud to drown out what I was really praying for, which was that she'd die. That God would take her. Not for her sake, but for mine." She jabbed her breastbone with her index. "For *my sake*. And now I gotta live with that. But you know what? God takes when he sees fit. And I loved my mother. And I know she's happier now. And somehow, knowing that, I feel stronger. You gotta take care of number one, else you are good for nobody. I got three kids. They need their mama."

I'd been staring at the chain around her neck for some time. Her name in gold script. I didn't like the idea of looking out for number one, but I was listening.

The moment came to announce your clean time. Five years. Ten years. Ten days. Ten days? It was a new guy, and he looked devastated. But the applause he got. And the cheers. He had no idea what was going on. I was in awe of him. Multiple years made no sense. I thought they were great, but really, I had no clue what that was about. But ten days! Ten days was like a week plus a few. Ten days could be me. I was, after all, nearing the close of my benzo wean. It'd been two months of decreasing doses. What I took now accommodated my preference for drugs over no drugs, but the physical effects were nil. Even so, I was scared of the end.

The meeting pressed on, it was Phil's turn. He said his baby was due in a month. He said also that when he was a kid, his brother got leukemia and that when it became clear the disease was terminal, he started wishing his brother were dead, too. At the time, Phil was only twelve, but he knew what to do with cocaine and bought a couple lines' worth right down the block from his house. He'd actually wished his brother dead. From his friends at school, he'd heard cocaine could make it all go away. And it had. His brother got worse and he felt nothing. His brother died, he felt nothing. Now, twelve years later, he was only beginning to mourn. But it was better this way. Much better.

I was starting to think tonight's meeting was designed with me in mind, but then that's what everyone thinks.

I decided to share about my own mother, thinking I could say something that'd be a help to us all. "I'm just back from rehab," I said. *Clapping. Welcome back.* "Please don't clap, I can't stand the clapping. I haven't done anything heroic and I could relapse tomorrow." *Keep coming.* "My mother was at rehab with me, though it didn't take. And right now, she's probably knocked out in her bathtub. And I'm here. Why am I here and not there? My father's been dead a year and today I came across a note he wrote my mom ten years ago that makes me think she spent her entire marriage to him longing for someone else. I also just found out my twelve-year-old sister has basically renounced membership in our family. Sound crazy? It's not. What's crazy is that I'm not high. I am dealing with all this clean. Sort of clean. I'm still in detox. But basically I'm clean. Sorta."

Miles, whose hearing had deteriorated badly in the last two months, rubbed my back and yelled, "You're doing all right, kid."

Allan raised his hand. "I'm feeling really messed up tonight and I wasn't going to say anything but fuck that. All this shit about 'looking out for number one' has got to have its limits, right? I got into a fight with my boss at work today. He called me a gook. I'm from Trinidad, for God's sake! So what, I should look out for number one to keep my job? What about my dignity? I told him to fuck off. Later I got a visit from a cop saying I beat up on the boss. And I kept saying, 'Look, if I beat up on him, he'd be dead.'

"You know what it is, you just can't escape your past. Once a con, always a con. It's like, what's it called, that law where all sex offenders have to announce themselves to the community. What the hell is that? If you let him out of jail, you're saying the guy's all right. If you think he's gonna strike again, why let him out of jail? There's just no fucking way to move on in this country."

One of the people I didn't know got in Allan's face so fast, no one saw it coming. He was screaming about how if you don't like the country, get out. The two men were separated. After, I invited Allan to join me, Fran, Drew, and Frank for a wholesome junket on the town.

Before we left, I made for the guy with ten days, who was smoking by the gate. I said he amazed me. He said he felt like shit. I said he gave me hope, which was near impossible. He said in that case, his day was worth living. I said mine, too, and I actually meant it.

I returned to my group, which was debating where to eat. Fran liked to visit places she'd been with a john, hoping someone on staff would recognize her. She proposed the Peninsula Hotel. Allan was still so furious, he didn't care where we went. Drew said a buddy of his was having a party, like a clean person's party, which sounded like the biggest yawn ever. What do people do at a clean person's party? *Talk?*

We went to our favorite dessert venue. I ordered the brownie whiplash. Drew went in for flan, flan being the most cloying and repulsive dessert ever. The rest had sorbet.

We talked about superplague, which flexed, inevitably, into talk about Bluebonnet and J.C., news of whom had dominated the papers for weeks. As it turned out, though ours was not the only center-turned-compound—across the country spas, hotels, and farming communities had closed ranks and secured their borders—Bluebonnet was the only one to experience death.

Fran said, "Think it was bad in Texas? You should have seen it here. Totally nuts. I been on the streets a long time and even in seventy-seven, during the blackout, it was nothing like this. I saw a man get punched in the face for a bottle of water."

"Punched?" Frank said. "I saw a couple get stabbed for their hospital masks. This little old couple. If it wasn't for my stupid brain, maybe I could have done something."

"Oh, Frank," I said. "You can't be responsible for everything."

He slurped at his peach sorbet. The traumatizing brain injury, sustained during speedball practice with friends atop a building, retarded the rate at which signals went to and from his brain so that even as his mind was saying, *Help these people*, his body would not move until several seconds later.

Allan, who was still smoldering, said, "I bet that fuck at the meeting is our highly patriotic American. I hate those fucks who say you're unpatriotic because you don't support the party line. I'm from Trinidad, I know what democracy means."

They asked for the scoop on J.C. I said how is it that people were getting beaten and stabbed here, but that the big news item was about some guy whose death was an accident?

"Because they buried him," Fran said. "Without telling anyone."

"So you're saying all people care about is ritual and protocol?"

Drew, who'd gone back to school for history and relished any chance to make it known, said, "It's what keeps law and order. You think anyone gives a crap what the president says at his inauguration? Unless you got Henry Harrison up there, because he spoke for two hours then caught pneumonia and died, no one cares. All that matters is that he gives a speech."

I demurred. "Okay, it's better to administer proper rites than not, but if we're choosing the worser sin, I'd say stabbing for a face mask beats out improper burial by a long shot."

"Say what you want," Fran added. "But J.C. is the one making the headlines. I bet they hang him."

Frank said, "Can they do that?"

We thought not, but then who knew what sort of abomination our justice system would mete out next.

"I feel bad for him," I said. "He was just really scared. He's got a pregnant wife. He's only a kid."

Fran stirred her coffee with a straw, which began to melt.

"I feel the worst for Travis," Allan said, addressing himself to the marble patterning on the tabletop, and afraid, it seemed, to make eye contact. He was still angry. I think guys who tend to anger are just compensating for inability to moderate feeling, and, owing to a stigma against hysteria in men—depressive unction in men, the sob without cause in men—the extreme of rage is often the only extreme allowed. Not so Allan. He could move from fury to desperation in seconds, and be equally histrionic in his experience of both. "Travis is heartbreaking. Here's a guy whose blind old uncle might have superplague—who, mind you, will die only a couple years ahead of schedule if he *does* have it—and who decides the only thing to do is to walk for two days in the desert trying to get help? Help that won't do a thing if the uncle's got it, but which might make things a little nicer anyway? To go through all that just to get knocked off by some jerk-off kid? How many people like Travis you think are out there? I bet he was just as scared as J.C. Isn't it amazing how different we can act? Or that our lives are so powerful that we are given the chance to make choices that can make of us men or dogs or something like God? It's crazy. No one gets the chances we do."

"Or the remorse," I said, "when you fuck up. Though maybe that's not fair. I mean, fear—panic—it's a chemical agent like anything else. Maybe J.C. just wasn't born with the strength to hold his liquor. It's not like you can study in advance and prepare for the test."

Fran shook her head. "That's just lazy. Every day you are alive is like studying. If you're paying attention, anyway."

"Well, la-di-da," I said. "Professor Fran."

She blew me a kiss.

Drew ran his fingers through his hair. "We're all scared. That's what's so messed up. Having to live with fear all the time. It's making people crazy. And people like us, we have the added problem of already *being* crazy."

We laughed. Nothing seemed to please us more than to acknowledge our own insanity.

"Well, maybe it's over," I said. "No new reports in a month."

Fran knuckled her forehead. Drew, for lack of salt, tossed a sugar substitute over his shoulder.

Allan turned to me. "That's fucked up about your dad's note. Can I ask what it said?"

"Just that my mom should return to this guy who was her fiancé a million years ago. He worked for her company for a long time after that. I guess maybe they stayed in love? I have no idea."

Fran asked what I was going to do.

"Do? What's there to do? I have to do something?"

"No. But I mean, now that you're back from rehab, just if you had any plans or anything. Get a job or go back to school. I don't know. I was just talking. Ignore me."

But this was not to be ignored. "No, really, I'm supposed to do something? With my life or about Dag Bersvendsen?"

"Is that his name? That's ridiculous." This from Allan, Allan from Trinidad whose parents were Gayatre and Doodon Ramsaroop.

Fran said, "I just thought maybe you'd talk to your mother. Or, um, Dag, if you can. Tying up loose ends, isn't that what you call it?"

Conversation stalled, the bill came. We forked over money, I covered Allan. While we were waiting for change, he said, "You know Mark skipped town? Moved upstate. I thought maybe you had something to do with it." He was looking at me intensely. "I thought maybe he went to that chicken farm."

I laughed. I could not even remember who Mark was. "Not me," I said. "Why, did a lot of people leave? And where's Ben, by the way?"

Expressions around the table said this was a touchy subject. Because the people who fled the city, they were scorned. They were craven.

I pressed. "Did Ben leave town, too?"

Fran said yes. He and his wife had bought a house and whelping dog in Maine.

Wait, what? Dirty Ben in Maine? With brindled collie and puppies?

"Christ," I said, and sunk low in my chair. "I don't have any plans for the future. I'm not doing anything."

Drew said, "Sure you are. You're seeing friends and trying out your life clean. That's plenty."

How nice. Like I was testing a new bra.

Frank had been quiet for some time. He'd get quiet a lot. You couldn't tell if brain injury or mood was responsible, so mostly you just waited for him to perk up, which he did, saying, "Good for Ben. Smart move. It's been a month since plague, yeah, but until they catch the guy, it's not over. It'll be back."

I went outside. We were three weeks into March, but the wind said otherwise, and the damp seemed to cleave to your bones. Frank was right, of course. The plague would be back. And this meant I had a very small window in which to address matters of the heart, chief among them Eric. I had decided to let him go, though not in any traditional sense. I was not going to grand-gesture him out of my life, there was just no way. What I could do, however, was to invite Kam back in. She was the solution. Our history conduced to friendship, and friendship was estimable and I was needing to do estimable things. First thing tomorrow: estimable things. Seeing my friends, testing my life.

Thirty-eight

had put Aggie in a giant *hangetsu* bento box. A bamboo case in which to present sushi. An urn seemed too austere and I imagined Agneth would enjoy the sight of her remains in a Japanese serving dish. Likewise the Japanese garden in Brooklyn, which is where I told Eric to be. I'd actually never been, so there was novelty in just about every aspect of our venture. My plan was to free Agneth and then to *talk*.

The garden had just opened, and everything in it appeared to be yawning. On the opposite side of the pond was a wooden gateway shaped like pi, whose persimmon gloss struck out against the greenery so that you couldn't look anywhere else. I gathered the pi announced a shrine in the grove behind, which might make for a good place to deposit Agneth. I'd heard enough stories where a breeze sends Grandma Del into everyone's hair and eyes, down a throat or several, to want to avoid this outcome at all costs.

Eric was late. I was nervous about seeing him, and then when I thought he wasn't coming, I started to worry, and then to get angry, like: How dare he deny Nana? When I saw him strolling past the giant stone lantern at the entrance, I was still mad. He waved. I folded my arms across my chest. He noticed just in time, else he might have hugged me, which I wanted so much I was even more furious when he pulled up short and said, "Hey," followed by the shoulder squeeze. The shoulder squeeze!

"You look really great," he said. "How are you feeling? Is it good to be back?"

"I can rope a steer."

It was finally warm out and he was in a jeans jacket, which I always found too femme on guys, except that Eric was beautiful in anything. His hair had grown out so that it came down the sides of his face. He'd also filled out his sideburns and gotten a new tattoo on the inset of his arm, which appeared to depict an Australian postage stamp of two large red-and-green flowers superimposed on a city by the water. It was quite delicate. And his mom, who was from Sydney, I bet she loved it.

"Okay," he said, "but can you *ride?*"

"Of course. My inner thighs can kill a man."

He laughed.

"I'm doing fine," I said. "World's going to shit, but why complain."

I looked at my shoe. This was not how I had meant to act, all tough and abradant. In my mind, we were to embrace with real joy because a lot had happened since last we met and we'd survived and grown stronger and more committed to the people we loved and less committed to all the shit in between and hey, by the way, let's you, me, and Kam go have dinner next week because I need you people to stay alive.

He said, "Amazing, isn't it? I can hardly believe the chaos of the last few months. It's really brought out the best and worst in people."

I could tell he was not feeling comfortable, either. When anxious, he tended to platitude. Me, I got combative.

"Best? Where? From everything I've heard, we're one case away from that movie, what's it called, where those schoolkids get put on an island and the only way to survive is to kill each other off."

He smiled and gestured at the path. I doubt he knew the garden any better than I did, but walking seemed in order.

"So contentious," he said.

"I prefer feisty."

"So feisty," he said.

I laughed, which had an unfurling effect on my mood. "I'm glad to see you," I said. "It was scary out there."

"Here, too. But you really do look good. I can see a difference."

I didn't know what to say, so I said nothing. I hated the idea of looking improved. I didn't want him to expect anything of me, least of all a successful experience of life now that I was clean.

"Now really," he said. "How are you feeling?"

"Okay."

"Are you lying?"

"I don't know. Today is my first full day off drugs. The wean is over."

"That's terrific! Really great. No wonder you're looking so well."

"I feel a little woozy. Just a little, though."

"Yeah, but that'll pass."

We came to a bridge and a small island shaped like a turtle. "This island is ridiculous," I said.

"It's supposed to symbolize longevity."

I stopped walking. "Is there an irony here? Because I can't scatter ashes in the presence of irony."

"None whatsoever." He sat in the grass, Indian style. "I've seen that movie, by the way, *Battle Royale*. My favorite are the ninth-grade girls who commit suicide rather than kill each other. No survival instinct at all."

"I know. But you think their behavior makes them better or worse people?"

"I'm not sure it's a moral issue. The will to live can't be qualified."

"I wouldn't say that. That's like saying all the Nazi collaborators were just acting out a survival instinct. Like it's okay to mass murder if it means saving yourself."

"That's an extreme case. But think about a father of three who can hide a Jew in the basement and risk all their lives or refuse to help. Say he refuses, you gonna call that immoral?"

"In that case, how are you feeling about Kam's parents? I still can't believe they wouldn't let you stay at their house."

"I wouldn't call it immoral."

"But you'd call it something bad."

"*Understandable*. That's what I'd say."

"Bullshit. And anyway, you would not have done the same to them."

"How do you know? We all think we'll act a certain way, hope to, in any case, but when the time comes, instinct can override anything. Just look at your guy at Bluebonnet."

"So you're saying it's okay that he killed Travis?"

"I'm not saying it's okay or not. I'm just saying he acted with no regard for these things. That a good man, a really good man, went down as a result is beside the point."

"Ah, so we're back to your *fuck it* theory. Haven't grown at all, I see."

"Nope, not an inch. You?"

I laughed.

"So that's Aggie?" he said, pointing to the box.

"Is it weird, this Japanese thing? I thought she'd like it."

"No, she would. It's nice. Should we do it here?"

"I was thinking maybe the shrine would be better. But I don't know. I thought this was going to be more emotional. That it's not is making me feel low."

"That's emotional. And anyway, you feel what you feel and whatever you feel is part of your response. And that's fine."

I smiled. "It's really nice of you to do this with me."

He smiled back.

In the shallows across the pond were two bronze statues glinting in the sun. Pelicans, maybe. Or storks. Ornithology wasn't my thing, but I was pretty sure a pelican had no business in a Japanese garden.

I pointed at them. "What if those were real birds in there? Like they'd been cryogenically preserved."

"Seems like wasted resources."

"No, but what if they were test-running the process for use on humans?"

"What for? You really want to wake up after the plague has wiped out humanity?"

I sighed. "Izzy and I just had this talk. She says she's too old to want to outlive anything."

"Now there's a cheering thought."

"Yep."

He skipped a pebble across the pond.

"I bet we get thrown out for that," I said. "For disturbing the peace."

"Then I hardly think spreading ashes is allowed."

"Good point. Maybe stealth is in order."

He stood and held out his hand. We crossed the bridge and followed the path to a waterfall. "A symbol of change," he said.

"You bring a crib sheet or something?"

"No, I just watch a lot of PBS."

"There's the shrine," I said. "Looks kind of like a tree house."

"With a *hogyo* roof?"

"Okay, who are you? Why do you know what that's called?"

He pointed at the learning station, which made me laugh. So much laughing. We mounted the steps and sat on the top one. I had the box on my knees.

"Are we supposed to say anything?" he said.

"I don't know."

"Are you going to open it?"

"I'm afraid her ashes will get all over us."

"How about if we put the box on the top of that little hill and just leave it open. That way the wind will take her when it wants. And we can watch from a distance."

"What if there's no wind and nothing happens so I go over to the box and just then a gust blows the ashes all over me? I only put some of them in there, so this could happen."

"We won't go back to it no matter what."

"Okay."

I put the box down, lid closed. We were both staring at it. The pressure to say something was much like what I felt having to talk to God. I wanted to do it, but I didn't quite believe it meant anything.

He rubbed my back and said, "Just be honest, it'll be fine."

I looked down at the box. "Okay, Agneth, I'm doing what you asked. I hope if you're out there, you're happy, and that if you're coming back, it's the way you wanted. I miss you. I guess scattering your ashes is just a gesture but I like knowing you'll grow into next year's flowers and grass. So as far as I'm concerned, you're definitely coming back, one way or the other. I love you."

I bent down and removed the lid. The air was perfectly still. Eric led me several feet away, where we stood like parents on the sideline. I hardly noticed his arm around my shoulder. Within minutes, a breeze picked up, warm and gentle, which took Agneth in a swell that toured the garden—the pond, the trees, the grass.

I leaned into him. "Just like you said." And I felt, I felt almost quiet.

We stayed that way for a minute or so. I thought I might even close my eyes. But then I felt him straighten up and the calm around us turn brisk. It was time for business, it seemed. We'd eaten and drunk, fucked whores, played golf, and now came the moment to divvy up New York. Only it was supposed to have been on my cue, not his, because I was the one with something to say. Unless he had something to say, which thought plied my body with cement. My worst fear? He was about to let me go in the most conventional sense of all.

We walked until the path split. He led us to a stone bench, where he sat forward with elbows braced on his knees.

I felt sick. I could not possibly make a speech about friendship among three knowing he was about to cut me loose. I figured for the heaviness I was experiencing already, I should just turn to stone and die.

"Luce," he said. "I need to tell you something."

"Uh-oh."

"No, no, it's nothing bad."

Then fine, don't tell me. "What is it?"

"It's Kam. She's pregnant."

I said nothing for a good three seconds. And it's not like I shattered but that I felt a rolling sensation, like I might just roll away. A rolling stone, I heard that before.

"Really? Congratulations. When is she due?"

"Two weeks."

And then I shattered. He was not throwing me over at all. He was, possibly, asking me to babysit. He was including me in his life with Kam. It was exactly what I'd wanted.

"What? And you're just telling me now? She's been pregnant this whole time? I can't believe it."

"Luce, we didn't want to say anything in the beginning, and then you were away."

"And you couldn't tell me on the phone?"

"I'm sorry. It just seemed too hard to talk about."

I perked up. "Why?"

"Because I'm terrified. Having a child is scary enough. But if plague hits New York—I've been hearing rumors. It's insane to bring a child into this."

"How's Kam handling it?"

"Same as me."

"And you still think her parents are *understandable*?"

"No. I think they are barbaric. Lucy, I'm really scared."

And I was miserable. So miserable it was almost bewildering. Did I really think there was a place for me in all this? Did I really want to *be* in all this?

"Don't be scared," I said. "It'll be great."

"It's a boy," he said. "A son."

"That's wonderful."

"I hope, maybe if things calm down, that you'll come see him later. Be like an honorary aunt or something."

I was getting clobbered. I wanted to hide under the bench. "Of course I will." And, "In the meantime, give Kam my best."

We stood. "I have to go see about Hannah now. You know she moved out to a friend's?"

"Is she coming back?"

"Yes. But I still have to go get her. Not looking forward to that at all."

"You'll do fine. I'm really impressed with how far you've come."

I was not going to be able to take this much longer. I began to count the steps to the subway, just put him on a subway.

We got to the entrance. "Aren't you coming?" he said.

"Nah, I think I'll walk for a while. Thanks again for doing this with me today."

"My pleasure."

"And congratulations. It's going to be great, you'll see."

We fumbled through a hug-kiss, and said bye. I waited for two subways to pass and then went down the stairs. I'd been a fool, of course, but then I almost found this reassuring. Even if I got better, kept clean, beat plague, mourning for Eric would be the hurt that stayed with me. And the thing that kept me sensitive to hope. Because in addition to slaughtering the most tender parts of your inner life, hurt also says: You are a person of feeling and people who feel have everything to offer.

Thirty-nine

Connie Denton lived in an apartment complex that spanned a city block in both directions. It was, I gathered, where old people went to die. If you could escape detention in a retirement home, West Twenty-third Street was the place to be. It had an indoor greenhouse maintained by the residents. The lobby floors were blanched marble. For every door a doorman. I had no idea why Connie would want to live here unless to forecast her future and be prepared.

The man manning the door was courteous. The desk guy, not so much. I looked past him to an assembly of strollers and scooters, which spoke to the intelligence of marble flooring—perfect for wheels, young and old. He wanted to help me—could he help me?—to which I said, No, thanks, to which he said, Ma'am?, to which I said, Oh, fine, Connie Denton, to which, And you are?, in a tone less querying than imperious, to which, Dorothy Hamill, okay? to which nothing, and down the hall I went, *jogged*, until safely behind elevator doors.

Forty-eighth floor. I hoped Connie did not have giant windows. On my way here, the wooziness of before had turned swoon; and the carpet underfoot, it felt downy. Like cotton. Or fluff. When the elevator opened, I swear I'd been levitating. From an adjacent apartment came sounds of wildlife—a bird or birds—like crampons against the blackboard. The effect was to make noticeable on my face the extent to which this headache was eroding my will to live, let alone visit with Connie Denton, who, if memory served, had a fairly shrill voice of her own. I knocked. I depressed the bell. I heard, coming closer, a shuffle of feet, of slippers, actually, whose sound was an index of old age, which had me thinking this was the wrong door and then, too late, that I should split, for there appeared a woman in puce robe and curlers asking what I wanted, Who are you?, and, in a shriek worse than any bird: Connie, there's someone at the door!

I staggered inside, holding my head like it might fall off. When did this pain in my neck start? Connie rounded a corner, saying, Mom, you're gonna wake the dead with that hollering, when she saw me and pulled up short. I love people in the instant before they make a choice; I love to watch them compute. It's probably the most spry and accomplished your mind gets. Chicken or beef may sound facile, but think how much you gotta factor in before making a decision, like what you ate yesterday, what you're gonna eat tomorrow, fat, protein, ancillary digestive issues, shrapnel in teeth, cost v. gain analysis—and that's all for a shitty fajita at Taco Bell, imagine me and Connie, do I throw her out, take her coat, and why does she look half dead?

"Lucy? What are you doing here? My God, are you feeling okay? Wait, tell me you did not come here on whatever drugs it is that you're on. Hannah told me everything."

I tried to follow her line of thought, but ended up asking for water. I really did not feel well.

Connie's mother said to her, "What's the matter with you? Get this girl some water." I laughed despite what felt like combat soldiers rappelling down my spine. Mothers. You never could outgrow them.

"Here," Connie said, and sat opposite. It was then I noticed they wore matching robes and that Connie's hair was just so flat as to have been newly ironed, which meant when I rang, they were doing each other's hair. How to describe the tenderness I felt for them except to say Connie's antipathy to me was of equal proportion.

"I think you'd better leave," she said. "The girls are in school and no way are you going to see Hannah like this. You have some nerve coming here."

I nodded and thought, Rain it on me. It was the first in many months where what was happening accorded precisely with how I felt.

She continued. "Do I have to call the doorman? Let's not make this ugly."

Meantime, Connie's mother had put a cold washcloth to my head. Apparently, I had slouched so aggressively that the slouch had turned lie-down, and I was sweating.

"Connie," she said. "This child is sick."

"Good, she probably has superplague—" After which mother and daughter froze for the other kind of instant I love, when you realize you are absolutely fucked.

"It's not plague," I said. "For God's sake."

"How do you know?" Connie said.

It'd be painful, but I rolled my eyes anyway. The last place I wanted to experience an onset of withdrawal was Connie Denton's apartment, but then I'd forgotten what happens, even after a wean, when your body realizes its only friend has not only been downsizing the relationship but ending it altogether. How else to respond but with what's at hand? A body in grief is unstoppable. Soon, I would be vomiting. The combat soldiers would mine every tendon and slash every nerve. Already, my head was changing shape, to swell and taper like a punchball. I felt braised. And my tongue was sere.

"Withdrawal," I managed.

"Oh, good Lord," Connie said. "In my house. Weren't you in Texas for this?"

"How's my sister?"

"Would you like some soup? Chicken or minestrone?" This from the mom, whose name was Gloria. "A child like you, you need to eat."

"She's not a child. She's thirty." Connie had moved to a recliner. Her tone was forbearing. I had maybe ten minutes left, though I needed more like twenty if I wanted to catch Hannah.

"Soup would be great." And to Connie I added, "It's very kind of you to see me. I'm sorry I came without warning."

"Uh-huh."

I sat up and focused on a discolored pinch of skin visible above the cleft of her robe, because that lazy eye was no antidote for nausea.

"So, can I ask about Hannah? I only found out recently she's been staying here."

"Living here."

"Right. Living here. If I had known, I would have come back sooner."

Connie sat forward. "And done what? I cannot believe the conditions under which that poor little girl has been living. She needs to be unlearned of most everything! And that man you left in charge, *Stanley*? Someone should have called child services."

"Say what you will about me, but leave Stanley out of it. He's a good man."

She glowered.

"Okay, I know," I said. "It's not been ideal. Things just got a little out of control this past year."

"A *little*?"

I could hear Gloria singing in the kitchen. And I swear the lazy eye winced.

"Don't look so put out," Connie said. "If this is the most honest you've been about what Hannah's gone through, you are in even more trouble than I thought."

"But how's she doing?"

Connie stood. "You've done a lot of damage. I found little cuts all up her legs and arms. She says she got banged up in gym."

"Oh, man. Kids are rotten."

"Are you listening? Are you retarded? She's been cutting herself."

"What? Like to hurt herself? No way."

Connie shook her head. "The school therapist isn't too swift, but he says it's more like punishing herself."

"Oh, God." I paused and went: *think, think*. "Look, it's very kind of you to have stepped in the way you did. But I'm here now, and I want to take my sister home."

Gloria appeared with a tray bearing soup and spoon. "Maybe she doesn't want to go," she said, and deposited the tray on my lap.

"Of course she does. It's her home."

Connie looked at her watch, resigned to Hannah's arriving while I was there. Gloria said eat your soup. It stung my cheek, which meant drooling it back into the bowl. On the bright side, the pain distracted me from the pain in my head and the irreclaimable condition of the muscles in my neck and mouth, knotted so tight as to be immobile. Lockjaw was setting in. Petrified neck. So as not to panic I thought, This too shall pass, and when that failed, I said a trench prayer that set me back weeks. I'd been making a point of talking to God thoughtfully and with equal regard for ambivalence and effort. A trench prayer was like racing for the finish line after weeks of learning to stroll.

Gloria said to Connie that she should cut me some slack. I was trying, wasn't I?

"You know," Connie said. "Despite everything, Hannah idolizes you. That's a big responsibility."

I grew ten feet and toppled; and at the door, laughter.

Both girls seemed to rear when they saw me, Indra adding a snarl to the mix so that no matter what emotion I had roused in her, she was going to look haughty feeling it. I did not expect Hannah to throw her arms around me. But then I didn't expect indifference, either. "Oh, hey," she said, and made for the kitchen, where she grabbed a can of Coke, cracked it open, and off to their room, Indra in tow.

I looked from Gloria to Connie and back. "That went well," I said. Probably I should have gotten up. Sundered relations between me and the couch. But the people's revolution in my gut was gaining momentum, and my legs now lacked for tensile strength, which meant from A to B, I'd have to ooze across the floor like pudding. Pudding! Gloria showed up with a garbage pail just in time.

The sound returned Hannah to the living room. On a scale of one to ten, how little did I want her to see me like this? After I'd come so far? I was retching in a pail, which was actually an ice bucket with antelope handles on either side.

She kept her distance, but asked Connie what was wrong with me.

"Withdrawal, apparently."

Hannah nodded. Her detachment was a horror. "So guess what?" she said.

I recognized that tone of voice. Droll and moribund. "Oh, no," I said.

"Yep."

"When?"

"Just now."

"Oh, no."

I glanced at Connie, whose pride was such that she'd sooner stay in the dark than ask what the hell me and my sister were talking about. By the same token, she likely guessed at the satisfaction I took in keeping her in the dark, which meant she knew I was petty, which all but soured the pleasure of the whole friggin battle.

Good thing, Gloria. She wedged the tip of her thumb between her upper and lower teeth and said, "What do you mean?" then lunged for the TV on which we interrupt this broadcast to bring you this special news report.

"Damn," she said.

Indra came flying out of her room, screaming. She had just heard it on the radio. "New Jersey? It's in New *Jersey*?! Holy crap it's in New Jersey! Mom, we have to go to the country!"

I watched her try to crawl inside her mother, as Hannah gently slid down the wall to a sitting position. She pushed up her sleeves, and it was true: Her arms were tracked with hatch marks.

"Oh, Hannah," I said. "Honey. What are you doing to yourself?"

She yanked at the cuff of each sleeve while Indra continued to mewl. "Mom, what are we going to do?"

"It's okay, baby. Everything's going to be just fine."

Indra was not consoled. She was way past consolation and into the hard facts. "Mom, you, me, Grandma, and Luther can barely fit in the car. If we have to take stuff—how are we all going to fit?"

Holy smokes. So much for the angel in every child, so much for the children are our future. This miserable little twit was trying to freeze out my sister.

"*Shhh*," Connie said. "Just settle down."

Gloria undid a roll of her hair, then another. She piled the curlers on the table. I braved the three steps between me and Hannah without incident. The floor tiles appeared cubed and motile. I tried to swipe them out of the way. Hannah slapped my hand. "Stop that," she said. "Go home."

"Honey, listen. It's just withdrawal. It's temporary. I didn't think it would be this bad. Besides the wean, I've been clean for almost three months. I swear."

Her face was stony, and again she told me to go away.

"Hannah, who do you think I'm doing this for? Me? Izz? I'm trying to straighten out for you. It's why I came back at all. Oh, look, don't cry. Just pack up your stuff and you can come home with me." I tried to stand on my own. Instead, I groped for the ice bucket.

Connie said, "You are a piece of work, you know that? What makes you think just because you're ready to say sorry, everyone else is ready to accept it? What kind of narcissism is that?"

I had nothing to say. I just felt tired. I just wanted to sleep.

"Hannah," I said. "Listen. This is a time for family. Especially if the plague is back. You me and Izzy need to stick together. You think when push comes to shove *Indra's* gonna look out for you? In this house, the gerbil comes before you."

"His name is Luther," Indra said. The spite in her voice was incredible.

"Hannah," I said. "Be reasonable. Just come home."

But my baby sister, somewhere along the line she got way smarter than me. "You can't just stop taking drugs and show up all of a sudden."

"What? Why? What's wrong with trying to be a better person so that you can help your family?" I put the question to her, feeling like I'd dodged a bullet.

"You don't even know me," she sniffled. "You never pay attention."

"I always pay attention! What do you mean? We've done tons of things together!"

She continued to stare at the floor. I've never had this dream, but I bet it's bad, when you wake up in court just as the judge renders his verdict against you. Was I on trial? I didn't even know! Only in my version of the dream, the dream as I live it every day, I go right back to sleep because what the hell, the judgment's been made.

Hannah took to the couch and drew a pillow to her chest.

Connie looked at me, shaking her head. "You are definitely leaving." She gestured to the door.

I looked at Hannah intently, thinking: What if I don't ever see you again? It was possible. With superplague en route to New York, anything was possible. She was my half-sister. Seventeen years between us. She'd grown up without my help, and she was right, I didn't know her at all.

"Today," Connie said, and pressed her palm to the small of my back.

Gloria, who had a bobby pin in her mouth, asked Hannah to assist with a hairpiece and comb, which, once in place, concealed the curls she'd just spent hours setting up.

I watched Hannah, the slant of her eyes picked up in the reed of each lip, and thought how much she looked like our dad.

"Thank you for taking care of her," I said to Connie. She was ushering me out the door. "Also, if you leave town, can you just call to say where you are?" More like shoving, she was shoving me out the door.

For a moment I considered her behavior a kidnapping and wondered how long before I engaged a lawyer or the police. On the other hand, Connie, Gloria, Indra, Hannah, and *Luther* in the country—a country house, I presumed—beat out, for safety, our apartment or the chicken plant. So it was pragmatic, this turn of events. In everyone's best interest.

"Hannah," I said, beseeching. But she didn't even look up, which added a new component to the afflictions of my body, such that the soldiers at war actually seemed to pause in their labors to acknowledge it: sorrow, chief assailant and keeper of secrets, for instance, how best to kill you over the course of your whole life.

I heard the chain lock in place on the other side of the door. I was not done being sick. And the door, it felt like wax against my forehead.

I wooed myself down the hall, down the elevator, past the empty desk, and outside, which was desolate but for an atmosphere of complete and utter panic.

Forty

At home, it was as expected: Stanley knocking on Mother's door, Mother embalmed in a high from which there was no escape.

I asked how long.

"Couple hours," he said. "At least."

I think I groaned, or growled, I don't know, whatever the sound of fury. I wanted to take an ax to the door.

We were standing in the hallway. Stanley continued to knock and call her name in the sort of voice meant to relax a wild animal.

"Stanley, don't be an idiot. Just open the door."

"It's locked."

"Break it!"

"I don't want to break it."

By now, the soldiers were losing conviction; some were even defecting to my side. The mission? *Loathe Stanley.*

"She's been in there a couple hours and you've just been standing here? Knocking on the door like a butler?"

There was no limit to how much abuse I could heap on him, which made me crazier still.

"Mother!" I hollered, and pounded on the door. "I'm coming in." Normally, my shoulder against wood was no contest, but as I was in a rage, as the thud against my skin was welcome, I managed to jerk the door open with three attempts.

Her room was dark, curtains closed. It smelled of sheets that needed changing. Not a bad smell, but thick and sleepy, like the musk of a house unaired for years.

She was curled up in bed. I could tell she had been crying from the swell of her pores and the spackle crusted at the levees of each eye. She'd been on a tear since the moment we got back from Blue-bonnet not even a day ago. She wore sweats that extended well beyond her hands and feet, and which ballooned well beyond her frame, so that if not for that pale face, she'd be hard to locate among the bedcovers in disarray.

I opened the curtains. Against the light, she took refuge under many throw pillows.

I said her name. She said close the curtains. They were opaque red satin, sold at auction from some dead lady's estate.

I sat on the edge of the bed, which was one of those NASA foam deals that cast your body every time you lay down. Personally, I found this disgusting. And revealing of people who want to be enveloped, even digested, by the oblivion of sleep.

"I don't feel well," she said. "Take my temperature?"

Because there are only so many gestures with which to express and possibly mitigate frustration, I pressed at my temples with an aim to dent the skin, to puncture the skin, and let my thoughts wheeze out.

"You said you were gonna eat."

"I have been eating."

"Crack is not food."

"Don't get high and mighty with me. I know where you've been, remember?"

I couldn't tell if she meant the womb, rehab, or chronic unhappiness, which, to be fair, I was still in.

"Plague's in New Jersey," I said.

"I know. I saw the news. What's happening out there?"

"Just what you'd expect."

"Hannah?"

"Connie Denton's. She's got a country house or something."

"You and Stanley?"

"I don't know. Probably back to Wanda's. You can come, of course. You should. Raymond could drive us. There's a decent hospital up there, too."

"Raymond quit. He went to Puerto Rico."

"There's plague in Puerto Rico."

"Try telling that to Raymond. Besides, what good's a hospital?

One thing your father was great at was total destruction. You get it, you die."

"Why do you have to say stuff like that? You all seemed happy enough."

"Even you can't believe that."

"Mom, you need to be in a hospital. You look awful."

"I do not."

I went to the bathroom and returned with a handheld mirror.

"Get that thing away from me," she said, swatting.

"When's the last time you looked at yourself? You're barely here. Mom," I said, and thrust the mirror back at her. "You're gonna die like this."

She lifted her head a little. "Now where have I heard that before?"

"You are the most selfish creature on earth."

"I know."

"What? What do you know?"

"That I'm dying." She sounded so weary, I knew she meant it. "But I also don't much care." And I knew she meant that, too.

"Mom, if you just stopped with the drugs. You were doing so much better at Bluebonnet. We could talk. You know, I'd tell you stuff and you'd listen."

So there it was: Mother was to me what I was to Hannah. We had learned by example or were programmed from the start; in either case, both of us filled our roles perfectly.

"My darling girl. I wasn't doing better at Bluebonnet. I just wasn't doing drugs."

The muscles in my neck were not getting paid enough for this shit; I hung my head. Everything this day had wrought was beginning to roil and bubble over. First Eric, then Hannah, now this.

"Mom, you can't just tell your kid that you don't want to live anymore. Don't I matter? Don't you care what happens to me?"

I was still sitting on the edge of the bed when I tipped over like a traffic cone. She touched my cheek with her palm, and kept it there. That her touch was consoling broke me down entirely.

"Of course you matter. And you will be fine. You won't turn into me, you are stronger. You certainly won't make the same mistakes I did."

"How do you know? I'm already a mess. And I can't learn if you won't stay to teach me."

"Because I know."

"This is crazy. I'm not going to back you on this one."

"You don't have to."

"I'm calling 911."

"And saying what? That your mother's dying and refuses treatment?"

"You don't have to die! Just shut up about dying!"

"Lucy, listen to me. Quinty has all my papers and he knows what to do and has assured me that even if all hell breaks loose, you will be provided for. The only reason I'm not just writing you a check is because probate will protect you come tax time."

I covered my ears. "Shut up! Shut up! I can't listen to this."

She stared at me with excessive calm, the calm of a mind made up for good.

I cheered up a little because I thought I'd found the glitch in her story. "You told Quinty you wanted to die? I don't believe that."

"No, you let Quinty think I had cancer. So I didn't have to say much at all."

"Okay, just tell me this is not happening. Do you understand that there's a maniac out there releasing superplague all over the country? Do you realize Hannah is so messed up she's been cutting herself? And you're just going to leave me all alone?"

She took a long breath that spasmed into a bid for air that grew her eyeballs tenfold. When it was over, she turned away from me and said, "We both know I've been gone for years."

Her resolve was almost magnificent.

"Can I ask you something?" I said.

"You found the letters? I knew you would."

"You wanted me to?"

"Yes. A person should be known by someone."

"I am not someone. I'm your daughter."

"And I wanted you to know."

"It's true, then? About Dag?" I could feel her nodding.

"I've made some mistakes."

"You're not supposed to say that! You're supposed to say, But if I hadn't met your father, I would not have had you."

More coughing. "I haven't been a good mother, I know. But if I had a choice to trade you for Dag, I would not have done it for anything. I never wanted to lose you. But if I had the chance to do it all over, from the start, so that if I chose Dag you would never have been, then I don't know. You can't miss what you've never had."

"Yes you can."

"Well, I don't know."

"Why didn't you try to start up again with him? You could have gotten a divorce."

She laughed. "Your father certainly thought I belonged with Dag. But I was not so sure."

Oddly, this came as a disappointment. Since learning of Aggie's sailor and then Dag, not to mention my circumstances with Eric, it seemed like our experiences were supposed to be some kind of referendum on love. All in favor? None. But Izzy's story didn't fit. It was more complicated. I wanted to despise her not just for messing up her kids, but for adding to Nana's legacy—the Monsen women forgo love. Instead, she was uncertain if she'd ever loved at all.

"Mom, you can get help. Your life is not over. You've got family. And chances. Maybe he's even still waiting for you."

She sighed. "Lucy, bring me that jewelry box?"

"Are you fucking kidding? You want to get high *now*?" I grabbed the box and turned it over. "Oh, sorry," I said, and picked up the rings from the floor.

"Give Hannah your father's. You can do with mine what you wish."

It fit perfectly. "I can't deal with this," I said. "I have no hope in my life."

With what energy she had left, Mother went upright. She was almost shouting. "Don't say that. If you didn't have hope, you'd be in the exact same place I am. Don't underestimate your strength. And your faith."

"Mom, just stop this. The people downstairs can probably hear you wheezing. I'm calling an ambulance." She did not protest. "I am," I said, and picked up the phone.

It occurred to me that I was trying to exact something from her in exchange for *not* calling an ambulance, and when I paused to gauge the options, it seemed like remorse, like I was wanting remorse.

I dialed as slowly as possible, which doesn't buy much time when you're dialing 911. After I hung up, I knew the ambulance would be here shortly. I tossed some underwear in a plastic bag. Grabbed her toothbrush. Told Stanley we were going. And throughout, I felt something like excitement, the old excitement, because people at the hospital would be distracted by the threat of plague, and the staff had probably been put on code red alert, which would leave no one to notice if I slipped behind the desk and into the med room, where the means to reprieve were several. I was not going to do this, but the thought conned me into feeling like I had something to live for, even if the rest of me knew it was not so. Not at all. Not even close.

Forty-one

hardly slept. No one can sleep in a waiting room and I am no exception. No sooner did Mother get set up in the ICU than she went into heart failure. I gather she has acute heart disease and that her lungs are working at only 20 percent. Beyond that, I don't know. The doctors have not been forthcoming, and I don't have the courage to press. They're so busy. And the chief, whenever a patient asks why this drug or what about the meds I was on or how soon or how long, he's like: Look, at your house, at your job, you might be the boss, but here, it's my show and I'm gonna run it. Okay? Don't worry. Try to get some sleep. Followed by a smile and opaque directives to the night nurse, who probably meant well when she took this job twenty years ago.

At the moment, I am being regaled by a child. He has just told me that a crocodile cannot expose its tongue. I'm not sure what to do with this information, but he seems to want thanks. He's been in this waiting room for two hours. Stanley got here at dawn so it's us, the kid, and his parents. The kid does not tire. He's about six. If not asking about the tubes down Grandpa's throat, he's playing Superheroes, in which arms are spread, flights made, and from the aforesaid, identities are revealed. Only not so much. Since every hero has the practice of circling the room, it's hard to know Captain Kipple from Luna Moth. The mother guesses the Hulk each time. I think she's playing the odds. The father makes up superheroes, which drives the kid nuts. "Sandwich Bologna Man!" he says. Not sure which is more painful, the scene in Mother's ICU or this guy who's obviously going to attempt humor for the rest of his life, to attempt and fail, and, in so doing, embarrass the crap out of his son and augment reservations long held by the wife—that her husband's a dufus, whose dufusness has no rival and which fawning, slurping gestures in bed do not forgive, have never forgiven, though it could be nice, right about now, that slurpy thing, since this hospital is the pits and she is depressed.

The kid's running in circles, going *swooooooosh*.

"Ghost Rider," I say.

"No, no, he's the Hulk. Definitely the Hulk."

The dad says, "Escape Panic Man! In a crowded situation, there is no one better."

I cock my head because this is actually funny, at least within the context of lethal plague among a people inclined to stampede any-way. Seems like hundreds go down at the Hajj every year. Soccer games in Peru. The morning Tickle Me Elmo hits Kmart. Just yes-terday there were rumors of an herbal plague talisman at a GNC downtown. Ten were injured, including one woman whose ribs were so trodden, it took surgeons eleven hours to find and remove the slivers and chips.

"DAD!" the kid says. "What's *wrong* with you?"

"Phantom Stranger," Stanley says.

I whack him in the arm. "Who the hell is that?"

"He's the one who just shows up, does his thing, and vanishes. At home nowhere. Could be he works for God, could be the Devil, but probably neither."

"Since when do you read comic books?"

"Aw, hell," he says, playing the rube.

I look him over and say, "Stanley, why are you still here? You've done way above the call of duty."

"You want me to leave?"

"I know the chicken slammer isn't much, but it's got to be bet-ter than this."

"I like hospitals," he says. "Besides, it'll save me the trip if I'm already here."

"What, for when superplague rips through Park Avenue?"

The mother shoots me an angry look, like: Watch your mouth in front of the kid. Because the kid lives on Mars? Everyone knows about the plague. And if you're into superheroes, you were into the plague way before it was into you. Figuring the average superhero's prototype is Jesus Christ, and that comeuppance in the Bible tends to manifest in the paranormal ague, survey says the kid who reads comics is as reared in apocalyptic bacteria as the next guy.

"At least go eat something decent," I say.

"I'll ask one of the nurses if she's got any sherbet."

"Stanley." I press a twenty in his hand. "Go have a meat item, please."

He grins. I know he's just going to buy jerky and a bag of Doritos, but maybe he'll buy jerky, Doritos, *and* a PowerBar, in which case: progress.

"I'm going to try to catch a nap," I say.

"Good."

"Not really. But what else am I gonna do? Stay awake while Izzy dies? This is horrible."

He kisses my forehead. "I'm sorry, baby. I'll be back in a sec, I'm just going to hit the cafeteria. You need food? A yogurt? We need to keep you strong, you know."

He is so doting, it's hard to take. I wish he would just go back to Wanda's.

I watch him leave, then turn my attention to the TV, which is, apparently, a dawn of spleen for the husband and wife, wife who wants CNN, husband who wants silence, husband who cannot carp because his wife's father is sick, which makes her right in all things until the father dies and for at least several weeks after that.

CNN it is. The husband cannot stand it. I try to divine the problem. Ah, here it is. The husband is irate because his sickly father-in-law has kept them in the city when he'd much prefer to flee to safer ground. The footage on the news is of people brawling for gas at a Shell station in East Hampton.

I watch him make for the coffee machine, which will engineer a cup according to criteria of his choice. He goes for three sugars, half-and-half, and full-body roast. I am just closing my eyes when I hear a voice I know saying, "Yes, in about two weeks or so," and Stanley saying, "That's wonderful news."

"Eric?" I say. It's him. "What are you doing here? Is it Kam? Is she all right?"

He squats by my chair and takes my hand. "Stanley called me. I'm so sorry."

I get up for no reason. I don't like anything that happens behind my back, but I'm also not thinking, so I just stand there while he fits his arms around me and pulls. My face is in his collar, I breathe in deep. There is cologne and hair gel, also a deodorant, but I'm in it for the smell of his room, his clothes and sheets.

He ushers me into a chair and sits down. I notice Stanley move to the other side of the lounge. He is so discreet. And he seems to know what I need, always.

"So everything's fine?" I say.

Eric nods. "How is your mom?"

"Not good. They don't think she'll last the day. She has a DNR."

"Oh, that's awful. You've been having such a bad run. I'm really sorry."

"It's okay. But look, there's no reason for you to be here. I've got Stanley. It's fine."

We look his way. He is entertaining the boy.

Eric says, "Wasn't he trying to find a surrogate or something? How's that going?"

"He gave up. Though not because of plague. There were other problems."

"Did he ask—"

"No, he didn't ask me. I couldn't deal with it then. Probably I can't deal with it now. Or ever, for that matter."

"Don't say that, Lucy. You will make a great mother."

"Oh, stop it."

"What? I'm serious. You're caring and loyal and attentive—"

I put my hand on his arm. "You really don't have to stay. I mean it."

He takes off his jacket and slings it over the chair. I look at his hands, and then I look at him.

"Listen," I say. "There's something I should have said yesterday."

"Yeah, I'm sorry about how I sprung that on you. I should have told you months ago."

"It's not that. It's just, you can't imagine how bad I felt about missing your wedding."

"That? Forget it. It's old news."

"It's not. I really meant to go. But I was such a wreck, I got the dates mixed up. But that's hardly the point. That's not why I didn't make it."

"What do you mean?"

I feel the urge to smack him for being so dense.

"If I'd really meant to go, I would have checked the invite more than once, or read it more carefully."

"You should probably be telling Kam this stuff and not me. She misses you."

"And I've missed *you*. So we have a problem."

"Lucy, we're about to have our first child."

"I'm all too aware."

He leans forward so I can't see his face. This is for the best. I had no plans to be having this conversation, but then that's usually how things go.

"And in case you're still not clear on it," I say, "the problem is that I still love you. I do. And I'm beginning to think I can't be trusted not to act on it, baby or not. So just help me. If I call, don't call me back. If I e-mail, don't reply."

He's still leaning forward, which can only mean he's afraid to look at me. I understand. No one wants to know how much he's hurt you. "Lucy," he ventures. "You're being dramatic. You're our friend. And because of everything that's been happening and how we've all been so afraid for so long, I'm coming to see not much else matters but your friends and family."

He looks at me by accident, so now he knows.

Tears withheld yesterday are now in free fall. I tell him to go home because this won't get any easier for me, and he's not helping. He asks if I'm sure. He asks if he can call me later. Yes I am sure, no he cannot.

I follow him out and make for the single-person bathroom down the hall. I keep it together as best I can until it's vacant. Soon as I'm behind the door, though, it all comes out. I droop to the tile. I stuff a wad of paper towels in my mouth to dampen the sound. The pain in my chest is exquisite, and the keening from my throat is pitched so high, no one at the door can detect how awful I feel, which is probably by design, too, nature's way of protecting us from evidence of the pain we cause each other.

I look like a basset hound. I have one of those faces that doesn't just pouch with grief, it billows. I could probably wipe each eye with my cheek.

The tears have stopped and I feel exhausted. How many times have I looked at myself like this? I lean over the sink. Again I am off schedule, but what the hell. Hands clapped, head down: God—I still don't know what else to call you—but God, I don't know that I can get over what just happened. I'm not that strong, and I don't know how long I can wait for you. Is the idea that you take away from me everyone I love so I can grow? Am I supposed to heal as a result? And then there were two? Lif and Lifthraser? I know that if you exist, you can *see me*. You know I'm trying the best I can. Why isn't that enough? It's not enough because I can try harder? Because I should want it more? What if I just can't? What if rehab has been no help? Or what if it *could* have helped if not for all the horrible shit you keep dumping on me?

I am self-centered, I am alone. And it just got worse. I have no one I can talk to. No, that's not true. There's no one I can get myself to talk to. If I am my own worst problem, then fix me. Or just send me the courage to give up. Any day now, they are going to lock down the city. No one gets in, no one gets out. I'm scared everyone I know is going to die. I'm scared I'm going to die. And not just in a flash, but in some gruesome, horrible manner. I'm scared of what's going to happen. I don't want to lose my mom. But I'm not asking you to save her. Or me. Not even the other people I love. My needs are just too crude for that. I am a child, I have the emotional wherewithal of a child, but at least that allows me to be honest. It might be the one thing I'm good at. So even though I don't have to tell you, because you're supposed to know, I'm gonna say it anyhow, or ask, or pray, okay, I'm going to pray.

Dear God, please take away this hurt because I cannot stand it, and I want a chance, maybe just one more chance to show up for my life and to enjoy it, even if it's only for a day or a couple hours, I just want a chance, the same as the next guy, though I know I deserve it less.

I return to the waiting room, but Stanley is gone. I guess he saw the whole thing with Eric. Meantime, the superhero kid is staring at me without restraint.

"Are you sick, too?" he asks.

His mother apologizes. Her face isn't far behind mine.

A nurse steps in, calls my name. She seems riled, like where was I when she needed me. I follow her through double doors, down a hall, down another hall, to Mother's area. The nurse opens the curtain, which has the air of exposing someone naked in the shower.

"Ten minutes," she says. "I'm sorry."

My mother's been intubated. Multiple IVs congregate at the roof of each of her hands. I can't see clear to a part of her body I can touch, and she can't talk, which means we are both denied ways to communicate that suit each other best. I ask if she's in pain. She nods. I say it'll be over soon. She nods. I sit by her bed, we stare at each other. I am glad I look so wretched because if I've never said it before, she'll know just from seeing me now. Ten minutes pass, but no one arrives to kick me out. From the wall extends a metal arm at the end of which is a TV I position in front of her bed. I say scoot over. She can't weigh more than eighty or ninety pounds, so when she doesn't move, I slip my arms under her knees and back, and lift. The IVs are not disturbed. She hardly seems to have noticed. I turn on the TV and lie down next to her. There is the local news—plague, plague—the national news—plague, plague—and, beautifully, *The Wizard of Oz*.

I left when it was over. I don't know exactly when my mother died, just that it was after our heroes walk down the yellow brick road, but before any of them gets what he wants.

Forty-two

If I only had a heart, that's what I checked out on. It was peaceful and a long time coming. The death with dignity initiative is a good one, though dying in hospital really isn't so bad, either. But now that I'm up here, I'm not certain the rush was advisable. My peer group is bizarre. And the one whose body is shellacked in welts—he's vile. What I need is to park myself in a corner and think. To think clearly, which I can do at last. What happened to me? I remember when Lucy was young, she'd watch that cartoon bunny who was always popping out of a bad hole and saying he must have taken a wrong turn at Albuquerque. She'd get fixated on that part, and I guess now I understand why. What provocation! To intend Denmark and get Sri Lanka, to mean well but ruin everything—there's no accounting for that kind of misfire except to throw your hands up and blame New Mexico, in which Roswell, in which aliens, in which all insoluble phenomena find a home.

Can I speak with authority about drug addiction? No. But I can say I didn't know how to stop, and that, in some measure, I didn't want to stop. That the pain of living without drugs was unsustainable. What did I do before cocaine? It's hard to remember. I loved and was loved. I started Syn, the company took off. I hired a team, came to the States. Even then, immigration law was so complex and xenophobic, I was denied a Green Card three times. What kind of story was that going to make? Return of the prodigal? So I could watch my parents molder on the shores of *Norway*? I met a scientist who proposed to keep me in New York for all my days. I accepted. And here is where things get banal. I had this, I had that, I was bored. And lonely. Michael was in D.C. most of the time, though his whereabouts didn't exactly impact my mood. Agneth was living in Paris. My sisters were estranged, from each other and me. I had loved and been loved, and began to think of it less like an opportunity missed than the only opportunity I was ever going to get. I started to obsess. I had never obsessed about anything in my life, I'd simply wanted and pursued and accomplished. It was singleness of purpose. But Dag, or thoughts of what might have been with Dag, came at me as if they'd been stalking me for years. Which they probably had. So picture it: tigress stalks doe for hours; you think, once she's got it, she'll let go for anything? Not a chance.

A heartbroken man with polio isn't likely to stray far from his place of woe; he was as I had left him in Bergen, working for an accountant. It was easy to hire him away. Easier still to move him to New York. We had business lunches once a week. He walked with crutches that cuffed his upper arms. We never once discussed chances past, but he never dated, never married, and it was by way of declaring status quo. And that was good. Less good was having to learn that Dag, his being there, would not placate my needs and, in fact, for having failed, would make them worse. What was I missing? Why so restless? I hardly noticed when the quest began, only that it was perpetual.

The years went by. I'm told I was austere. My staff was afraid of me. My friends were afraid of me. *Fortune* said I was cutthroat, and several colleagues quoted in the piece agreed.

When Syn stock went public, Michael and I split a bottle of champagne. When the CDC bumped him up, Bulgari helped us celebrate. And so my marriage. We had an understanding, and in the sense that we'd both choose our work over each other, we had much in common. Even when I began to doubt my priorities, I respected his enough not to let on. I had brought Dag over in secret. On the sly, I steeped my body in remedial herbs of the Orient. I ate slabs of Lindt chocolate by the dozen. Wine spritzers were a vice. Pottery classes thrice a week. Asatru blots at the ambassador's residence, for which you had to sign a nondisclosure agreement. Acupuncture, yoga, jujitsu, origami. My days were plentied, but I was bored.

And then, an accident. I was waiting to meet a Balkan astroler who rented office space from an ob-gyn on the Upper East Side. An odd arrangement, but then I got the impression the astrologer was part tenant, part escort. While she was detained, I picked up a baby magazine. Later, after the astrologer had promised change—could be financial, emotional, salutary, shocking—I was having conjugal thoughts in which ratio of unprotected intercourse to months of no consequence suddenly seemed indicative. And then devastating. I could not have a child? But I wanted a child! That was it, a child! I went home and began to research the problem like a fanatic. The first IVF baby was still six years off, but hormonal treatments were available. I do not recall what the problem was, something about low estrogen or progesterone and exigent fallopian taper, but I did what had to be done, and when it finally took, I thought I was fixed.

Postpartum depression? Not really. Soon as the initial euphoria wore off, I knew that even as I'd love my child, my child was not going to make things bearable. Because that's what had happened, I don't know when, but one day in my third trimester I came to understand that my life was unbearable. Thirty-six hours and one C-section later, I had a baby girl. And a man I once cared for. Also: a husband in D.C., a business with no rival, money money money, the envy of friends I didn't much like, a dilettante's interest in Norse mythology, some stocks, and an invitation to the Met to see *La fille du régiment* with the then moderately known Luciano Pavarotti. February 17, 1972, and I was there. Let me try to explain. The first two minutes of the aria "Pour mon âme" are pleasant enough, jaunty and bright, with a modicum of gravitas. The next two minutes bring in the chorus and another singer, and it, too, is pleasant. Donizetti wrote some lovely music. But even if it were tripe, Pavarotti's tenor voice is inimitable. At five minutes in, the real beauty of the aria begins. Melodic and lyrical, the sort of music that actually makes your heart soar. Unless you love opera, I don't know if that expression does anything justice. He sang it beautifully, and we were delighted. But the real test was on deck. "Pour mon âme" is notorious for its high Cs, nine to be precise, and for how no one sings them except in falsetto, which is, technically, cheating. Of course, when everyone cheats, cheating's fine. In '72, a Met audience knew its stuff and what it could expect. So when Pavarotti ripped through the first two high Cs, it was, perhaps, the most breathtaking thing any of us had ever heard. It made your skin bristle. That sweetness, the brilliance and fire. I could not breathe. I looked down my row and no one else was breathing, either. All you could see was the twinkle of eyes wide, many crying. I cried. And when he held that last C, for *seven seconds*, the rapture was almost too much. I wonder now if the experience was what some call a religious transport. I don't know. Certainly we were too frenzied then to recognize what had become of us. The cheering and ovations. The inability to applaud enough, to express enough—when I left the hall with my friends, I wanted only to retain that feeling of utter abandon. My baby was at home, needing to be breast-fed; a few blocks away was the Rainbow Room, with cocktails and banter and oysters and vista. Neither would continue the ecstasy we'd just experienced, but I wanted to try. February 17, 1972. Lucy was just over a month old. I'd left her with a German nanny, daughter of my PR director, and gone to the Met. Then the Rainbow Room. The second of the Twin Towers would open next year. We were sixty-five floors up. I imagined the excess of the city—the hubris of these buildings prodding the sky—might approximate something of that God-given voice and, I don't know, stoke my temperament, because, as I was beginning to understand, the only way to treat mania is with *more* mania.

No such luck. I stared out at the city, listless. I felt certain I would not make it home. Certain I could not go home to face the life I had created for myself. Nor the life I had literally created, this thing that needed me all the time, every second, always and always. When Nancy Davenport tapped me on the shoulder, she could have been a gorgon for the difference it made. I recall her linking her arm in mine and saying some things just had to be lived, you couldn't explain them otherwise. I recall the clack of my heels on the bathroom floor and several women bent over the vanity. There were introductions—this is Isifrid—and a flaunting of pertinent information—she runs Syn, yes *that* Syn—followed by a parting of women at the vanity and Nancy Davenport saying, "Welcome home." I don't know how many lines of coke made their way into my body that night, just that whatever I had known of abandon and rapture, whatever I would know in years to come, it would never suffice again.

From then on, the only fix I got was to my intentions. I knew my goals. And hardly anything suffered as a result. The company ran itself, my marriage ran itself, and motherhood, insofar as I delegated the job, ran itself. With all that free time, I aspired only to procure and use drugs, which required none of the chicanery that often attends abuse. I had money and I had friends, and when I ran out of friends, I bought more. If anyone asked why I was doing this, I'd say because I could think of no other way to live that would work for me. Even as I'd sit in the bathtub, sobbing for the pain of addiction, wanting to stop, praying to stop, I'd light up with the idea that one more pull and I'd be healed.

I snorted cocaine for ten years. It took that long to get creative. But after that, the learning curve wasn't so steep. I sniffed coke, ate coke, shot coke. Sniffed, shot, and smoked dope. I put them together and thought I'd done something new. Meantime, AIDS was starting to make news. AIDS was in, needles were out. Needles were out, *crack* was in. Crack. My friends were aghast. Crack was for junkies and bums and *black people*. It had no social cachet whatsoever. God knows you couldn't buy it at the Mud Club or Area. The hedonists would only go so far. You saw footage on the news of crack houses and black people looking like those famine babies Michael Jackson was always talking about. Crack was poison and if you weren't careful, it could turn you into one of those distended-belly, doe-eyed Negroes.

So on the one hand: doe-eyed Negro. But on the other: crack. Most electric sensation ever. A supernova in every cell of every part of your body. Negro, nova. I took my chances and started to make my own. If you could make pasta, you could make crack. They say things acquired with difficulty are sweeter than those acquired with ease, but, as with most truisms, the drug addict need not apply. Further, there is something of the Barbie Baker to it all—blend, heat, strain, dry—that could make you feel like the Queen of England doing cupcakes. Alternately, you could outsource the job to a high-end chef for whom *rethink, revise, revamp* is second nature. The result? Take Benedictine, twelve-year-old

Scotch, Pellegrino, fresh mint, and some extremely expensive un-cut cocaine; mix, dry, cut (centrifuge tubes and Bunsen burner are a plus); serve in obsidian stem fashioned by Italian glazier of repute, and enjoy.

Enjoy for a second. Maybe two. Then despair. Followed by your daily life. What did I care for Michael's affairs? His illegitimate daughter come to live in our house? My own daughter, retarded in all ways but technical? I was a crackhead! But take away the crack and I was still an addict. And, apparently, a Viking. I guess I'm not surprised. At bottom, both are people who depredate their souls in pursuit of a misery so comprehensive and insane, it satisfies—albeit in the short term—a need whose brutality might kill you otherwise. A need for what? Who can say. Scholars continue to dispute the ety-mology of the word *viking*, though the consensus is that Northmen regularly used the phrase *i viking* to mean trading and plundering across the open sea. A Viking: *one who fared by the sea to his adven-tures of commerce and war.* A sensitive, artistic people of whom a great number were possessed of the need to venture out, to maraud, murder, trample, and steal. One tends to forget that because the Vikings were brutal, they were also disposed toward the acquisition of land and power, an enterprise no less sober than, say, Andrew Jackson's liquidate-the-Native-American initiative. No one knows for certain whether Jackson approved the distribution of smallpox-infected blankets to Mandan Indians in 1837, or if the pandemic arose by accident; suffice it to say that a highly patriotic American will kill most anyone for love of We the People. Enough with the interweaving? The parallel stories? I'm afraid not. From my van-tage, I see there can be no growth without the understanding and application of principles developed over time, because of time, times past, histories made.

Also, I can ponder matters of universal import, or I can mingle with my kind, among them that man doing unspeakable things to himself with a cow prod and a midget weeping for her solitude, here, there, everywhere.

Forty-three

We were terrified. The first case of superplague to hit New York, you'd think it had never struck anywhere else. That no one had heard of the thing—What *is* this? And, Oh my God, this is the end.

The victim worked in Coney Island—a shill for one of those bust-a-balloon, win-a-fish derbies. He died within hours of presenting a first symptom. For the next couple weeks, his girlfriend, family, and immediate colleagues were quarantined with little hope of return. I cried for them. They'd had no time to say goodbye, some even had small kids. Usually, when death comes emergent, the tragedy of not being able to prepare gets mitigated by the benefit of not having to see it coming. But these people sitting in quarantine, they saw it coming every second of every day. I could not imagine anything worse.

I had a certified check for six million dollars in my wallet. Hardly made a dent in what Mother left me. I planned to give most of it to charity, assuming such things still existed postplague. Probably all the good Samaritans would die from helping the sick, and all the poor people for whom charity is intended would die for lack of six million dollars to buy a converted missile base on eBay, which is what I did. It was a race against time. The owner had his own base, so he was fine, but the check had to clear and we needed to find a pilot willing to fly us out, and all this assumed we could escape before lockdown.

The city didn't have space for emergency hospice, so it did the crazy thing of sprucing up North Brother Island, home to Riverside Hospital, once a TB sanitarium, then a rehab that hadn't been operational since the sixties. No one really knew it existed except maybe the guys on Rikers, for whom the shores of Brother meant, possibly, escape. The island was overgrown with weeds and wildlife, which had colonized the ruins and lighthouse. No way could the buildings be made functional, so in came the Quonset huts. Helicopter cams broadcast pictures of chicken-coop-type structures arriving by barge, and the National Guard deboarding cots and IV bags. The whole thing was repulsive, and from the scale of the operation you got the impression the city was bracing for a lot of inmates, beginning with the Coney Island Twelve. Thing is, none of them got sick, and eventually they had to be released. NBC filmed the reunions. The reporters asked questions like: How emotional has this been for you, having your life all but ended, only to be given this second chance?

No program got higher ratings that month. And while this happy turn of events relieved some of the grief suffered by people elsewhere in the country, it drove the rest of us in the city that much closer to madness. If it was unhuwting always to be asking who's next, at least you should be able to rely on the promise that once your mom got superplague and you were living under the same roof, you'd get it, too. Only it wasn't happening that way. The bacillus would not conform to a pattern, which meant no scientist or doctor had been able to model a likely scenario of transmission. Despite the thing's virulence, only 3,067 people had died nationwide; by all accounts, the toll should have numbered well into the hundreds of thousands, if not more. At any moment, the plague could fell a locker room or act as if dropping an atomic bomb whose casualties are one. Autopsies, biopsies, cultures, there was no explaining whence or how immunity conferred itself on the fortunate. Clearly those susceptible to plague released by our highly patriotic, *highly elusive* American were in the minority, but you had no way of knowing your karma in advance.

There came a week of inactivity followed by a recrudescence that killed a family of four in their townhouse on the Upper West Side. The kids—Benis and Geoff Spence—had been schooled privately; the parents—a psychiatrist and an impresario of world renown—were trustees of the public library. In short, no advantage had been denied them except impunity, which meant nearly everything was denied them in death. Next of kin were refused access to the bodies. Local police and hospital staff refused to *collect* the bodies. Neighbors began to protest. Mercenaries offered themselves by the dozen. Because of the Coney Island Twelve, quarantine—never appealing to begin with—had lost credibility. What good had it done? After all, one of the twelve was Geoff's Spanish tutor, conduit of terminal infection, a Typhoid Mary among us. And no doubt there were more. Having experienced quarantine, there was no going back; soon as the tutor was named culprit, she vanished. As did the Spence family's friends and associates. Because if it wasn't enough to isolate for a couple weeks, if you could be a carrier whose ability to transmit was impossible to gauge, you might as well be jailed at Guantánamo. Forget habeas corpus, you were there to stay.

The situation was escalating out of control.

For weeks I'd been making arrangements to get out with Stanley, but without the gusto an exodus of this nature required. There were people to bribe, a silo to renovate, and amenities to be bought. Think there was soap in that place? It was worse than an abandoned coal mine. At least underground. Above ground was a two-thousand-square-foot house—a log cabin really—with basement access to the launch control center and the silo, which was about 185 feet deep and 50 feet wide, whose roof doors at 230,000 pounds had to be opened hydraulically.

The Atlas-F was one in a twelve-missile squadron decommissioned in 1965. It could travel six thousand miles and carried a nuclear load of about four tons of dynamite. It was also the booster that put John Glenn into orbit. Coulda been the missile that sparked holocaust in '62. No clue what happened to the actual warhead; all that remained at my base was a bunch of computer equipment, enough asbestos to kill off Kansas, and an underground facility that almost nothing could destroy. I'd read a pamphlet saying if you had seasonal affective disorder, maybe underground housing was not for you, but otherwise, it was today's mansion for tomorrow's truth.

I made the calls and signed some papers, but was still having trouble acquiring the deed. Something to do with contracts as yet unfulfilled by the U.S. Army Corps of Engineers, something something remediation of contaminants in the ground water as per legislation dictating how to deal with formerly used defense sites, affectionately termed FUDS. Some days I'd send out e-mails that used phrases like *colossally inconvenient*; other days I'd be so depressed by how bureaucracy kept to the script no matter THE SUPERPLAGUE, I couldn't even get out of bed. Plus there was little excitement in self-preservation now that people I actually knew were dying.

My favorite doorman, the one who taught me how to tie my shoes, he died. Our board refused to disclose cause of death but come on, we all saw him coughing up gore into the lapels of his blazer monogrammed with the building's insignia. I had long suspected the new porters were subject to investitures, because how else to account for the pride they took in house livery? Frederick was dying, but he was still pained by sputum on his jacket. Maybe he was pained *because* he was dying, knowledge of which made him reorder priorities like a crazy man.

All the other residents in the building had fled. Likewise the building staff. Frederick was, perhaps, the last straw. And so, after thirty years, I finally got what I wanted, which was to open the front door for myself. To walk in unacknowledged. Less appealing was having to take the back stairs, but better them than stalling in the elevator with no one to call for help.

Day by day the city appeared to exfoliate, as if the affluent who escaped revealed in their stead the marrow that gives this town life. In other words, whole sections of Manhattan began to empty of white people.

By August, you could still get in and out of the city, though you had to prove residence in either direction after seven p.m. New restrictions were enacted daily, though they rarely made sense. Ships were permitted to dock and unload, but a guy wanting to see his grandparents in Long Island? Forget it.

I'd heard from Hannah once. Or from Connie on Hannah's behalf. They were ensconced somewhere in Oswego, way the hell upstate. When this thing was over, Hannah wanted skiing lessons. Would I pay? Of course. I'd pay for anything she asked. Could she have my room if she came home? A thousand times over. Yes, yes, and yes.

The city forbade public gatherings for fear of providing a target or exacerbating conditions in which plague thrived. I don't know how people continued to hold religious services, but I bet they did. Of course they did. Duress unites a congregation better than anything.

We had a routine: Stanley would get up, eat, watch cartoons, movies, eat, nap, lay out furniture for the launch control center—picture a giant underground spool with cement spindle—go to bed and start anew the next day. I would wait for Eric to call, but pretend it was the last thing on my mind.

Mother had not asked to be cremated; in fact, she'd left no instructions at all, just that I tell Dag of her death. Until now, I had not mustered the stamina to hound the story between them. What could I learn that I wanted to hear? If the loss of Dag could explain Mother, that'd be one thing. But it didn't. It was just a love affair like any other. Even so, the day I called I was nervous and extremely disappointed to find his number disconnected. I guess I'd wanted something from him after all. Maybe just to hear him talk about her the way I hoped to remember her, but wouldn't.

One morning the phone rang. The phone never rang, which made me think Hannah, which made me answer. It was Fran. She heard my voice and said, "Oh, honey, I found you! We've been so worried. How is it you've never given anyone your number except Ben?"

"Do you even have to ask?"

"No, honey pie, I don't. Are you okay? We miss you."

I recapped the last few weeks.

She said, "That's a whole lot of shit to deal with."

"You been to any meetings?" I asked. "Are they even possible these days?"

"Sort of. It's been hard because of space and the police. Still, the people who haven't pussied out and left seem to get off on the hardship. So we've been managing here and there. Recovery stops for no one!"

"You know, my mother used to fit two hundred lunatics in this apartment and pray to Thor. At least once a month. I'd say, Isn't this a bit much? And she'd go: Thor stops for no one!"

"Good grief. We should just have the meetings at your place."

"We could have a convention, now that I think about it."

"I like it! A meeting in the famous pink room. I'll wear chain mail."

I laughed. "It's really good to talk to you."

"You, too. So I'll tell everyone seven tonight. That okay? Or is six better?"

"Tonight?" I'd thought we were kidding.

"Of course. Everyone will be psyched."

"Tonight? In the pink room?"

"That's what I'm saying. What's the address again?"

I told her, then went tearing through the house, yelling for Stanley. "Stanley! I just did a bad thing!"

He showed up with a two-liter bottle of orange soda. "What? What's even left to do that's bad?"

I paused because I understood the subtext here. We'd stopped having sex ages ago, so whatever wrong he'd advanced by sleeping with a girl out of wedlock was gone. He had not smoked pot in almost a year. And it'd been a good three months since alcohol. There really were no vices left to us except those of a spiritual nature, but you couldn't call them vices because *vice* implies deviance, which is okay for stuff like drinking—you may be drunk now, but you were born sober—but less okay for spiritual poverty since I maintain people like me and Stanley were born poor and just stayed that way.

"I sort of agreed to host a meeting tonight. In the pink room. We don't even have any food. We need food! Maybe we can use those restaurant coffeemakers in the pantry. Should we make dinner, too? Like pasta salad? Pasta salad for twenty could be gross. But maybe I could make a lot of small things."

Stanley put his hands on my shoulders and said, "Slow down there. Have you considered the dangers at all? Or that you might have wanted to ask me, since I live here, too?"

"I should have told Fran about the stairs. No way Derek gets up here. Or Neil. Jesus, half these guys are hobbled. This place isn't wheelchair accessible! Okay, think. What would Izzy do? Get the elevator fixed. Is it even broken? Probably not worth it to find out."

I told Stanley to stop laughing. What did I know about hosting? I could make fun of people, sure, but to take responsibility for the quality of time they spent in my home?

"It's not a gala, Lucy. It's a meeting. And just bringing people into your house these days, you're doing something good. In fact, I can't believe they're all sticking together. What if one of them is sick? Or gets sick?"

"Are you worried?"

He shook his head.

"Exactly. I knew you wouldn't be. Which is why maybe this is our moment. Maybe this is the moment when we find out why we were put on this earth as addicts."

"That might be the craziest thing you've ever said." But he was smiling. And so was I.

"Can you believe it? A meeting. In my house, with my friends."

He took a swig of orange soda and said, "Cheers."

Forty-four

There was one market that still catered to the foodies among us. Most other places had shut down. We drove across town and loaded up. We bought *platters*. Vegetables, cheeses, international bonbons. I liked these platters despite the wilted broccoli and that strange dill paste you never saw anywhere else. We got fried chicken and roasted chicken and chicken breasts marinated in chicken stock. Stanley wanted peanuts. I wanted teddy grahams. Spinach pie by the slab, enough for fifty, was on sale. Likewise ginger ale and ginger beer. I worried the pink room was too pink. I worried that for some people, the pink, yellow, blue triptych of the rooms might cause seizure. I'd heard of this before, a color scheme that clashes with the retinal bias of your eyes. I worried the lighting was maudlin, and the rugs too Persian. *Too Persian.*

I dedicated the yellow room to the enterprise of buffet. Mingling went to the blue room, meeting in the pink. The apartment had never felt more like a game of Clue. All I needed was a hank of rope and motive to spare.

I put on lipstick. I wore a necklace whose gold spangle sat in the base of my throat. I plucked a white hair from my scalp. Several white hairs from my scalp. When did I start getting white hair?

People began to roll in at about six-thirty. From walking the stairs, they all had the wheeze. Rheum at every hatch—eyes, nose, mouth. I think substance abuse can affect your glands well into abstinence so that you're always leaking, sweating, shedding no matter what. On the other hand, the summer broil did tend to solicit whatever coolants you had. It was August, and the weather was behaving according to type. You'd think anything that conformed to type might allay fears that life would never be the same, could never be the same, postplague. Or that a chance to complain about things prosaic might come as a welcome departure from complaining about the end of the world. But mostly, it wasn't like that. It was too fucking hot to be like that.

By seven, we were thirty-five addicts and a whole bunch of cheese. No one went for the cheese. In ante-party mode, I had thought the cheese wise for its ease of consumption—cube, toothpick. By midswing, I realized the cheese was a horror. Who cubes Brie? And what sort of Brie clots around a toothpick? My platter hailed from Mars. I hailed from Mars. And everyone else had the wheeze.

We grouped in the pink room. The petit-point loveseats came in handy. Likewise the Victorian parlor chairs. Plenty of space to sit in a circle. Take us back a couple centuries and we were Napoleon's court deciding to sell off Louisiana.

Long-timer Morgan had agreed to run the meeting, so all I had to do was read some stuff and introduce him. I was not even nervous. There was, in my home, a spirit of fellowship that seemed committed to including me no matter what. I'd been trying to win points by having these people over. I'd made up my face to look pretty so that when I smiled, people would smile back. What kind of behavior was this? No one minded at all.

Morgan took the floor and asked for quiet. He was in his sixties, clean for twenty-two years. Three children, no wives. I'd seen him before, he was hard to miss; he sold a line of sportswear for the nocturnal athlete that managed to glow in the dark and blind in the day. Tonight he wore a carrot jog suit with reflective chevron medallions sewn into each arm and leg.

"I'm glad to be here," he said. "It's so great to see everyone, especially now. I see you people together and I know God is at work in my life."

Stanley nodded.

"Tonight we're talking about the decision to ask God to take away our shortcomings, all the stuff we do and feel that's bad for us. I'm a selfish guy—let me put that on the table—and I don't want to give up on anything that's mine. I *like* my defects. I cling to them for dear life."

I noticed the webbing at his neck lacked for color. It was pigmented white.

He leaned forward. "Here's the thing I've learned, and learned the hard way: My defects never got me anywhere. At the same time, they are so a part of me, I can't get rid of them on my own. And that's why we ask for help. I have a lot of anger and from keeping it inside, I used drugs. And for letting it out, I went to jail. So what's the alternative? Ask God to release you from whatever will turn you to drugs. And He will. He does."

More nodding. Even *I* was nodding. Because though the God thing was still a problem, I knew well what it meant to want to be released from yourself—in the good and bad sense. I also knew what it meant *for me* to articulate the desire to be rid of my worst self. It meant the compulsion to feel well outweighed the compulsion to do bad. And that was already an achievement.

When Morgan finished, I raised my hand and I guess because this was my house, he called on me first. I said, "You know, I totally sympathize with wanting to hold on to your character defects. I have a million, but the worst is just wanting to self-destruct. So even though I don't much believe in God and certainly don't think anyone's gonna release me from anything, it's good even to want that release. Because if your worst problem is wanting to die, but you are somehow able to want to *not* want to die, that's a step closer to, you know, not wanting to die. Know what I mean?"

No one had any idea, but Fran scratched my back by way of support.

Morgan called on the Blade, who said, "I'm glad to be here. I like what you had to say about defects. My problem is that I forget to ask for help and then it's too late. I get into trouble with my anger and do something dumb and then realize later I should have prayed. Just the other night my mom was busting my balls about making her coffee too hot and I got so mad I hit her. My own mom. Now she's praying for superplague to come to our house and I go, Mom, that's not funny, and she goes, Good, because I'm not kidding."

Half of us were laughing. The other half were too busy wondering what had become of his lisp. Underneath, of course, all of us were stricken.

Glenn cut through the noise. "This is really hard," he said. "A woman on my block died of plague yesterday. Nice woman, three grandkids. Always sitting out on her front steps. I suspect there are all these people dying and no one is reporting them for a reason. I want to get out of here, but I have no place to go. I can't prove residence anywhere else. I can't even prove it here. Is this the way I'm supposed to go down? After everything I've gone through to get here? All I ever wanted was to fit in and be liked, I never wanted the choices I made, and now that I'm clean—for four months— now that I've stopped killing myself, the superplague is going to do it for me? What sort of reward is that? I know I should be asking God to take away my urge to question His authority. But instead I pray for a way to get out of here. When push comes to shove, I just can't act with the selfless nobility people are always talking about. And then I feel like shit. Yeah, yeah, we're not saints and no one acts with anything like perfect adherence to our principles, but that doesn't change the fact that I feel like shit."

This meeting was getting good. We all felt like shit.

Stanley raised his hand. I could not believe it. I'd heard him speak about his alcoholism in passing, but that was it. He said, "I've been living with a woman for a year or so now. Before that, I had barely spoken to a woman since my wife died in a car accident with me at the wheel, drunk. But this new woman I met, she got me excited enough about life to think about actually trying to *have* a life. After that, I had some ideas, but they didn't pan out. Now I just live with this woman and it's fine. I love her. It's not painful, I don't suffer, I just live. I live with a woman I love. And that's my bottom line for today. Just for today, just for me, I don't really need anything else."

People who didn't know me thanked him for sharing and moved on. People who did know me smiled like a parent smiles at her child's graduation or marriage. And even as I was conscious of them delighting in me, or me and Stanley, I was still able to feel touched. I loved and was loved, so what if I didn't keep the feeling between us? So what if I relayed? Isn't that what we do? Relay feeling from person to person, from one life to the next?

I slipped my hand into his and squeezed.

After, we mingled in the blue room. Another meeting over. Fran was double-fisting Cokes; Neil was checking his blood glucose with one of those strip meters. In a corner, several people had congregated around the Blade, who sat cross-legged on the floor, doing something fancy with a dishrag.

"Says he can make a chicken," Glenn said.

"Oh, boy," and I went for Stanley. Given our specialized horror of all things chicken, I figured this trick was meant for us.

It was just after nine. The phone rang. Hannah at nine? I felt a whole bunch of cheese nosedive in my gut, and ran for the extension in the pink room, in which all the sconce lighting had been turned off. Facing my friends, the effect was of looking through a window at the office Christmas party.

I said hello a couple times. I heard breathing, or weeping, actually, and said hello again. All I could think was that Hannah was sick. But it wasn't Hannah. And for an instant, I was disappointed because I was so rotten, I'd rather she be sick and forgiving than never talk to me again. No, no, that wasn't right. I just wanted to hear her voice.

It was the last coherent feeling I would have for the rest of the night.

I returned to my friends. Stanley said, "What's wrong? You look like death. Who was that?"

Fran came up beside me.

"It was Kam."

"Oh no," they said, in tandem.

"Eric went to North Brother this morning."

"Oh my God."

"They just came for him with a van. No warning or anything. He'd been sick for a day. She's coming over."

Stanley sat me down.

"With the baby," I added.

"Oh no," they said, in tandem.

Fran took on a look I'd never seen on her before. It was fear. I could sense she was having racing thoughts. She gave me a hug and said, "I wish I could stay, but I've got to get downtown, honey. You can handle this. Will you call me tomorrow?"

I nodded. I understood. "You could go even if you didn't have an appointment."

"But I do!" she said.

I stood and smiled.

Word spread quickly that plague might well be entering this house. You got the feeling people were trying to take their leave politely, but then flying down the stairs. Most left without saying goodbye because the shame just wasn't worth it. Morgan half sighed and said his kids were waiting at home. Everyone's excuse was fine with me; the apartment emptied in three minutes.

I sat on a couch and stared.

"When's she coming?" Stanley asked.

"Now."

He put his arm around me. I was conscious of my eyes blinking. Slowly, slowly.

"Eric's going to die?" I said. "On some island with all those strangers? But he's got a new baby. He's got a life."

I was starting to feel hysterical. "What the fuck sort of divine plan is that? He could have taken me, instead. I'm ready! How many times have I said I'm ready? There is no God. There's just not."

"Lucy, listen to me." Stanley put hands on either side of my head and looked me straight on. "If you can't believe, just believe I believe. It's enough."

I leaned into him and closed my eyes. Sometimes before falling asleep at night, I'd think about what if my dad had left a suicide note. What it would say, what it would have felt like to see it. I'd imagine him instructing Izzy to take care of me and Hannah. That he loved us, but could not endure a world in which his work imperiled the lives of those closest to him. That he suffered and did not know another way out. And then I'd imagine a scenario in which I didn't have to read his note because he'd waited for me. Because we'd died together.

"Stanley," I said. "Don't say stuff like that."

"Why?"

"Because you will leave me, too."

"I won't leave you," he said. "Even if I die, I won't be leaving you."

"That doesn't mean anything to me. I don't know what that means."

"Yes you do."

And so we sat. Well into the night, waiting.

Forty-five

We left in the morning. We had breakfast and packed our bags. Outside, the silence was comprehensive.

I hired a pilot for ten thousand dollars. On the way to the heliport, the baby nursed. We stopped for diapers and Clif Bars at a deli. The reek of dairy gone bad suggested the owners had evacuated some days ago. They probably took what they could, and the rest was plunder.

In the car, Kam and I agreed to talk in the air. And in the air, we agreed to talk at the base. Now we are only half an hour away, five thousand feet up.

She's sitting with the baby in her lap. Her eyes are closed, she is unwell; and the times we had, they belong to a different life altogether. She seems to know my thoughts because when she opens her eyes and locks onto mine, she looks mournful for things too abstract to cry over. We will bawl for Eric later. Right now, we're talking about us. And where we were. And who we will be.

I feel the rise of grief in my chest, which is when her face breaks and she coughs into her palm.

Stanley reaches for the baby. The way he cradles him to his heart, he's a natural. Kam wipes her lips on a tissue and presses her forehead to the glass. There is blood spatter on the cuff of her shirt. I try to look elsewhere. Her eyes have the most beautiful almond shape.

They named the baby Travis. After the man who died trying to get help for his uncle. I couldn't believe it at first, but then apparently a lot of babies born that summer were named Travis.

We are almost at the base. The pilot says it's been a good day to fly. Outside my window, there are trees and lake and a swath of land, in which our home, cut from a forest centuries old.

My father is dead. Three thousand, three hundred and ninety-eight people are dead. Agneth and Isifrid. Benis and Geoff Spence. Kam has made no requests, only that we find Eric and put her nearby. I know this won't happen, but I say we'll try.

The baby is too much fat for you to say which parent he resembles more, but when I hold him, and I have just learned how, I think he looks very much like Travis. It is uncanny, and I am so scared. But the baby, he doesn't mind. He smiles a lot. He laughs for no reason. And some days, when he's just woken up, he looks on me as if I am the dawn and we have plenty of time.

Acknowledgments

For the completion of this novel, I owe many thanks to many people and organizations, chief among them:

The Lannan Foundation and the Corporation of Yaddo.

Oliver Broudy, Martha Cooley, Steven Ehrenberg, Claudia Gon-
son, Michael Hearst, Amy Hempel, Brigid Hughes, Rick Moody,
Peter Rubin.

Also:

Lydia Wills and Paul Elie, miracle makers.

JJR, for staying, for everything.

And, with all possible gratitude, Jim Shepard, for whom, even so,
there can never be gratitude enough.

A Conversation with Fiona Maazel
by Bret Anthony Johnston

Why do you write?

Well, I want to say it's because there's moral fortitude to be had in the rendering of other people's problems. That writing is one of the best ways to make sense of the mess and pathos of being alive. That it gives me the illusion of imposing a sensibility on the world that will last. I want to say these things—and I think they're true—but I can't because none actually gets at why I chose this life. Truth is, I do it because it's fun. Writing is the most fun I get. I'm sure this says more about my private life than necessary, but never mind. Even when the writing goes badly—and it frequently does—it's fun. Even when I think I can't do this, this is too hard, I enjoy it. I love the *craft* of storytelling and the mental labors therein. Every sentence feels like its own universe, and so I think long and hard about how to put that universe together. Likewise every paragraph and every page. It's a tremendous challenge and I often feel like my brain is being exercised to its detriment—like holding a bad yoga pose—but then I also find it exhilarating. And addictive.

What is your writing process or habit?

I think it's important to be writing all the time, no matter the genre. Lyrics, poems, letters, journals, anything to keep the muscle going. Me, I like to write found poems. I know that finding a poem isn't quite *writing*, but it is about organizing words on the page. And it can teach you a lot about how to generate possibilities with language by forcing you to think outside your comfort zone. Sometimes I look at an incredible sentence by Cormac McCarthy and try to imagine a state of mind in which I might have written that sentence. On what planet do I need to be for those words to have arranged themselves thus in my head? Probably I can't get to his planet, but I can get off my own. So I'm always messing around with language to see where it gets me, and that is certainly part of my routine. As for the more prosaic stuff, I do best in concentrated spurts. If I am writing a novel, I will go to some remote location, forget the rest of the world exists, and put in twelve-hour days at the computer. Then I come home and despair and count down the days until my next retreat.

Where does revision fit into your writing process?

Revision *is* my writing process. Revision is where the real work happens. A draft will always make certain promises, so when I revise, I start by looking at these promises to see (a) which ones I want to keep and (b) how to ax the ones I don't. I try to ask the big and small questions. Is this interesting? Do I care? The assonance at work in this sentence—is it aurally pleasing or just annoying? I feel a little like one of those grooming monkeys when I revise: I look at the thing from all angles, I tinker, I cut, I savage. I also try to show my work to at least one other person whose aesthetic I value and trust. I will go over and over a story or novel or even a sentence and never actually feel satisfied. To paraphrase someone smarter than me: a work is never finished, just abandoned. Eventually, I have to let it go. And this would be fine if I never had to see it again. As is, I read from *Last Last Chance* at bookstores, and feel mildly horrified by sentences here and there and so I often revise as I'm reading. Maybe this explains why my events have yet to pack Giants Stadium.

Where does reading fit in?

When it comes to reading for pleasure, I am very behind. I can't keep up with what my peers are doing, and I am ashamed. That said, I am also careful about what I read when I am working on a book because I am easily maneuvered into confidence or self-disgust, and neither is all that helpful when it comes time to write. Some writers are enabling in their brilliance—I read a great thing and then I want to do a great thing and I get very ambitious for its own sake and the work ends up being pretentious and awful. Other writers, for their brilliance, shut me down entirely. I read their work and think: Oh, forget this; I'm throwing in the towel. Oddly, I experience neither problem when I read old books—early twentieth century, nineteenth century, etc. As long as I'm milling around there, everything goes fine. *The Mayor of Casterbridge, Crime and Punishment, Moby-Dick*. I like a good yarn. But I also like a discursive novel so long as the mind behind it is exquisite and so is the prose. I like most anything that puts language first and plot second, though with the same caveat. I like to be wowed. I am not often wowed, but when it happens, there is nothing better.

Where did you get the idea of Last Last Chance *(LLC)?*

The book actually started as a short story. I'd seen a promotional video for a kosher-chicken plant in upstate New York that stars a rabbi who asks people if they know what *kosher* means. Of course, no one had any idea, myself included. Anyway, this guy and his lo-fi, handheld encomium for orthodox chicken, it made me laugh with a kind of horror. I figured I'd use it for something because if it's funny and awful, these are good criteria for what's likely to end up in my fiction. Ideally, anyway. Meantime, I was reading John Kelly's book on bubonic plague and finding the whole thing really dark and harrowing. So I filed that away, too. Next thing, I started to write about a drug addict who'd been sent off to a chicken plant a few months after her father manufactures a deadly strain of plague that gets stolen from his lab—and off I went. This is generally how stories come to me—in parts that I stitch together.

What other kinds of art inspire you as a writer, and specifically, did any other kinds of art inspire LLC?

I live under a rock. I am woefully disconnected from what's happening in the art world. I have not seen a new movie in months. I don't have cable. I think I embarrass my friends. So it's probably safe to say that *art* does not inspire me at all. I mean, I *like* it, I appreciate it and can be roused in all the ways art tends to rouse anyone, but it's not a huge part of my writing life. Mostly I am inspired—though I don't like this word, it seems silly—but mostly I am stirred to action by other people. Their stories. Their motives. People are so ugly and fascinating and pathetic and lovely, there's just no shortage of what can be made of these qualities in congress with each other. So I listen a lot. I eavesdrop. I try to see what people are up to in their hearts and go from there.

Advice for writers?

Write.

What was the process of getting LLC published like?

Not so bad, really. I was very lucky because the book found its way into the hands of a great editor who really believed in it. Throughout our work together, I could feel his enthusiasm and it kept me going. It's sort of a slow process—almost anticlimactic, really—but there were many highlights along the way. I kept having to remind myself to *enjoy* it. You only get one first novel. There were page proofs and galleys and the cover and advanced reading copies and flap copy and my first blurbs and my first reviews, and each of these felt like a milestone or minideath (depending), and each came at a bit of a price because I was scared and wanting, mostly, to (a) not get slaughtered by the press and (b) start work on something new. Happily, both came to pass, and it all went just fine.

Why, in a world like ours, does writing matter?

Oh, well, why does anything matter? Things aren't going so well these days—our politics are appalling, the country's a mess, and everyone is broke—so it's possible all our artistic pursuits are vapid and pointless. But I don't think so. The arts are how we communicate. How we reinvigorate our humanity when it seems lost to us forever. How we bring the perpetrators to task for what they have done. How we solace each other. Dismantle, ennoble, educate, and love. Writing is *the* record of note. The diary that matters. We might be regressing into the barbarism of our forebearers, but I'd like to think that literature—*art*—is and has always been the tide that turns us around.

One of the wonderful things about LLC is its ambition. You've braided together seemingly disparate narrative threads. Was it your intention all along to write such a "big" book, a novel that incorporated Vikings and addiction and plagues and reincarnation and, you know, everything else?

Not exactly, no. I knew I wanted to write about narcotics recovery and plague because I thought the solipsism of addiction might rub up nicely against a national crisis so that the stakes of one would always be dwarfing the other in a constant battle for which misery reigns supreme. As for the rest, the reincarnation stuff, it happened by accident. I got lucky that the substance or principle of reincarnation dovetails so nicely with many of the novel's other obsessions. After all, the cornerstone of reincarnation is that you keep coming back—how excellent that this same mantra dictates behavior in narcotics recovery: Keep coming back to meetings, keep trying, and while you're at it, tell your story, which is, of course, exactly what the reincarnated people do. Still, even without the luck, there was little chance I was going to write a small-scale novel. As it turns out, I have a lot of energy that will incline to absurdist and somewhat questionable prose if not repressed or put to good use. For this novel, the oddness of the reincarnated people was a good outlet, and what allowed me to stay focused with the main narrative voice and not start making everyone a troll for no reason. If I can't harness the energy, I'll just start getting weird, or *more* weird, and no one wants that. So I have to marshal my energies but also find ways to let them rip—which means conjuring dead people and, possibly, bloviating on topics that interest no one but me. My mind wanders—I'm interested in so many things—so my task is to find a way to bring it all together.

What role did research play in the writing of LLC?

A huge role. I know very little about pretty much everything, so for the novel, I had to research plague and reincarnation and infectious disease and crack pipes. I didn't even know what one looked like. I also had to read about fourteenth-century Europe and the Vikings and World War II just to make the dead people credible. The most harrowing material was about infectious disease. I learned much more than I wanted, and there were several weeks during the writing of this novel that I swore off meat and chicken and vegetables and food and *air*, it all seemed so deadly. Incidentally, there's a bibliography on my Web site, which I debated long and hard about posting, because I didn't want to seem pretentious. But in the end, I posted it anyway because, come on, this is interesting stuff! Vikings! Fatal disease! Well, my reading list is on there, if anyone's interested.

LLC is dark and funny, the latter of which is very rare in books dealing with recovery from addiction. Did you set out to write a funny book or was it a product of Lucy's perspective and experience?

Hard to say. I didn't mean to be funny, but then the material is so unpalatable, I didn't think I could get at how horrible addiction and egotism and terror really are without being funny about them. The risk is that the narrator, for her humor, seems unavailable or at least impenetrable, and so I worked hard to break her down as the book went along. Part of recovering from drug addiction is ego diminishment, the ego being a terrific defense and insulator. Much like humor, in a way. So I had to be careful about it.

Most readers will read the interview after having read the novel. What can you tell them about the title?

If you concede the possibility of a last *last* chance, then you essentially concede that your chances are infinite. And that's pretty much what the book is about. This is your last last last last, etc. You just keep coming back—in body (as per recovery), in spirit (as per a reincarnated person), or in story (as per, well, all the stories that get told throughout the novel, including the protagonist's). The book wants to dispatch the concept of apocalypse, even in the face of a slate-wiper like plague, and so that's what the title is getting at.

How did you arrive at Lucy's voice? Did you always imagine she'd be the window through which we see the book?

She came easiest of all—this angry, miserable girl who's so shackled to her own egotism, she just can't rise above herself. I had compassion for her from the start and figured she'd be a good way to tell this story because already in her plight would be the elements of a good story, just the homogenizing struggle we have with ourselves every day: to be better, stronger, more loving and courageous.

Also with Lucy—and Izzy, Hannah, and pretty much everyone in the book—how did you manage to make such stereotypically "unlikable" characters appealing and alluring?

I don't think they are unlikable. *I* like them. I don't even think they are all that weird. Okay, so they've chosen to manifest their problems in particularly destructive ways, but I hardly think these depart radically from how most of us conduct our lives, at least our inner lives, when we sit down alone with ourselves. Most people, when you look at them long and hard enough, are struggling and traumatized and confused and hurt. So what's interesting in all this is not that people are good or likable, but that they *try*. And try really hard because there's so much to overcome. I think there's nobility and pathos and humor in all this, and so maybe that's why some of the people in the book seem appealing. Because they are trying. Even Izzy tries. It's just that not everyone succeeds.

The trauma (plague, etc.) is twofold in the novel, and it works on both a macro and micro level. That is, the national crises mirror, in many ways, the characterological crises. Was this your intent or did it evolve from draft to draft, revision to revision?

I certainly wanted the plague-as-meltdown to interact and foil the emotional crises that fell the main characters. But I also wanted to use it as the one thing a drug addict could play down by way of aggrandizing her own problems and, in this way, to illustrate the stupendous narcissism of addiction. Not even the *plague* is more harrowing or deadly than *my problems* and *my life*. The problem, though, with wanting to downplay the plague was that I almost lost it altogether and, from draft to draft, had to revive it. I also wanted to look at how a national crisis tends to mobilize things like fundamentalism, racism, and xenophobia, because these, too, are freakishly selfish in their trappings and stuffings.

The ending of the book is intentionally ambiguous (at least to my reading). Has that been a point of contention either with your editors or your readers?

Some people have asked me to clarify the ending, to tell them what happens. But what they really want to know is what happens *next*, which is a different question entirely. And one I can't answer because I don't know. In any case, I am suspicious of resolution and rarely find in its craft anything that satisfies me. I actually believe in ambiguity as an organizing principle, which is counterintuitive only in the way *chaos theory* is counterintuitive. Things don't end neatly, if they end at all, and certainly not when there's a plague still out there whose virulence and contagion are unknown. For me, the big thing was reincarnating Travis in the baby—that this guy who was just trying to do the right thing would end up in this child, who may or may not die of plague himself, and who may or may not take Lucy and Stanley down with him. Does it matter? No. Lucy has made progress. If she gets to *act* on what she's learned is just not the point, only that she has learned at all.

What's the best experience you've had relating to LLC since it's been out in the world? The strangest experience?

Oh, I'm not sure I can answer these questions. It's been very odd listening to people respond to the novel—discussing its characters and intentions—because they often credit me with more ambition or intent than I ever had. Sometimes a bone is just a bone. Sometimes it's a metaphor for peace on earth, but with me, usually, it's just a bone. So that has been weird. It's also been a little embarrassing to grapple with people who've gotten intimate with my work because I am, in the main, pretty shy. Mostly, though, it's been nice. I wrote a book and a few people read it, how amazing is that?

For those of us who know you, visiting your Web site feels like hanging out with you. One of the things that contributes to that is your movies. Can you talk a little about them? Do they in any way relate to your writing process?

It feels like hanging out with me? Is that a compliment? But yes, my movies. They are ridiculous. But also very fun to make. My first movie was about cheese. It ended with a picture of a woman wearing a cheese bra (the moral? Cheese is salvific). Probably my best showing to date is about tumbleweeds in Marfa, Texas. They fall in love. They argue, they part, they nap. As for the films on my Web site, they happened by accident. I spend a lot of time alone and I can't write all the time. But I also have guilt when it comes to watching TV or brainlessly cruising the Internet. So if I'm not reading or working, I am probably making a movie. I suppose I enjoy making narrative in any way I can. Also, I figured since there were these weird reincarnated people in my novel, why not make a short film about each? So I started in on them. Turns out, I don't know how to use my editing software at all, so the films are raw and lo-fi, and a lot of the time I end up treating my ineptitude like it's part of the work, which seems like a decent way to pass the hours. I made a little movie for the *New York Times*'s Web site. When they posted it, I was *almost* as excited about that as I was to sell my novel. Right now I am making one about bears. The protagonists are my sneakers.

What are you working on now?

A new novel. It's about loneliness and a kidnapping and how good people turn awful. It's also about surveillance and our fractured politics and North Korea and a big love story gone very wrong. There might also be some salacious activity happening under Cincinnati. The other day someone explained to me what *prog rock* is. So now I think I might be writing a *prog novel*.

Bret Anthony Johnston is the author of *Corpus Christi: Stories* and the editor of *Naming the World: And Other Exercises for the Creative Writer.* He directs the creative writing program at Harvard University. For more information, please visit www.bretanthonyjohnston .com.

Discussion Questions

In *Last Last Chance*, Fiona Maazel paints a darkly comic portrait of the emotional and spiritual turmoil of Lucy, a thirty-year-old drug addict about to venture her seventh attempt at rehab. As daunting as this might be under normal circumstances, Lucy's family is still reeling from the suicide of her father, formerly an esteemed government scientist now held in universal contempt after vials of an incurable "superplague" disappeared from his lab. People across the country start getting sick, panic ensues, and, as Lucy's family falls into chaos, rehab suddenly seems like the safest place to be in this gritty novel about learning to have hope in a world full of anxiety. The complexities of Lucy's story and the nuance of her wry yet vulnerable character provide many avenues for discussion.

1. Lucy struggles with self-loathing and a sense of worthlessness. Why do you think she feels this way? Nature or nurture? Do you blame her neglectful parents or something else?

2. On page 35, Lucy describes how she fell in love with Eric, but that this love wasn't enough to stop or even curb her drug abuse. Why not? Why might the support and presence of someone you love not be enough to help a person like Lucy cope with her suffering?

3. Similarly, Lucy is convinced that rehab and therapy—basically all the services available to people with problems—will not work for her. Why does she think so? What do you think she has to surmount before she's able to believe she can change or be helped?

4. Throughout *Last Last Chance*, the narrative gives voice to the main characters after they have died, or before they were born. How do these scenes affect the overall tone of the novel? Are they meant to give the action in the story a spiritual setting? To create some historical patterns? Do these voices help explain anything about Lucy and her family? How so?

5. A lot of the characters in the novel do awful things and behave badly, and yet you still root for them. Why? Do you root for some characters more than others?

6. At her grandmother's funeral, Lucy despairs about not being able to cry because she can't express her emotions like everyone else. Why do you think she's so withdrawn and stunted in her emotional development? What accounts for the sense of disconnect between her and the rest of the world?

7. When Lucy's mother, Isifrid, narrates her story, do you believe her explanation for why and how Isifrid became a drug addict? Can you think of other reasons why her life turned out so badly? Do you think she loves Lucy at all? Do you think that anyone could have saved her, or was her case always hopeless?

8. Why do you think Maazel chose to write a novel about a character trying to kick her drug addiction in the midst of a plague? Is there something about the panic and sickness of a plague that seems to mirror the experiences of the addict?

9. Do you think Maazel's account of what could happen in the advent of a biological attack seems realistic? Do you think you'd react and behave the way people in the novel do? If not, what might you do instead?

10. What do you think is going to happen to Hannah? Do you think she'll ever forgive Lucy? Should she? Is there a chance she could turn out a drug addict like her mother and her sister? Why or why not?

11. When Isifrid has a breakdown in Texas, Lucy is stirred to grief and wishes she could pray for her despite her reservations about God and prayer in general. How is she able to make that leap? Do you think that helping others might help Lucy overcome her own suffering?

12. Are Lucy and Stanley a good match? What do you think they see in each other?

13. Do you think the plague will end and things will go back to normal? Or will things only get worse? Will they ever catch the lunatic who unleashed the plague? Are we meant to have hope about the future of the world at the end? Are we meant to have hope for Lucy?

14. Have you or anyone you know ever experienced addiction or rehab? Do you think the feelings Lucy expresses are universal?